PEOPLE OF THE BOOK
PART ONE: MASADA SCROLL

ALSO BY ROBERT VAUGHAN

The Tenderfoot

On the Oregon Trail

Cold Revenge

Iron Horse

Outlaw Justice

Western Fiction Ten Pack

The Founders Series

The Western Adventures of Cade McCall

Faraday Series

Lucas Cain Series

Chaney Brothers Westerns

Arrow and Saber Series

The Crocketts Series

Remington Series

...and many more

PEOPLE OF THE BOOK PART ONE: MASADA SCROLL

ROBERT VAUGHAN

PAUL BLOCK

ROUGH
EDGES
PRESS

People of the Book Part One: Masada Scroll
Paperback Edition
Copyright © 2023 (As Revised) Robert Vaughan and Paul Block

Rough Edges Press
An Imprint of Wolfpack Publishing
9850 S. Maryland Parkway, Suite A-5 #323
Las Vegas, Nevada 89183

roughedgespress.com

Paperback ISBN 978-1-68549-351-6
eBook ISBN 978-1-68549-350-9

PEOPLE OF THE BOOK
PART ONE: MASADA SCROLL

ONE

A SPARK OF LIGHT FLARED AS GAVRIEL EBAN LIT A CIGARETTE. SHIELDING his eyes against the afternoon sun, he glanced over at the low stone structure that two millennia ago had held grain and other provisions for the final holdouts at the fortress of Masada. Silhouetted in an open doorway were a half dozen men and women, members of the archaeology team spending their break huddled around the door to take advantage of the cooling breeze spilling from within. Eban was too far away to make out more than an occasional word, but he fantasized that they were Zealot fanatics debating how to defeat the Roman troops who had laid siege to their mountaintop stronghold. And he pictured himself a Zealot guard with a broadsword strapped to his side rather than the 9mm Jericho 941 handgun that was standard issue for Israeli security police.

In his musings, the final assault had begun, and it would soon fall to him and the handful of other security officers—no, Zealot warriors —to bring glory to the Jewish nation at the point of their swords.

But this wasn't the first century, it was the twenty-first, Eban reminded himself. There were no Roman soldiers, no Zealot uprising to alleviate the numbing boredom of another long, hot day working security at an archaeology dig where the only enemy assault was by the dust devils that swept across the desert valley surrounding Masada.

Eban took a long drag on the cigarette and dropped it to the ground, crushing it into the dirt with his boot, remembering his promise to Livya that he'd quit. He smiled at the image of her waiting for him in their Hebron apartment. A few more hours and he'd be home, climbing under the covers beside her.

A shuffling movement caught his attention from off to the side. Turning directly into the sunlight, he saw the figure of a man approaching from around one of the fort's small outer buildings.

"Moshe?" he called, squinting as he tried to make out if it was one of the other guards on duty. "Moshe, what are you doing out here? I thought you were at the—"

A silver blade flashed once, then sliced across Eban's throat. He felt a sting, then wetness as blood from his carotid artery spilled down his neck. He opened his mouth, but the windpipe was severed, his scream silent as he dropped to his knees and clawed at his neck. He looked up at his attacker, his expression beseeching, his lips forming the word: *Why?*

Only the man's fierce, blazing eyes were visible from behind the dark headdress that covered his face. His reply was as cold as the steel in his hand as he leaned over and thrust the blade upward into Eban's heart, then kicked his lifeless body onto its back in the dirt.

The assassin's raised arm and clenched fist summoned others, and eleven more men in dark headdresses and clothing materialized from behind the nearby rocks and stone walls.

With hand signals and gestures, he directed their gruesome task. Unsuspecting and unarmed, the victims went down under the knives and garrotes of the assault team.

———

EVEN THROUGH THE thick stone walls, they could hear the terrifying sounds from above, the moans and cries and prayers of the dying.

"Hurry," she said. "We must not let it be found."

Her companion dropped to his knees to scoop up dirt with a short-handled shovel, the pungent odor of freshly turned earth assailing his nostrils.

"Hurry," she urged. "We don't have much time!"

"I'm almost deep enough." He gasped for breath as he increased his labor.

Another scream, this one so close as to make both of them jump. Then a mournful dirge:

Yeetgadal v' yeetkadash sh'mey rabbah
B'almah dee v'rah kheer'utey.

"Give it here," he said, dropping the shovel and reaching toward her.

"Is it deep enough? This must not fall into the wrong hands."

"It has to be. We have no time left."

Y'hey sh'met rabbah m'varach l'alam u'l'almey almahyah.
Y'hey sh'met rabbah m'varach l'alam u'l'almey almahyah.

Above, the chanting of the Kaddish grew fainter as the voices trailed off one by one.

———

THE ASSASSIN WALKED among the bodies, rolling each onto its back to examine the face, as the rest of his team searched the area. One of them came hurrying over and said with a shrug, "It's not here."

"It's nearby," he replied, not bothering to look up at the fellow. "She said it was here, and I believe her."

"Look for yourself, it's not here, I tell you."

"Have you checked inside all the buildings?" he asked.

"Of course."

"Search them again." He gave a dismissive wave. "Find the woman." He didn't bother with her name. His team had been drilled for countless hours; they knew all too well who and what they had come here for. "Find her, but be careful she isn't harmed. She will lead us to it."

DOWN IN THE basement of the stone building, the woman kept vigil by the stairs as the man quickly filled the hole, tamped the dirt, and tossed the shovel to one side. "The shovel," she whispered excitedly, gesturing at where it lay.

"Of course," he said, realizing it was evidence of the burial site. He snatched it back up, then scraped his foot over the ground, hiding any remaining marks of the dig.

She was again peering up the stairs at the doorway above as he came over and placed a hand on her shoulder.

"It's time for us to go."

"Do you think it's safe?" she asked, fear evident in her eyes as she looked up at him.

"We have done all we can do. Whether the door opens upon Heaven or Hell is now up to God."

Outside, the cries and prayers were stilled, replaced now by the soft whisper of the wind.

———

THE SOFT WHISPER of the wind slipping by the MD-III gradually emerged into his consciousness. Opening his eyes, he blinked against the harsh light streaming through the window of the airliner, then squinted down at the shimmering surface of the Mediterranean.

"Father?"

He half-heard the voice, his thoughts concentrated on what he had just experienced. Ancient desert ruins...hooded terrorists dressed in black...steel blades slashing through skin as a man and woman buried their treasure in the ground. Was it a dream? A vision? Was he recalling some distant memory from a book or movie?

"Father Flannery?" the woman persisted. "Are you Father Michael Flannery?"

Shaking himself out of his reverie, Flannery turned to see a young flight attendant looking down at him with eyes such a brilliant green they had to be the work of contact lenses. "Yes," he acknowledged with a forced smile.

She held forth a slip of paper. "The captain received this for you." Her eyes narrowed, her expression almost conspiratorial as she leaned across the empty aisle seat. "You must be an important man. It's not often a passenger gets an in-flight fax from the Israeli government."

"Thank you," Flannery said, taking the fax. He waited until she left the first-class cabin before reading it, though he was sure she had already done so:

Fr. Michael Flannery:

Upon arrival, please report directly to the office of the chief of airport security. I will meet you there to expedite you through customs. I look forward to seeing you again. I think you are going to find this visit quite illuminating.

Preston

Preston Lewkis was a professor of archaeology at Brandeis University. He and Michael Flannery had met and become good friends almost a decade earlier when the Irish priest taught a semester course on "Christian Artifacts in Israel" at the campus in Waltham, Massachusetts. They had maintained contact ever since, and Preston's recent e-mail had been both mysterious and intriguing:

Michael, come to Jerusalem as soon as you can. Trust me, my friend —you don't want to miss out on this. Ask no questions now. Just write back with your flight information. All expenses will be reimbursed.

If Preston's e-mail had been crafted to pique Flannery's curiosity and guarantee his compliance, it had done the trick. Now, less than 24 hours later, he was about to find out what this was all about.

"Masada," Flannery whispered as if in reply. The last he had heard, Preston was serving as a consultant to the team excavating the ancient Jewish site.

Which likely explains my dream, he realized with a nod. *But what has Masada to do with me?*

Flannery tried to clear his mind of the questions that had consumed him since receiving that e-mail. All would be answered soon enough, he knew. Better to use the remainder of the flight to catch up on the sleep he had missed during the whirlwind of preparations for this trip.

Tucking the fax into his jacket pocket, he lowered the window shade and closed his eyes. To still the jumble of thoughts, he inwardly voiced the Lord's Prayer, sounding the Latin tones slowly in his mind almost as a meditative mantra.

The second time through, he became aware of a faint glow, as if the sun were rising in the distance. It filled and slowly supplanted the darkness of his inner vision, highlighting the barren landscape, the stone ruins that peopled his surroundings. A flicker of movement caught his attention, and he made out two figures, a man and woman moving arm-in-arm away from him, framed by the rising light. And then a whispering sigh...the wind, or a voice? he wondered.

"Heaven or Hell...it is now up to God," the woman repeated, glancing over her shoulder as if directing her words at the priest watching from the distance.

The man spoke words Flannery could not make out, then the couple embraced and began to intone a Hebrew prayer. They took a few more steps forward, then vanished into the burst of light as the sun lifted above the horizon.

Flannery remained motionless but felt his body rushing forward to where they had been standing. He found himself at the edge of a precipice, gazing out upon a desert valley hundreds of feet below. The sun flashed ever more brilliant, beams of light piercing his head and throat and heart. There was no sign of the man or woman...only the searing white light. And the cry of a thousand voices vibrating within him as he took up their Kaddish dirge:

> *May His great name be blessed forever and ever.*
> *May His great name be blessed forever and ever.*

TWO

THE PILOT LOWERED THE COLLECTIVE AND THE BELL JET RANGER helicopter began its descent, the blades popping loudly as they cavitated down through their own rotor-wash. Leaning through the open door, Preston Lewkis looked out at the yellow-brown dirt below.

"This is it," he called over his shoulder to Michael Flannery, who was seated in the middle of the helicopter, as far from the open doors as possible.

Flannery, obviously uncomfortable by the helicopter ride, gave a tight-lipped nod.

"Two years ago, a buried wall was located by using satellite imagery," Preston shouted over the noise. "They're pretty sure this is part of some previously unknown section of the fort."

"The old Jewish fort?" Flannery called back.

"Yes."

Preston gazed down on the fortress that had been abandoned by the Zealots a few years before their final defense against the Romans and mass suicide in the year 73 of the Christian, or Common Era. It had been constructed on a mountain plateau 440 feet above the Dead Sea. The summit had a rhomboid shape, elongated from north to south and isolated from its surroundings by deep gorges on all sides.

Once the fortress wall had been discovered, the Israeli Antiquities

Authority began a thorough exploration, sponsored largely by a grant from Brandeis University, where Preston was a professor. He had been brought in as part of the field team, specifically requested by Daniel Mazar, an antiquities scholar from Hebrew University and one of the principal members of the Israeli research team.

Mazar was something of a mentor to Preston, who had taken an internship at Hebrew University during his senior year at Washington University at St. Louis. It had been a fascinating and rewarding experience, working with the venerated scholar on the Dead Sea Scrolls. In fact, after graduating, Preston had returned to the ongoing digs at Qumran for another full year.

He and Mazar had been friends ever since and had co-authored *Liturgical Archaeology: Lessons learned at Qumran*. The New York Times said of the book: "A readable and comprehensive examination of apocalypticism in the Qumran scrolls. Professors Mazar and Lewkis have a remarkable sense of proportion; this gem of a book will be helpful in courses not only on the Dead Sea Scrolls but also on Second Temple Judaism, apocalypticism, and the New Testament."

For Preston, this current project was the dream assignment that might come once in a lifetime. At thirty-six, with most of his teaching and field career ahead of him and no wife or children, he was still on the rise. Perhaps a departmental chairmanship or a prestigious fellowship lay ahead.

Preston pulled a St. Louis Cardinals baseball cap, a reminder of his hometown, snug over his dirty-blond hair as the helicopter landed in a swirl of sand that quickly dissipated when the pilot flattened the pitch and killed the engine. Unfastening his safety belt, Preston stepped out, ducking slightly, though it wasn't strictly necessary, as he hurried from under the *whoosh* of the rapidly slowing blades. He waved his thanks to the pilot and waited for Michael Flannery, who had just emerged from the helicopter and was looking a bit wobbly back on solid ground.

The priest was tall, with a runner's lean frame, an athletic man in his mid-forties who looked unaccustomed at being so unsteady on his feet. He ducked far lower than necessary to protect his head, one hand flattening his thick, dark-brown hair as if it were a cap about to be swept away by the helicopter blades.

As Flannery came up beside him, Preston gestured toward an open area near the ruins of the old fort where a shallow, thirty-foot-wide pit had been dug. "Before we examine our find at the lab, I wanted you to see where we found it. The location makes it all the more astounding."

"You still haven't told me what *it* is," Flannery said, sounding more than a bit frustrated at Preston's continued air of secrecy.

"Patience, Michael, patience. All in due time. I want you to be exposed to it the same way we were, so you'll feel something of the same impact. And it might help you help us get to the bottom of it."

"*It* again?" Flannery forced a smile. "Well, I don't like being left in the dark, but I'll play along." He chuckled. "As if I had any choice."

They approached the pit, where a dozen or so young men and women in overalls were working the dig under the supervision of two scholarly looking men in white lab coats. At various positions around the site, armed security guards from the Israeli military were keeping watch.

"As you can see, the dig is ongoing," Preston said.

"Is this where the Yishars were killed...what, three years ago?"

"That was nearby." Preston nodded to the left. "Their team was excavating some buildings at the northwest edge of the ruins."

Flannery gazed down into the pit. "I thought all work at Masada had been halted after the attack."

"Yes, for almost a year. And with tensions heating up on the West Bank, the government was leery of committing additional troops out here. But things turned around with the satellite findings and when new information surfaced about the terrorists who—"

He was interrupted by the arrival of an Israeli officer. The woman—in her late-twenties, thirty at the most, Preston guessed—was disconcertingly attractive, with high cheekbones, olive complexion, chocolate-brown eyes, and raven hair pulled up beneath a military beret. So much so, that Preston felt a twinge of embarrassment at his reaction, given that his companion was a Roman Catholic cleric. But he relaxed upon glancing over at Flannery and seeing that the priest was equally affected, though perhaps by the incongruity of such beauty packaged in khaki battle-dress utilities and heavy black boots, accented by an Uzi over the right shoulder, barrel pointed down.

"I'm Lieutenant Sarah Arad," the officer said smartly in English, eschewing a salute. "You're Dr. Preston Lewkis?"

"Yes," he answered, taking out his photo ID from the Antiquities Authority.

Preston had visited the site numerous times, and it seemed as if each time a new officer was overseeing security and was as displeased with the assignment as the person before. From this lieutenant's expression, he assumed she would be no different.

"And this is Father Michael Flannery?" she asked, turning to the cleric, who nodded and held forth the security badge Preston had given him in the helicopter. "They told me you were coming, Father Flannery." She hesitated, then asked, "That is a proper form of address?"

"Yes, that's fine," he replied with a smile.

"If you'll lead the way, Lieutenant Arad," Preston said, mindful of security protocol at the site, "I'd like to show Father Flannery where the discovery was made."

"Right this way." The lieutenant pointed toward a long, narrow ditch, the base of which made a gradual descent to a depth of about twenty feet below the floor of the pit, where it ended at an opening in the wall.

"Have they found anything new?" he asked.

The officer shook her head. "The shards of some broken jars, but nothing else. If there was ever anything in any of those other jars, it is gone now."

"Shall we?" Preston said, motioning his friend ahead as the lieutenant started down the incline.

———

MICHAEL FLANNERY DUCKED through the arched opening in the stone wall. Whatever door had once hung there had long since rotted away, but there were clear markings where hinges had been inserted in the stone frame. Entering the chamber beyond, he blinked against the glare from a tripod of lights. As his eyes adjusted, he found himself in a room approximately ten feet wide by twenty feet long, with a hard-packed earthen floor and walls made of closely fitted stones. The ceiling, just inches above his head, was a marvel of construction, fashioned of long stone slabs that traversed the entire width of the room. The tripod lights were fixed on a shallow pit about six feet in diameter that had been dug in the ground.

Moving forward into the chamber, Flannery drew in a breath and smiled. The cool dryness was permeated by a distinctive fragrance—musty but not unpleasant—that he had experienced before. It was the bouquet of the ages, the product of a self-contained bubble of air that had remained undisturbed for some two thousand years.

"This is where Azra found it," Preston Lewkis said, interrupting his reverie.

"Azra?"

His friend pointed toward the far end of the room, and for the first time Flannery realized someone had been there when they entered, shielded by the glare of the lights.

Upon hearing her name, the woman approached, and Preston said, "This is Azra Haddad. She's been with the digging team since the excavation began."

Azra was a mature yet youthful-looking woman of indeterminate age, with skin that would be described as weathered or seasoned, rather than wrinkled. She wore a head scarf of checkered cloth that suggested she might be Palestinian, making her presence something of a surprise in the wake of the deadly raid on the Yishar dig. But it was her warm, dark eyes that caught Flannery's attention. He felt a strange familiarity and thought he saw a mutual recognition as she looked back at him. He was certain they had never met and was about to ask if such a thing were possible, when Preston broke the silence.

"Azra, tell Father Flannery about the finding."

With a demure smile, she came forward a few paces and knelt at the edge of the pit. She indicated a spot almost exactly in the middle. "It was right there that we unearthed the urn," she said in an accent blending her Arabic heritage with a hint of British nobility. She was obviously well-educated, possibly at a British university.

Flannery moved closer and examined the pit. There were shovel marks but nothing remarkable to indicate a great find. "An urn, you say?" he asked. "And you made the discovery?"

"She noticed a subtle change in the floor surface," Preston interjected. "As if it had been disturbed. Isn't that correct, Azra?" Without awaiting a reply, he continued, "All right, you've seen where we found it. Now, what do you say we go back to Jerusalem, have dinner, and get you checked into your hotel? Then first thing in the morning, we'll go to the lab and you can see what was inside that urn."

"We can't go see it now?"

"You've worked with the Israeli Antiquities Authority before. You know how they are," Preston said. "They insist their people be present whenever we examine it, and by the time we get back, it'll be too late."

Flannery gave a resigned shrug. "All right, whatever you say."

"Let's go, then." Preston gestured for Lieutenant Arad to lead them back to the helicopter.

As Flannery followed them from the chamber, he paused to look back in at the site of the discovery Preston Lewkis had promised would fundamentally change how the world was perceived. Azra Haddad was still kneeling on the ground, eyes closed as if in prayerful repose. Suddenly the scene shifted, and he saw a man and woman burying something in a freshly dug hole, their movements punctuated by the prayers and screams of the dying. He shook his head to clear the vision he had first experienced while asleep on the plane.

Dreams, foolish imaginings, he mused. Somehow he had pulled together disparate events—Preston's promise of unearthed antiquities, the tragic terrorist attack on Masada three years before when Saul and Nadia Yishar and their team of archaeologists had been brutally murdered by Palestinian terrorists.

As he started to turn away, the woman named Azra looked up at him. No words passed between them, yet he was certain it was her voice he heard whispering within: *At last we meet again.*

Flannery backed through the doorway into the harsh afternoon light. He gazed into the ruins a final time but could no longer see Azra. The woman again had vanished, returning to the shadows beyond the globe of light that pulsed at the heart of the chamber.

THREE

THE NEXT MORNING THE ROMAN CATHOLIC CLERIC AND THE BRANDEIS professor showed their photo IDs to four armed Israeli soldiers in the lobby of a nondescript, purposely unmarked building on the campus of Hebrew University on the outskirts of Jerusalem. One of the guards checked their names against a clipboard list, then motioned for them to proceed down the hallway.

As Michael Flannery followed his friend, he asked, "Is this the Catacombs?" He had heard of a secret, secure facility by that nickname where the university undertook its most politically sensitive research.

"Precisely," Preston acknowledged.

"But aren't the Catacombs on a military base?"

His friend gave a conspiratorial grin. "Oh, a lab's been built on one of the bases, but that whole facility is little more than a subterfuge. The real work happens right here." He opened a door at the far end of the hallway and ushered the priest inside.

As Flannery entered the room, his eyes were drawn to a woman standing in the far corner, speaking in hushed tones to the soldier on guard. When the woman saw them enter, she nodded in recognition.

With a shock, Flannery realized she was the same lieutenant he had met at the Masada dig. Today she was not wearing military garb but a decidedly civilian sun dress with a bright floral pattern, cut flatteringly low in front. She looked nothing like an Israeli officer, and when Flannery glanced over and saw Preston's expression, he guessed that his friend shared that opinion.

There were three other men in the room, all standing around a central work table. About ten feet long, it was covered by an exquisite blue cloth with delicate gilt needlework—a shroud of sorts that Flannery would expect to find in a synagogue rather than a laboratory. The cloth lay flat upon the table except for a bulge at each end. To the right it covered something cylindrical, as wide as the table but only a few inches high. To the left, it was draped over an object almost three feet tall.

"Michael, let me introduce you to the others," Preston said, steering him toward a short, thin man, balding except for a little hair over each ear. "This is Dr. Daniel Mazar. He was my professor during my internship here, and he's still my mentor, sponsor and friend."

Flannery extended his hand. "I'm very pleased to meet you."

"The pleasure is all mine, Father."

"You worked with Yigael Yadin, didn't you?" Flannery asked.

"Yes, I'm proud to say that I did."

"I studied some of his work; he was brilliant. And courageous, fighting with the Haganah."

"Truly, one of the fathers of our country." Mazar turned to acknowledge the younger man who came up beside him. "This is Dr. Yuri Vilnai, administrative director of the Institute of Archaeology."

Flannery and Vilnai shook hands.

"And this is Rabbi David Itzik, minister of religious affairs and head of the Council of Religious Orthodoxy."

"Ah, Rabbi Itzik, it's good to see you again," said Flannery, his smile eliciting little more than a stiff nod. What could be seen of the rabbi's expression behind his wiry white beard and equally bushy eyebrows was an air of patronizing tolerance, at best. "The rabbi and I have worked together before," Flannery explained, turning back to the others.

"Good, good," Preston said with the hint of a grin. "Then you won't be put off by his reputation as a gruff and combatant politician and defender of the faith."

"Not at all."

During the introductions, Flannery had noticed his friend's eyes darting more than once to the lieutenant, who seemed amused by the attention.

As if in response, she started toward them, saying, "So good to see you again, Professor Lewkis...Father Flannery." She nodded to each in turn.

"Oh, I believe you've already met Sarah Arad," Dr. Mazar said.

"Yes, we have," Flannery replied. He saw that Preston was having a hard time keeping his smile professional.

"Why, yes, uh...hello again," Preston stammered. Then, almost as if he couldn't resist temptation, he added, "A much nicer uniform today, if I do say so."

"Uniform?" Mazar interjected. Looking over at her, he chuckled. "Oh, yes, you were in uniform yesterday, weren't you? Sarah is here today in a different capacity."

"I'm with a reserve unit, and they allowed me to finish my monthly rotation yesterday at the Masada site," she explained. "It's my day job that brings me here today."

"Yes," Mazar said. "Sarah is a specialist in antiquities preservation."

"What kind of restoration work do you do?" Preston asked.

"Not restoration. It's more overt destruction of our nation's treasures that concerns me."

"Sarah's with Israeli security," Mazar told them. "Rabbi Itzik and I twisted a few arms and got her assigned to our project." He smiled at Sarah, then turned back to Preston and Flannery. "We had something of an ulterior motive, I confess. You see, Sarah also has a degree in forensic archaeology, and she's something of an expert on the Masada ruins. We intend to keep her busy on more than just matters of security."

"I will hold you to that promise," Sarah told the professor.

"Forensic archaeology?" Preston asked her, looking eager to pursue the subject.

Mazar cut him off with a raised hand. "Enough of these pleasantries," he declared, tugging at the arm of Flannery's black suit jacket like an impatient schoolboy. "It's time for the real introduction."

His colleagues moved aside, parting the way as Mazar led their guest to the table.

"The Masada urn," Mazar announced as Yuri Vilnai carefully raised the covering from the left end of the table. He folded the cloth back onto itself, revealing the urn but leaving the rest of the table hidden from view.

As Flannery approached, Preston brought over a box of surgical gloves, and they each donned a pair. At first Flannery was hesitant to touch the urn, holding his hands a few inches away as he followed its contours. But Mazar assured him it was all right and encouraged him to make a thorough examination.

The urn was fashioned of reddish brown clay, and any paint that once may have graced the outside had long since vanished. It had a slight barrel shape and was about two feet tall and twelve inches in diameter at the widest point. It flared in slightly near the top, forming a lipped opening about ten inches across. A flat cover of the same reddish clay sat on the table beside the urn.

"Exquisite," Flannery whispered, running his hand over the raised surface, which bore the carvings of a menorah and ram's horn.

"Yes, it is." Preston moved up beside him. "If you were asked to date it, Michael, where would you place it?"

Leaning forward to more closely examine the design, Flannery noticed some flecks of gold paint in the crevices of the flickering flame tips. "I'd say early to middle first century. But I'm sure you already know that, just as I'm sure this urn is not the reason I'm here. Something inside the urn, perhaps?"

"We've removed the contents," Mazar said. "But before doing so, we took an MRI scan. Here's a composite image." He held up a computer printout.

The MRI scan had produced cross-sectional views of the interior that, when pieced together, revealed in remarkable detail a scroll, almost pristine in appearance, neatly rolled and bound by a cord.

Flannery nodded, not at all surprised. The scrolls discovered at Qumran had been hidden in jars not unlike this urn. What did surprise him, however, was the apparent condition of this find. Most of the Dead Sea Scrolls were little more than scraps of writing that had to be painstakingly pieced together.

He tapped the MRI image with his forefinger. "From its condition, this appears much newer than first century."

"It's been carbon dated at about two thousand years old," Sarah Arad replied. "The same as some ashes from a cooking fire also unearthed in the chamber."

"Father Flannery," Yuri Vilnai said from the opposite side of the table, "I'm sure we have tantalized you long enough. Would you like to see the scroll?"

"No, I think I'll go home now," he quipped, drawing a cautious smattering of laughter.

Vilnai turned to Professor Mazar, who gestured for him to proceed. With Preston Lewkis assisting from the near side of the table, the two men rolled back the cloth, beginning alongside the urn and making their way to the far end of the table. As they did, the scroll was revealed laid out beneath a protective sheet of thick glass that was raised from the table so as not to touch the paper.

Flannery realized at once that it wasn't actually paper, invented in China in the second century, but papyrus, made from Cyperus papyrus plants, which grew in the fresh waters of the Nile and in biblical times were called bulrushes. Only a few of the Dead Sea Scrolls were of papyrus, the vast majority written on animal skins.

Flannery stared down in amazement at the scroll, which was in remarkably good condition. It was about a foot wide, with three feet of its length visible, the rest still in a roll near the right-hand edge of the table. The surface was covered with a patina of dust, the color of ocher. Was this the very dust, he wondered, stirred up so long ago by the martyred Zealots of Masada during their glorious apocalyptic battle against the Romans?

As he focused on the writing, he marveled at how perfectly preserved the lettering was. But then he blinked in surprise. "It's in Greek," he exclaimed. He looked up at the group gathered around the table. "This document came from Masada?"

"From the very place we were standing yesterday afternoon," Preston said.

"But it's neither Hebrew nor Aramaic. That's strange."

"It gets stranger," Preston replied. "We've already been able to translate much of it."

"I'll read the first section aloud," Mazar said.

Yuri Vilnai brought Mazar a manila folder containing a stack of papers. Clearing his throat, the older professor began to recite:

The Account of Dismas bar-Dismas.
Recorded in his own hand
in the 30th year from
the Death and Resurrection of the Christ,
set down in the City of Rome
at the command of Paul the Apostle
by a Servant and Witness.

I, Dismas, son of Dismas of Galilee and messenger of Jesus Christ by the will of God the Father and commissioned by the Holy Spirit, do hereby set down a testament for believers and those who may come to believe, according to His will.

The witness I have made of all that Jesus did and taught before his Crucifixion by sentence of Pontius Pilate, the Roman prefect of Judea, was by the word passed from the mouths of the holy Apostles themselves to me, but of His crucifixion I bear direct testimony and of the aftermath until He ascended to Heaven at the right hand of the Almighty Father.

These are the things which the believers hold to be true: that a child was born unto Mary of Nazareth, in whose womb the Lord Himself by the power of the Holy Spirit entrusted the Son to be King of the promised Kingdom of Heaven; that the child of Mary, wife of Joseph of the House of David, she without stain of sin and Mother of the Lord, was foretold by the prophets of Israel as the Savior and sign of God among us, His covenant people; that His name was called Jesus...

Michael Flannery felt his head spinning. He reached out to support himself on the table bearing the scroll.

"Father, are you all right?" Sarah Arad asked, moving quickly to his side.

"Yes." He breathed deeply a couple of times. "Yes, I'm fine." He looked at Preston, then at Mazar and the others. "Is this...is this real?"

"We believe it is," Preston assured him.

"Of course, we don't want to go out on a limb just yet," Vilnai put in. "We all know what happened with the so-called ossuary of James."

"Yes, we don't want another error like that," Mazar said almost beneath his breath, his jaw set tightly.

Flannery noticed the exchange of glances between the two men, and he recalled that Daniel Mazar had authenticated the ossuary as the burial box of James, the brother of Jesus, only to have his authentication ultimately challenged and disproved by his younger colleague, Yuri Vilnai. The incident had not only caused hard feelings but had come close to ending Mazar's career.

"All evidence, so far, points to the authenticity of the document," Preston said.

"If this is true, you know what that means, don't you?" Flannery said, still barely able to breathe from the very thought of what was in front of him. "This could well be the only recorded word of someone who actually saw the living Christ."

"It may be the Q document," Preston declared.

Everyone present was well aware of the rumored Q document, a theoretical gospel for which there were no direct, or even indirect, historical sources. Its existence had been postulated by theologians who discovered they were better able to reconstruct the development of the New Testament by assuming a written source that the authors of the three synoptic Gospels—Matthew, Mark, and Luke—had used in their own writings. The name came from the German word for source: *Quelle*.

"Which brings us to why you are here," Preston continued. "Why everyone—Rabbi Itzik included—agreed when I suggested you be consulted." He laid a hand on his friend's arm. "I know it's too soon to say, but what does your gut tell you? Have we found Q?"

"Wouldn't that be incredible?" the priest muttered.

Flannery allowed his imagination to think it, to wish it, to hope against hope. There was something remarkable about this discovery, beyond its startling immediacy, something that touched him deeply and spiritually. He had not felt this way since he was a young seminarian about to embark upon the studies that would qualify him for the priesthood, to be a minister of the very gospel they were discussing so casually and academically.

All the while that he was musing about what could be the greatest find in centuries, Flannery was scanning the Greek characters that had been so carefully and lovingly laid down upon the papyrus—and cursing himself for having been such a poor student of ancient Greek. He moved toward the left, to where the author had first signed the scroll and begun to recount his tale.

"Dismas bar-Dismas...the son of Dismas of Galilee. Do you really think it could be...?" He shook his head in wonder and disbelief.

"The Good Thief," Preston said, completing his friend's thought. "Yes, if the document is real."

"Apparently so," Professor Mazar put in. "Later in the document, he describes his father's death on the cross at the right hand of Jesus."

"If this is real," Flannery said, "it would be the only recorded incidence of the Good Thief's name, for it has come down to us in legend only, not substantiated by any gospel account."

Flannery could hardly fathom what he was seeing or hearing. Could this truly be a gospel written by a Christian convert whose father was one of two Jewish prisoners who shared Christ's fate at Golgotha? But just as he was allowing himself to think it possible, allowing himself to believe, he saw beside the name of Dismas a symbol not unlike an Egyptian *ankh* but far more elaborate. It shook him back to reality, and he let out a gasp.

"We noticed that, too," Preston said when he realized what Flannery was looking at. "We haven't been able to identify it as yet. Do you have any idea?"

Flannery stood back from the scroll, shaking his head. "I seriously doubt this is Q or even an authentic first century document. Not if that symbol was drawn by the same hand as the rest of the scroll."

"What do you mean?"

"That's the Via Dei—or a very close representation," Flannery replied.

"Via Dei? The way of God?" Preston said. "I've never seen it before."

"It's rarely been seen, and never on a document as ancient as this purports to be."

"I've never even heard of Via Dei." Preston turned to professors Mazar and Vilnai, who shrugged to indicate the term was unfamiliar to them, as well.

"It's Christian, but not well known," Flannery explained.

"Why does it throw the scroll's authenticity into question?" his friend probed.

"The Via Dei is from a much later period—the Middle Ages, at least. Definitely not first century."

"Are you certain?"

It was Flannery's turn to shrug. "But I know where I can find out."

"Where?"

"The Vatican."

Despite the silence that greeted his remark, Flannery saw the disapproval in their eyes—and even a good measure of hostility on the part of Rabbi Itzik. The very presence in the room of a representative from Rome was undoubtedly a source of controversy and a testament to Preston Lewkis's power of persuasion. In order to convince these Israeli scholars, theologians and government officials to bring in someone from the Vatican, Flannery had agreed he wouldn't reveal anything of what he learned to the public or the Church. Now he was suggesting that they risk opening that door wider.

Flannery smiled at Daniel Mazar, who was leading the team, but then turned to the rabbi, who wielded much of the power, and said in as reassuring a tone as he could muster, "Of course, any such inquiries would be handled with the utmost secrecy. No one in Rome need know my purpose."

When the rabbi did not object but merely lowered his gaze, Flannery knew he would be allowed to proceed.

Preston Lewkis seemed to sense that his friend had prevailed, and he announced, "Well, then, if you're returning to Rome, there's much we first must review."

"Show him the other one," Professor Mazar interjected, turning back to the scroll. "The other...what did you call it? Via Dei."

"Another symbol?" Flannery asked, his doubts about the scroll's authenticity overshadowed by intrigue at the mystery of its origin.

"Yes, right here."

The professor tapped the glass about halfway across the visible portion of the scroll. There, sandwiched between two Greek words, was a smaller version of the Via Dei symbol. Flannery noticed that the ink was a bit fainter than the surrounding words, and he compared it to the other one and realized that the larger symbol, too, appeared to be of different ink than the rest of the document.

He looked back at the smaller one and tried to read the surrounding text. "What does this say?" he asked, indicating the words on either side of the Via Dei symbol.

"It's a name." Mazar pointed to the word on one side of the symbol. "Simon." Then the other. "The Cyrene."

Flannery shook his head in disbelief. "Simon of Cyrene? The very one who...?" His words trailed off, as if he could not voice what he was thinking.

The room fell silent as Rabbi Itzik stepped forward. Closing his eyes, the Jewish cleric raised his left hand and recited from memory a passage from the Christian Gospel of Mark:

> And they began to salute him, "Hail, King of the Jews!" And they struck his head with a reed, and spat upon him, and they knelt down in homage to him. And when they had mocked him, they stripped him of the purple cloak, and put his own clothes on him. And they led him out to crucify him.
>
> And they compelled a passerby, Simon of Cyrene, who was coming in from the country, the father of Alexander and Rufus, to carry his cross. And they brought him to the place called Golgotha.

FOUR

SIMON'S JOURNEY FROM CYRENE HAD TAKEN SEVERAL WEEKS, THE ROADS crowded with pilgrims en route to Jerusalem. He would have postponed his visit until after Passover, but he had heard that the Roman soldiers in Judea were seeking additional providers of olive oil, and he was determined to get there before their contracts were filled.

Late in the afternoon, he stopped to rest in the shade of a fig tree in a small hollow beside the road. He intended to remain only a few minutes, but the grass was soft and the shade was cool, and he drifted to sleep.

Pleasant images of boats, blue water and beautiful women were disturbed by the strident voices of his sons, Alexander and Rufus. In the dream they were still boys, arguing over some imagined slight. As their shouting escalated, he looked around to see what they were up to, but it was as if a fog had descended over his eyes, pierced only by an unfamiliar voice crying out, "Get away, thief!"

His boys were mischievous, but never malicious. Yet he was certain they were the ones being accused.

Simon strained to hear if it was Alexander or Rufus who said, in a low and threatening tone, "Give us your purse and you won't be harmed."

Rufus? Simon asked himself, no longer certain the dream voices belonged to his sons or that he was even still asleep. Struggling to awaken, he raised himself on one elbow, disoriented in the darkness, disconcerted to discover that his short rest had lasted until after sunset.

"There's no point in fighting," the man continued. "There are three of us and only one of you."

"If you want my money, you're going to have to take it from me," came the reply.

Fully awake now, Simon realized a robbery was taking place on the road just above. Snatching up his staff, he climbed the embankment and saw, silhouetted in the moonlight, three men accosting one. As two of the thieves tried to grab hold of their prey, Simon strode quickly forward and, before anyone could react, swung his staff at the nearest man, knocking him unconscious to the ground. With his staff at the ready, he leaped to the side of the victim, then faced the two remaining thieves.

"Now there are two of you and two of us," he hissed, his black skin glistening in the blue-gray light.

The thieves, realizing they no longer had the advantage, dragged their comrade to his feet and fled.

"Run!" their intended victim shouted after them. "You are not only thieves but cowards."

"Did they harm you?" Simon asked when they were alone.

"No, and I've you to thank for that. I am Dismas bar-Dismas." The stranger said his name in Hebrew rather than Aramaic, the common language they had been using.

"Dismas, son of Dismas," Simon repeated in Aramaic. He looked the man over. It was hard to see clearly in the moonlight, but he guessed Dismas was in his early twenties—a few years younger than Simon. He had a trim brown beard and large, striking eyes, though Simon could not determine the color. His expression was open and warm. "I take it you are a Jew. On pilgrimage, perhaps?"

Dismas nodded. "And I take it you are neither pilgrim nor Jew." He gestured, indicating Simon's skin color.

"I am Simon of Cyrene in the province Cyrenaica. There are Jews among my people, but no, I am not of your faith."

"Yet you are on the Jerusalem road during pilgrimage. Your reasons are not my affair, but I am thankful for it. And I am in your debt. I could have been lying in the ditch now, badly beaten or worse, without a coin to my name."

"Why do you travel alone?" Simon asked. "Most pilgrims go by caravan."

"Caravans cost dearly, and I prefer to put my paltry few coins to other uses. And what of you? Afoot and alone?"

"Like you, I choose not to squander my wealth, meager though it may be, on the back of a camel." Simon shook his staff. "This rod is companion enough."

Dismas grinned. "I may not be as sturdy as that staff, though my hotheaded younger brother thinks me as wooden. But I daresay I'm at least as good a conversationalist. Since we're headed the same way, why don't we travel together? Not only for safety, but for companionship, for I feel I have made a new friend this day."

Dismas bar-Dismas held forth his hand. With a broad smile, Simon clasped the young man's forearm in a gesture of friendship, and they set off down the road.

———

JOSEPH CAIAPHAS DIPPED his bread into a dish of olive oil and placed a piece of goat's cheese upon it. Taking a bite, he washed it down with water, wishing it were wine but knowing that must wait until a verdict had been rendered in the case at hand.

The Hall of Hewn Stone was a chaos of noise as those for conviction and those for acquittal shouted their questions and arguments at one another. On hand were forty-seven of the seventy-one members of the Sanhedrin, the supreme council and court of justice of the Jews. That was far more than the quorum of twenty-three required for the Beth-Din, or House of Judgment, to render a verdict in a criminal case. They sat in a semicircle so that each could see the other as they argued their positions.

Caiaphas appeared to be paying little attention to the proceedings, which had gone smoothly at first, with members voicing their opinions in order of age, youngest to oldest. But feelings had grown heated until all semblance of order vanished. Caiaphas looked unperturbed, waiting until he finished his light meal before finally raising his hand. As High Priest of the Sanhedrin, he commanded the respect and attention of all the members, and his signal brought instant quiet, with those who had jumped to their feet during the debate now taking their seats.

Caiaphas touched a linen cloth to his lips, then gingerly folded it onto his lap. "I have listened attentively to both sides in this matter," he began. "There are those among you who would pardon the Zealots because their acts of murder and revolt are to end the oppression of our people by Rome. But we are here to decide a matter of law, not to validate motives. Therefore, as subjects of Rome, we are bound by their laws in everything that does not defy the laws of God. To do otherwise would be to invite the wrath, not only of Rome, but of our Lord."

Caiaphas paused for effect, looking from one member of the council to the next, until all eyes were on him alone.

"You must, by law, consider only the pertinent facts when casting your vote. The question is a simple one. Did this prisoner, like the two prisoners before him, commit the act for which he is being tried? You have heard and questioned witnesses who have sworn that he did, and none have come forth to dispute their testimony. As High Priest, I now bring this discussion to a close and call a vote."

Two clerks were summoned, and voting commenced in the trial of Dismas of Galilee, a Zealot accused of being a member of the Sicarii, a secret group that used small daggers, or *sicae*, to assassinate fellow Jews believed to be collaborating with Rome. Although conviction required a two-vote majority, acquittal needed only a majority of one. The advantage was given to the accused because the penalty, should he be found guilty, was death.

As the judges were called upon, each in turn delivered their verdict in the manner prescribed by law.

"I, Rosadi, was for conviction, and I remain so."

"I, Dupin, was for acquittal, but I now stand for conviction."

Thirty members voted for conviction and seventeen for acquittal. When the votes were duly noted in the official record, Caiaphas pronounced the prisoner guilty and ordered the clerks to submit his name, along with the names of Gestas and Barabbas, to the Roman prefect for execution.

———

DISMAS BAR-DISMAS CLAMBERED onto a large boulder and gazed down upon the east wall of the city. Sundown marked the start of Passover, and the faithful had flocked to Jerusalem by the thousands for this most holy of weeks. He could see hundreds of pilgrims gathered at the Golden Gate. Many had just completed their exhausting journey and were streaming through the gate and into the city. However, an equal number were using the final minutes before sunset to conduct business with entrepreneurs who had set up stalls just outside the wall. On sale was everything from food and drink for the travel weary to prayer shawls and sacrificial pigeons for worship within the Temple.

Dismas dropped down off the boulder and approached Simon, who stood leaning upon his staff. "I'll wager there isn't a vacant bed in the entire city," he said. "Why not join me tonight and deal with all that in the morrow?"

"It would only postpone the inevitable," Simon replied, looking less than enthusiastic about having to face the crush of the crowd. "It's been a pleasure traveling with you, Dismas, but now I should be going about the business that brought me to Jerusalem."

"But the sun is almost down. You'll find no Romans in a mood to negotiate olive oil contracts, nor businessmen willing to break Passover to attend to your needs."

"True enough, but..." Hesitating, Simon shook his head with uncertainty.

"Is my company so wearying that you're eager to be away?" Seeing he had elicited a faint smile, Dismas pressed his advantage. "Come to the garden. You'll feel at home camping under a canopy of olive branches. And perhaps the Rabbi will be on hand. He spends much of his time there."

"I'd love to meet this teacher of yours, as well as your other friends, but—"

"Not friends, really. More companions on the path."

"Ah, you seem to pick up companions on whatever path you travel."

"It's the Rabbi," Dismas said. "He has a way of drawing people together—even the most unlikely folk."

"Such as a Cyrenean olive merchant and a pilgrim from Galilee?"

"Precisely."

"It's just that I'm not a religious man...not a seeker like you. Just now I'm more concerned with feeding my family in the life at hand than the one hereafter."

"What about feeding your own belly? You've been complaining about hunger all afternoon, and my friends are sure to have a welcoming pot at the boil. These are good, everyday people—fishermen and farmers such as yourself."

"If they're friends of yours, then I'd be honored to meet them." Simon clapped Dismas on the shoulder. "Let's see this garden of yours."

"Gethsemane," Dismas said, nodding with anticipation as he led his friend off the main road and across a field toward the Mount of Olives beyond.

FIVE

ENTERING GETHSEMANE, DISMAS BAR-DISMAS WAS JERKED TO A HALT BY Simon grabbing the sleeve of his robe.

"That's the Rabbi, isn't it?" Simon asked, nodding toward the men seated around a campfire at the far end of the grove of olive trees.

Dismas heard lighthearted banter but couldn't tell what was being said. Then the fire flared enough to make out the face of the only one in the group who was standing.

"Yes, that is him...Jesus of Nazareth," he said. "The others are his disciples."

"Disciples?" Simon asked, clearly confused by the comment. "I thought they were companions, not followers. Who exactly is this Nazarene?"

"A teacher whom some are proclaiming the Messiah," Dismas replied somewhat dispassionately, as if relating a bit of historical fact. "But there are also those who call him a false prophet, a blasphemer."

"And who do *you* say he is?"

Dismas thought a moment, then replied, "I have seen healings and other miracles at his hands, and I believe him to be a man within whom the spirit of God abides."

"What sort of man would claim for himself the spirit of God?" Simon asked,

"He makes no such claim, but speaks to all who will listen of love for God and neighbor."

"Many a prophet, real and false, has spoken the same."

Dismas grinned and held up his finger. "Ah, but do they also preach that we should love our enemy?"

"Love our enemy?" Simon scoffed. "Even those thieves who attacked you on the road?"

"Especially them. And if they should strike us, we are to turn the other cheek so they may strike us once more. Now, that's true love."

Simon chuckled. "I saw little love between you and those highwaymen."

"It isn't easy to put into practice all that he teaches. But those who hear him and seek to follow his precepts are forever changed," Dismas declared. "Would you like to meet him?"

"A man who wants me to love my enemies?" Simon rubbed his big hands against his chest as if they were unclean, then held them forth. "These hands have dispatched many an enemy. What if Jesus finds me unworthy?"

Dismas laughed. "Be you rich or poor, beggar or thief, sinner or Sadducee, Jesus of Nazareth will receive you with open arms. He says he is building a temple with stones the builders have rejected, and I daresay you and I equally fill the bill. Come... I promise, you will like him."

———

"AND SO WHAT does the Rabbi do? He feeds every one of the thousands with just five loaves and two fishes," a disciple was saying as Simon of Cyrene approached the campfire. "Now, some may call that a miracle, but the fish were mullet." The speaker wagged his forefinger and gave a disapproving scowl. "Not carp, mind you, but mullet, so repulsive it would hardly take one to feed a multitude." His comment elicited a chorus of laughter.

Simon had expected the Rabbi to be older and more serious-looking and was surprised to see Jesus laughing as hard as the others.

"Andrew," the Rabbi said, coming forward into the light, "your appetite is so prodigious that had the boy brought carp, I fear you would have eaten it all while others went hungry, regardless of the bounty."

"I think the Master knows my brother too well," a big man said as the others laughed at the good-natured ribbing.

Just then Jesus noticed the two men approaching and called out, "Bar-Dismas...how good to see you. And you have brought a friend."

"Master, this is Simon of Cyrene," Dismas said, then turned to Simon. "The one with the appetite is Andrew, his brother and fellow fisherman is Peter, and that tall fellow there is John. The others will introduce themselves, if they care to. Beware, they're a scruffy, discontented lot." He leavened his words with a smile.

Indeed the group looked a shabby, Simon thought, their hair long and unkempt, their robes of plain, almost threadbare cloth, their thin sandals cracked and caked with dirt. Either they had been on a long journey or simply did not concern themselves with the impression they made.

But while the group looked not unlike the thieves who had accosted Dismas—or perhaps the ascetics who called themselves Essenes and lived a wild existence in the desert—there was something different about the one they called Master. Like the others, his coarse Semitic features had been burnished by long hours under the sun, but there was an added light about him that wasn't a mere reflection of the campfire. His eyes positively glowed with a warmth that dispelled the hunger Simon had been feeling all afternoon.

Turning away from those deep, disarming eyes, Simon looked around the group and noticed the short broadsword at Peter's side. "You are armed?"

"Many wish the Rabbi harm," Peter explained, patting his huge fisherman's hand against the hilt. "If they do, they will have to deal with me."

"But aren't we to love our enemy?" Simon countered, recalling Dismas's words. "Not love him to death."

The quip brought an immediate round of laughter, with several men motioning for Simon to take a place among the group. As the Cyrenean sat on the ground between Dismas and Peter, the fisherman patted Simon's arm and gave a rueful smile. "You speak wisely, friend, but for me it's a lot easier to love my enemy knowing he fears me just a mite."

"Like the money changers," Andrew put in. "You should have seen them, when the Rabbi drove them from the temple." He mimicked Jesus upending benches and sweeping money off the tops of tables as he shouted, "'This is the house of the Lord! Get out! Get out you defilers!'"

Pretending to be one of the money changers, John affected a look of shock and fear, his eyes and mouth open wide. The others, Jesus included, laughed at their antics.

"Bar-Dismas, tonight we shall partake of our Passover supper. You and your friend must dine with us." Peter invited them with the authority of one used to leadership.

A thin, serious-looking man had been stirring the embers, and he thrust his stick deep into the flames and glowered at Peter. "I have not made preparations for extra guests. That would require more money than our meager—"

"The world does not turn upon the coin," John interjected. "We can accommodate more by eating less."

"No, Judas is correct," Jesus proclaimed, coming up behind Judas and placing a hand upon his shoulder. "Bar-Dismas and Simon will not be able to eat with us."

"I don't understand, Master," Thomas said. "You would have us be fishers of men, yet these two good fellows you would reject?"

Jesus raised a hand. "I say this to you all..."

Simon noticed a change—an urgency—in Jesus' tone as he moved away from Judas, toward the firelight at the center of the circle.

"As you, my faithful disciples, have served me during my mortal life, so too shall Dismas bar-Dismas and Simon of Cyrene serve after I have gone. But tonight, other service calls them."

There was such sureness in Jesus' tone that for an instant Simon found himself believing the pronouncement. Then his usual doubting nature resurfaced, and he asked, "Rabbi, why do you say I will serve you? I am not of your faith or your race."

"But you *are* of my faith, Simon," Jesus replied. He walked toward the Cyrenean, one hand placed over his heart. "And are we not all of the race of man?"

As Simon gazed up at Jesus, he saw in amazement that the man they called Master now had skin as dark as his own. None of the others took any notice, either unaware of the transformation or all too familiar with the Rabbi's powers.

"Master!" Simon exclaimed, dropping forward onto his elbows and touching his forehead to the ground.

"Simon?" Dismas asked in genuine wonder at his friend's seemingly instantaneous conversion.

"Master, how can I serve you?" Simon asked, his head still pressed to the ground.

"When it is time, you will know," Jesus answered. "Now, rise, Simon. Open your eyes so that you may see."

Simon looked up and blinked in bewilderment, for the man who but a moment before had features as ebony as the Cyrenean's was once again the ruddy-faced, brown-eyed Jew he had met upon arriving.

"My friend Dismas spoke truly," Simon whispered. "Within you the spirit of God abides."

DISMAS BAR-DISMAS WATCHED with pride and jealousy as Jesus and the disciples gathered around Simon of Cyrene as if welcoming home the prodigal son the Rabbi was so fond of sermonizing about. His pride was understandable, having been the shepherd who brought this black sheep to their fold. The jealousy, however, surprised and disturbed him, yet he could not shake the desire to be the one standing there in the group's warming embrace.

His thoughts were interrupted by someone calling from the far reaches of the garden.

"Dismas! Bar-Dismas! Please, someone, help me! I seek the eldest son of Dismas of Galilee. I am his brother, and I bring him news!"

Recognizing the voice, Dismas hurried toward the edge of the darkness and called, "Tibro! I am over here!"

There was a rustling of the underbrush, and then a young Jew stepped into the circle of light. Though a bit taller and more muscular than Dismas, he looked much like his older brother, with the same trim beard and disarmingly green eyes. And like the disciple Peter, he wore a short broadsword belted around his waist. Hanging from that same belt was a dagger.

Though alike in appearance, the brothers differed in temperament. Dismas shared their mother's gentle spirit and was a man of letters, able to read and write Greek, Latin, Hebrew, and Aramaic. Tibro, who at nineteen was younger than Dismas by three years, had their father's fiery and mercurial nature, quick to judge, equally quick to act upon that judgment.

"Praise be, I have found you," Tibro exclaimed, clapping his brother on the shoulders. "We must act quickly. Father is in danger."

"What happened?"

"We were set upon by Roman soldiers. I managed to get away, but Father, Gestas, and Barabbas were captured."

The news did not really surprise Dismas. Their father had long been driven by a fanatical nationalism. He and his younger son followed Barabbas, leader of a faction of the Zealots. They believed that anyone who would impose or even acknowledge any other law but that of the Hebrew God was an evildoer to be eradicated—not only Romans but any Jew who collaborated with them.

"The Romans have him?" Dismas asked.

"They turned him over to the Sanhedrin for trial. Can you imagine a treason so great that Jews would try Jews for a crime against Rome?"

"I have long feared this," Dismas said. "But come, we will do what we can." They started from the garden.

"Bar-Dismas," Jesus called, and the brothers halted and looked back. "There is nothing you can do. Your father must play the role written for him, as even I must do."

"The role written for him?" Tibro mocked, striding a few paces toward the Rabbi, his hand reaching instinctively for the dagger at his side. "You, a false prophet who leads our people away from God, would tell us that our father has a role to play in your heresy?"

"For paying homage to me, your father will be remembered and honored until the end of time," Jesus said.

"My father pays you no homage! He is in prison, awaiting crucifixion by the Roman dogs because he is a man of honor and principle who bows to no man. And he will die a man of honor and principle!"

"Come, Tibro," Dismas urged, tugging at his brother's robe. "You said Father needs us."

Pulling free, Tibro shook a fist at Jesus as he raged, "Homage? I would rather see him die than blaspheme himself by paying homage to the likes of you!"

"Let me teach that insolent pup some manners, Master," Peter said, gripping the hilt of his broadsword.

"No, Peter. For even Tibro has a part to play in the great mystery." Smiling, Jesus turned from the angry young Zealot and opened his arms as if to herd his followers ahead of him. "Come, it is time for our supper."

———

As THE DISCIPLES headed toward a nearby building where they would hold the Seder meal, Simon stood immobilized between his new companions and the one who had brought him to the garden and was now retreating into the darkness.

He felt a hand upon his shoulder and turned to see the Rabbi looking at him with compassion and understanding.

"Follow him," Jesus said softly. "Our time together is yet to come. But your friend is still in need of your wise counsel."

Simon hesitated, then felt himself surrendering to the Master's will. "Shall I see you again?" he asked.

"Truly, we shall walk together from this day forward," came the reply.

Nodding in acceptance, Simon turned and hurried into the night.

SIX

DISMAS AND TIBRO WAITED IN AN OUTER CHAMBER OF FORTRESS
Antonia, hoping to hear they would be granted an audience with the
prefect. They had spent all night going from one Jewish official to
another, until finally they learned that their father had already been
convicted by the Sanhedrin and sent back to the Romans for
execution.

When the clerk who had taken their request returned, he shook
his head and announced bluntly, "His Excellency Pontius Pilate will
not receive you. Now be gone."

"Perhaps he did not understand our purpose," Dismas said with
forced calmness, holding a restraining hand in front of his more
hotheaded brother. "We did not come to seek the release of Dismas of
Galilee, only the prefect's permission to visit with the prisoner before
sentence is carried out."

"This is not a propitious time," the clerk replied with a flick of the
hand. "That man Jesus of Nazareth has just now been brought before
the prefect. The Sanhedrin called for his crucifixion, as well."

"What?" Dismas blurted. "Jesus is to be crucified? But why? What
crime has he committed?"

The man shook his head. "His Excellency is perplexed by that very
question. The poor fellow seems little more than a self-proclaimed

prophet, and this cursed land is rife with their kind. Yet Caiaphas insists upon his execution, and Herod Antipas supports him."

"What has Herod to do with this? He rules Galilee, not Judea."

"But he is spending Passover here in the capital. And since this Jesus is from Nazareth in Galilee, the prefect thought it politic to send him to Herod."

"So it was Herod who condemned—"

The clerk smirked. "Herod? They say he is petrified of this prophet —thinks him the resurrection of that baptist he agreed to behead. No...he wanted to keep his own hands clean, as usual. He sent him back here with word he would support whatever the Sanhedrin recommends."

"And the council recommends whatever Caiaphas tells it to," Dismas muttered, his hands clenching.

The clerk shrugged and walked away across the chamber.

"I don't understand you," Tibro hissed. "Our father stands convicted, yet your concern is for this man Jesus?"

"He is guilty of nothing more than preaching the word of God."

"And Father?" Tibro asked, grasping his brother's sleeve. "While your Jesus talks of a better life for us Jews, Father works to bring it to fruition."

"Yes, the work of a Zealot," Dismas whispered. "And he has always known such work could lead him...well, to such an end."

Seeing that the clerk was about to exit the chamber, Dismas pulled free of his brother's grasp and called after him, "One more thing, if you please." When the man halted and looked back from the open doorway, Dismas continued, "You said the Sanhedrin is calling for Jesus' crucifixion. Then his fate is not sealed? Pontius Pilate may yet commute the sentence?"

"If you hurry to the courtyard, His Excellency intends to display his beneficence by pardoning one prisoner as a Passover gift to your people."

"Which one?" Tibro asked.

Again the man shrugged. "Jesus? Barabbas? Perhaps your friend Dismas? The choice will be the people's."

"Come," Tibro said, pulling on his brother's arm. "Let us go quickly and make a plea for our father."

DISMAS AND TIBRO joined a crowd that soon numbered more than two thousand packed tightly into the Praetorium, the paved courtyard of Fortress Antonia. All eyes were fixed on the head of the stairs, where Pontius Pilate, the Roman prefect of Judea, sat on the *Sella Curulis*— the ivory chair used by high officials of Rome as a seat of judgment. Although not born into the senatorial caste of Roman society, a descendant instead of horse trainers and traders, soldiers and merchants, Pilate had risen through the army and into imperial government service through wit, intelligence, cruelty, and an appreciation of the art and science of bribery.

"There he is," Dismas said, pointing to a figure, flanked by soldiers, who had just been brought out and stood now near Pilate. Even from a distance, the bloody lash marks were quite visible, and it was apparent that it took a great effort of will for him to remain on his feet. "Oh, look at him, how he is injured. They have beaten him."

"Father?"

"Jesus."

"Why do you show such concern for this Nazarene? Have you no love, no compassion for your own blood?"

"Of course. But we have seen this trouble coming for a long time now, and I am not its cause."

"Are you suggesting, my brother, that I am?"

"You were with him," Dismas replied.

Before Tibro could answer, Pilate rose from his chair and walked to the head of the stairs to address the crowd. He wore the purple stole of imperial office as if he had been born to it, and spoke in ringing, authoritative tones that could not mask his displeasure at being in Jerusalem during the Jewish holy season rather than in the comfort of his own palace in Caesarea on the Mediterranean coast.

"This man, this Jesus, was brought before my tribunal," Pilate began, "charged with blasphemy to the Jewish religion, which does not fall under my jurisdiction, and inciting the nation to revolt and accept his kingship, which most certainly does. But I have myself questioned him, and I find no guilt in him."

"Then let him go!" Dismas bar-Dismas shouted.

Several in the crowd looked toward him, frowning in disapproval.

"Still yourself," Tibro said, gripping his brother's shoulder. "We mustn't draw attention."

Dismas shook his head, breathing deeply to calm his emotions.

"Herod Antipas also questioned him and found no guilt, and so returned him to me," Pilate continued. "Therefore, this shall be my finding: He has done nothing to deserve the penalty of death."

"Crucify him!" someone shouted. "Put him to death!" Others in the crowd took up his cry.

"Why do they call for his blood?" Dismas asked, shocked at the vitriol around him.

The prefect held up his pale hands, calling for quiet. "I intend to discipline him, then set him free."

"No!" came a chorus of voices.

"He must die!"

"Put him to death!"

"Crucify him!"

The shouts filled the courtyard and echoed from the walls of the fortress.

Again Pilate held up his hands. When the crowd quieted enough for him to be heard, he continued, "In honor of the celebration of your holy day, I will release one prisoner to you. Who would you have me release?" He gestured to the soldiers behind him, and they brought forth three other men to stand beside Jesus.

"There he is!" Tibro said, nodding in the direction of their father, who stood at the extreme right. "This is our chance." He cupped his hands around his mouth and shouted, "Dismas! We would have Dismas of Galilee!" Turning to his brother, he ordered, "Shout! Shout out Father's name as loudly as you can."

The elder brother hesitated, wanting to proclaim to all assembled that they were on the verge of condemning the very man who had it in his power to save all of Judea, all of mankind. But it was as if he heard the Rabbi telling him that even this moment had been written in God's book, that he must now don the mantle of a son and honor the father who bore him. Before he realized what he was doing, he heard himself crying out, uncertainly at first and then with growing conviction, "Dismas! Give us Dismas!"

"Dismas!" Tibro joined in, clapping his brother on the back and then turning to those nearest to them. "Please, help us demand the freedom of Dismas!"

A few others took up the shout, but from another part of the courtyard voices began calling the name of the better-known Barabbas. That call became a chant, picked up by more and more, until it engulfed those who had been shouting for the other prisoners.

"Dismas!" the brothers continued to yell, their voices buried beneath the roar for Barabbas.

Once more, Pontius Pilate raised his hands in a plea for quiet and civility. "Who would you have me release? Barabbas the Zealot or Jesus the Messiah?"

"The Messiah? He is not the Messiah!"

"Barabbas!" the crowd roared. "Give us Barabbas!"

"Insatiable beggars," Pilate muttered. Turning to a servant, who brought forth a large silver washing basin, he placed his hands in the scented water, as if washing himself clean of any association with the release of a known criminal and the death of an innocent man.

Knowing now that any attempt to free their father was futile, Tibro and Dismas pushed their way back through the crowd. As they passed from the courtyard, they could still hear strident voices demanding the crucifixion of Jesus.

"Surely, they do not know him," Dismas said, his shoulders slumped as he followed his brother down the street. "They have not met him, they have not heard him speak. If they had, they would not call for his blood."

"You disgust me," Tibro railed as he halted and spun toward his older brother. "Our own father is to go to the tree, yet you decry the fate of this false Messiah."

"He is not false."

"Then who is he?"

Dismas hesitated, then said with conviction, "The Son of God."

Tibro raised his hand palm forward, as if creating distance between them. "I cannot listen to such heresy," he declared. "Get away from me. You are no brother of mine." Turning, he walked away.

"Tibro, wait!" Dismas called, reaching out for him.

"No!" Tibro gave a dismissive wave. "I do not know you!"

SEVEN

DISMAS BAR-DISMAS WANDERED AIMLESSLY THROUGH THE STREETS, thinking of the appalling turn of events. Yesterday he had arrived at Jerusalem on a joyous pilgrimage to celebrate Passover. He had looked forward, with deep pleasure, to prostrating himself on the stone floor of the great Temple. He had made a friend during the journey, and last night he had enjoyed a visit with Jesus, the man he truly believed to be the Son of God.

But one long, sleepless night later, Dismas found himself alone on the crowded streets, tired, dispirited, hungry, his brother having abandoned him in anger, his father hours, perhaps only minutes, from the cross, his teacher awaiting a fate too horrible to comprehend.

"Dismas, my friend!" a voice called.

Turning, Dismas saw a dark, smiling face among the growing multitudes that had spilled into the streets from the Praetorium. "Simon!" he called.

Simon of Cyrene pushed through the crowd to Dismas's side, and the two men gripped forearms in greeting.

"Did you see your father?" Simon asked.

"No. We tried all night but without success."

"I'm truly sorry."

"Simon, have you heard? Jesus is to be crucified."

"Yes, but I don't understand. Why would your people kill one of their own holy men?"

"Not all think him holy," Dismas replied.

"Then they have not seen him as we have."

They were interrupted by the shouts of a Roman soldier. "Make way! Make way!" he commanded. Two other soldiers followed, the armed trio forming a wedge that separated the crowd.

"What's going on?" Simon asked.

"They must be bringing the prisoners." Suddenly Dismas realized this might be his last opportunity to speak to his father. "Simon, we have to get closer."

"Stay with me."

With powerful thrusts of his muscular arms, Simon pushed forward, opening a path until they were at the front of the crowd, which now lined both sides of the road.

Two soldiers on horseback led the procession, riding side by side down the narrow, stone-paved street, pressing the spectators against the buildings and into the alleys to further widen the passage.

"Back! Get back!" they ordered, punctuated with an occasional lash of their whips.

Behind the horsemen were six foot soldiers in breastplates and helmets, followed by the three condemned men. Jesus was first in line, barely able to carry the heavy, awkward timber that was to become the crossbeam of his cross. A crude crown of thorns had been thrust atop his head, piercing the flesh and streaking his face with blood. Around his neck hung a sign reading: King of the Jews. A tattered robe revealed his torso striped with bloody lacerations, and his legs quivered with fatigue. Even those among the crowd who had shouted most vociferously for his crucifixion now recoiled in pity, and many began to weep.

Gestas was next in line. Looking angry and defiant even now, he carried his own crossbeam easily, for he had not been beaten. It was unusual for the Romans to beat a man condemned to death, which confirmed to Dismas that the prefect had intended to punish rather than execute Jesus.

Following Gestas was Dismas of Galilee. Although as strong as his fellow Zealot, he did not have the same defiant look. Rather his expression was one of resignation as he plodded along the street, dragging his crossbeam upon his shoulder.

"Father!" the younger Dismas shouted as he pushed to get closer.

Hearing his son's voice, the condemned man's face brightened. He searched the crowd lining the street, and when he saw his eldest son, he smiled.

"My boy!" he cried happily. "How glad I am that God gave me the opportunity to look upon you once more."

"Tibro and I tried to see you during the night," bar-Dismas told him. "They wouldn't allow it."

"I felt your presence," his father assured him. He nodded toward Jesus, ahead of him. "Is he not the man you told us about? The one you call the Messiah?"

"He *is* the Messiah, the Son of God," the young man declared without hesitation.

"I am sorry for him. If one is to be crucified, it is not right that he should be beaten."

"How are you, Father? Is your faith strong?"

"God is with me."

"Put your trust in Jesus, as well," bar-Dismas urged. "God will not desert his own son, and neither will his son desert you."

Just ahead, Gestas glanced back and gave a mocking laugh. "Son of God, is he? Look at him. The man who calls himself our king can barely walk."

———

NEARBY, Simon was caught up in the drama playing out on the road between Fortress Antonia and Golgotha that one day would be known as the Via Dolorosa—the Way of Suffering. He was aware of the poignancy of Dismas bar-Dismas carrying on a final conversation with his father, but he was equally aware of the suffering of Jesus, and he moved down the street to keep pace with the Rabbi. Jesus had told him to see to his new friend, and in truth Simon had been following Dismas the entire night and day, only pretending to accidentally come upon him a short while ago. But Jesus had also promised that he and

Simon would walk together always, and this seemed the last chance to do so.

Suddenly Jesus staggered and pitched forward. He hit the ground hard, unable to break his fall because his hands were tied around the crossbeam. The beam slid free and tumbled forward with a loud thump.

"Get up!" the Roman soldier demanded, hurrying over to Jesus and kicking him in the side. "Get moving!"

Simon rushed out from the crowd. He hoisted the crude wooden beam onto his own shoulder, then reached down to Jesus with his free hand. As Jesus grabbed hold and regained his feet, Simon gazed upon his face, streaked with rivulets of blood that ran from the puncture wounds of the mocking crown of thorns. Then, without thinking, Simon tore a wide patch from the hem of his shirt and used it to wipe away some of the blood.

Simon felt Jesus gazing deep into his soul. Once, when Simon was a child, he had fallen from a tree and had the breath knocked from him. It was a moment of panic, lying on the ground, unable to draw any air, wondering if he would ever breathe again. He had that same feeling now, a dizzying loss of breath and disassociation with reality. For an instant he imagined he was looking ahead into the ages, seeing things he could understand only in the abstract: wondrous cities and fields of shame, feast and famine, war and peace, triumph, tragedy.

"What are you doing?" one of the Roman soldiers demanded, threatening Simon with his raised whip. He motioned for the black man to give back the heavy beam, but then he hesitated, staring uncertainly into Jesus' eyes. At last he shook his head as if to clear it and gestured for Simon to continue with his task. "Move it on, move it on!" he grunted, shaking the whip to indicate he would not hesitate to use it.

As Simon started forward beside Jesus, he knew that, regardless of what happened today, his life had been forever changed.

———————

IT WAS a few minutes after noon, and the sun, high and hot, glistened off the leaves of a nearby grove of olive trees. The three condemned men hung from their crosses upon Golgotha, facing the holy city of Jerusalem. Most of the crowd had left, once the spectacle of roping and nailing them to the crossbeams and hoisting them onto the uprights had been completed. There was nothing to see now, except the final agonizing moments of dying by asphyxiation. And because hanging from the cross so quickly sapped them of their strength, there was little sound or spectacle, little to hold an audience's interest.

Several did remain, however: the morbidly curious, friends and families of the condemned men. But Jesus' followers were precious few, most of them fearful that they would be arrested by the Romans or butchered by the crowd if recognized as members of his inner circle.

Some detractors and doubters were on hand, and one of them shouted up at Jesus on the center cross, "If you are the Son of God, come down from the cross!"

"It is said that you have helped others. Can you not help yourself?" another challenged.

Gestas, in his agony, gasped his own contemptuous plea. "You claim to be the Messiah? Then, save yourself! Save yourself, and us as well!"

Dismas of Galilee, who had been silent from the moment they lifted him onto the right-hand cross, now looked over at Gestas. "Have you no fear of God?" he asked. "We are receiving the same punishment as the Messiah. But we are guilty of our crimes, whereas he is an innocent man."

Bar-Dismas had been watching, feeling his father's pain in his own heart, praying for him. Now he heard his father refer to Jesus as the Messiah, and he looked around the thinning crowd, hoping to see his brother, but Tibro was nowhere in sight. In fact, he had not seen his brother since they had separated in anger earlier that day.

The senior Dismas looked down upon his son and managed a smile. Then, grimacing, he struggled to turn toward Jesus. "Remember me, Jesus of Nazareth, when you come into your glory," he said contritely.

Jesus looked over at Dismas. "Truly I say to you, this day you shall be with me in Paradise."

EIGHT

As Simon began the long return journey to Cyrene, he could not get the events in Jerusalem out of his mind. It wasn't just the brutal scourging and execution of a good, gentle man that had so moved him, but the strange sensation he experienced under Jesus' gaze as he took on the burden of the cross. It was as if he had been shown the future—not just his own but that of mankind. In what must have been only an instant, he had seen wondrous things he could not now fathom. Who was he to have such a remarkable vision? He was not of the race or the religion of this Jesus, so why had he been so affected?

He recalled the Rabbi's words that night at the campfire—"Are we not all of the race of man?"—and how his skin had appeared as black as Simon's. That could have been a trick of the light, of course, for the shadows had been growing long in the Garden of Gethsemane.

"Simon," a voice intoned, interrupting his musing as he walked alone down the deserted road.

He halted and looked around, half expecting to see his friend Dismas bar-Dismas come in search of him. "Yes?" he called, but he saw nothing, so he shrugged and continued along the hard-packed roadway.

"Simon."

Simon spun around, and again he saw no one. But this time when he turned back, someone was blocking the way in front of him. For a moment he didn't recognize the man. Then with a gasp he realized he was looking at Jesus.

"No, it cannot be!" Simon fell to his knees, muttering the Rabbi's name.

"Rise, Simon," Jesus said. "Did I not say we would walk together again?"

"My Lord, forgive me for my doubts," Simon whispered, afraid to look up at him.

"In my travail, you used your shirt to wipe blood from my eyes. Look now at that garment, Simon."

Simon had clutched the torn patch of cloth all during the crucifixion, later discovering it still gripped tightly in his fist. It was so drenched with blood that he had considered throwing it away. But something had compelled him to save it, as if unwilling to let go of Jesus. This morning he had stuffed it in his traveling bag, and he opened the bag now and took it out.

"Open it," Jesus declared, "and gaze upon the sign."

The cloth was approximately one-foot square and stiff with dried blood as Simon unfolded it. He looked at the cloth, then glanced up questioningly at Jesus, who merely smiled. When Simon looked back at the cloth, his eyes widened in wonder, for the brownish, encrusted blood was reddening and becoming moist again. It began to flow from the cloth onto the dirt at Simon's feet, leaving the material a lustrous white—a white more brilliant than the fabric had been the day it was woven.

Not all the blood drained away. Some of what had been a random pattern remained now in the form of a strange, unfamiliar symbol. The top looked like a crescent moon resting with the points facing upward and just touching at the peak. Centered in that circle of moon was a five-pointed star, with the bottom two points shooting downward like beams of light and forming a pyramid with the horizontal line of the ground. Connecting the ground to the crescent circle was a T-shaped cross, much like the one that bore Jesus upon Golgotha.

"What...what is this wondrous thing?"

"Trevia Dei—the three great roads to God that are one," Jesus said.

"It is a symbol of the different paths men shall take in seeking their Father."

"I don't understand."

Reaching out, Jesus touched Simon first upon the forehead and then the heart. Simon felt a tingling sensation, then found himself surrounded by a bubble of light. All of his senses were intensified: Colors became more vibrant, smells sweeter, sounds more resonant, even the hard earth felt exquisite beneath his feet.

Still gazing at the image on the cloth, he saw the Trevia Dei transform into three separate symbols that slowly lifted into the air and pulled away from one another. The top turned and formed a crescent moon and star. The pyramid doubled and folded upon itself into a six-pointed star. Finally, the transept of the cross lowered, forming a cross with four arms.

Suddenly Simon was transported to a new time and place, and though the experience was unlike anything he could have conceived, he was neither frightened nor mystified. From some distant vantage point, he gazed back upon a bright blue ball suspended in a black void, and he knew without understanding how that this sphere was the home of man.

His vision expanding, he saw marvelous, winged machines streaking like chariots through the sky, cities ablaze with lights that never flickered, buildings taller than the Tower of Babel. But he also saw men and women with skin as dark as his own being chained and crowded onto slave-trading boats, Jews being herded by the thousands to slaughter in death-camps, millions of men and women of all races and nations being killed by terrible engines of war.

Finally he became a part of the image, feeling himself not just viewing but physically present in a great temple, though unlike any structure he had ever seen. He was standing in an enormous chamber with a domed ceiling so high and wide that he couldn't help but wonder what kept it from crashing to the ground.

The walls appeared fashioned of gold itself, with incredible statues and paintings of God and His angels. Images of the cross were everywhere, and on each cross, a crucified man who appeared to be Jesus in spirit if not precisely in form.

The temple was filled with hundreds of people who stood in

orderly groupings around the sanctuary, many wearing opulent red robes, the one at the altar dressed entirely in white. He heard the subdued murmur of men and women at prayer and felt a gentle movement of air that carried upon its breath the aroma of incense.

No one seemed to notice Simon standing there in his dusty traveler's robe, alone in one of the aisles leading to the altar. Then he became aware that someone was staring at him—one man alone among the assembly. He turned to that man, whose demeanor and whose curious black garb with stiff white collar were far simpler the others'. Something about this man bridged the long leap of time between them, and their eyes locked in mutual recognition.

Simon held forth his hand, and the gesture was repeated by this man of elegant simplicity. Then, even as Simon took a first step toward him, the image began to fade, the great domed cathedral shimmering like mist as it disappeared, until once again he found himself on the road from Jerusalem.

Simon looked at the cloth in his hands. The Star and Crescent, the Star of David, and the Cross had once more come together into the blood-red symbol Jesus had called Trevia Dei.

"You have seen?" Jesus asked.

"Yes, Lord," Simon answered. "I don't know why I was chosen to view such astonishing things, but I have seen and will never forget."

"In time you shall see and understand more, for the Trevia Dei shall teach you," Jesus told him. "It is a sign for man's journey to God. I have chosen you, Simon, to be keeper of this sign until you are no longer able. Then you must find one who is worthy, who in time will find another, who will pass it to yet another for fifty generations to come...until the time Trevia Dei is to be revealed."

"Yes," Simon replied, looking again at the marvelous symbol upon the cloth. "I will do as you say, my Lord, always..."

There was a faint rustle of wind, and then Simon looked up to discover he was again alone. For an instant he thought it had all been a dream, but then he saw in his hands the cloth bearing the Trevia Dei, and any remaining doubt vanished. He fell forward on the ground, giving a prayer of thanks that he had been chosen, and a prayer of entreaty that he be worthy of so great a trust.

NINE

FR. MICHAEL FLANNERY STOOD AMONG THE GATHERED ASSEMBLY THREE-quarters of the way back in the great nave, watching the spectacle and grandeur of a Pontifical Mass. It was a pageant nearly as old as Christianity itself, one Flannery had witnessed many times, but it never failed to move him, for at such times the very stones of St. Peter's Basilica came alive.

It did not seem a stretch for Flannery to imagine the scarlet-clad cardinals as the blood of the Church, as Christ's blood. They were the wine of the Sacrament.

"This is my blood of the new covenant, which is shed for you."

The new Pope, dressed in white and on the throne of St. Peter but a year, was Corpus Christi—the body of the Church.

"This is my body, which is given for you."

Flannery strained to hear the Holy Father's words.

"O risen Christ, the source of fresh vitality, capable of softening even hardened hearts and renewing courage in those who have lost their way, Lord and redeemer of the human race, enlighten and guide the peacemakers. O victor over death, give strength to those who fashion justice and peace in the world, and especially in the Holy Land, where hopes for peaceful coexistence are still jeopardized by misguided souls who would resort to force and violence."

Force and violence, Flannery thought. The terrorists' bombs and Israeli gun ships may differ in method from the force and violence that was perpetrated in the Holy Land two thousand years ago, but there was no difference in the hatred that spawned it, nor was there any difference in the killing that resulted from hardened hearts. And what sickened Flannery's soul was that the most vitriolic of these events were brought about by religious intolerance.

As Flannery contemplated these things, he was aware of a shimmering golden glow in the nearby aisle. At first he took it for a trick of light, the interplay of divergent beams of sunlight. He looked around for the source but found nothing, and when he turned back toward the glow, it was gone. In its stead was a man, a rather powerfully built black man, dressed in a coarse homespun robe.

This was no apparition; this was a flesh and blood human being who was looking around the cathedral in wonder. And not the kind of wonder Flannery had seen in many first-time pilgrims to the Vatican, but the amazement of someone seeing more than his life experience had prepared him for. And there was something else about the man, something beyond his expression of awe...a peace beyond all understanding. Flannery felt drawn to him in a way he had never been drawn to another human being, a powerful connection that seemed to spring from their very souls.

Their eyes connected, and Flannery felt something akin to an electric shock. He almost called out as he reached toward the stranger, whose own hand stretched out to him. The golden bubble of light reappeared, so brilliant that Flannery had to shield his eyes against its intense glow. When the glow subsided, the figure was gone.

"What?" Flannery muttered aloud.

Those standing nearby glanced over at him, a few in curiosity, most in irritation, for the Holy Father was still speaking. Apparently Flannery alone had seen the apparition—if indeed it had been an apparition. And if so, what had it meant? he wondered. What did the dark-skinned pilgrim in the homespun robe want of him?

Closing his eyes, Flannery struggled to fix the stranger's image in his memory. As he did so, the Pontiff's quavering voice seemed to fill with intensity and light.

May His great name be blessed forever and ever.
May His great name be blessed forever and ever.

————

SARAH ARAD'S balcony terrace had the same cream and royal blue floor tiles as the rest of her Jerusalem apartment, and it was furnished as if it were another room, with wicker sofa and ottoman, and a steel and glass dining set. As a result, the terrace did not feel separated but like an integral part of the living quarters. Indeed, with the sliding doors fully open as they were tonight, the activity flowed effortlessly from inside to outside.

Preston Lewkis, who had accepted an unexpected but very welcome invitation to dinner, stood at the balcony railing, gazing out over the city. The night was pleasant, the air soft and aromatic.

"I hope you're hungry," Sarah called from behind him.

"I was born hungry and I've never gotten over it," he replied, turning and leaning against the rail. He recalled that the first time he had seen Sarah he had found her attractive, even in her battle fatigues. The woman he was looking at now was considerably more so. Her blue-black hair, almond-shaped eyes and olive features were set off perfectly by a short black sweater-dress that draped easily over her body. She looked feminine, sexy, and stunning.

Sarah's face reddened slightly, and she smiled almost in embarrassment. "You're staring."

"You should be used to men doing that," Preston replied, heading inside.

"Why, thank you...I think." She opened the oven and removed a broiler pan that held twin skewers of glistening meat and vegetables.

"Mmm, it smells good."

"Lamb kebobs," she said, lifting the skewers. "Would you pour the wine while I get the rice?"

Returning outside, Preston uncorked the bottle and poured a bit into one of the wine glasses, then swirled it took a sip. Satisfied, he poured for both of them, just as Sarah brought over their plates. He held her chair as she sat down, then sat across from her.

Sarah raised her glass. *"L'chaim."*

"*L'chaim,*" Preston replied, then added, "and mud in your eye."

"Mud in your eye?" She gave a questioning grin.

"Sort of a back home thing."

"And where is that?"

"Well, right now it's Waltham, Massachusetts, where the university's located. But I'm from St. Louis."

"Oh, I've been there," she said with enthusiasm. "My father once gave a lecture at Washington University."

"Your father lectured at Wash U?"

"Yes, on archaeological finds in the Holy Land."

"Hmm, I must've already been out of school then. I don't remember a lecturer named Arad."

"My father was Saul Yishar."

Lowering his glass, Preston stared at her in bewilderment. "Saul Yishar?" he finally said. "You mean to say, *the* Saul Yishar was your father?"

"You know of him?"

"Of course. Who in this field hasn't heard of Saul Yishar? And your mother, as well... I take it Nadia was your mother."

"Yes."

"I attended that lecture. I did my undergraduate work at Washington U. So you were there with him? That means we were in the same building at the same time."

She grinned. "Now, half a world away, we meet again."

"But your last name—"

"Arad is my married name," she explained.

"Married...?"

"My husband was a major in the Israeli Army." Her voice grew softer. "Two years ago, he was killed at a military checkpoint."

"I...I'm very sorry to hear that." Shifting to more comfortable ground, he continued, "Saul and Nadia Yishar were archaeologists without equal. It's no wonder you took an interest, growing up with that inspiration."

"It can also be quite intimidating. While I don't keep it a secret, I usually don't mention they were my parents, lest someone expect more than I can deliver."

"The world lost two of its most brilliant scholars when they—" He paused, as if just realizing a painful fact. "How stupid and insensitive of me. Your parents were killed when..." His voice trailed off.

"Yes, when Palestinian terrorists attacked their dig."

"That was the early dig at Masada, right?" he asked, and she closed her eyes and nodded. "Which is why you've asked to work there now."

"Continuing their work is honoring their memory," she said, offering a faint smile.

"Your husband *and* your parents. I can't tell you how sorry I am."

"Yes, well, such things are a fact of life here," Sarah said. "One just goes on."

There was an awkward silence, during which Preston tasted the kebob. "This is absolutely delicious."

"I'm glad you like it. It's an old family recipe. Well, not kebobs—everyone makes kebobs. I mean the herbs and spices."

"Which is what makes it so delicious. What are they?"

"I can't tell you. It's a secret as old as...as old as the Masada scroll."

"As a Jew, what do you think of the scroll?" he asked.

"What do you mean, 'as a Jew'?"

"Well, does it challenge any of your beliefs? It speaks of Christ, yet it was found at Masada, which is one of the holiest Jewish sites—and until now, totally unconnected with early Christianity."

"Why should it challenge my beliefs? Jesus was one of our boys, after all," she said with a slight smile. "So, Jewish history and early Christian history are bound to overlap. If anything, I'll bet it ends up challenging your beliefs as a Christian."

"Me? Nah," he scoffed. "Perhaps if I were Catholic, like the good Father Flannery. But we Protestants are used to challenging and being challenged."

"I've been wanting to ask you about Father Flannery," Sarah said, her tone cautious.

"Yes?"

"Are you sure it was wise bringing him onto the team?"

"Michael Flannery? I trust him implicitly."

"Perhaps. And while he may have rightfully earned it, he has placed a higher trust in..." She struggled to find the right words.

"In God?"

"No, in the Vatican and in papal authority," she declared.

"He gave his word that he won't say anything of the scroll, not until we—"

"We're not talking about some ordinary antiquity," she cut in, dropping her fork onto her plate. "If the scroll proves to be authentic first century—and especially if it turns out to be the Q document—he may feel compelled by a higher authority to break his earthly vow."

"Not Michael." Preston leaned across the table and placed a comforting hand over Sarah's. "I trust him with my life...with all of our lives. And with the secret of the scroll."

Sarah gave a half sigh. "I hope you're right."

"And we need him," Preston continued. He patted her hand, then picked up his fork and stabbed another morsel of lamb. "There's no one better to help us unravel whatever mysteries the scroll may yield."

"It's not really Father Flannery that I'm worried about," she said. "It's the idea of the Vatican being involved on any level. I just don't want the integrity of the scroll to be compromised."

"How do you mean?" he pressed.

"While I've always admired Christianity as a quintessentially Jewish movement, I can't say I feel the same fondness for the Vatican. Is there a more close-minded organization in the world than the Roman Catholic Church?" she asked. "Their prime motivation is defense of the faith...not truth or knowledge. If we find anything in this document that in any way calls into question their doctrines, they'll spare no effort to discredit or destroy it...or more likely, bury it in their vaults with all the other ancient writings that don't quite square with their rigid ideology."

"I don't think we need worry about that," Preston said. "Your government may be willing to share photocopies of the scroll, but never its possession. And the Vatican would have to contend with us Americans first."

"You?"

"My university is funding the Masada dig, remember? Brandeis would have something to say if Israel tried to turn the scroll over to the Vatican."

"I hope you're right," she said, shaking her head in doubt. "But when politics gets mixed with religion, who knows what might happen? What deals might get struck? Ahh, but that's best left to the priests and politicians." She raised her glass and smiled. "What was that you said? Here's dirt in your eye."

Preston chuckled, then raised his own glass and clinked it against hers, and they each drank deeply.

"Now, enough talk of sacred scrolls and religion," Sarah declared. "If I had wanted to discuss business tonight, I'd have invited you to the laboratory."

"Oh?" Preston said, momentarily confused. Then, seeing the look in her eyes as she studied him over the rim of her wine glass, he nodded in understanding. "Oh," he repeated, returning her smile. "Yes, of course."

TEN

FATHER SEAN WESTER POURED TWO CUPS OF COFFEE FROM A SILVER POT, then added copious amounts of cream and sugar to Michael Flannery's cup. "I know, Michael, m'lad, how you like a little coffee with your cream and sugar," he teased.

Flannery suppressed a smile as he leaned across the table and accepted the cup. "You know me too well, Father."

"I knew you better when you were a young priest, eager to learn everything and spending all your free time in the archives. Irish we were, in a foreign land, and we had some fine conversations, we did. But you don't come around much anymore, and this old fellow gets lonely."

"Come now, Father. How can you possibly be lonely in a place like this? Surrounded as you are with all the saints and their works."

Wester sipped his coffee and looked around at the stacks of books and manuscripts. In his late seventies, he had spent a good portion of those years sequestered among the artifacts of the Vatican archives, some of which were from before the birth of Christ.

"There's surely some truth in what you say." He let out a faint sigh. "The wisdom of the ages is gathered in these old walls. And if you're here long enough—and the good Lord knows I more than qualify—

you don't even have to open some of the covers to read them, for the saints themselves will come and whisper in your ears."

"Has that ever happened to you?"

"Aye, lad. How can it not in this place?"

"No, I'm not speaking metaphorically. I mean have you ever seen something you can't explain? A figure, a saint perhaps...?" Flannery paused in midsentence when he saw the way the older priest was looking at him. "Well, I was just, uh..."

"Have you seen something?"

Flannery took a swallow of his coffee, purposely avoiding Wester's question.

"Michael m'lad, have you seen something?"

Flannery nodded.

"And what would that be?"

"During yesterday's Mass in St. Peter's. I thought I saw something, someone..."

"One of the saints? The Virgin Mary herself?"

"No, nothing like that. He was an ordinary man, a black man, muscular and oddly dressed. He was there one second, then he was gone."

"Is there no chance you merely lost him in the crowd?"

"I...I suppose that could've happened," Flannery said. "But I never looked away. I mean, I was looking right at him, and he...well, he simply vanished."

"The heat," Wester declared. "It can run awfully long and get terrible hot."

"Yes, but you didn't answer my question, Father. Has anything like that ever happened to you?"

Wester chose his words carefully. "Michael, you've not gone back to—"

"No, Father," Flannery interrupted. He was resolute, but not defiant. "I have been sober for twelve years."

"Wondrous things have appeared in the Holy See over the last several hundred years. Visions that have been reported, as well as many that have not. Who is to say that you have not been blessed by such an event?"

"But what does it mean?" Flannery asked. "A black man in a coarse-spun robe, reaching out to me...touching my soul in a way I cannot explain. What could it mean?"

Wester shook his head. "I don't know, though I'm sure that here, among two thousand years of sacred history, there is an answer. If you were selected to see the vision for some holy purpose, then I have no doubt you will discover the reason why."

"I have another question," Flannery said, putting down his cup. "And this one is more concrete. Once long ago, I saw this somewhere." He showed Wester a piece of paper on which he had drawn the symbol at the beginning of the Gospel of Dismas bar-Dismas. "Recently, I saw it again."

Wester looked at the symbol, and for just a moment, Flannery thought he saw a flicker in the old cleric's eyes.

"Where was this?"

"I don't remember where I saw it first." Taking care not to mention the Masada scroll, Flannery continued, "But someone in Israel showed it to me recently, and I recalled having seen it before. I believe it is called the Via Dei."

In a whisper, the old priest replied, "Aye, Via Dei."

"Then you've heard of it?"

"I believe I have."

"Do you know anything about it? Are there any references to it in the archives?"

Wester stroked his chin a moment, then nodded. "Let me see what I can find."

Flannery drummed his fingers on the table as he watched the older man move away. Wester was not very tall, and his long cassock covered his feet, creating the illusion he was gliding rather than walking across the marble floor. Flannery had known the Irish priest for as long as he had been in Rome, meeting him first because he had an intense interest in the archives, then befriending him because they shared an Irish heritage—and something more. Something Father Wester had noticed and called to Flannery's attention well before anyone else.

"Careful, lad," he had told Flannery not long after they met. "Don't let your fondness for spirits impair your love for the Holy Spirit...for the Lord."

Wester had confided that he, too, had devils to fight, and it was partly his gentle prodding that averted what could have been a disaster for the younger priest. Flannery would always be grateful for that.

When Wester returned, he was carrying a leather-bound manuscript. He opened it on the table and pushed it in front of Flannery, who saw it was neatly rendered in a clear and legible hand. It looked to be no more than a hundred years old.

"This is unpublished," Flannery said, looking up at Wester.

"Unpublished, yes. It isn't a Catholic book but one that was written —or channeled, so the author claimed—by the famed psychic and founder of the Theosophical Society, Helena Petrovna Blavatsky, better known as Madame Blavatsky. She was working on it at her death in 1891."

"How did we get hold of it?" Flannery asked as he began to turn the pages and scan the writing.

"Who can say?" Wester replied with a shrug. His mouth quirked into a smile. "Perhaps a Catholic spy among the Theosophists. But it ended up here, and I daresay it's the only copy, because it isn't among the fourteen volumes of her complete writings."

"Have you read it?"

"Aye. Like you, I had seen the symbol once or twice in my youth, and when I stumbled upon it in this manuscript, I was curious and read the whole thing. Fortunately it's in English, though a bit hard to make out in places. Madame Blavatsky's native language was Russian, but she moved to England as a young woman. Only the last chapter refers to Via Dei."

Wester leaned forward and flipped pages of the fairly thin manuscript until he found the correct one. The passage included a hand-drawn symbol almost identical to the one Flannery had shown him.

"That's it," he said, tapping the symbol. "It's the only place I've ever seen it described. This may be the lone recorded reference, and from a dubious authority, at best. But I'll let you draw your own conclusions. Take all the time you need." He backed from the table. "You can work right here; you'll not be disturbed."

"Thank you."

Over the next few hours Flannery pored over the manuscript, first reading the final chapter on Via Dei, then starting the book at page one. Other clerics came and went, but he didn't see them. Distant doors opened and closed, echoing through the chamber like the beat of a kettle drum, but he didn't hear them. Dinner hour came and passed, but he felt no hunger as he again came to the passage where he had begun earlier that day:

> Via Dei, meaning God's Path and commonly called The Way of God, is one of the oldest organizations in Catholicism. Its origins are lost in ancient history. Some say it had roots in the Druid religion and survived the conversion to Christianity. Others say it was a military society formed by the Crusaders and used as their authority to kill, without compunction, Muslims and other non-believers. Some put the origin all the way back to contemporaries of Jesus, in particular one Gaius of Ephesus, who traced his spiritual lineage to Dismas, the so-called Good Thief who was crucified beside the Savior.
>
> Many scholars credit Via Dei with keeping alive the deeper mysteries of Christianity during the Dark Ages, when true believers were systematically put to death as heretics by their own church. Since the Reformation, however, Via Dei is said to be a highly secretive society charged with preserving Catholic purity by destroying any group or individual they deem a threat to Mother Church. The symbol of Via Dei—a pyramid and cross capped by a circle—is considered by some to have been influenced by the Freemasons and Rosicrucians, by others to have been a source for both societies.

While Flannery was not surprised at having found a reference to Via Dei as a secret society from the Middle Ages, he was stunned that Blavatsky had made a direct connection between the purported founder of the group and Dismas the Good Thief, father of the author of the Masada scroll. There were several men named Gaius in the New Testament, and while none was specifically called Gaius of Ephesus, all but one were connected to the apostle Paul, who spent much of his ministry preaching in Ephesus.

Flannery examined the Via Dei symbol as rendered by Madame

Blavatsky, noting the similarities and very minor differences to the one on the Dismas scroll. The main variation was at the top, where the crescent moon with tips touching was instead a perfectly symmetrical circle, and the five-pointed star atop the pyramid was less a star and more like thin rays of light, giving it something of a Masonic appearance. But the similarity was unmistakable.

As Flannery painstakingly sketched the symbol in his notepad, a cheery voice intruded upon his reverie.

"Will you be spending the night here, then?"

"What?" Flannery asked, looking up from the manuscript.

"It's ten o'clock," Father Sean Wester said, coming around the table and into his line of vision.

"Ten o'clock? At night?"

The old priest chuckled. "Aye, lad, two hours before midnight. You've been here all day; you've had no supper."

"I guess I was distracted."

"I would say so."

"Father Wester, do you know of any Catholic writings that confirm or deny what is written here?"

"Let it go, lad."

"What?"

"There are some things best left alone. I know little about Via Dei, but what I do know tells me to leave it in the archives."

"Then there are Catholic writings on the subject?"

"I've given you all I know," Wester said, but even as he spoke, Flannery could see the falsehood in his eyes.

"You aren't telling me the truth, are you? Not all of it, at least."

"Michael, 'tis like my own son, you are," the priest said, his voice tender. "Lay down this quest."

———

IN HIS QUARTERS in Vatican Hall, Michael Flannery warmed a pastry in the microwave and ate it slowly, following it with a glass of orange juice. It wasn't much of a supper, but he wasn't really hungry. Too much had happened during the past two days, from the apparition in

St. Peter's Basilica to his conversation with Father Wester to the discovery of the Blavatsky manuscript.

One thing he knew for certain. The society Via Dei, or at least its symbol, predated the Crusades. It predated even all the known Gospels, for he had seen it clearly displayed on the Masada scroll. He didn't know what it was, but he did know what it wasn't: a symbol created by some knight-errant in order to justify the murder of Muslims.

Whatever secret society it once represented, that society was still around. Flannery knew that because of something he had not shared with Father Wester or even the archaeologists in Israel: the circumstances under which he had seen the symbol the very first time. During his early years at the Vatican, he had been courted by a fellow priest who wanted him to join a group called Via Dei. The courting was so secret that when he asked for more information, he was told that nothing more could be said.

"You must take us on faith," the priest had declared.

It was intimated that membership in Via Dei was a guarantee of quick promotion through the Catholic hierarchy. Did he want responsible jobs in the Vatican? Did he aspire to the purple? Might he some day want to be a cardinal? Though membership in Via Dei didn't guarantee those goals, it would certainly enhance his chances.

Flannery neither accepted nor declined the offer, waiting to see what would happen. As it turned out, nothing happened, and he had nearly forgotten about the whole thing until he again saw the symbol, this time boldly drawn upon a document two thousand years old.

The priest tried to put all thought of Via Dei out of his head as he undressed and climbed into bed. He fidgeted for a while before finally settling into sleep. It was a restless sleep, however, filled with images of Jerusalem, the scroll, and the strange black man who had appeared before him during Mass. But as he dreamed of that man, the image transformed into a more familiar face, though one he hadn't seen in perhaps twenty years.

"Father Leonardo Contardi," he exclaimed, bolting upright in bed and waking himself in the process.

He spoke the name again, this time in a whisper, as he more fully recalled the man who had first mentioned Via Dei when they both were seminarians here in Rome. He had lost touch with the priest not long thereafter, when Contardi was assigned to a mission in the Middle East.

One thing was certain, Flannery told himself as he lay back down on the bed and closed his eyes. "Tomorrow I must find Father Leonardo and learn what he knows about Via Dei and its symbol."

ELEVEN

It took Michael Flannery two weeks to track down Leonardo Contardi. The last he had heard, the young, enthusiastic priest had departed Rome for service at a monastery in Israel. But as Flannery now discovered, the Monastery of the Way of the Lord had shut down a few years later, with Contardi being transferred to a tiny village in Ecuador's Amazon lowlands. There, living among the primitive Huaorani tribe, the priest first lost his health and then his emotional stability. Only three months ago, he had been sent back to Rome to the San Giovanni Hospice for Priests. He had come home to die.

As Flannery was ushered into a small, private room at the hospice, he couldn't believe that the gaunt, contorted figure stretched out on the bed was the same man who could once beat him so easily on the handball court. Only twenty years had passed since they had studied, relaxed, and laughed together. Like Flannery, Contardi was only in his forties, though he now looked several decades older.

"Leonardo," Flannery whispered, taking the frail priest's hand in his own. The hand had no strength. "I wish you had let me know you were back in Rome."

Contardi looked up at the visitor, his gray, rheumy eyes betraying no hint of recognition. In a surprisingly strong voice, he said in English, "Lentils."

"Excuse me?"

"Lentil soup—all we are ever served in here, you know. Lentil soup." His voice was a bit reedy but clear, his eyes wide with what seemed a note of excitement. His formerly thick Italian accent had softened remarkably, no doubt the result of years overseas in the company of men of many nationalities.

"Oh, I'm sure the menu is more varied than that. Perhaps there's some medical reason why—"

"Are your belongings safe from the rain?" Contardi interrupted. "The rains are terrible, you know. Sometimes it comes down like a waterfall."

"Yes, I'm sure the rains were terrible." Flannery tenderly stroked the priest's hand.

"The Holy Father is angry with me."

"Now, why would the Holy Father be upset?"

The priest's eyes narrowed, and he whispered conspiratorially, "There are three hundred twenty-two of them, you know."

"Three hundred twenty-two? Leonardo, I'm sorry, I don't know what you are talking about."

"Why, lentil beans, of course. Sometimes it rains in the lentil soup. All the nurses are Protestant, you know. Why would they have Protestant nurses in a Catholic home?"

Flannery sighed. Father Contardi's condition was worse than he had imagined. They were quiet for a time, then Flannery made the Sign of the Cross over his friend and breathed a prayer. He turned to leave.

"Michael, why are you here?" Contardi called after him with surprising clarity.

Flannery turned back quickly. "I have come to visit with you," he said, returning to the bed, hoping there would be no more talk of soup or rain. "You should have let your friends know you were back in Rome."

"You see how I am," Contardi replied. "I did not wish to impose upon anyone."

"The opportunity to help a friend is never an imposition."

"Help me? Tell me, Michael, how would you help me?"

"I can pray with you."

"Save your prayers for those who have not lost their faith."

"Leonardo, you don't mean that."

Contardi tilted his head slightly. "No, there is something else... some other reason you have come."

"Why do you say that?" Flannery asked, suddenly uncomfortable about troubling a man in such condition with his own burdens.

As Contardi's lips cracked into a smile, Flannery realized just how emaciated and sick he was, and the reality set in that this was a hospice and that his friend would only leave this bed when lifted from it by the Lord.

The priest raised a bony finger and tapped his cheek just below his right eye. "You see, I learned a few things from my years in the jungle. I no longer only see what is on the surface...but deeper. The truth is invariably revealed." He paused, narrowing his eyes as he asked, "What is it? Why have you really come?"

Thank God, he is lucid now, Flannery thought. "Yes, there is a reason," he admitted. He took out the paper on which the symbol of Dismas was drawn. "Do you remember when we were much younger, how we once discussed an organization called Via Dei? This was their symbol, I believe."

Contardi looked at the paper. If it was possible, his complexion grew even more ashen, and he threw his arm across his eyes and turned away.

"No," he said, shaking his head, his voice rising in fear and anger as he continued, "No! Take it away! Take it away! Can you not see the flames? Do you not smell the sulfur? Satan, get thee behind me!"

"Leonardo, what is it? What's wrong?" He placed a comforting hand on the priest's forearm, only to have the ailing priest jerk free.

"Nurse! Nurse!" Contardi shouted.

A male attendant hurried into the room. *"Padre? Che cosa?"* he asked.

"Diavolo!" Contardi pointed an accusatory finger at Flannery, who gaped back at him in open-mouthed shock. *"Chi l'anima mi lacera?"* the priest muttered, rolling away from the two men and again covering his face, as if seeing some sort of demon. *"Che inferno! Che terror!"*

"What is it?" Flannery beseeched of his friend. "What have I done?"

"So sorry, Padre, he gets sometimes this way," the attendant said in heavily accented but understandable English as he inserted himself between Flannery and the ill priest, who was babbling now in some unidentifiable language. "Perhaps you better should leave. I give him a sedative and he can rest."

"Yes," Flannery agreed. "Yes, I'll leave."

By now Contardi's ravings had dissolved into audible sobs. Flannery crossed the room, looking back a final time before stepping into the hall. His friend was struggling to sit up as the attendant tried to ease him back down.

With a final burst of energy, Father Contardi exclaimed, "L'anima! The soul, it is eternal! It is all I have left. I'll not relinquish my soul!"

REALIZING he'd get no more help from Father Wester in the Vatican archives and unwilling to upset Father Contardi any further, Michael Flannery continued the search for information about Via Dei on his own. He looked through all the Vatican libraries to which he had access, then removed his collar so as not to attract unwanted attention and visited the libraries and antiquarian bookstores of Rome.

He was about to give up when he stumbled upon a book entitled *Black Mass*. The whole concept of a black mass was so repugnant, so evil, that he could almost feel the book burn his hands as he held it. Forcing himself to look through it, he found a reference to Via Dei:

The Marquise de Montespan, mistress of Louis XIV, sought the services of a defrocked priest to conduct a Black Mass over her, because she thought the King was interested in another woman. Using Montespan as a naked altar, the priest invoked Satan and his demons of lust and deceit, Beelzebub, Asmodeus, and Astaroth, to grant Montespan whatever she desired. He consecrated the host by sticking pieces into her vagina. More than two hundred people, including some of France's highest ranking nobility, attended the ceremony, which concluded with a great orgy.

Learning of the heresy, the Catholic Order of Via Dei conducted a secret trial, obtaining confessions by means of torture. Most of the nobility received prison sentences or exile, but thirty-six commoners were executed, including the defrocked priest, who was burned alive in 1680.

———

WHEN FLANNERY RETURNED to his quarters that evening, his telephone was ringing. Snatching it up, he heard Father Contardi say in a clear, strong voice, "Michael, you are back. This is Leonardo."

"Leonardo! How are you doing?"

"I have moments of confusion. Apparently they are coming with more and more frequency. I hope you understand and forgive me for my outburst the other morning."

"There is nothing to forgive, my friend," Flannery assured him.

"You asked about Via Dei."

"Yes."

"I wonder if you could visit me again. We should talk. I think it is important that we talk."

"Yes, of course. I'll come over right away."

"No," Contardi said. "It's late; any visitor now would be subject to the utmost scrutiny. It would be better if you came in the morning, after breakfast."

"All right, I'll be there at nine."

"Michael, if it isn't too much trouble, would you bring some lemon drops?"

Remembering his friend's penchant for the confection, Flannery laughed. This was much more like the lighthearted young priest he had known. "I'll bring the biggest package I can find," he promised.

———

IN ANOTHER PART of the hospice, someone stood in the shadows, holding his hand over the mouthpiece of a telephone as he listened to the conversation. When he heard both parties hang up, he broke the connection. Then reacquiring the dial-tone, he put through a call.

"It does not look good for Father Contardi. I think his time has come," he told the person on the other end. "It is time to administer Last Rites."

He set the phone back on the cradle.

"May God receive him into his kingdom," he intoned as he retreated even deeper into the darkness.

———

"*IN NOMINE PATRIS, et Filii, et Spiritus Sancti. Amen.*"

Hearing the blessing, Father Contardi opened his eyes and, in the subdued light of his small chamber, saw a man in a hooded-cassock standing over him. A hand protruded from the voluminous sleeve of the robe, two bony fingers extended forward, tracing the Sign of the Cross in the air.

"Extreme Unction?" Contardi said. "Have I come to this?"

"Now, Father, the Second Vatican Council decreed that we no longer use the term Extreme Unction," came the reply. "We anoint the sick."

Contardi could not see the man's face, hidden in the shadows of the hood. But he could hear the voice, a quiet hissing, like the sound of the wings of Gabriel.

With oiled, skeletal fingers, Contardi's night-time visitor anointed him on the forehead and hands.

"Through this holy anointing may the Lord in his love and mercy help you with the grace of the Holy Spirit. May the Lord who frees you from sin save you and raise you up."

The celebrant paused, then continued in Latin.

"*Misereatur vestri ominipotens Deus, et dimissis peccatis vestries, perducat vos ad vitam aeternam.*"

The celebrant stepped back into the shadows of the room, completely disappearing from sight. For a moment, Father Contardi wasn't sure his mysterious visitor was still in the room, or even if he had ever been here.

Had this all been a hallucination brought about by his delirium?

Contardi closed his eyes, and thus he didn't see the second man come forward and place the pillow over his face, pressing it down so hard that he couldn't breathe. He knew then that he was dying, and he tried to say a quick prayer, but he couldn't mouth the words, except in his mind.

Kyrie eleison. Christe eleison.

Because Father Contardi did not struggle, it was over very quickly, and the man who wielded the pillow looked into the shadows at the one who wore the hooded cassock.

They exchanged nods. No words were spoken. None were needed.

———

MICHAEL FLANNERY HAD a dozen or more questions he wanted to ask, and he hoped his old friend was as lucid this morning as he had been during the unexpected telephone call the previous night. Carrying a bag filled with packages of lemon drops, Flannery bounded almost giddily up the stairs of the hospice and crossed the lobby to the front desk.

The young nun on duty looked up and, recognizing him from his previous visit, said, "Good morning, Father." She seemed eager to practice her English and asked, "Who desire you to visit with this morning?"

"Ah, good morning to you, Sister. I'm Father Michael Flannery, and I'm here to call again on my dear friend, Father Leonardo Contardi."

Flannery saw a flicker of reaction on the sister's face. "One moment, Father. I will get Father Guimet."

"Father Guimet?"

"*Si.* The director of the hospice."

Hoping to keep his visit as low-profile as possible, he said, "Why must I see him? I didn't have to last time."

"I must get for you him," the sister said, picking up the telephone.

Flannery was about to protest again but thought better of it. Apparently there had been a report about Contardi's outburst the other day. He would talk to this Father Guimet and explain what had happened.

Flannery crossed the room and dropped down onto one of the lobby chairs. Fiddling with the bag on his lap, he considered opening one of the packages of lemon drops and taking one for himself. It was neither whiskey nor sweet coffee, but for the moment it would suffice. He resisted the temptation. He knew his friend would be generous with them, but better for him to make the offer.

"Father Flannery?"

The priest who came toward him was in his sixties, very thin, totally bald, and with pendulous ears much too large for his head.

"Yes," Michael said, rising from the chair. "Father if this is about my previous visit—"

"I'm sorry," Father Guimet said abruptly. "But Father Contardi...I am sorry to tell you, but he passed away during the night."

TWELVE

DISMAS BAR-DISMAS STOOD IN JERUSALEM'S STREET OF WEAVERS, greeting the congregants as they arrived at the church meeting house to hear Stephen preach of the risen Christ. During the six years since Jesus' crucifixion, Stephen had gathered a growing band of believers into a movement he called The Way, and Dismas was one of his most enthusiastic and effective supporters.

Dismas recognized most of the people who had already arrived but was pleased to see several new faces. The gatherings were larger with each meeting, and he knew that the other churches that were sharing the message of Jesus were drawing similar crowds.

A middle-aged tradesman came hobbling down the street and stopped in front of Dismas, fixing the bearded young man with a challenging gaze. "Is this where they preach of the coming Messiah?" His eyes narrowed with distrust.

"Please join us and hear the good news." Dismas motioned toward the doorway. "I am Dismas bar-Dismas."

"Hershel the butcher," the man introduced himself.

"May the spirit of Jesus the Christ be with you always, Hershel."

"Jesus? You speak of the Galilean prophet, the one who was crucified for his blasphemy?"

"He was crucified for speaking the truth," Dismas said. "He was the Messiah."

"How could *he* be the Messiah, if he is now dead?"

"He was dead, yes, but he rose from the dead and now lives in Heaven, at the right hand of the Lord."

Hershel raised a hand as if to ward off evil. "Oh, sir, now I fear *you* are being blasphemous. For no one could rise from the dead without usurping the power of God."

"Or being of God," Dismas replied.

"You say he has risen from the dead. Have you seen this miracle with your own eyes?"

"I have not, but there are many who have. If you wish to know more, come listen to my friend Stephen."

The butcher gave a hesitant nod. "Yes, I think I would like to know more about him."

Dismas escorted Hershel into the large meeting room and introduced him to the gathering. On hand were about three dozen men and women of all stations, from landowners to slaves. Within the church there was no differentiation between them, and wealthy and pauper greeted each other in the name of Jesus, then took their places on simple plank benches to listen to Stephen. Dismas stood in the back, where he could welcome any latecomers.

The conversation stilled as Stephen mounted a raised platform at the front of the crowd. He was a tall man with angular, almost harsh features, dressed in sandals and a plain brown robe. Most striking were his dark, close-set eyes that blazed like black coal. He stood there, looking out over the assembly, his eyes seizing their attention. When the silence was complete, he began to speak.

"When Moses was in the desert near Mount Sinai, he saw a bush that was burning, yet not consumed by the flames. He moved closer to examine this wondrous thing, and that's when he heard the Lord's voice ring out, 'I am the God of your ancestors. Take off your sandals, because you are standing on holy ground.'"

Upon saying this, Stephen removed his own sandals, and most of the congregation followed his lead.

"Moses received commandments from God that offered life, and he presented those commandments to us, but we did not obey them.

Later, Joshua led our ancestors to this promised land and Solomon built us a temple."

Stephen raised his hand and held it still for a moment. Then shaking his finger, he continued in a voice so loud that it rattled the windows.

"But the Most High does not dwell in houses that people build with their hands."

The congregation gasped at what seemed a direct attack against the Temple, the holiest place in all of Jerusalem.

"As the prophet says, 'Heaven is my throne, and the Earth is my footstool. So do you think you can build a house for me? Do I need a place to rest? Remember, my hand made all these things!'"

Some of the newcomers stirred uneasily and looked ready to bolt from the presence of the blasphemer, but Stephen held them fixed in their seats with the power of his gaze and the certainty of his voice.

"You stubborn people! You have not given your hearts to God, nor will you listen to him. Your ancestors sought to destroy every prophet who brought word that the One Who is Good would come. They killed the prophets, and now you have turned against and killed the One Who is Good."

Stephen looked up, then pointed toward the rafters.

"Look!" he shouted. "I see Heaven open wide, and the Son of Man is standing at right side of the Lord!"

Suddenly a man in the front row leaped to his feet, and as if on signal, three other congregants rushed forward with him and grabbed hold of Stephen. The rest of the assembly remained transfixed, thinking it a planned part of Stephen's sermon.

Dismas, too, was taken in by the action, but then he recognized the leader of the four as the newcomer who had claimed to be Hershel the butcher, and he realized the truth: A number of today's celebrants had not come to worship but to take the fiery orator prisoner.

"Leave him be!" Dismas shouted.

He started forward but was grabbed by two other men who had been seated near the back. A third man, small in stature but power-fully built, burst through the outer doorway and moved in front of Dismas to block his way. He was completely bald and had a large, hooked nose and eyebrows that converged in the middle. Dismas recognized him at once as Saul, one of the most dedicated persecutors of the followers of Jesus.

Saul pointed to Dismas. "Do not interfere with the law, bar-Dismas," he declared.

"Where are you taking him?" Dismas demanded.

"That is none of your concern."

Some of the congregants, realizing at last what was happening, stood and began to shout as Saul and his men dragged Stephen from the church. With Dismas at their head, they followed outside, where an even larger contingent of Saul's men were waiting to take the prisoner into custody.

Dismas and his fellow Christians were far outnumbered and powerless to do anything but watch in fear as Stephen's captors carried him out of the city to the Kidron Ravine. There, they encircled Stephen and began picking up large stones, with Saul gathering up and holding their cloaks.

Knowing what was about to happen, Dismas charged forward at Saul, trying to break through the ranks of his followers. He almost made it before he was beaten to the ground by several of the men. They started to drag him over to where Stephen was standing alone in the center of the circle, but Saul motioned for them to take Dismas away. Apparently he was acting on orders—possibly from the Sanhedrin—and he would not overstep his authority.

As Dismas was pulled to his feet and dragged off, Saul stepped back into the ring of men and nodded. At his signal, first one and then a second threw his stone at the victim. The others joined in, and Stephen was struck again and again, blood flowing freely from the gashes to his head and body. He dropped to his knees and bowed his head as the stones continued to rain upon him.

"Lord Jesus, receive my spirit!" he cried out.

From just outside the ring of stone throwers, Dismas gasped upon hearing Stephen's cry, for it was almost identical to the words Jesus had said from the Cross. Stephen's next words were even more astonishing.

"Lord, do not hold this sin against them."

Those were his last words, for the next stone proved fatal.

Saul's men looked at Stephen's body for a moment, then one by one they dropped their remaining stones and walked over to their leader.

"It is good," Saul said as he handed each man his cloak. "You have done God's work here today, and it is a good thing."

———————

FOURTEEN YEARS LATER, Dismas bar-Dismas was many miles from Jerusalem, seated on a rock bench in a garden in Ephesus, gazing at the sunlight dancing on the surface of the Aegean Sea. As he thought back to the brutal stoning of Stephen, he felt far older than his forty-two years, with a bone-deep tiredness from his extensive travels during the two decades since the crucifixion of Jesus. Those travels were due in large measure to the man responsible for the stoning, for soon afterward Saul had come to arrest Dismas, forcing him to flee Jerusalem. Later, Saul had been instrumental in bringing Dismas here to Ephesus. But this time it was not out of hatred but out of love.

"Dismas?"

Turning, he saw a short, bald man with a hooked nose. "Ah, Paul... you have met with the priests?"

"Yes," Paul replied. "We will no longer be allowed to use the synagogue for our teaching. But I have found an auditorium at Gymnasium Tyrannus that you can use."

"*I* can use?"

"Yes, my friend. I must continue my travels and teaching, but you must stay here and carry on the work we have started. I leave you in the company of young Gaius of Ephesus, who will help ease your burden as you lead our flock. Will you do this?"

"Yes, of course I will," Dismas said.

Even as Dismas felt a wellspring of love pour out toward the man standing before him, he wondered how he could have such feelings for the very person who had stoned his friend, Stephen. Back then, if anyone had told Dismas that the most dedicated persecutor of the followers of Jesus would one day become an apostle, Dismas would have said they were lying. If they had claimed that Dismas, himself, would go on a preaching journey with Stephen's killer, he would have called them crazy. Yet that is exactly what had happened, for Paul, the loving and dedicated servant of Jesus the Christ with whom Dismas was now traveling and preaching, was indeed the same man who had organized the stoning of Stephen.

Paul, known then as Saul, was a Pharisee destined for the Rabbinate by birth, education, and temperament. En route to that lofty station, he had accepted a commission from the Sanhedrin to defend Judaism and had entered wholeheartedly into the persecution of those who believed Jesus was the Messiah. But he had experienced a miraculous conversion on the road to Damascus when he had been stunned by a flash of light and heard the voice of Jesus.

Soon after, Saul was baptized and took the name Paul, and he went to all the synagogues preaching that Jesus was the Son of God. It was on the third journey that Dismas joined him, their path ultimately leading to Ephesus, whose temple of Artemis—Diana of the Ephesians—was a great center of paganism in the Mediterranean world.

As Paul moved closer and placed a hand on Dismas's shoulder, Dismas felt the weariness drain away, replaced with a surge of energy like sap renewing a tree.

"I have been truly blessed to have you traveling with me," Paul declared with a smile, "for you saw the living Christ, and your own father was saved by him, even as he hung from the Cross. And you were on hand in the Kidron Ravine, a witness to those dark days before I came into the light. Yet, though you have every reason to bear me ill will, I feel from you only the love of the Lord."

"And I have been equally blessed to have had such a teacher as you," Dismas replied.

Paul stepped back a few paces, then halted and said, "There is one task I must ask of you, my brother."

Dismas noticed a strange solemnity in the older man's expression. "I will do whatever you ask."

"It is not I, but someone far greater who requires your service."

"What must I do?"

"While here in Ephesus, you must begin to write an accounting of the life of our Lord, as you have known it."

"Me?" Dismas asked in stunned disbelief. "I am not a writer like you. I am but—"

"You are someone who was with the Christ when he still walked upon this land. No matter how educated my words may sound, they are those of a man whose faith lies in believing, not seeing. You were graced with the gift of having seen and having believed. It is a gift you must share with all."

Dismas started to protest, but Paul held up a hand.

"Give it no more thought, my brother. When it is time, our Lord will place pen and papyrus in your hand and command you to write." Paul moved closer to his friend. "And now I must be on my way."

"Remain safe on your journey."

"Go forth, my brother, in the love of Christ."

They clasped forearms, then turned and headed in their separate directions.

THIRTEEN

In the ministry room of the governor's palace, Rufinus Tacitus stood behind his elevated chair of state, staring through the window at the boats in the harbor, wishing he was returning to his homeland aboard one of them. In his mid-fifties, the provincial governor of Ephesus resented having to waste his career in an outpost so far from Rome.

A young woman entered the room bearing a bouquet of flowers. "Isn't it a lovely day today?" she mused as she arranged the flowers in a vase on one of the side tables. "And our garden is so exquisite."

"Did you cut them yourself?"

"Yes."

"Marcella, I have told you to have the servants do the work. How do you think it looks for the governor's wife to be engaged in such trivial labor?"

"Oh, but Rufinus, I don't consider it labor at all," Marcella said. "It pleases me to walk through the garden."

The governor turned back to the window, concealing his anger. A petty and vindictive man, Rufinus Tacitus was fiercely jealous of his attractive young wife and had been known to cruelly punish a soldier for merely looking at her with anything approaching familiarity.

Rufinus was not only jealous of Marcella, he secretly feared her, since she was of higher birth, with family connections that were largely responsible for the success of his diplomatic career. Some of his resentment at being in Ephesus was directed at her, but he held it in check, since he would need her family's support if he ever hoped to make it back to Rome.

Marcella was in her late twenties, almost thirty years younger than Rufinus. Their marriage had been arranged by her parents, as most marriages were, and while he knew she wouldn't have chosen him for herself, he had to concede that she tried to be a good wife. The task was made more difficult by his brooding discontent, which often flared into rage and even violence.

"There," Marcella said, stepping back to admire the floral arrangement. "That will brighten the room for you."

Rufinus glanced at the flowers but said nothing, then turned back toward the harbor and the boats.

"I will leave you to your thoughts," Marcella said.

He waited as the sound of her footsteps faded down the corridor. Then he turned away from the window and took a swallow of wine from the goblet he was holding. Spitting the liquid back into the goblet, he threw it against the wall and shouted, "Tuco!"

"Yes, Your Excellency," his head servant replied, entering the room.

"Get some wine I can drink, not that bilious vinegar."

"Yes, Your Excellency." Tuco bowed obsequiously.

"And get that cleaned up!" he ordered.

Tuco clapped and two other servants hurried in to tend to the mess. He left the room, then returned a moment later with a fresh goblet of wine. He held it forth tentatively, then stepped back to await the governor's response.

Rufinus took a swallow but made no reaction at all. It was almost as if his outburst had never occurred. He pointed to a boat that was sailing out to sea.

"They will be in Rome in a few days," he said, "while I am stuck in this place forsaken by the gods."

"But Your Excellency, it is beautiful here," Tuco said. "And you have a most responsible position. Everyone in Ephesus respects you for your wisdom and courage."

"They do, don't they?" Rufinus agreed. "Not many could rule such a backward people as well as I do."

"I know of no one who could," the servant declared.

"Tuco, have you heard much of this new religion, these Jews who worship a man who was crucified some years ago?"

"Yes. But it isn't just Jews. Right here in Ephesus they number Gentiles among them. Some have taken to calling themselves Christians."

"What does that mean?"

"The man who was crucified was called Jesus the Christ."

"Christians, are they?" Rufinus took another sip of his wine. "Are you a Christian, Tuco?"

"Of course not," Tuco responded emphatically. Your Excellency, why are you so interested in this religion?"

"Because one of our soldiers is enamored with this strange cult and seeks to resign his commission. And not just any soldier, but an officer in my own private guard."

"You are talking about Marcus?" Tuco asked.

Rufinus looked up in surprise. "You know of this?"

Tuco nodded. "Marcus has been telling other soldiers of Jesus and urging them to hear the Christian leaders in Ephesus, Paul of Tarsus and a man named Dismas."

Pinching the bridge of his nose, Rufinus shook his head. "It is worse than I thought. Summon the commander of the guard."

Tuco withdrew, and Rufinus turned again to the window. The boat that was bound for Rome was far out to sea now, so far that it was barely visible.

A few minutes later, heavy footsteps pounded the tiles, and a voice said, "Governor Tacitus."

As Rufinus turned, the legatus, or legion commander, brought his fist to his breast in salute. Rufinus returned the salute with a haphazard hoisting of his cup as he asked, "Legatus Casco, did you know that Centurion Marcus Antonius has asked to resign his commission?"

The silver-haired officer looked a bit uncomfortable. "Yes. He has spoken of it to me."

"What did you tell him?"

"I believe he has fallen in love with an Ephesian woman," Casco said. "I counseled him about it. I told him that all soldiers in foreign lands have liaisons, but he must not let such a thing go to his head." The legatus chuckled. "Bed her, share a house with her if you must, I told him, but there is no need to resign your commission."

"You are an idiot," Rufinus barked.

A flash of anger, then of hurt replaced the officer's smile. "I beg your pardon, Governor?" he said.

"His wanting to resign has nothing at all to do with a woman. He has joined that new religion."

"You are speaking of the religion that is being preached by those two Jews?"

"You know of this Paul and..." he struggled for the other name.

"Dismas," Casco said. "Yes, I do."

"And what are you doing about it?"

"I have sent men to listen to their teachings and report back if they are saying anything treasonous."

"You have sent spies?"

"Yes, Your Excellency."

"Let me guess, Casco. Could one of those spies have been Marcus Antonius?"

Casco was silent for a moment, then he nodded.

"And were you not aware that he was taken in by these people? That he has become one of them?"

Casco shrugged. "Your Excellency, as far as I was concerned, it was just another religion. There are many religions. I saw no harm."

"It is not just another religion," Rufinus snapped. "It is a very dangerous one. And now Marcus is preaching this new religion to his comrades. What would happen if more of them become Christians and desert from the ranks? Would you have us be left here, defenseless?"

"No, Your Excellency."

"I would hope not," Rufinus said. He made a waving motion with his hand. "Go. Bring me Marcus Antonius."

"At once." Casco again pressed his fist to his breast.

————

"GOVERNOR," Legatus Casco announced, "Centurion Marcus Antonius is just outside."

"Send him in."

Casco turned toward the door, but Rufinus called after him, "No, don't send him in. Bring him in, under guard."

Rufinus crossed the room and sat in his chair of state. A few moments later, Marcus Antonius entered and saluted, escorted by a soldier on either side. Marcus was a little taller than the average Roman, with dark curly hair, blue eyes, and a muscular build.

Rufinus did not return the salute but immediately began his questioning. "Centurion, I am told you have embraced the religion of this false prophet, Jesus."

"I do not believe Jesus to be a false prophet, Your Excellency," Marcus replied.

"Oh? And, what do you believe him to be?"

"He is the Son of God."

Rufinus laughed out loud. "Which god? Jupiter? Mars? Perhaps he was the son of the Ephesian Goddess Diana."

"The son of the one true God."

"One god? How can there be but one god? What about the gods of Rome?"

"I believe those gods to be false," Marcus declared.

Rufinus's head began throbbing, and his face turned red with anger. "False?" he shouted so loud that he sprayed spittle on Marcus's face. "You are a blasphemer!" Turning away, he called out, "Legatus Casco!"

"Yes, Governor," Casco said, hurrying into the room.

Rufinus pointed at the centurion. "Place this man in irons. And prepare a tribunal. I intend to try him for treason against the state." He turned and glowered at the prisoner. "And then I intend to execute him."

FOURTEEN

MARCELLA PLACED THE FLOWERS ON A TABLE IN HER BEDROOM, STEPPED back to admire them, then decided they would look better on a chest. She had just relocated the vase when one of the women on her personal staff came into the room.

"What do you think, Tamara? Better here, or over there on the table?"

"Oh, here, Mistress, definitely."

Stepping back across the room, Marcella looked first at the vase on the chest, then at the table. "Yes," she said, nodding. "Yes, I believe you are right." Her smile faded when she saw tears in the young woman's eyes. "Tamara, what is it?" she asked.

"Mistress, please, you must help me," Tamara blurted. "Governor Tacitus has arrested Marcus."

"Marcus? Do you mean Centurion Marcus Antonius?"

"Oh please, Mistress, I love him, and I fear for him."

"Why would my husband arrest one of his own officers?"

"I don't know," Tamara replied. "Can you find out? Please, go to your husband, ask him to spare my Marcus."

"I'll speak with him," Marcella promised as she embraced the woman.

———

WHEN MARCELLA RETURNED to the ministry room, her husband was again at the window. "You spend all your time looking out to sea," she said.

"I should be in Rome," Rufinus answered. "Not wasting my time and my talent in this dismal place." He turned from the window. "What do you want now?"

"Is it true that you've placed Centurion Marcus Antonius under arrest?"

"I have."

"Why, may I ask?"

"You may not," he retorted, then thought better of it and said, "Why does it concern you?"

"One of my staff, Tamara, has feelings for him. She is concerned for his well-being."

Rufinus gave a humorless grin. "She has good reason. He has committed treason, and I intend to execute him."

Marcella gasped. "Treason? Marcus Antonius? But no, that is impossible!"

"Oh? And why is such a thing impossible?"

"I know Marcus well. His father served my father. They have always been loyal citizens of Rome. Why would he commit treason? What has he done?"

"As to why, you will have to ask him," Rufinus said with a dismissive wave. "But I can tell you what he has done. He has become a..." He paused a moment, then let the word slip through his lips in a sneer: "Christian."

"Christian? What is a Christian?"

"There are Jews in the city preaching to the Gentiles about a self-proclaimed prophet known as Jesus the Christ. I should have stopped them earlier, but what matter is it which god the Ephesians worship?"

"Jews, or Christians? I am confused."

"Believe me, my dear, it gets much more confusing," Rufinus said, his tone dripping with condescension. "They are Jews, but they are not accepted by their own people, who consider this Jesus a false prophet. Yet they continue to teach that he is the son of God, and your friend

Marcus believes them. He has abandoned the gods of Rome, the gods and state he is sworn to defend, in order to worship this false prophet, this Jesus the Christ."

"And that is why you have arrested him? Because he has accepted this new religion?"

"Isn't that enough?"

"But Rufinus, you understand religion," she said, moving closer and placing a tender hand on his forearm. "There are gods enough to go around. Almost everyone has their own god to pray to. Why have you so little tolerance for this one? He is just one more god, isn't he?"

Rufinus pulled away. "No, this one is different. This one is dangerous." He rubbed his arm as if erasing her touch. "You are too young to remember, but I do, only too well. Many years ago Pontius Pilate had the man Jesus crucified. One would expect that to have ended it. Yet people are still going about, preaching in his name."

"How dangerous can he be if he is dead?"

Rufinus looked at his wife with eyes that were wide and deep. Oddly, she thought she saw some fear in them.

"That's just it," he said. "There are some who proclaim that he isn't dead, that he has been seen since the crucifixion."

"You mean a ghost?"

"No. A ghost I can understand. But he is said to have appeared in the flesh."

Marcella laughed. "Rufinus, surely you don't believe such a thing?"

"Of course not. But many do, including your centurion. And he has asked to resign his commission so that he might join those who preach of this Jesus. What if others are infested with this disease? What if it runs rampant through the army? You can see what a problem that would cause."

"Suppose Marcus renounces this man Jesus? Would you spare him then?"

"Renounces Jesus?" Rufinus thought a moment, then took a few paces closer to his wife and declared, "Yes, if he renounces Jesus and this...this Christian religion, I shall spare him. In fact, I shall reward him, for it will reveal this petty prophet for the charlatan he is."

"Is it all right if I visit Marcus in jail?"

"Why on Earth would you want to do that?"

"I've known him a long time. Perhaps I can convince him to renounce this false prophet."

Rufinus nodded. "Visit him if you wish."

———

THE DUNGEON WAS DIMLY LIT by dusty beams of sunlight that stabbed through the brick-sized holes left in the walls to let in air. Not enough fresh air to overpower the stench, however, and Marcella had to hold a perfumed handkerchief to her nose as she followed one of the guards. She glanced left and right into the iron-barred cells that lined the stone corridor.

The men who occupied the cells were gaunt, miserable-looking creatures, with long, stringy hair and beards. Some were dressed in rags, but many were completely naked. If any of them were surprised to see a beautiful young woman in their midst, they were too far removed from reality to react. Very few even glanced her way, and the ones who did look up registered no reaction in their dark, vacant eyes.

"He is the last prisoner on the right, Mistress Tacitus," the guard announced.

"Thank you," Marcella replied. "You may go now."

"But my Lady, I should not leave you unprotected."

"I will be all right," she insisted, and when he hesitated, she said more forcefully, "Leave."

"As you wish, my Lady." The guard saluted, then turned on his heels.

When the man was gone, Marcella approached the centurion's cell. Marcus still wore his red cloak of office and was seated on the floor, his knees drawn up before him as he leaned against the far wall.

"Marcus?" Marcella called quietly.

Startled to hear a woman's voice, Marcus leapt to his feet and approached the bars. "Mistress Marcella!" he exclaimed. "What are you doing here?"

"I've come to talk some sense into you," she replied. "Marcus, your father served mine for many years. We have known each other since childhood. Isn't that correct?"

"Of course."

"And you know that I care for you as if you were my own brother."

"You have always been most gracious."

"Then surely you must know that I don't want you to die. And certainly not for something as foolish as your infatuation with some foreign god."

"He is not a foreign god. Jesus is the son of the one true God."

"Who or what Jesus may be is of no concern to me. What I care about...what Tamara cares about...is that you not sacrifice yourself out of stubborn allegiance to some petty belief."

"How is she?" Marcus asked, his eyes betraying his concern.

"Tamara? How do you expect? The man she loves is locked up in —"

"She said she loves me?"

"She cares about you deeply. Surely you know that."

Marcus let out a sigh. "And I care about her. More than she realizes."

"Then get yourself out of this place and back to her. All Rufinus wants is for you to say you were mistaken about this man Jesus and —"

"But I'm not mistaken, and I cannot renounce him. That's one thing I will never do."

"Look, Marcus," Marcella said soothingly, reaching through the bars to him, "it doesn't really matter what you believe. It's what Rufinus believes that's important. You can figure out a way to say what he wants to hear, whether or not you believe it in your heart."

"I will never deny my Lord or his son, Jesus Christ. I'm sorry, but it's something I cannot do. Not for you. Not even for..." His voice trailed off.

"Not even for Tamara? But she loves you."

"If she does, then she'll understand what I must do."

Marcella stared at him a long moment, then asked cautiously, "Tamara...is she a Christian, too?"

The centurion's shoulders slumped. "It is something I pray for every day, but no, she has not yet found her way to the Lord. I have tried to convince her to attend one of our meetings, but she steadfastly refuses." He looked up at Marcella, his eyes beseeching. "I believe she refuses out of deference to her mistress."

"These meetings," Marcella said, changing her approach. "Is that where you first heard of this religion?"

Marcus nodded. "I learned of the Christ from a man named Dismas. He is here in Ephesus now, preaching the word of Jesus."

"Where can I find this man?" she asked. "I wish to attend one of his meetings."

Marcus's expression brightened. "Yes, you must hear what he has to say. It will change your life."

"How do I find him?"

"He preaches nightly at Gymnasium Tyrannus."

"Tyrannus...yes, I know the place," Marcella said. "I will go there and—" She started to say "talk to him" but knew that wasn't what Marcus would want to hear, so she altered her comment in midsentence. "—and listen to him."

Marcus nodded enthusiastically. "Yes, this is good. And please, take Tamara along. You will see with your own eyes and hear with your own ears what I have been saying." He reached through the bars and boldly touched her cheek. "The Lord be with you, Marcella."

FIFTEEN

GYMNASIUM TYRANNUS WAS A PRIVATE SCHOOL FOR BOYS, AGES SEVEN TO fifteen. The building included rectangular exercise grounds surrounded by colonnaded porticos, off which opened instructional rooms. Here, students learned physical training, music, some mathematics and science, but especially literature, speech, and social behavior.

Marcella, accompanied by Tamara, stood under the colonnades, watching as people started gathering to hear a sermon from Dismas.

"My Lady, do you think...?" Tamara started, but Marcella held up her finger in caution.

"Remember, I am not 'my Lady' tonight," she whispered. "I must not be recognized as the governor's wife."

"Yes, my...Marcella," Tamara said, uncomfortable at using such a familiar form of address.

Instead of the fine silks of her station, Marcella was wearing one of Tamara's dresses, a knee-length tunic of coarsely woven cloth. With her head covered by a gray shawl, she looked very much like the other women who were attending the meeting.

An earnest-looking young man about Marcella's age was seated at a table just outside the door to the meeting area, and when he saw the two women hanging back, he stood and greeted them. "Welcome to our gathering. I am Gaius." When they did not reply, he went on, "Ladies, be not bashful. The message of our Lord Jesus Christ is to be heard by all. Come, find a comfortable seat before the meeting room is filled." He motioned for them to enter, his smile failing to soften his serious expression.

Nodding and averting her eyes, Marcella started forward, Tamara hanging close to her side. Gathered inside were Jews and Gentiles, Ephesians all, including common laborers and members of the wealthier class of merchants and professionals. She chose a seat near the wall, then pulled her shawl about her so as not to be recognized.

After a few minutes, a bearded, middle-aged man rose and stood before them. He did not need to raise his hands in a call for quiet, because all conversation immediately ceased as everyone turned full attention toward him.

"I am Dismas bar-Dismas," the man began. "Grace be to you, and peace, from God our father and from his son, the Lord Jesus Christ."

His blessing was punctuated by a few amens and hosannas from the audience. Their murmurings faded, and Dismas fixed them with a stern yet sympathetic gaze as he began his recitation.

"Do not tell falsehoods but speak only the truth, because we all belong to one another in the same body.

"When you are angry, do not fall into sin, and cease your anger by day's end, so that you not give the Devil a way to defeat you."

As he continued, he moved through the room, fixing his gaze on one and then another of the assembly, as if each commandment spoke to a failing within that person alone, as if even their darkest secrets were open to his sight.

"Do not steal, but earn an honest living. Then you will have something to share with those who are poor.

"When you speak, say not harmful things, but say only words that will do good to those who hear you.

"Do not be bitter. Do nothing evil. Be kind and loving to all you encounter, and forgive one another, as God forgives you in Christ.

"Be you slave or master here on Earth, remember that your true master is in Heaven, and as he loves each one of you, so you must love and respect one another."

Dismas moved to where Marcella and Tamara were seated. He

looked back and forth between them, his gaze settling at last on the governor's wife. She tried to look away but was transfixed by a force that seemed to emanate from his startlingly green eyes.

"And should you find yourself in a position of great influence among the people, be it in your own right or reflected through one you love, do not hesitate to proclaim the truth of our Lord. For all power, all position, comes from him alone, and all who deny his grace shall lose their standing in Heaven even as they gain it here on Earth."

Dismas returned to the front of the room and continued his sermon. But Marcella heard little of it, her thoughts instead on the words he had spoken directly to her, words now seared into her soul.

Concluding his address, Dismas said, "And finally, pray for me that when I speak, God will give me words so that I can tell the secret of the Good News without fear."

Again there was a murmur of hosannas in assent.

"Peace and love with faith to you from God the father, and his son, Jesus Christ. Grace to all of you who love our Lord Jesus Christ with a love that never ends."

When the sermon was completed and people started filing out of the room, several in the audience went forward to speak with Dismas. But Marcella just sat in place. His words had resonated within her in a way she had not expected, and she felt her head spinning dizzily.

Tamara stood and looked down at her mistress with concern. "Aren't you going to speak to him about Marcus?"

"Yes," Marcella replied, blinking to force herself back to the present. "But wait until the others have left."

"All right," Tamara agreed and sat back down.

It took several minutes for the worshippers to greet Dismas and depart. Finally, Dismas and the young man named Gaius started from the room as well, but when Dismas saw the two women still in their seats, he stopped in front of them. He seemed somewhat smaller, gentler now, his broad, easy smile brightening his green eyes as he inquired, "Are you women all right?"

"No," Tamara replied, choking back tears.

"Oh? Is there something I can do?"

"Tell him, my Lady." As the appellation slipped from Tamara's lips, she placed a hand over her mouth.

"My Lady?" Dismas said as Gaius eyed the women with suspicion.

She stood and lowered her shawl. "I am Marcella Tacitus, wife of the governor. But you already knew that, didn't you?"

Dismas bowed his head. "I am honored that you came to our meeting."

"We didn't c-come to hear you," Tamara stammered, lowering her head to her hands as she began to sob softly.

"It's all right, Tamara," Marcella soothed, rubbing Tamara's shoulder.

Dismas looked confused. "If you didn't come to hear my sermon, why are you here?"

"We came about Centurion Marcus Antonius," Marcella told him.

"Marcus? What about him?" Gaius put in. "I was surprised he wasn't here tonight."

"He couldn't come," Tamara blurted, looking back up at Dismas. "He's in prison, because of you."

"Me?"

"He has declared himself a Christian," Marcella said.

"We know," Gaius said. "Dismas himself baptized him."

"What you don't know is the governor has thrown him in prison for that. He intends to try him, then execute him."

Dismas looked genuinely surprised. "But why? Rome is usually tolerant of religion and hasn't even tried to stop the Ephesians from worshipping Diana."

"Marcus asked to resign from the army," Marcella explained. "My husband...that is, the governor fears that others may be influenced to do the same. He considers Marcus's conversion an act of treason, not faith."

"I see," Dismas said, frowning. "I'm sorry. I'm truly sorry. If there's anything I can do about it—"

"There *is* something you can do," Marcella said. "You can go see Marcus. Convince him to renounce this Jesus you were preaching about. If he would declare that he is not a Christian, I have the governor's word he will forgive him."

Dismas shook his head. "That's one thing I cannot do."

"Of course you can. You must, for it is the only way Marcus will be spared."

"No, I cannot. If Marcus were to renounce Jesus, he would do so at the peril of his own soul. I could never live with myself if I were responsible for such a thing."

"But you'll be responsible for him losing his life," Marcella said. "How can you live with that?"

"Our mortal existence is only temporary. If he dies now, or fifty years from now, the result is the same. Like all of us, he will die someday. But the soul is eternal. He must do nothing that would risk losing his soul."

"It need not be a true declaration," Marcella countered. "He need only speak the words; what he really believes can remain between himself and his God."

"But the Lord hears not only what comes from the mouth but from the heart," Dismas replied. "And if Marcus were to bear false witness for the sake of saving his body of flesh, he would truly be renouncing his body of spirit and his God." He shook his head emphatically. "No, I cannot do what you ask."

"So, you are just going to let him die?" Tamara said, her tears turning to anger as she stood and faced the man.

"I didn't say that." The hint of a smile formed at the corners of his mouth as he glanced at Gaius. "While I won't counsel Marcus to sacrifice his soul for the sake of his earthly life, perhaps I can offer the governor something of more interest than the life of one centurion."

"What are you suggesting?" Marcella asked.

"An exchange."

"Exchange? What sort of exchange?" she pressed. "What are you talking about?"

"I shall go to the governor's tribunal," Dismas declared. "And I shall offer myself in place of Marcus."

"You mustn't! It would be suicide!" Gaius exclaimed, but Dismas gestured for him to remain silent.

Marcella looked at Dismas in confusion for a long moment, then slowly shook her head. "No, he is right. No one expects you to do such a thing."

"But he must!" Tamara blurted. "My Lady, please, let him do as he wishes. It's the only chance for Marcus."

"It wouldn't be right," Marcella muttered, more to herself than the others.

Dismas reached out and took her hand. "Marcella, I want to do this. I must do this."

She noticed that he used no deferential title in addressing her but simply spoke her given name. And oddly, it pleased her.

"I suppose if you feel so strongly about it..." she mused aloud, uncertain what she was thinking or feeling.

"I do. For the sake of Marcus and for our Lord."

"For our Lord..." she repeated, the words tasting like sweet wine on her lips.

SIXTEEN

SEVERAL HUNDRED EPHESIANS WERE CROWDED INTO THE PRAETORIUM TO witness the trial of one of Rome's own. Not only was the prisoner a Roman citizen, he was an officer, a centurion in the governor's private guard. Rufinus Tacitus was waiting on the Sella Curulis—the seat of judgment. Marcella was seated nearby, though out of her husband's immediate area.

"Bring in the prisoner," Rufinus called.

A drum sounded as Marcus Antonius was brought before the tribunal. His hands were bound behind his back, and a metal collar was affixed around his neck. A rope ran from the collar to the hand of one of the guards, who led him in as if he were an animal.

Marcus was dressed in his finest uniform, with a bright red robe slung from his shoulders and a highly polished brass breastplate that flashed golden in the morning sun. This was by design, for Rufinus wanted his subjects to understand that the law applied equally to Roman and Ephesian alike. The object lesson wasn't lost upon them, and several in the crowd gasped at seeing such a high-ranking Roman subjected to such treatment.

Tuco took his place on the stone floor before the Sella Curulis and unrolled a document, then began to read: "Your Excellency! There comes before you on this day one Marcus Antonius, centurion of the

Anatolian Legion of Rome, seeking fair and just judgment from the tribunal of Rufinus Tacitus, who by order of Claudius, emperor of Rome, is the fair and mighty governor of Ephesus."

"For what reason does he seek justice?" Rufinus asked.

"He is charged with treason, Your Excellency."

"How do you plead, Centurion Antonius?"

"Your Excellency, I have committed no treason against you, and no treason against my emperor or against Rome."

"Yet you proclaim yourself to be a Christian. Is this not true?"

"Yes it is, Your Excellency. But the Lord says, 'Render unto Caesar that which is Caesar's, and render unto God that which is God's.' I have committed no treason against Rome, neither by thought nor deed."

"If that is so, then you will renounce this false prophet Jesus here, publicly," Rufinus demanded.

"I am sorry, Your Excellency, but I cannot do that," Marcus said.

"If you do not renounce him now, I will have you crucified like your God, like your Jesus."

"Your Excellency," Legatus Casco quickly interjected, "Centurion Antonius is a citizen of Rome and as such cannot be crucified."

"Then I will have him beheaded," Rufinus said easily.

"May I address the court?" a voice called from amid the crowd.

There was a murmur of surprise and curiosity as everyone looked around to see who had called out.

"Who addressed me?" Rufinus demanded.

"I did, Your Excellency." A bearded man in the robe of a mendicant pushed forward through the crowd and bowed his head slightly. "I am Dismas bar-Dismas."

"Dismas?"

Tuco leaned over to whisper into Rufinus's ear.

"You are the Jew who is preaching of Jesus? The one who converted Centurion Antonius?" Rufinus asked.

"I am."

"For what reason would you address me?"

"I have come to beg you to spare the life of this good man," Dismas said, gesturing toward Marcus.

"If you wish to speak, you may do so." Rufinus motioned away a pair of guards who were closing in on the man who had disrupted the proceedings.

Dismas turned so that he could see not only Rufinus but the crowd and Marcella, seated just beyond her husband.

"Some of you will remember Paul, who for many years was here among us preaching the word of God," he began. "I wish to tell you a story about him. Before His Excellency Rufinus Tacitus came to Ephesus, Paul and his companion, Silas, were put into prison. They were praying and singing songs to God when suddenly a strong earthquake shook the foundation of the prison. Then all the cell doors broke open and the prisoners were freed from their chains. The jailer, fearing the prisoners had escaped, drew his sword and was about to kill himself, when Paul called out in the darkness, 'Do no harm to yourself, for we are all here!'

"The jailer fell down before Paul and asked, 'What must I do to be saved?' His answer was the same as I preach to all who will listen: Believe in the Lord Jesus Christ, and you will be saved. The jailer then took Paul and Silas to his home, where he washed their wounds and gave them food. The next day, the Roman officers set them free."

As the sermon finished, the crowd buzzed in excitement, some of them moved by the power of his words, all of them expecting a violent response from Rufinus. To their surprise, he merely laughed.

"Tell me, Dismas bar-Dismas, do you expect your God to send an earthquake that will free Marcus Antonius and my other prisoners?"

"No, Your Excellency," Dismas replied. "Though if God wished to do so, it is within his power and there would be nothing you could do to prevent it."

"I see," Rufinus said, nodding in thought.

"Governor, I would make a bargain with you," Dismas said, taking a step closer.

Rufinus looked at him suspiciously. "And just what is this bargain you would make?"

"I offer myself in place of Marcus," Dismas announced.

"To what purpose?"

"I will take his place beneath the sword. Let him go, and kill me instead."

There was a collective gasp from the crowd, especially from Gaius and other followers of Dismas, who couldn't hold back their cries of protest.

Rufinus stroked his chin. "An interesting offer. You do understand, don't you, that as a Jew you won't be going before the sword? I would have you crucified."

"I will go to the cross with joy in my heart," Dismas proclaimed.

"Joy in your heart, eh?" Rufinus scoffed. "We will see how much joy you have when the breath is being squeezed from your body and you are wracked with pain on the cross."

"Then you accept my bargain, Your Excellency?"

"I accept your offer to die on the cross," Rufinus declared, his lips twisting with a smirk. "Guards, seize this fanatic. Place him in the same cell with Marcus Antonius. We will have a double execution."

Some in the crowd shrieked in protest, others with excited glee. Gaius had to be restrained by his companions as he rushed forward, shouting that the streets would run with Roman blood if the governor did not revoke his edict. Near the Sella Curulis, Marcella leaped from her seat to beg her husband to reconsider. But Rufinus Tacitus was already gone, departing the Praetorium in a swirl of robes and the clatter of swords of his private guard.

SEVENTEEN

SARAH ARAD TURNED ONTO THE BOULEVARD FROM A SMALL SIDE STREET near her apartment, spinning the silk-green Mini Cooper's steering wheel with her left hand as she held the cell phone to her ear with her right. As the little car straightened and sped off down the road, she glanced in her rear-view mirror and saw the dusty black Mercedes pull out onto the boulevard behind her. Probably coincidence, she told herself. Still, she kept an eye in the mirror as she gave the Mini some gas and pulled away from the banged-up old car behind her.

She had lowered the cell phone briefly to shift gears, and as she put it back to her ear, it was still ringing. She was about to hang up, when she heard the click of a phone being picked up and a breathless, "Hello?"

"I was about to give up on you," she said, adding in a slightly suggestive tone, "Did I catch you at an inopportune moment?"

"Shaving," Preston Lewkis replied. "It's a noisy electric; I didn't hear the phone."

From the sound of his breathing, she guessed he had run from bathroom to bed stand in the small three-room apartment he was renting during his stay in Jerusalem. She imagined him standing there with a towel around his waist, his skin still glistening from his morning shower.

Shaking away the image and forcing herself to focus on the road, she asked, "Would you like a ride to the lab? That is, if you haven't received a better offer."

"By better offer, do you mean the city bus? If not, then yes, I'd be delighted."

"I'm in my car now. I'll be in front of your flat in fifteen minutes. Is that too soon?"

"I'll be waiting outside," he promised.

Sarah snapped closed the cell phone and tucked it into the cup holder, then glanced in the rear-view mirror. The old Mercedes was still behind her. Seeing a service station just ahead, she slowed and turned into it, watching as the black vehicle drove by without stopping. The driver kept his eyes straight ahead, but his comrade in the passenger's seat seemed to be paying close attention to her.

Or am I just being paranoid? she wondered.

There was that possibility. But Sarah had learned the necessity of vigilance the hard way, by the deaths of her parents and husband at the hands of terrorists.

But didn't most terrorists strike randomly, their victims in the wrong place at the wrong time? Why would these men be specifically targeting her?

Sarah pulled back onto the street. Less than two blocks away, she saw the car again, this time parked at the side of the road.

When the Mercedes swung behind her into the boulevard, she didn't wait to give them a second chance at her. Jerking on the hand-brake and spinning the steering wheel, she whipped the Mini into a squealing, fish-tailing, 180-degree turn. The pursuing car now gave up all pretense of subterfuge. The driver made a U-turn in the face of traffic and, to the loud honking of angry drivers, sped after her.

Sarah accelerated to 100 kilometers—more than 60 miles—per hour, a phenomenal speed on the busy Jerusalem boulevard. She ran a traffic light and threaded her way between a bus, a taxi, and several cars, then glanced in the mirror to see her pursuers gaining ground on the straightaway. The Mercedes had more horsepower, she knew, but it was no match for her nimble Mini in the turns, so she marked a position in the upcoming intersection, made sure there were no vehicles or pedestrians in the way, and spun the steering wheel to the right. The little car reacted instantly, negotiating the 90-degree turn at full speed with only a slight squeal and barely a roll.

As she raced down the side street into a neighborhood of old warehouses, she heard the screeching roar of tires and looked back to see the Mercedes spinning wide in a cloud of smoking rubber. But somehow the bigger car managed to hold the turn as it wildly fishtailed onto the street behind her.

Sarah braked slightly, turned sharply left and accelerated into a narrower side street. As she gunned the car forward, she saw the road ahead blocked by a large delivery truck backing sideways across the road toward a loading platform on the left. Two cars were halted in the right lane, waiting for it to clear the road.

Honking her horn, Sarah pulled into the empty left lane to pass the waiting cars. A worker beside the loading dock waved and shouted, "No, stop!"

As the Mini came on hard past the waiting cars toward the narrow opening between the loading platform and the rear of the truck, the worker dove into a nearby trash bin to avoid being hit. The truck driver, who had heard the commotion and slammed on his brakes, jerked open the door of the cab and leaped from his perch to escape the expected collision. But Sarah had perfectly judged the gap, and the Mini slipped through with an inch or so on each side. She was almost clear when her right-hand mirror caught the edge of the truck's tailgate and snapped off with a sharp crack.

Almost immediately upon reaching the open street ahead, Sarah heard a tremendous crash as the Mercedes followed her into the opening and, halfway through, slammed to a shuddering halt. Sarah braked to a stop and turned around to see what was left of the vehicle, which had pancaked on either side before becoming hopelessly stuck, wedged between truck and loading platform. The two men inside were scrambling to free themselves from the wreckage, but they were unable to open their windows or doors as smoke began to billow around the vehicle.

Sarah climbed out of the Mini Cooper and started toward them. She tried to take note of their features—dark skin, black hair, Semitic features that could be Palestinian or Israeli—but what stood out most was the stark fear in their eyes as smoke turned to flames that licked up into the passenger compartment.

As the shorter man in the passenger seat banged on what was left of the windshield and tugged at his seat belt, unable to free himself, the driver raised a small handgun and stared at Sarah with something akin to resignation. She wondered if she should dive to safety but instead stood transfixed, watching as he pointed the gun not at her but at his own open mouth. He closed his eyes, and as the flames leaped up around him, he pulled the trigger, his head jerking backward with the impact. His comrade screamed now but was drowned out by the ferocious roar of the Mercedes exploding.

Sarah was knocked almost off her feet. As she retreated toward her car, she looked back a final time and tried to make out what was left of the license plate. The first three symbols were legible; the rest of the plate had been sheered off in the impact.

Climbing back into her Mini, Sarah snatched up her cell phone and dialed the police emergency number. Without giving her name, she quickly reported the location of the crash and fate of the victims. Then she called her office and spoke with Specialist Roberta Greene, one of her colleagues at Yechida Mishtartit Meyuchedet, better known as YAMAM, Israel's elite counter-terrorism unit. She asked Roberta to gather information on any Mercedes with a plate that began AL9—and to keep Sarah's name out of any police inquiries.

As she drove around the corner to head back to the boulevard, Sarah glanced at the dashboard clock to see how late she was. Incredibly, only thirteen minutes had passed since her call with Preston Lewkis. She was only a mile or so away, with two minutes to spare.

Stepping on the accelerator, she pulled out onto the wide boulevard and eased into the morning traffic.

EIGHTEEN

PRESTON LEWKIS WALKED UP TO THE MINI COOPER AS IT PULLED TO THE curb beside his apartment building. Opening the passenger door, he eased into the seat and propped his briefcase on the floor in front of him. He smiled at Sarah. "Fifteen minutes, on the dot. I like punctuality..."

"In a woman," she added, her grin broadening. "You were going to say 'in a woman,' weren't you?"

"In anyone," he defended himself. "But yes, especially in a woman. In my experience—which, believe me, is mostly work related—they are seldom punctual."

Sarah chuckled. "I detect a hint of chauvinism."

"I guess I do sound a bit like that, don't I?"

As Sarah pulled from the curb and they headed down the street, Preston glanced through the side window and saw the twisted metal where the right-hand mirror should be. He had been so focused on Sarah that he hadn't noticed it when getting into the car. The metal was jagged and sharp-edged, as if from a recent collision.

"What happened here?" He gestured toward the mirror.

"Vandals," Sarah replied with a slight shrug. "I've been meaning to get that fixed."

She changed the topic to the recent find at Masada, and they spent the rest of the ten-minute drive to the campus of Hebrew University discussing the condition of the scroll that had been unearthed at the site.

When they pulled up at the parking area entrance, Preston noticed several more security vehicles than usual, with armed guards walking the perimeter of the unmarked building that housed the antiquities laboratory. The guard at the gate took extra time scrutinizing their photo identity cards and checking his clipboard before finally waving them through.

"They've beefed up security," Preston noted as they crossed the lot and found a parking spot near the lab entrance. "Is there a reason we should be more concerned?"

"Vigilance is a way of life here," Sarah said as they got out of the car and walked to the entrance.

Her tone was matter of fact, but Preston noticed a concern in her expression as she glanced around at the security precautions that had been instituted during the previous day. Even as she spoke, an additional police car raced through the parking area to where the other security vehicles were parked.

"Yes, vigilance is becoming a worldwide way of life," he remarked. "I suppose it will remain so until this war on terror is won."

"I'm afraid that our descendants, fifty generations from now, will be fighting terrorism. As long as there's one person willing to strap on a bomb in the name of his god, the war will remain unwinnable."

Preston held the door, then followed her into the lobby. They headed toward the security desk.

"Surely, you aren't suggesting we just give up?" he asked, lowering his voice as they approached the guard.

"Not at all. It's like the battle against evil. It will always exist in the world. The fact that we can't eradicate evil doesn't mean we shouldn't fight it."

Sarah placed her handbag on the scanner and handed the guard a slip of paper. "The scanner will show a 9mm Glock," she told him. "This is my authorization."

The guard examined the permit, then watched the screen as the handbag passed through the scanner. "Very good," he said, motioning her through the metal detector.

Preston watched it all in surprise—and admiration. Then he placed his briefcase on the scanner and muttered, "All you'll find in there is a sandwich. Not even kosher."

He saw Sarah suppress a grin. The guard, on the other hand, looked unamused as he reviewed the contents of the briefcase, first via the screen and then by direct inspection. Indeed, there was only a paper lunch bag with some manila folders containing research papers.

Clearing inspection, Preston caught up to Sarah and followed her down the hallway. "I didn't know I was working with James Bond," he whispered. "Or is it Jane Bond?"

"Don't be ridiculous." Sarah patted her handbag. "This is a Glock. Bond carries a Walther PPK."

"Of course, I should have known."

Sarah chuckled. "I'm a security officer—and a lieutenant in the reserves, remember?"

"Oh, yes, I remember it well. The beautiful young lady in the BDUs."

"BDUs? I'm impressed. Where did a civilian like you learn about battle-dress utilities?"

"How do you know I didn't serve in...? Oh, yes, your people know everything about me."

"Well, we know enough," she said with a grin.

"Then you should know I'm an avid fan of the History Channel. Great source for military jargon."

They headed down the hallway to the laboratory where Preston had first seen the scroll of Dismas. It was stored in the lab's large, double-lock safe, which required two people to open, and was brought out only when absolutely necessary. The scholars were able to continue their work even without the document on hand, thanks to digital images that were stored in a computer directory that could only be accessed and decrypted by a code that changed daily.

As they entered the lab, they found professors Daniel Mazar and Yuri Vilnai huddled over one of a half-dozen computer monitors that lined a long table along the side wall, where they were engaged in a spirited debate about a passage from the Dismas Gospel.

Mazar acknowledged Preston and Sarah with a smile and motioned for them to come over. Then he pointed at the monitor and said to his younger colleague: "Here's the passage." He read a line aloud from the photo of the scroll: *"He appeared after his resurrection, first to Simon, who was on the road to Cyrene, and to whom he gave the symbol, then to Cephas, then to the twelve, and after these to five hundred brethren at once."*

"That's little different from First Corinthians," Vilnai said, looking up from the monitor. He quoted from memory: *"He appeared after his resurrection first to Cephas, then to the twelve, and after these to five hundred brethren at once."*

"It is very different," Mazar insisted.

"It adds but one name. What is one more name? Even the four Gospels disagree on the particulars of who saw the risen Christ and when." He waved his hand dismissively. "It is a difference of no consequence."

"I agree with Daniel," Preston said, having heard enough to voice an opinion.

"Of course, Professor Lewkis, you agree with your mentor," Vilnai said disdainfully. "Please explain how the addition of one name can make this passage so significantly different from the same passage in Corinthians."

"There are two reasons," Preston replied. "One is the person's name. The fact that he is encountered on the road to Cyrene makes it almost certain he's the same Simon who helped Jesus carry the cross. The other is that he was given the symbol."

"What symbol?" Vilnai challenged.

"The symbol Father Flannery is researching for us."

"The Via Dei," a woman said, and Preston turned to see that Azra Haddad had just entered the lab.

"Via Dei, yes, that's what he called it." He looked questioningly at Azra. "But how do you know of this symbol? You weren't here when Father Flannery mentioned it."

"It is an ancient symbol," Azra replied. "I'm sure others have heard of it."

"How did you get in here? How did you get by security?" Sarah asked.

Azra held up some papers. "Professor Mazar asked me to prepare a report on what I was doing when I found the urn," she said without directly answering Sarah's question.

"Yes. I did ask for the report," Mazar confirmed, "though, it wasn't necessary to bring it to me here."

"I have the necessary clearance," Azra replied. Her tone was matter-of-fact, not defensive, as if to remind Mazar that without her discovery at Masada, there would be no document at all.

"Of course you do," he said. "I meant no challenge."

"Will that be all?" Azra asked, and Mazar nodded. She headed from the lab, closing the door behind her.

"To get back to the symbol," Vilnai said, gesturing toward the image on the screen, "While I know about the Via Dei, my point is that the passage in question never specifies what symbol it refers to. Isn't that so, Professor Lewkis?"

Before Preston could reply, Mazar said, "Perhaps not, Yuri, but I think it's reasonable to surmise—"

"Surmise?" Vilnai cut him off. "We're scientists. We don't surmise."

They continued to argue, and when it became clear the conversation was going nowhere productive, Preston decided to shift things in another direction. He waited for a rare moment of silence, then commented, "I've been wondering about the presence of Hebrew passages scattered among the Greek. I've been trying to research other documents that contain both Hebrew and Greek, and I can't find many."

"Yes, it's most unusual," Mazar agreed. "I've wondered about that, too."

"You are making my point for me," his younger colleague declared. "We've got a scroll that mixes Greek and Hebrew and bears a symbol not encountered until the Middle Ages." Vilnai jabbed a finger toward Preston's chest. "That's straight out of the mouth of that Vatican expert of yours." He shook his head emphatically. "While I'm not claiming this is a modern-day forgery, I don't see how it can be authentic first century. Middle Ages, a bit later perhaps, assembled by an organization that had its own agenda but wasn't privy to the wealth of knowledge we benefit from today about first century literature."

"I think you're jumping the gun," Mazar said.

"Think...or surmise?" Vilnai countered.

"I admit the symbol troubles me. But Father Flannery may turn up evidence that pushes it back to the early days of Christianity. And it's drawn in what appears to be a different ink, so there's the possibility that the scroll is authentic but the symbol was added at a later date."

"What about the Hebrew and Greek?" Vilnai pressed. "We don't see that in authentic first century manuscripts."

"I don't think it all that strange," Mazar replied. "Don't forget, Dismas was a Jew, and many scholars believe his father was a Zealot. He may have been making his appeal to both the Gentiles and the Jews. So why not include Hebrew to make particular points?"

"Daniel, you cannot authenticate a document by using as a yard-stick something that itself has not been proven," Vilnai lectured. "You say Dismas was a Jew, as if we know for certain he even existed at all. There's no real historical evidence for the elder Dismas of Galilee. We know him only as one of the thieves on the cross. His name comes to us by legend only. And as for Dismas bar-Dismas? We have only the word of the scroll, and it cannot be used to validate itself without some sort of corroboration."

"Yuri, the scroll exists, and the author gives his name as Dismas bar-Dismas," Mazar said. "Now, while we can argue the authenticity of the claims made by this document, I don't think we can argue over the fact that it does exist, and its author was one Dismas bar-Dismas."

"I believe you made a similar case for the ossuary of James, did you not?" Vilnai asked rather pointedly.

Preston saw Mazar's lips quivering, but the older scholar said nothing in response. Instead, he returned to work at his computer station.

"Forgive me, friend," Vilnai said, walking over to stand beside Mazar. "I meant no disrespect by that rather ill-chosen remark. I mean only to urge caution as we examine this admittedly fascinating document."

"There is nothing to forgive, Yuri," Mazar replied. "Progress can only be made by bold extrapolation. Validation can be achieved only by challenge. We bring to the table what we must."

Vilnai chuckled and patted Mazar on the shoulder. "Well stated, Daniel. Well stated."

Preston noted the uneasy smile that passed between the two men. It was clear that while the scholars shared a measure of mutual respect, they shared little beyond that.

NINETEEN

FOR THE NEXT HOUR, SARAH ARAD WORKED AT THE COMPUTER STATION to the left of Preston, with the two university scholars seated at their own terminals at the far end of the table. She spent most of the time calling up images of different portions of the scroll, comparing sections side by side for any sign that the calligraphy was the work of more than one person. Even more challenging was determining if the same hand had fashioned the Greek and the Hebrew characters. As she worked, she became increasingly convinced that a single person had produced the scroll. Furthermore, she believed that the person who had written down the words had also authored them. While that would be difficult to prove, there were indications this was an author's first or second generation copy rather than a transcription of a previously written work.

Her near-silent reverie was broken by an audible sigh from Preston. He seemed deep in thought and she did not want to disturb him, but when he sighed a second time, she asked, "Is something wrong?"

"I don't know." He gestured at the image of the scroll on his computer screen. "There's something strange here."

Sarah grinned. "We unearth at the Jewish site of Masada a two-thousand-year-old gospel, purportedly written by the son of the Good

Thief who died on the cross beside Jesus, and you say there is *something* strange? If you ask me, the entire thing is beyond bizarre."

"Well, yes, there is that," he said with a hint of a smile. "But I'm talking specifically about the way so many Hebrew words and phrases are scattered throughout."

"I don't find that so strange," she said. "It's not unlike today. Nearly everyone in Israel speaks English and Hebrew. Many also speak Yiddish, and in one sentence you often find all three languages in collision."

"Yes, I can understand that. Something from a second language fits better than the language you're using, like the word *chutzpah*. You'd be amazed how often that shows up in conversations among Americans. But this is different."

"In what way?"

"Well, for one thing, the author will use the Greek word for something, then three sentences later, he uses the Hebrew word for the same thing. What makes it strange is the seeming randomness with which he employs the words."

"Do you think it undermines the validity of the document?" she asked.

"No, I wouldn't go that far. But I do find it very interesting."

Their conversation was interrupted by the ring of the telephone and the clipped voice of the younger scholar announcing into the receiver, "Yuri Vilnai here." He listened a moment, then said, "I'll send her right out." Hanging up the phone, he turned to Sarah. "Someone at the front desk wants to see you."

"Did they say who?"

"It's the police."

She deflected Preston's questioning glance with a shrug, then excused herself and headed to the lobby, where she found two men waiting for her by the security desk. They were in civilian clothes, but their demeanor gave them away as clearly as if they had been in uniform.

"Sarah Arad?" the shorter one asked as she approached. He was older than his partner, and with his crumpled suit and haggard expression he looked as if he'd been around the block quite a few times more.

"Yes. "Is there something I can do for you?"

"I'm Special Agent Alan Steinberg, this is Special Agent Bruce Gelb."

He held out the broken side mirror from her car. It was banged up pretty badly, the plastic housing misshapen from extreme heat. It undoubtedly had been found amid the wreckage of the Mercedes.

"Is this yours?" Steinberg asked.

"Of course," she replied. "Surely you've already matched it to my Mini Cooper outside."

"Then you admit you were involved in an accident this morning?"

Sarah sighed. "I'm sure you aren't special agents with the traffic bureau."

"We're not with traffic," Steinberg said brusquely. "Witnesses said the two men in the car that hit the truck appeared to be chasing a light-green Mini Cooper."

"Silk green," Sarah replied. "And that color was discontinued after the first year of production, so there must be very few in Jerusalem."

"And even fewer that have recently lost their side mirror," the one named Gelb put in, his tone much softer than his partner's.

"Yes, I was at the scene of the accident."

"And they were chasing you?" Gelb asked.

"They appeared to be."

"Do you know why?"

Sarah shrugged. "I have no idea."

"Surely, Miss Arad—"

"Mrs. Arad," she corrected.

"Surely, Mrs. Arad, you must have some idea. Otherwise how would you even realize you were being followed?"

"I saw them in my mirror. I don't know, there was something suspicious about them. I made a few turns and they turned with me. I stopped, they stopped, then I did a U-turn and sped away, and they came after me."

"Why didn't you call the police?" Steinberg interjected. "A simple call might have prevented a fatal accident—and putting all those bystanders at risk."

"It's rather difficult to use a cell phone while being chased down alleys. As for calling the police, I did as soon as I was able."

"After the crash." Steinberg glanced down at his notes. "So it *was* you who made that first call reporting the accident." He looked back up at her, his eyes narrowing. "But you didn't give your name."

She gestured at his thick notepad. "Surely you already know more about me than the color of my car. Or do I need to show you my security ID?"

Steinberg tapped the pad with his pen. When he spoke, his tone betrayed his disdain for other branches of the security forces, especially when they jeopardized his jurisdiction. "Yes, we know where you work."

Sarah directed her comments at Steinberg's partner, who she sensed was more sympathetic. "Then surely you understand why I wouldn't want my name listed in a police report—or worse yet, on the local news. Until we know more about those men, it's better that this remain a traffic accident, the result of some high-speed hijinks."

"Perhaps if you had worked with us from the start," Gelb said in a conciliatory tone, "we'd be closer to knowing some of those answers."

"If you check with my office, you'll see that I've asked YAMAM to offer whatever assistance you might need. But I have good reasons—some admittedly personal—for keeping my own distance."

"Personal...?" Gelb pressed cautiously.

"You've heard of Saul and Nadia Yishar?"

"Of course," he replied. "They were killed by terrorists a few years ago at Masada."

"They were my parents," she said bluntly.

"I didn't know. I'm so sorry." Gelb hesitated a moment, then added, "Arad? Sarah Arad? Yes, I remember now. Your husband was Major Ariel Arad. He was killed at a military checkpoint, wasn't he?" he asked, and she nodded. "I can understand why you'd be more than a little sensitive about today's...incident."

"Thank you." Sarah's expression softened. "And to complicate matters, I've recently been assigned to the same Masada dig where my parents died. While there's likely no connection between that terrorist attack and the Mercedes, we need to confirm that through our own investigation." She turned back to Steinberg and said pointedly, "And those inquiries go far beyond the scope of the local police."

Steinberg was about to reply, but Gelb cut him off. "It seems we have mutual interests here. There's no reason we can't keep your name out of our report for the time being. Isn't that right?" He glanced at his older partner, who gave a begrudging nod. "In return, we'd be grateful for any information you turn up about those men following you."

"Then you haven't identified them?"

"Any papers they may have been carrying were destroyed in the blaze," Gelb explained. "And they were so badly burned, it's unlikely we'll match them up to any photos of known operatives. There's DNA and dental records, but if no one files a missing person report, we'll have nothing to compare against."

"Unless we already have a file," Sarah suggested.

"Prison?" Gelb asked, and she nodded. "Yes, we'll check the DNA database. Did you get a good look at them?"

She found herself turning away as she shook her head and replied, "No, I'm afraid not." While technically it wasn't a lie, because it had not been a good look, she felt confident she could identify at least the driver. But she wanted to pursue that through her own department rather than the police.

"Perhaps you could look through some photos at the station?" Gelb asked. "Someone might look familiar. Anything would help."

"Of course. But can it wait until—?"

"Later today would be fine," he cut in, not giving her a chance to suggest a time too far in the future. He handed her his business card. "Call my cell phone, and I'll meet you at the station."

"Yes, of course, she said, glancing at the card.

"And if you think of anything else, or if anything suspicious happens, please call at once."

"I will. And thank you for your concern." Sarah smiled at Gelb, then gave Steinberg a perfunctory nod and headed back down the hallway.

————

SPECIAL AGENT BRUCE GELB waited until Sarah Arad disappeared around the end of the corridor, then he clapped his partner on the shoulder. "Let's get out of here, Al."

"You seemed quite smitten with her," Steinberg said with a snicker as they left the university building.

"Prissy little bitch," Gelb muttered.

"You sure sounded different back there. I thought I'd have to pull you two apart."

"Just working the case," the younger partner replied.

"Yeah, and she was probably working you, as well."

"Nah. She's YAMAM. They don't work a case, they bulldoze it."

"Do you think she's holding back?"

"She saw them," Gelb said flatly. "No way she didn't see them. But she'll never share that with us."

"Which is why you didn't insist she check the mug books right away?"

"What's the point?"

"Why didn't you tell her about the driver's ring?" Steinberg asked.

"Maybe if she'd been more forthcoming..." Gelb shook his head emphatically. "No, we'll keep that bit of evidence for ourselves. Let her waste her time poring through mug shots and tracking down Palestinian terrorists. We'll follow the ring." He patted the evidence bag in his jacket pocket.

"*In Nomine Patris,*" the older man intoned with an air of mystery.

"Amen," his partner declared, chuckling. "Now let's get the hell out of here."

———

JUST AFTER NOON, Preston Lewkis accompanied Sarah to her car on their way to a neighborhood restaurant for lunch. As they neared the vehicle, she suddenly put a hand on his arm and halted.

"What is it?" he asked.

She gave a silent nod across the parking lot, and he turned to see Yuri Vilnai standing beside his Audi sports car, engaged in intense conversation with the Palestinian woman named Azra.

"I thought she left a long time ago," Preston said.

"So did I."

Just then Azra looked over and realized they were being observed.

She made a final comment to Vilnai, then turned and briskly walked away.

"Let's see what that was about," Sarah said.

"Are you sure that's a good—?" Preston started to reply, but Sarah was already heading across the lot.

Vilnai was climbing into his car when Sarah called out, "Professor, wait."

He hesitated, then stood from the vehicle and turned toward them. His smile looked forced, and it was clear he resented the intrusion. "What is it?" he asked impatiently.

"What were you and Azra talking about?" she asked.

Vilnai's annoyance grew more obvious. "It was a private conversation between the research director and a field operative."

Preston was used to Vilnai's imperious attitude. What surprised — and impressed—him, however, was the cool confidence in Sarah's reply.

"You may be research director, professor, but I'm in charge of security for the project. So I'm going to ask you again, what were you discussing?"

Vilnai also seemed unsettled by her tone, and he sighed in acquiescence. "Before Azra Haddad was transferred to the Masada site, she was working at the old monastery excavation on the road to Sdom. She asked to return there, and I agreed to the transfer. Does that present any security problems for you?"

"Not as long as you keep me informed," Sarah replied.

"If that is all, I have things to do." Without awaiting a reply, Vilnai climbed into the car and shut the door. Revving the engine, he pulled away rather quickly and headed across the lot toward the street beyond.

"He's a most unpleasant man," Sarah said, taking Preston's arm and steering him back toward her car. "Why they made him research director instead of Dr. Mazar, I'll never know."

"I think that's where the resentment comes from," Preston said. "Yuri has the title, but Daniel still enjoys the greater international reputation."

"All the more reason he should be director," she commented as they got into the Mini Cooper.

"I agree, but after that ossuary fiasco, the committee was effectively forced to give Yuri the nod. After all, he was correct and Daniel was wrong. And it grates on him that we all still turn to Daniel on matters of scholarship."

Sarah started the engine. "I suppose you're right. He's one of those little men trying to establish authority by force, rather than respect."

She flipped open her cell phone and gestured that she would just be a moment. Preston noticed that she used the speed dial feature, and a moment later she had the other party on the line.

"Hello, Roberta. This is Sarah. I want you to run a complete security check on a woman named Azra Haddad." She paused a moment, then said, "Yes, she made the Masada find... I know, but I need you to run it again." Closing the phone, she turned to Preston. "Do you like Chinese? I know an excellent little place. Come, I'll take you there."

"Damn," Preston said with a chuckle as the car darted forward. "You are not only punctual and well armed, you are decisive as well."

"Do you find that off-putting?"

"No. Quite the contrary. I rather like that." He noticed the way Sarah looked over at him, and he grinned. "No, I wasn't going to say, 'I like that in a woman.' I was going to say, 'I like that in *this* woman.'"

TWENTY

Fr. Michael Flannery was awakened by a knock on the door of his room in Vatican Hall. It was still dark, and the soft gleam of the digital clock by his bed read 4:37.

Who could possibly be calling at this time of day? he thought groggily.

There was a second knock, louder and more insistent, and someone called, "Father Flannery?" Though the call was a quiet hiss, it projected a sense of urgency.

"Just a minute," Flannery answered, switching on the bed stand lamp.

He reached for a housecoat and slipped into it as he padded over to the door. Pulling it open, he saw a familiar face staring intently at him. At first he wasn't sure where he had seen the young man before, then he recognized him as the nursing home attendant who had been on hand during Flannery's visit with Fr. Leonardo Contardi. The nervous man glanced up and down the hallway, obviously agitated.

"Come in," Flannery said, realizing that, for some reason, the visitor did not want to be seen here.

"*Grazie.*"

As the man stepped into the room, Flannery stuck his head outside and looked up and down the hallway. None of the other doors were open, so he was reasonably certain that no one had seen anything. He closed the door and said, "You were Father Contardi's attendant."

"Sì. I am Pietro."

"If you don't mind my asking, Pietro, what are you doing here at this hour of the morning?"

"Please to excuse me, Father, for I disturb you at this time, but I wish not to be seen." He held forth a small box. "To Padre Leonardo this belong, and he asked for me to give it to you, if to him something should ever happen. There is a letter."

Flannery opened the box and took out the letter, which rested atop a leather notebook. Unfolding it, he read:

Michael:

If you are reading these words, then I have left this mortal life and my eternal soul is standing before God's final judgment. I ask your prayers that He may judge me mercifully.

The young man standing before you is Pietro Santorini. He has been very kind to me during my stay in this place, and I have prevailed upon that kindness to have him, upon my death, deliver my journal to you. He is doing this at great personal risk, so please do nothing that would put him in graver jeopardy.

Michael, I know you are involved in a quest of some kind regarding Via Dei. I would ask that you end this search, but knowing you, such a request will only make you the more curious. So, if you are bound to do this thing, I beg of you, my friend, be very careful, for you risk not only your life, but your eternal soul.

IHS, Leonardo

Flannery looked up at Pietro. "Father Contardi says you are taking some risk in doing this. Thank you."

"I can go now?" Pietro said nervously.

Flannery held up his hand. "Wait, let me look outside." Opening the door, he glanced up and down the hall and, seeing nobody, motioned for the young man to depart. "Go quickly, and God be with you."

Pietro hesitated, and Flannery thought he saw tears glisten in his eyes. "I...I very much like the old Padre Leonardo. He was to me like... like my own padre." Turning, he hurried through the doorway and down the hall.

Alone once more in his room, Flannery made coffee in a small Krups brewer, which along with the microwave oven were among the few luxuries residents were allowed in Vatican Hall. Then he sat in a chair beside the bed stand and began reading Fr. Leonardo Contardi's journal.

The first page noted that Contardi had begun recording his thoughts soon after becoming a priest as a means of practicing his English, and indeed most of the journal was in that language, with a smattering of Italian and Latin. At the time, he and Flannery had been novice priests together, and he mentioned Flannery several times:

Yesterday I played handball with Fr. Michael Flannery, an Irishman who has left his green island to work in the Vatican. As a rule, I do not like the Irish. I find them boastful and loud, and to be sure, Fr. Flannery possesses some of these disagreeable traits. But there is much about the man to like. He is pious, intelligent, and quick to give himself in friendship. And most important, I can easily beat him in handball.

Flannery smiled as he read Contardi's evaluation. As he continued perusing the journal, he found the passage where Contardi had been sent to his first overseas mission, a desert monastery in Israel.

I wish Michael would have accepted the invitation so that he might serve with me in this place where, for two thousand years, we of The Way have been initiated into His service. But Via Dei is not for everyone, for indeed, to protect the faith we must sometimes move outside the faith, to do things that, were it not for a higher purpose, might destroy our very souls.

Flannery felt a charge of adrenalin. There it was, the first mention of Via Dei. He tried to recall those early years, when Contardi had wanted him to join the secret organization he called The Way. Flannery hadn't pursued the possibility, and apparently Via Dei had decided against pursuing him, as well, for no actual offer of membership had ever been made. Over the years he had all but forgotten the incident, until recent events brought his old friend and Via Dei back into his life.

From outside his apartment, the first golden bars of sunlight spilled through the window. He could now hear the shuffling of feet as other Vatican Hall residents headed down the hallway for morning prayers. Flannery, with a silent prayer asking to be forgiven for his absence, remained glued to the journal.

In my willingness to serve Him, and in my eagerness to be accepted by the others in The Way, I have undertaken every mission put before me. Intellectually I can see the necessity for these operations, no matter how terrible they may seem, for indeed it is of vital importance that the Holy Catholic Church be strengthened. It is also important that subterfuge be employed so that the Church be shielded from any hint of scandal or guilt.

But I am beginning to think I may not have the moral or emotional strength to continue. For to have on my hands the blood of innocents, regardless of how noble may be the purpose for their dispatch, I am sickened to my very soul.

If only I would be allowed to leave Via Dei. But I have made a commitment of service that binds me for eternity. Where that eternity is to be spent, I shall leave in God's hands.

Flannery felt a growing uneasiness and even dread as he continued to read. It was almost as if he were hearing his friend's confession, and perhaps that was what Contardi had intended in arranging for him to receive the journal. Shockingly the entries became even more confessional when Contardi left Israel to serve at a small parish in Ecuador.

Her name is Pilar. She is a nurse with the medical mission, and at first our work together was filled with the love of God and the joy of helping others, and that was enough to satisfy us. But one night when she was treating patients in my church, the rains came, and with them the wind and lightning and thunder, and she could not leave. We found ourselves alone in the sanctuary, a single candle lighting the distance between us.

Pilar came to me as an innocent young woman, and I defiled that innocence, taking her before the altar. I know what I did was wrong, but as God is my witness, there was more love than lust in my heart.

Our affair continued for three months, but it got more difficult each time. The poor child was torn between her love for me and her guilt at having relations with a priest. She begged me to leave the priesthood so that I could lift the burden of guilt from her. But how could I tell her that I was held by double ties, my priestly vows and the even more terrible and indissoluble chains that bind me to Via Dei?

She could not live with her guilt and was found one morning, dead from an overdose of sleeping pills. In order that she may be buried in consecrated ground, the doctor said that it was an accidental overdose, but he knew, and he knew that I knew, that it was suicide. Only Pilar, God, and I know why she committed this most dreaded of unpardonable sins.

Now, this poor girl, the woman I truly loved, burns in Hell, the victim of my own indiscretions. I cannot pray for the forgiveness of my own soul, for it is linked with the eternal damnation of the soul of my beloved Pilar.

After the death of Pilar, Contardi's journal became more and more disjointed, sometimes deteriorating into absolute babble, such as references to the rain and lentils he had raved about during Flannery's visit. It was now obvious to Flannery that guilt over Pilar's fate had been a major factor in Contardi's nervous breakdown.

The remaining pages also contained occasional passages of complete lucidity in which Contardi hinted that he had committed unpardonable acts in the name of Via Dei. In every case he used the same justification.

Though on the surface these acts appear terrible transgressions, Via Dei washes away the sin because of its greater service to the Church.

There were also a few intriguing references to Masada, which was a few kilometers from the desert monastery where Contardi had served. Unfortunately, the entries were so vague as to shed no light at all upon the recent discovery of the Dismas scroll or the Via Dei symbol it contained.

Leonardo Contardi's journal was as depressing as it was frustrating, and Flannery found himself awash in sympathy for his friend. What was this Via Dei that had so tragically destroyed Contardi? What did

he mean when he said that he had on his hands the blood of innocents? Was he referring to Pilar? If so, why did he use the plural?

No, whatever guilt he felt over Pilar was compounded by guilt over
acts he had committed in the name of Via Dei.

Could there really be a connection between such an organization
and the Gospel of Dismas? Surely the symbol he saw on the scroll had
nothing to do with the Via Dei that had so ravaged the mind, life, and
ultimately the soul of his friend, Fr. Leonardo Contardi.

Flannery was about to close the journal, when the pages flipped to
the last one, and he saw Pilar's name in his friend's final entry. As he
read, he felt a knife piercing his heart:

> *Years, so many years of imagining my beloved Pilar, a suicide lost to the fires*
> *of hell. But today it is clear, and I know at last that she does not share the*
> *fate that awaits me.*
>
> *They let me believe she had taken her own life, as if she would throw*
> *away something so precious for the sorry likes of me. Had I known of our*
> *child, I would have known how much more of a reason she had to live. I*
> *would have seen the truth of her death and their hidden hands at work. But*
> *they could not let me know, for I would have moved Heaven itself to see them*
> *in Hell.*
>
> *Now I can only pray that Pilar rests in the arms of our Lord, and that*
> *our daughter, wherever she may be, thinks on occasion of her poor mother*
> *and father and smiles.*
>
> *I see the flames ahead, and I am ready. Let Pilar's murderers remain*
> *masked in life. The Way upon which they walk shall lead them to the same*
> *fiery retribution. And then, even in the depths of Hell, my soul at last shall be*
> *at peace.*
>
> *Chi l'anima mi lacera? Chi m'agita le viscere? Che strazio, ohimè, che*
> *smania! Che inferno, che terror!*

Closing the journal and his eyes, Michael Flannery repeated in
English the final cry as Mozart's Don Giovanni is engulfed by the fires
of Hades: "'Who lacerates my soul? Who torments my body? What
torment, oh, what agony! What hell! What terror!'"

Overcome by a spirit of compassion and love for the man who had once been such a close friend, Flannery dropped to his knees and called out to Fr. Leonardo Contardi:

"I confess to almighty God, to blessed Mary ever virgin, to blessed Michael the archangel, to blessed John the Baptist, to the holy apostles Peter and Paul, to all the saints, and to you, Father, that I have sinned exceedingly in thought, word, and deed..." He struck his breast once, twice, a third time, intoning, "through my fault, through my fault, though my most grievous fault. Therefore I beseech blessed Mary ever virgin, blessed Michael the archangel, blessed John the Baptist, the holy apostles Peter and Paul, all the saints, and you, Father, to pray to the Lord our God for me."

Crossing himself, Flannery repeated the Confiteor in Latin: *"Confiteor Deo omnipotenti, beatae Mariae semper virgini, beato Michaeli archangelo, beato Joanni Baptistae, sanctis Apostolis Petro et Paulo...*

As he recited the penitential prayer, he felt a dizzying sensation, and opening his eyes, he saw all four walls of his room flashing before him as if he were on a whirling disk, spinning round and round.

"What is this?" he called aloud, and he fell onto his back, spreading legs and arms to regain some stability. "Please, stop! Stop!" he called.

Mercifully, the room slowed to a halt, and he lay on the floor for a long moment, breathing deeply, fighting the nausea the spinning sensation had caused. Slowly, gingerly, he sat up.

He could hear a choir. But that wasn't possible, he was too far away from any of the chapels. Perhaps one of the other residents of the hall had a CD player.

But even as he considered that possibility, he knew this was something different. Though it wasn't actually music as such, he was hearing an ethereal chord, several melodic octaves in a wide range of rich voices, from the deepest and most resonant bass, to the sweetest tenor, to the highest and purest soprano. It was as if Bach, Beethoven, Vivaldi, and all the great composers had combined their genius to create this singular, unimaginably beautiful tapestry of sound.

As he surrendered to it, the music eased his nausea, calming his spirit and enabling him to accept the apparition that began to play out before him. For with the music came a vision of wonder that transported him far across the sea and the centuries. Flannery found himself at Masada, not far from where the Dismas scroll had been discovered. But this was a different Masada, before wind and time had laid ruin to its once imposing walls. And standing before him in the fortress, bathed in a shimmering aura of light, were two men. One was Leonardo Contardi, but not the dying priest he had encountered in the hospice. This was the youthful, athletic Contardi, his skin taut and tan, his eyes sparkling with humor and life. At Contardi's side was the same man Flannery had seen in the Pontifical Mass at St. Peter's.

"Ah, Michael!" Contardi called, raising his arms in greeting. "Come. There is someone you must meet."

The black man looked up at Flannery, and as he did, Flannery felt a shock pass through his body—not of pain, but an overwhelming sensation of love and acceptance. Flannery started toward him, but the man held up his hand.

"The time has not yet come," he intoned.

The chorus of music, which had continued in the background, rose now to a crescendo, and the aura of light surrounding the two men grew brighter than anything Flannery had ever seen—yet so exceedingly gentle that he did not need to shield his eyes,

Then, in what seemed an eternal instant, the music and the light were gone and Flannery found himself alone again in his room, not prostrate on his back but kneeling in prayer, as if he had been reciting the Confiteor all along.

"...*mea culpa, mea culpa, mea maxima culpa.*"

He stopped in mid-prayer, his clasped hands trembling.

What had just happened to him? Had he experienced some sort of astral projection, some out-of-body manifestation? Was it the work of an overactive imagination, or had he been graced with a true vision? And if so, was it a vision from God or from Lucifer?

Flannery struggled to hold in his mind's eye the image of Leonardo Contardi and the now-familiar stranger. But they were already fading, like a photograph too long in the sun. Left in their place was the background landscape, the walls of Masada again fallen into disrepair.

"Masada..." he whispered, rising to his feet.

Michael Flannery had no idea how to interpret his vision, yet it left him with an overwhelming desire to return at once to the Holy Land and continue his quest.

TWENTY-ONE

RUFINUS TACITUS STRUCK A POSE FOR HIS PAINTER. WITH ONE FOOT slightly forward, he held his stomach in, his chest out, his chin up, and his eyes squinting as he gazed into the distance, into the future. On the canvas, the painter had added a laurel wreath that wasn't there, a purple cape, and a sword with a golden hilt.

"Oh, you are making a marvelous presentation, my Lord, simply magnificent," the artist fawned. "Not even Caesar is more regal in bearing or more glorious in pose."

Rufinus preened even more—if that were possible—under the painter's mawkish compliments. His eyes widened slightly upon seeing his wife enter the room. "Marcella," he said through clenched teeth in order not to break his pose. "I intend to send this portrait to your father. Do you believe he'll be pleased?"

She moved behind the painter and looked first at the canvas, then up at her husband. "I believe he will."

"Pleased enough, perhaps, to help secure a posting worthy of me, back in Rome?"

"Yes, I am certain of it."

"Good, good. And I will be counting on a letter from you, soliciting him to that effect."

"Your Excellency, please," the artist said. "If you insist upon talking,

I will not be able to do as well with the portrait."

"Leave us," Marcella ordered the artist.

"I beg your pardon?" the man replied in surprise.

"I said go," she repeated. "You can finish the portrait later. I want to speak with the governor now."

"Do as she says," Rufinus ordered, dropping his pose and dismissing the fellow with a backhanded wave. "My bones are weary from standing. We shall resume after our meal."

"Very good, Your Excellency," the artist replied, bowing as he backed from the room.

Rufinus came over to look at the portrait, which was about one-third done. He studied it for a moment, his head cocked uncertainly.

"I think he has captured your strength and intelligence quite well," Marcella said as she gingerly touched his forearm.

"I suppose so. But the eyes..." He shook his head uncertainly as he examined the dark, lifeless orbs.

"It is not yet finished," she assured him. "The eyes must always come last. They are windows into the man."

He sighed, a mixture of acceptance and resignation, then turned to his wife. "Of what did you wish to speak?"

"Rufinus, I want your permission to visit Centurion Marcus Antonius and the holy man who shares his cell."

"Why would you do that?" he asked in surprise. "I allowed it once, and what good came of it?"

"I've known Marcus since we were children," she said. "He is like a brother to me."

"I know you have a soft heart for him. But you must understand that my hands are tied. How can I show my subjects that I am a just ruler if I grant mercy to a condemned man simply because he's a Roman officer? Or worse, because he's a friend of the governor's wife."

"Perhaps I can convince him to recant," Marcella said.

"You tried that, I believe, with little success."

"Yes, but now you have condemned Dismas to die alongside him. Marcus must understand that Dismas is sacrificing his life for him. What a waste it would be if both were to die. If I could get Marcus to recant now, it would unmask Dismas for the charlatan he is. And it would show your subjects the power you have over this false god."

"If I accede to your wish, will you write to your father, asking him to recommend me for a post in Rome?" Rufinus asked. "And not some perfunctory trifle from a dutiful wife, but a letter that only a daughter knows how to write when she desires to tug at her father's heart?"

Marcella nodded. "Yes, I promise that I will."

Rufinus smiled, then spun toward the doorway. "Tuco!"

"Yes, Your Excellency," his head servant said, sweeping into the room.

"Send word to Legatus Casco that my wife is to have unrestricted visiting rights to prisoner Marcus Antonius."

"Very good," Tuco said with a bow as he left the room.

"Thank you, Rufinus," Marcella whispered demurely.

"It will avail you nothing, you know," Rufinus told her. "Marcus is a stubborn one. He will not change his mind. He will die for his false messiah."

———

As BEFORE, Marcella was forced to hold a perfumed handkerchief to her nose to overcome the powerful stench of feces and urine, festering sores, rotting food, and unwashed bodies that permeated the dank, dimly lit dungeon.

A pair of guards escorted her through the overcrowded cobble-stone hallways that she had visited before, bringing her this time to a remote corridor that held but a single cell at the far right-hand side. A lone, smoky torch flickered outside the iron-barred cell, bathing it in a grayish pool of light.

Starting down the corridor, she signaled that she wished to visit the prisoners alone. Under orders to obey the wishes of the governor's wife, they bowed and withdrew.

Marcella halted a few feet from the cell door, out of sight of the two occupants but able to hear their conversation. She recognized at once the commanding voice of Dismas bar-Dismas intoning what appeared to be a prayer. When Marcus Antonius responded "Amen," she started to call out to him, but something made her hold back, unnoticed in the shadows, listening as Dismas continued to speak.

"There were two others who went to the cross with Jesus, Zealots whom the Romans called thieves, because they desired to steal back their Holy Land from Rome. One of the thieves was Gestas, the other was Dismas."

"Dismas..." Marcus repeated, his tone indicating he had heard the story of the Good Thief. "Your father."

"Yes. When they came to a place called the Skull, the soldiers crucified Jesus and the two thieves, one on his right and the other on his left. Jesus cried out, 'Father, forgive them, for they know not what they do.'"

"Is that true?" Marcus asked. "Did Jesus seek forgiveness for the very soldiers who were crucifying him?"

"Yes. With my own ears I heard him beseech his Father to forgive those who nailed him to the cross."

"When our time comes, should we do the same?"

"Yes. And not just the soldiers, but also the one who gave the order they will carry out."

"I can forgive the soldiers, for I was one once, and I count many friends among them. But I don't think I can forgive Rufinus Tacitus."

"But you must," Dismas insisted, "for it is only with forgiveness in your heart that you can enter Paradise. In so doing, though we die in the flesh, we will not die in the spirit."

"No!" Marcella called out, stepping from the shadows into the pool of light. Through the iron bars, she saw the two men seated in the far corner of the cell.

"My Lady!" Marcus blurted, standing quickly and coming toward her. "I had no idea you were here."

"Do not listen to him, Marcus," she implored.

"Why not? He is my friend. Did he not offer to die in my place?"

"But he's not going to die *for* you, he is going to die *with* you," Marcella said, her voice catching with emotion. "And he welcomes death. By his own words, he welcomes it."

"I do not welcome death," Dismas said from where he stood at the rear of the cell. "But neither do I fear it, for through my Lord Jesus, I have conquered death."

"You speak the words of a crazed man," Marcella said. "Marcus, please, disavow his Christian god. Do that, and you will be saved."

Marcus shook his head slowly. "I'm sorry, my Lady. I cannot do that."

"Oh, what is it with you and your Jesus? What kind of god would want you to die for him?"

"He who died for us," Dismas replied. "He died for us all."

"No!" Marcella shouted. "He didn't die for me! I do not want anyone to die for me!"

Turning, she ran off down the corridor.

————

MARCELLA COULD NOT STAY AWAY for long. The very next day, the wife of the governor of Ephesus returned to the prison, this time carrying a basket of fruit.

"My Lady, you have come back," Marcus said, delighted to see her. "I feared I would not see you again."

"Yes, I have come." Marcella held the basket up to the cell bars. "I brought fruit for you."

"Figs!" Marcus exclaimed as she pulled back the cloth. "A dozen or more figs! My Lady, what a wonderful gift."

"It is a gift we must share with the others," Dismas said, coming over to the cell door.

"Yes," Marcus agreed, though his expression betrayed a hint of disappointment. "Yes, of course you are right." He took a single fig from the basket. "We will share this one. Please distribute the others to the rest of the prisoners."

"But I brought these for you," Marcella told him. "You need to keep up your strength. Share them between you, but there aren't enough for the men in the next corridor, let alone the entire prison."

She was about to protest more, but she fell silent as Dismas reached through the bars and placed his hand over the basket. Closing his eyes, he said a silent prayer. Then he looked directly at Marcella. Under the power of his penetrating green eyes, she felt the breath leave her body. Her legs weakened, and she reached out to grab the bars of the cell to keep from falling.

"Give one fig to each of the prisoners," Dismas told her. "There is enough fruit for everyone."

"You are wrong," she said, her voice tentative, uncertain. "I...I myself filled the basket. I know how many there are."

"Give one to each prisoner," Dismas said firmly.

Marcella tried to argue, but the words caught in her throat, and she found herself nodding. Though she was certain it was an exercise in futility, she headed back down the hallway and into the next corridor.

As she came to each cell, she held forth the basket. The prisoners, crammed five or six to a cell, rushed to the bars, reaching with emaciated arms and clawing fingers. Nearly all showed scars of torture and many were naked, but none were ashamed, for they were no longer aware of humanity in themselves or anyone else. And while most seemed disconnected from reality, she saw the same grateful awe in their eyes as she handed each poor soul a fig.

She moved through the prison almost without thinking, handing the figs to one man after another, until the last of nearly fifty prisoners had been served. Finally she found herself standing before the guard's station, and she looked down at the basket to discover that a few figs remained. Not until she had served the last soldier was the basket finally empty.

Marcella returned to Marcus's cell, her eyes filled with wonder. "How was that possible?" she asked.

"Through God, all things are possible," Dismas said. "Thank you for your kindness."

"My Lady, will you come back again?" Marcus asked.

"Yes, I..." Marcella started to say, then she shook her head. "No, I can't. The sentence is to be carried out within the week. I do not wish to see you die."

"Come tomorrow," Dismas told her. "And bring materials so that I may write."

"Didn't you hear me?" Marcella said. "You are to be executed within the week."

"That is not possible," Dismas replied, unperturbed by her declaration. "I need time to fulfill a task Paul set out for me when he left Ephesus, and it requires more than a week. You will find a way to delay the execution."

"Delay it? I want to stop it! And I *can* stop it, if you will just renounce this Jesus."

"You have seen with your own eyes," Dismas said, dropping his gaze toward the now-empty fruit basket. "Can you disavow the truth of what you have witnessed?"

"No, I...I cannot," she said. "But that's not the same as—"

"Then you can understand why we cannot renounce our Lord," Dismas said, his voice softening as he continued, "You will find a way to delay the execution. He has told me that you will."

———

"ARE you going to hold the execution at midweek?" Marcella asked her husband over breakfast the next morning.

"You know that I am," Rufinus Tacitus answered as he speared a piece of cheese with his knife.

"If you do so, I fear you will be making a mistake."

Rufinus sighed. "We have been through all this, Marcella. I cannot spare your childhood friend."

"That's not what I mean," she said, her tone calm, almost matter-of-fact. "I confess, I have given up on Marcus. If his new god is so important that he will turn his back on me and on Rome, then I wash my hands of him."

"Oh?" Rufinus said, an eyebrow rising. He spread some date preserves on a piece of bread. "I must say, that surprises me. I thought you wanted him spared."

"Well, I did. But no more."

"Then why not hold the execution at midweek?"

"Did you know that the Christians of Ephesus have organized a celebration to be held at Passover?"

"Passover? But Christians and Jews are at odds."

"Yes, but the Christians believe Jesus was resurrected during Passover week, so they have organized their own celebration to mark the occasion."

"Interesting," Rufinus said. However, he seemed far more interested in the bunch of grapes he was reaching for.

"There will be great crowds and prayer services on the day of Passover," Marcella said. "That's why you should delay the execution." Seeing her husband's look of confusion, she continued, "Think of it,

Rufinus. What greater show of your power over this false god than to choose the very day of his supposed resurrection to crucify his holy man, Dismas, and his convert, Marcus."

Rufinus shook his head. "Marcus Antonius is a Roman citizen. By law, I cannot crucify a Roman."

"Hasn't Marcus renounced his citizenship? You are free to deal with him as you wish."

"I don't understand. Once you wanted me to spare Marcus. Now you want me to crucify him."

"It was his choice," Marcella said disdainfully. "I offered him the path to freedom, and he chose death. He as much as humiliated the wife of a governor of Rome." She paused a moment, then went on, "No, he had his chance. Now you must use him to assert your own power over these...these fanatics. What better act to convince my father to intercede on your behalf for an assignment in Rome."

Rufinus stroked his chin. "Perhaps you do have a good idea." He rose from the table, still holding the bunch of grapes. "All right," he declared. "I will have Legatus Casco postpone the executions." He laughed. "Won't it be glorious to look into the faces of those Christians as their holy man is crucified on their day of celebration."

As Rufinus strode from the room, calling for Legatus Casco, Marcella felt a dread of desperation. She had done her part to buy Dismas and Marcus some time, but to what end? Execution in several weeks rather than several days? And while she was convinced neither man would ever renounce the one they called Jesus the Christ, in her heart she still held a glimmer of hope. Surely they weren't meant for so horrible a death. Surely they would realize they could deny this Jesus, they could proclaim whatever Rufinus required, just long enough to escape their fate.

But now, she feared that her actions had only served to harden her husband's heart, and nothing Marcus or Dismas could say or do would stop him from carrying out their crucifixion. Had she postponed fate or only made matters worse, turning their execution into a public spectacle?

She shook her head, clearing the horrible images that flooded in. She would find a way, she promised herself. She would not only buy them time but their lives.

TWENTY-TWO

MARCELLA DID NOT KNOW IF IT WAS VISION OR DREAM THAT CARRIED HER from her bedchamber. She had been sitting alone, eyes closed in meditation, when she felt the chair move beneath her, bearing her across the fields surrounding Ephesus to the banks of a stream that flowed to the nearby sea. A small gathering stood in the water, their eyes and arms welcoming her as she floated out to them.

She was no longer in her chair but in their comforting embrace, the water rising around her as they whispered a secret name, one she could not hear or speak but could feel resonating deep within her. As she sank beneath the surface of the stream, she breathed deep of its life-giving water and prayed to that nameless one, to the one they called—

Marcella jerked open her eyes, her hands clutching at the arms of the chair. She gasped for air as she looked around the bedchamber, making certain she was indeed back at the palace. Clasping her hands together, she gave a silent prayer of thanks.

Hearing footsteps, Marcella unclasped her hands and looked up at the doorway, feeling a flush of embarrassment that someone might think she had been in prayer. It was a silly reaction, she knew. She had merely been thinking about that strange dream, she told herself. And even if they suspected she had been praying, they would assume it was to the Roman gods, not to the one God who had been on her mind so incessantly since her last visit to the prison.

When she saw her servant, Tamara, she relaxed her shoulders and smiled. "What is it?" she asked, motioning the young woman to come forward.

"Is it true what they are saying, my Lady, that Marcus and Dismas are to be executed on the day our Lord rose from the dead?"

"*Our* Lord?" Marcella replied. "Tamara, have you become a believer? A Christian?"

The servant lowered her gaze and said softly, "Yes."

"You surprise me. How can you accept the very religion that is to be the cause of Marcus being crucified?"

"I...I have come to believe," Tamara said, adding boldly, "How is it that you do not? Did you not tell me, with your own lips, of the miracle of the basket of figs?"

Marcella shook her head. "I was distraught, confused. I'm sure I just miscounted. There was no miracle."

"My Lady, I helped fill the basket with figs. There were not enough for every prisoner."

"I'm sorry, but I just cannot accept it as easily as you. But to answer your question, yes, the execution is now set for the day Jesus supposedly rose from the dead."

"Not 'supposedly.' He *has* risen."

"How do you know?"

"I have been told, and I believe," Tamara said, as if that were explanation enough. "That seems a particularly cruel thing to endure, to be crucified on such a day."

"I know." Marcella sighed. "That's why I chose it."

"*You* chose it?" Tamara's eyes welled with tears.

"Tamara, they were to die tomorrow," Marcella said, seeing the disappointment in her servant's expression. "I had to get it postponed. Indeed, Dismas asked me to buy him some time, and this was the only thing I could think of that would convince my husband to delay his plans. I knew it was something he couldn't resist."

"Yes, of course, my Lady. I am sorry I doubted you."

"Tamara, I am told that the believers are no longer meeting at Gymnasium Tyrannus."

"When Dismas was arrested, they moved the location."

"Do you know where they are meeting now?"

"Yes, Mistress Marcella. I know."

"Will you take me there?"

Tamara hesitated.

"Tonight?" Marcella added. "Tamara, if I am to help you and Marcus, then you must trust me."

"I will take you," Tamara agreed.

———

THE MEETING PLACE was near the outskirts of Ephesus in a house that was windowless on the street side. The entrance was at the rear, through a door with attached half columns surmounted by a triangular pediment. A narrow entry corridor led into an atrium covered by a roof that tilted inward on all four sides. An opening in the center, called a *compluvium*, allowed rainwater to run through into an ornately tiled pool, or *impluvium*, from which the excess drained into a cistern below. Around the atrium were grouped bedrooms and, at the far end, a large living room.

It was in this living room that the church services were held. About two dozen men and women were already present, talking quietly among themselves around a marble bath set into the stone floor.

As Marcella and Tamara entered the room, one of the women looked over at them and gasped in recognition. "You are the wife of Governor Tacitus."

"The governor's wife?" a man asked in alarm.

"Has she come to do us harm?" still another said, moving toward the two women.

"Wait, please!" Marcella said. "I mean no harm."

"She is my mistress," Tamara said quickly. "I will speak for her."

"It's all right," a voice said, and Marcella turned as a young man came forward. "If our sister, Tamara, speaks for you, then you are welcome among us, my Lady."

It was the same man who had greeted them at Gymnasium Tyrannus when they went to see Dismas. He was perhaps thirty, with a close-cropped brown beard and light-brown eyes that failed to soften what seemed a forced smile.

"I am Gaius, and I shall be leading the service in Dismas's absence."

When everyone had settled into chairs that had been positioned around the bath, Gaius began by recounting the baptism of Jesus. "It is said that Jesus came from Galilee to the Jordan River, and he asked John to baptize him. 'My Lord,' John replied. 'Why do you come to me to be baptized? It is I who should be baptized by you.'"

As he spoke, Gaius walked over to the bath and, kneeling beside it, dipped his hand into the water.

"But Jesus answered, 'Let it be this way for now. We should do all things that are God's will.' So, John baptized Jesus, and as Jesus rose straight away from the water, Heaven opened, and God's spirit came down on him like a dove. And a voice from Heaven said, 'This is my son, whom I love, and with whom I am well pleased.'"

There was a slight sigh among the gathering, as if they were awestruck that God had spoken, and that he had called Jesus his son.

"And now," Gaius said, lifting his hand and letting the water flow through his fingers, "I invite each of you who has not yet done so, to give your soul to the Lord, to be baptized in the name of Jesus Christ, and to be sealed by him forever."

As if driven by an outside power, a power beyond her comprehension, Marcella felt herself approaching the bath. It was as if she were floating, not moving of her own accord, and as Gaius and the others reached toward her with open arms, she saw herself wading into the waters of a stream rather than a ritual bath. Gentle hands guided her down into the swirling water. She felt no wetness but was aware only of its warm embrace. Gaius wrapped one arm behind her back, the other over her forehead. His voice was muffled, yet sounded like sweet music as he lowered her head beneath the surface, then lifted her up again.

"Marcella, I baptize you into the kingdom of the Lord, in the name of Jesus Christ."

She felt a strange shudder deep in her chest, and then she began to cry, softly at first, then sobbing aloud as Gaius and his fellow believers gathered her in their arms and carried her from the bath.

MARCELLA SPENT the next hour seated among well-wishers in an adjoining room. She wore a simple white robe they had given her to use while her clothing was taken away to dry. She had regained her composure and felt strangely at peace, though still uncertain about what she had experienced.

"Is it true that you have seen Dismas in prison?" one of the women asked her.

"Yes," Marcella replied. Oddly, until that moment, she had all but forgotten why she had come tonight. "Yes, I have spoken to him many times, and to Marcus Antonius."

"How are they faring?"

She shook her head. "It is a bad place...a very bad place for anyone to be. But they make the best of it. At least they share a cell and can converse freely."

"Tell us of the basket of figs," Gaius asked.

"The figs? You know of this?"

Tamara, seated beside her, said a bit nervously, "I told them, my Lady."

Marcella put her hand on Tamara's. "We are both baptized now, are we not?" she asked. "Here, I am not your mistress, I am your sister."

"Yes...Marcella," Tamara replied with a smile.

Marcella looked at the others. "I am glad my sister told you of the figs and the basket. It is true. I saw it with my own eyes."

"We would hear the story from your lips," Gaius pressed.

To gasps and exclamations of awe, Marcella recounted how a basket containing only a few figs provided fruit enough for every prisoner and every guard. Concluding the story, she described how Dismas had begun to work on a commission given him by the apostle Paul.

"They were to have been executed tomorrow," she explained. "But Dismas asked for me to arrange more time so he could complete his work."

"And were you able to do so?" Gaius asked.

"Yes. But it is only a delay. I convinced my husband to hold the execution on the same day as the celebration of the resurrection of

Jesus. I convinced him that an execution on that day would dispirit you."

A man sighed. "Yes, that will greatly dispirit us."

"How could you do such a thing?" a women asked, her face flushed in anger. "To even suggest that he crucify Dismas and Marcus on the very day we dedicate ourselves to the glory of the Lord's triumph over death?"

"I'm sorry," Marcella said. "It was the only way I could think of to persuade my husband to grant Dismas the extra time he needs."

The woman started to object, but Gaius held up his hand. "We must not blame our sister for doing what she thought was right. And perhaps this is God's plan. What greater way to go to glory than on the day that Jesus Christ himself conquered death?"

"And in the same manner," another offered. "By being nailed to the cross. How glorious!"

Marcella looked at the others in shock. "How can you celebrate that Dismas and Marcus are to be killed?"

"We aren't celebrating their deaths," Gaius said, "for indeed one day we shall all die. We are celebrating their eternal life and that they will soon be in Paradise."

"Well, I'm not ready for them to die," Marcella replied. "That is why I have devised a plan."

"A plan? What plan?" Gaius asked.

"A very simple one. You must help me convince Marcus and Dismas to make a public denial of Jesus."

There was a collective gasp.

"They don't have to mean it," Marcella quickly added. "Once free, they can say what they will. But first we must convince them to live, and to do so, all they need do is speak words Rufinus demands. The words need hold no truth."

Gaius frowned. "They cannot do such a thing."

"Of course they can."

"No, they can't. Marcella, you were just baptized in the name of Jesus. Could you, honestly, stand now and declare to all that Jesus is false?"

"Well, no, not of my own volition," Marcella admitted. "But words proclaimed under the threat of death do not bear the weight of truth and later can be denied."

"We live every day under the threat of death," Gaius countered. "And so, each and every day we must proclaim the truth, even though we find ourselves between the tip of a sword and the edge of the abyss."

They were interrupted by a loud voice announcing, "I seek Gaius of Ephesus. I am told I may find him here."

The crowd moved aside to reveal a tall, cowled stranger standing in the doorway. As the man drew back his hood, several people exclaimed in unison, "Dismas!"

"How did you get out?" Marcella cried, jumping up and hurrying toward the man, who shook his head, looking confused by their reaction.

As Gaius approached, he halted in mid-stride and declared, "You are not Dismas bar-Dismas."

Marcella examined him more closely and also realized he was not Dismas, though he bore a striking resemblance.

"I am Tibro, brother of Dismas." He looked from one person to another, his eyes, as green and disconcerting as his brother's, settling at last upon Marcella.

As she returned his penetrating gaze, she felt a curious sensation, not unlike what she had experienced during the baptism. She was certain that she and this man had already encountered each other, perhaps in the distant past. Yet she knew in her mind that they had not.

"Tibro, yes, of course. Your brother has spoken fondly of you," Gaius said as he clasped the visitor's forearm in greeting. "I am the one you seek."

Tibro turned from Marcella, sounding a bit disoriented as he said to Gaius, "My brother speaks fondly of me? I find that surprising, as we disagree on most everything."

Gaius grinned. "He has told us that, as well."

"Dismas wrote to me in Jerusalem, saying he intended to trade his life for that of a Roman soldier. Can such a thing be true?"

Gaius nodded solemnly. "Yes, he attempted to."

"Attempted? I don't understand. As I came in, you were planning how to free him from prison."

"He tried to exchange places with Centurion Marcus Antonius, and the governor accepted the offer, but reneged. Now both Dismas and the Roman are sentenced to death."

Tibro's expression hardened. "At least the Roman pig will die."

"Oh, sir, how can you be so cruel?" Tamara called out as she pushed through the crowd.

Turning to her, Tibro said, "You don't look Roman."

"I am Ephesian."

"Then how is it you are so concerned about a Roman? And a Roman soldier, at that?"

"I love him," Tamara declared.

"Love?" Tibro scoffed. "Roman soldiers don't marry the women of occupied lands. You are nothing but a diversion."

"That is not true of Marcus," she insisted.

"And why not? He's a Roman soldier, is he not?"

"He's not like the other soldiers," Gaius said. "He is one of us, now. He has accepted Jesus as Lord."

"That only makes it worse," Tibro said. "A Roman who has accepted a false god."

"We do not believe Jesus is false," Gaius replied. "And neither does your brother."

"Dismas is a fool," Tibro muttered, then gave a sigh. "But the fool is my older brother, so, if something can be done to save him, I want it done."

"I have talked to him many times," Marcella said, moving closer to Tibro. "I have tried to convince Dismas and Marcus to renounce Jesus, even if they don't mean it. If they will only say the words, I believe my husband will free them as a testament to his own mercy."

Tibro looked puzzled. "Your husband?"

She felt herself weaken under his gaze. "I...I am Marcella, wife of Rufinus Tacitus, governor of Ephesus."

"Oh, by the beards of the prophets, you are not only married, you are married to the governor?" he said, and she lowered her eyes. He looked in disbelief at the assembly. "You are Christians, you are Ephesians, and yet you accept in your midst Roman soldiers and," he took in Marcella with a wave of his hand, "even the wife of the Roman governor?"

"We are all brothers and sisters in Christ," Gaius proclaimed.

Tibro turned back to Marcella. "You, a Roman, have accepted Jesus?"

"Yes," Marcella answered resolutely, looking back up.

"Well, I'll have to get used to that," he replied, stroking his chin. "But as I came in, I heard your plan to save my brother, and I can assure you it will not work. Under no circumstances will he renounce Jesus. I am a Jew, I do not countenance this cult religion of yours, but I know Dismas to be a man of great honor who would die before he would betray his beliefs."

"There must be a way to convince him," Marcella replied.

"You say you have accepted Jesus. If you were in my brother's place, would you renounce your God?"

"No, I would not."

"Even if it meant your death?"

"Even then," Marcella declared. As she looked up into Tibro's eyes, she thought she saw a glimmer of approval. She found that strange, since he did not share her belief.

"Then you could not expect Dismas or this Christian centurion to do any less, could you?"

"No, I could not," Marcella said in resignation. "And so, all is lost."

"Perhaps not." Tibro turned to Gaius and the others. "Perhaps, with this good lady's permission, you will allow me to suggest a plan of action of my own."

TWENTY-THREE

WHEN MARCELLA RETURNED HOME THAT EVENING, SHE WAS ALMOST dizzy with conflicting emotions. She had just given her soul to Jesus. But what exactly did that mean? She had never thought much about religion, because none of the many Roman gods and religions had resonated within her. Upon first arriving in Ephesus she had flirted with the worship of Diana, but ultimately that proved unfulfilling. Why, then, had she been so moved by these Christians as to allow herself to be baptized into their new faith?

She knew the reason. The steady strength of Dismas and Marcus, the warmth and acceptance of Gaius and the others in the group, convinced her that this was not a false teaching but a true path to the one true God.

Although she was filled with emotions, she had no second thoughts about what she had done. On the contrary, she now believed her conversion to Christianity the most significant and moving event of her life.

But there was also Tibro, and she could neither understand nor explain the tumult of sensations she experienced as she thought of him. She found herself replaying in her mind every word he had spoken at the gathering. What had he meant when he said that she was not only married, she was married to the governor?

Not *only* married.

It was as if he was disappointed that she belonged to another man. Why would such a thing have any impact on him?

Even as she asked the question, she knew the answer: He had reacted to her the same way she had to him.

She had to confess there was something about the younger bar-Dismas that quite unsettled her. She knew she felt an attraction of sorts to his older brother, but that attraction was to the holy man's words and spirit. Almost from the day she first met Dismas, she had considered him a teacher, a guide—so devout as to be unapproachable.

Tibro was different. He exuded the same fiery spirit, but in an earthier manner. And when she looked into his deep green eyes, it was not a teacher she saw but a man—a man who held her gaze with unnerving power and passion.

As she thought of Tibro, her body warmed and she felt a tingling sensation in her skin. She was a married woman, but never before had she experienced anything like this.

As Marcella entered her husband's anteroom, all the sensations she had been experiencing shut down instantly. She felt a chill, almost a sense of revulsion as she saw Rufinus Tacitus sitting in his chair, studying the nearly completed portrait he had commissioned.

"What do you think?" he said upon seeing her. He gestured eagerly at the painting. "Is this image of me not magnificent? Does it not capture my very essence?"

Marcella forced a smile as she walked over to the painting. The artist had been particularly kind. Along with adding the laurel wreath, purple robe, and gold-handled sword, he had also made Rufinus much better-looking, while managing to keep enough of his actual appearance as to preserve reality. The portrait Rufinus was graced with a flat stomach, broad shoulders, and well-proportioned limbs. A bulge had been removed from his nose, the unsightly mole on his chin was missing, and his eyes, which had a tendency to wander in different directions, were fixed and steely.

"What a clever artist," Marcella exclaimed truthfully.

Rufinus continued to admire the painting. "It is wonderful how an artist so far from Rome is able to portray me with such accuracy."

"His depiction of your likeness is truly..." She groped for the appropriate word. "It is truly incredible."

The governor grinned like a giddy child. "Yes, I am most pleased."

Choosing her words carefully, Marcella said in a soft voice, "Husband, is the execution still planned for the Christians' holy day?"

Rufinus's expression darkened. "You haven't lost your resolve, have you? Everything is scheduled, just as you proposed. The very morning they celebrate the so-called resurrection of their Jesus, I shall put Marcus Antonius and that Christian holy man to the cross. You haven't changed your mind, have you?"

"No, I am in full accord," she lied, fighting the revulsion she was feeling. "But Rufinus, I...I don't want to be here."

"What?"

"When you crucify Marcus, I don't want to be here."

"But of course you will be here. It was your idea, after all. Or were you lying when you said you no longer care what becomes of that treasonous cur?"

Marcella moved closer to his chair. "What I said about Marcus doesn't change that we were friends once. I don't think I could bear to witness—"

"Bah. You're being sentimental," Rufinus chided. He wagged his finger at her. "Believe me, sentimentality has no place with people such as us. You must understand, Marcella, that you and I were born into the ruling class."

Kneeling in front of her husband, Marcella placed a hand on his knee. "I am also frightened."

"Frightened, my dear?" he said with far more compassion than he had exhibited in a long time. "Of what?"

"Suppose the crowd becomes unruly. Suppose a riot breaks out. If they turn on us, we could be killed."

"There is no reason to be afraid," he said, patting her hand. "We will be well protected by our soldiers."

"I know, and I am certain they would be able to protect us. Still, it would be a frightening experience. And...and there is another thing."

"What?"

"My parents. They are old and ailing, and it has been so long since

I've seen them. I would feel awful if something were to happen before I see them again."

"There is always that possibility when you are on duty in a foreign land," Rufinus said.

"Yes, I know that, my husband." Marcella looked over at the portrait, then smiled. "I have an idea." Rising, she walked over to it. "You had this made as a gift for my father. Suppose I take it to him myself, and as I hand it to him, I will tell him how much better it would be if we were brought back to Rome. A letter he could refuse. But to his own daughter?"

Rufinus nodded, gently at first and then with growing conviction. "Yes, that might be just the thing to win him over. All right, Marcella, you shall have your wish. I will make a boat available for you to depart on the morning of the festival. While the crucifixion is going on here, you shall be at sea, on your way back to Rome, to deliver my gift to your father and news of how I have dealt with these religious fanatics."

———

"My Lady," Tamara said, gently shaking Marcella as she lay sleeping in her bed.

Opening her eyes, Marcella struggled to focus on a moon shadow projected on her wall, the lacy pattern of a cornelian cherry tree that stood just outside her bedroom window. "What—what time is it?" she asked groggily.

"It will be sunrise before long, my Lady. The day of our Lord's resurrection is at hand."

Pushing aside the bed coverings and lowering her feet to the floor, Marcella sat up and looked around the darkened room. "Is the rest of the house still asleep?"

"Yes."

Nodding, Marcella stood up. "Help me get dressed."

———

THE TWO WOMEN walked quickly down Cuertes Way, their sandaled feet padding softly on the cool pavement. Here and there the glow of a candle could be seen in the window of an early riser, but for the most part the only illumination was the silver moon glow.

It was only a five-minute walk to the drab stone edifice that housed the Roman prison. Marcella pulled the bell chain, and a few moments later the heavy door swung open and the commandant of the guard peered out at them.

"My Lady," the soldier said in surprise. "What brings you here at this hour of the morning?"

"The prisoners are to be executed today, are they not?" Marcella asked.

"That is true."

Marcella indicated Tamara. "My servant was betrothed to Centurion Marcus Antonius, and I have brought her for a final goodbye."

"I don't know," the commandant said, stroking his short beard and looking back and forth between the women. "This hardly seems an appropriate time for such a thing."

"Later will be too late, don't you think?"

"But at such an hour? Wouldn't it be best to return before their sentence is to be carried out?"

"That is not possible, for my maiden and I sail for Rome on the morning tide. And neither is it necessary, for I have been granted unrestricted access to the prisoners," Marcella reminded him. "But if you want me to summon my husband and bring him back with me…well, I must warn you that Governor Tacitus can be quite irritable when he is awakened in the middle of the night."

"No, no, of course not," the commandant said, backing from the doorway to allow them to enter. "You are right, my orders are to give you full access, and there is nothing limiting the time of day." He looked quite contrite as he added, "Please excuse my unpardonable behavior. I was just taken aback by—"

"There is no need to apologize," Marcella assured him as she stepped across the threshold into the dimly lit interior. "You were only doing your duty."

The soldier scurried across the room. "Let me get a lamp, and I'll lead you to the cell."

"I shall tell my husband of your kindness," Marcella called after him. When the commandant returned, she reached for the lamp and said, "You have been most gracious, but I know the way quite well. I would like Tamara to have a private moment with her betrothed."

Moments later, Marcella was leading Tamara through the prison corridors. As they approached the one holding Marcus and Dismas, she raised the lamp in front of her, revealing a pair of bodies curled up on some grass matting that served as a bed at the far side of the cell. She called out softly, "Marcus, are you there?"

One of the prisoners stirred, then sat upright, peering toward the glowing light at the barred door.

"I am here, my Lady," Marcus said as he stood and came forward into the light. Then, recognizing Marcella's companion, his face lit with joy and he cried out, "Tamara!" He rushed to the cell door and clasped the young woman's hands through the bars.

Marcella gave them but a moment as she nervously looked down the dark corridor. Then she whispered, "Go wake up Dismas. There isn't a moment to spare."

TWENTY-FOUR

RUFINUS TACITUS STOOD AT AN OPEN WINDOW, LOOKING DOWN AT THE growing crowd that had gathered in the palace courtyard. "Legatus Casco, how are they composed?"

"Most have come to enjoy the spectacle, Governor, but there are some among them who pray for the release of their holy man and the Christian centurion."

Rufinus took a sip of his wine and continued to study the crowd as he asked, "How do our soldiers feel about the crucifixion of one of their own?"

"Some do not like it, Your Excellency, because they feel it violates Roman law to crucify a citizen of Rome."

Rufinus spun around and glowered at the silver-haired legion commander. "By his own words and actions, Marcus Antonius has renounced his rights as a Roman citizen."

"Still, the soldiers believe that he should receive a quicker punishment."

"All of the soldiers?"

"No, not all."

"If the crowd gets unruly, can we count on them to protect us?" the governor asked in some concern.

"All my men are loyal. They shall do as you command."

"Yes, well, that's what we thought about Centurion Antonius, is it not?"

"You need have no fear, Your Excellency," Casco assured him.

The governor's eyes narrowed. "I am not a man who is easily frightened."

"I meant no disrespect. The courage of Rufinus Tacitus is well known to all."

Satisfied by the answer, Rufinus turned his attention back to the throng below. Some people had begun yelling openly for the crucifixion, while others were on their knees, hands clasped together as if praying for a miracle. A few of the more enterprising Ephesians were moving through the crowd, selling pastries, fruit, and drink.

"The courtyard is too small," Rufinus mused aloud, then turned back to Casco. "Have our soldiers move the spectators to the amphitheater. We shall hold the crucifixions there." He grinned. "It will be the best day of theater these simpletons have ever seen."

"A brilliant move, Your Excellency," Casco declared. "And it will be easier to control the crowd there."

"Oh, and my wife—did she get away safely this morning?" he asked, almost as an afterthought.

"Yes, Your Excellency. Accompanying her were her handmaiden, Tamara, and two Ephesian servants."

Rufinus nodded. "Good. Now, call for my sedan chair. I will enter the theater as governor."

Casco saluted, then marched briskly from the room.

———

RUFINUS WAS CARRIED through the streets of Ephesus, protected from the late-morning sun by a feathered fan held above him by an African slave. As the procession of guards bore the governor to the open-air amphitheater, they passed the town hall and the Baths of Scholastika, then turned onto Marble Street at the Hellenistic *agora*, where artisans fashioned gold and silver offerings for the goddess Artemis. Finally they reached Arkadiane Street, which ended in front of the theater.

The great amphitheater, built into the side of Mount Pion, measured five hundred feet in diameter and could seat about twenty-four thousand people. The *cavea*, or auditorium, was divided into three bands that each contained twenty-two rows of seats, with twelve stairways dividing the cavea into huge wedge-shaped sections. The semicircular area between the raised stage and the seats measured eighty by thirty-seven feet, with the stage itself eighty feet wide and twenty feet deep, supported by twenty-six round pillars and ten square ones.

The theater was nearly filled, with most of the crowd looking eager for the spectacle to begin. A far smaller number, scattered about in small groups, were praying for their Messiah to save the two condemned Christians.

Many called out to Rufinus as his sedan chair was borne into the theater and placed on the forward part of the stage. The crucifixion would take place in the open area between the stage and the seats. Because it was composed of great paving stones, the crosses could not be set in the ground but would be supported by wooden frames. These structures had already been built, and two crosses lay on the ground alongside them. A small contingent of soldiers stood beside the crosses, two of them holding hammers to nail the prisoners to the beams, the others with ropes and tackle to lift the crosses into position.

In addition to the soldiers who would take part in the crucifixion, there were many others, dressed in shining breastplates and helmets as they formed a semicircle between the crowd and the execution site. They stood shoulder-width apart, each with his left arm folded behind his back, right hand extended and grasping a spear, its point upright and tilted toward the crowd.

The effect was quite impressive, though Rufinus realized there were only a hundred guards to hold back twenty thousand should the crowd get out of hand.

As soon as the sedan chair was in place, the governor strode to the front of the stage. He raised his hand and the conversations stilled. When all was quiet, he called out, "Bring in the condemned! Let the entertainment begin!"

There was a ripple of excitement as the prisoners were led through a door that opened in the front of the stage, directly below where the governor was standing. As Rufinus gazed out upon the crowd, he heard both mocking taunts and expressions of pity.

"You, Holy Man!" someone shouted. "You are about to be crucified. Soon you, too, can be a god!" His exclamation was greeted with laughter.

"Will you rise after three days?" another called to increasing laughter. "If so, tell me, so I can come watch the show!"

"Oh, look at them," a voice filled with pity cried out. "They are so badly beaten that they can't even walk."

And indeed the spectator was right, for as Rufinus looked down from the stage, he saw that the two condemned men were seemingly unconscious as they were dragged in, face down, by a pair of guards each. Marcus Antonius was dressed in the red cloak and breastplate of his office, and there was a particular buzz of excitement as he was hauled across the open area to one of the crosses. Rufinus felt certain that his decision to crucify the centurion would strengthen his hold over the Ephesians.

The other prisoner was wearing a crown of thorns, his head dripping blood onto the stones as he was brought forward into the sunlight. His appearance drew a collective gasp, followed by cheers of approval at the spectacle the governor was providing. Rufinus thrilled at the adulation, for the crown had been his own idea, designed to mock both the condemned holy man and the so-called Christ.

The prisoners were dropped, face down, beside the crosses they would soon occupy. The guards backed away as the ones wielding hammers came over to attend to their task. Kneeling beside the prisoners, the soldiers rolled them over onto the crosses and lifted their hands into position on the crossbeams. Their faces were bloodied and unrecognizable from the beating they had endured.

"Wait!" Rufinus Tacitus called out, raising his arm as they were about to pound nails into the wrists of the condemned men. He gestured toward Legatus Casco, who stood down in the pit with his men. "Revive the prisoners!" he ordered his chief of guards. "I want them to enjoy the proceedings, as well."

Casco signaled to some of his guards who stood nearby with buckets of water. Hurrying forth, they dumped them unceremoniously on the prisoners' faces. The two men shook their heads and sputtered as they regained consciousness.

Casco started to signal for the crucifixion to proceed, but then he held up a hand and moved closer to the crosses, staring first at the condemned centurion and then the holy man with the crown of thorns. He moved back and forth between them, then turned to one of the guards and shouted, "What is this? What has happened here?"

Puzzled by the growing confusion, Rufinus descended the stairs that led into the pit and went over to Casco. "What is it?" he demanded.

Casco pointed to the two men who were struggling to get up from the crosses but were being held in place by the soldiers. The water from the buckets had washed most of the blood from their faces, and though they were badly bruised, their features were recognizable.

"These are two of my guards," Casco said, keeping his voice low. The crowd could see that something was amiss but had no idea what it was. "They were on duty at the prison."

"What?" Rufinus snapped in anger and frustration. He looked down at the prisoners and saw that, indeed, they were not Marcus Antonius or Dismas. He glanced around and saw how the crowd was stirring. Restraining his anger, he whispered sharply, "How did this happen?"

Casco turned to one of his centurions. "Where are the four guards who brought in these prisoners?"

There was a flurry of activity as the centurion consulted with other soldiers, and then he returned and announced, "They are gone, Legatus!"

"Find them!" Casco shouted. "Find them and bring them to me!"

By now the amphitheater was abuzz with excited rumors. A few seemed to realize what had happened, while others thought it a part of the spectacle, and they shouted, "Crucify them! Crucify the prisoners!" as Casco's men went rushing out into the seats in search of the missing guards. The soldiers began to find bits and pieces of the uniforms the guards had worn, a helmet or breastplate here, a sword or cape there.

After a few minutes, the centurion returned with some of the items, which he dropped at the governor's feet. "They're gone, Your Excellency," he reported, then turned to Legatus Casco. "Somehow they broke into the prison this morning; two other guards have been found locked in the prisoners' cell, and these two were substituted for the condemned. The attackers exchanged clothing with the guards to carry out their ruse, then slipped into the crowd and removed the uniforms."

"Did anyone get a good look at them? Did anyone recognize them?" Casco asked.

The centurion shook his head no.

"Find them," the governor ordered. "Search every house in the city if you must, but I want them found and brought to me this very day!"

"What about those two?" Casco motioned toward the guards who were still being held upon the crosses.

Rufinus scowled at Casco, then at the badly beaten guards. He looked up at the crowd, which was growing increasingly restless as it continued to shout, "Crucify them! Crucify them!"

"Give them their damn crucifixion!" he cursed with such anger and intensity that he sprayed spittle.

Legatus Casco looked at his governor with momentary puzzlement, then struck his chest with his fist and turned to his soldiers, giving the order to proceed.

As the governor ascended the stairs and returned to his sedan chair, he heard the pounding of hammers and the gleeful cheers of the crowd as they witnessed the promised crucifixion. They either didn't know or didn't care that it was neither the centurion nor the holy man but a pair of unfortunate Roman guards who were being put to death.

Rufinus could only hope that in time the story would spread that Marcus Antonius and Dismas bar-Dismas had indeed been crucified, and his own stature would increase as the legend grew. Or he might as easily become a laughingstock at having been tricked by a ruffian band of Christians in such a backwater province. If that were his fate, would he ever be welcomed back to Rome? he wondered.

He turned away from the spectacle before him as the crosses were lifted from the ground and raised into position. Waving a hand at one of his aides, he ordered, "Take me back to the palace."

Leaning back in the sedan chair, Rufinus Tacitus closed his eyes and imagined himself somewhere, anywhere but Ephesus.

TWENTY-FIVE

Tibro bar-Dismas, now totally divested of the garb of a soldier, stood near the front of the Harbor Gymnasium and Bath House, watching as the crowd dispersed from the theater. There was an air of great perplexity, with people arguing over what they had just witnessed. Some shouted praises to God that Dismas and Marcus had been spared, others insisted just as vociferously that the two condemned Christians had met their proper fate on the cross.

"Come, Tibro," Gaius urged, tugging at Tibro's arm. "We must leave before the soldiers get here."

"I am not known in Ephesus," Tibro replied. "No one can say I was one of the guards."

"But you so resemble your brother, someone may mistake you for him."

"Yes, you may be right."

"Come, I will show you the road to Jerusalem." Gaius led Tibro away from the crowd and down a narrow alley.

"It will be a long, lonely journey without my brother."

"Dismas has more work to do for the Lord," Gaius said.

"For Jesus? How can he—how can any of you—be so blind?" Tibro said in frustration. "It was all that false preaching about Jesus that nearly got him killed."

"And being a Zealot in Jerusalem is so much safer?" Gaius said with a half-smile. "Perhaps we should focus not on theology but on getting you away from here safely."

Gaius was a native Ephesian and knew well the city of nearly three hundred thousand. He kept to small streets and back alleys through which soldiers rarely passed as he led them away from the center of the city.

As Tibro followed, he thought back on his final moments with his brother, before Dismas and Marcus were spirited from the prison by their fellow Christians and Tibro, Gaius, and two others took the place of the guards.

"I risked my life for you, not for your false prophet Jesus," Tibro had told his older brother as they shared a brief moment in the cell. "Now I want you to return to Jerusalem with me. Our parents are gone; there are only the two of us left."

They had embraced, but then Dismas had pushed away from Tibro and said, "I'm sorry, but I have given my life to the Lord and must go where he leads me."

"If I had known you'd be so foolish with this second chance, I wouldn't have even come to Ephesus."

"I'm sorry, but I must do what I must."

Tibro had responded with an expletive, and he winced now as he recalled his anger. He would have come regardless of the consequences or of what Dismas did thereafter. He was driven by love for his brother and also by a sense of guilt at not having been able to save their father. He was determined that such a fate would not befall his brother.

The Romans are the enemies, he reminded himself, *not these Christians, no matter how misguided they may be.*

Though Tibro professed to be angry with his older brother, in reality he respected Dismas for standing by his principles. Dismas considered himself bound to a higher duty, and not even familial bonds could cause him to abandon the man he called his Lord. It had been little different for Tibro or their father, both of whom had sworn allegiance to the Zealot cause of ridding the Holy Land of the scourge of Rome.

But what about the woman Marcella? he asked himself. She was not only a Roman, but also the wife of the governor. Was her religious conviction as powerful as his brother's? Was that what gave her the strength to defy her own people and take up with such a ragged lot?

Had Tibro not actually met Marcella, he would never believe that a Roman woman could hold so strong a belief. Yet, at considerable risk to herself, she had agreed to help Tibro. Indeed, there would have been no hope of success without her involvement in the rescue mission, for she had gained them entry to the prison.

Why had he so quickly taken her into his confidence? Tibro wondered. Had she wavered, had she lost her nerve and told her husband what they were planning, many lives would have been lost. But he had known, almost the instant he met her, that she could be trusted. He had seen that truth in her eyes...and something more powerful and mysterious. There had been an undeniable attraction—no, a connection—between them. Were she not the wife of the governor, and a Christian one at that, and were she not sailing that very moment for the despised Rome, he might have allowed himself to imagine what he knew could never be between them.

"There's Epaphras," Gaius said, interrupting Tibro's reverie. He pointed to an older man seated on a stone marker at a crossroads a short distance ahead.

Seeing Gaius and Tibro, Epaphras waved, then walked toward them. He had a large bundle tucked beneath each arm.

"This is Epaphras, my brother-in-Christ," Gaius said by way of introduction. "And this is Tibro bar-Dismas."

Epaphras bowed to the younger man. "For your service to Dismas and to our cause, I thank you."

Tibro waved his hand impatiently. "I do not serve any cause other than our joint dislike of Rome."

"Nevertheless, you helped us free our brother Dismas," Gaius said. "For that you have our prayers and our thanks."

"You may call Dismas brother, but he is my brother in the flesh, and it is for that reason alone that I came."

"It is not blood alone that makes men brothers," Gaius said with something of a patronizing smile. "All who have been baptized in the name of Jesus Christ are one family. Therefore, Dismas is as much a brother to us as to you."

Tibro started to object, then thought better of it. "I suppose I have less cause to worry, knowing that Dismas is among brothers."

"Do not fear," Gaius replied. "I will watch over him."

"From Ephesus, with Dismas in Rome?" Tibro said dubiously.

"No. At his side, for I'm headed that way, to Rome." He pointed to the road that led west from the crossroads. "And there lies the way to Jerusalem." He indicated the road heading east.

"When you see Dismas in Rome..." Tibro began, then struggled to find words to express what he was feeling.

"I will watch over him always," Gaius promised. "And I will make sure he sends word to you in Jerusalem."

"I am in your debt," Tibro said.

"As we are in yours."

Epaphras held forth one of the bundles he was carrying. "To help with your long journey, our brothers and sisters in Christ have prepared cheese, olives, figs, and nuts. Take this purse with you, eat and enjoy." He handed Tibro the bundle, then gave the second one to Gaius.

Tucking the package under his left arm, Tibro grasped Epaphras's hand in thanks. Gaius added his hand to theirs, and they stood a moment joined as brothers.

"I hope you'll allow me to say a prayer for your safety," Gaius said, "and for the safety of Dismas and those who are traveling with him."

Tibro wanted to protest that he did not need a prayer in the name of someone he considered a false prophet. But he had measured the quality of these two men and found them worthy, if misguided. Not wishing to hurt their feelings, he nodded and said, "Yes, a prayer."

"Our Father in Heaven, guide this good man on his long journey home. Give eyes to his feet that they do not strike a stone and injure him. Fill his mouth with food and song until he is safely at his destination. Look also with favor upon our brothers, Dismas bar-Dismas and Marcus Antonius, and our sisters, Marcella and Tamara. Give their vessel fair winds and good seas so that their journey to Rome may be without peril. These things we ask in the name of your son, our Lord, Jesus Christ. Amen."

Mentally removing the reference to Jesus, Tibro added his amen to what otherwise was a fitting prayer for a Jew. He then took leave of the men and started down the road.

As he followed the right-hand path, he looked back a few times until he could no longer make out Gaius and Epaphras at the crossroads. Then he turned his gaze to the blue waters off in the distance. He could not see the boat but knew it was out there somewhere, sails full in the afternoon breeze as it plowed the waters toward Rome. He imagined his brother standing at the bow, and near him the woman Marcella. He wondered if she was thinking of him just then, and if he would ever see her again.

———————

MILES AWAY AT SEA, a small boat sailed swiftly toward the coast of Greece, bearing the wife of Governor Rufinus Tacitus to Rome. The three other passengers were mere servants, at least as far as the boat's crew was concerned.

Dismas bar-Dismas found it difficult to play the role of a servant. While he considered himself a servant of Jesus Christ, he did not know how to properly humble himself as the attendant to a mere mortal, even one as prominent as Marcella. And so he tried to avoid notice as he stood alone at the rail, gazing into the distance.

Marcella came up beside him, interrupting his meditations. "Look at them," she whispered, nodding toward the stern, where Marcus Antonius and Tamara were seated arm in arm on a pile of canvas sail. "I am glad we were able to secure Marcus's freedom. It means so much to both of them."

"Yes," Dismas agreed.

"Oh, how rude of me!" Marcella declared, drawing her hand over her mouth. "Of course, your freedom means as much to you, as well."

"Does it?" Dismas replied, looking back to sea.

"Do you not value your own freedom and the things you can now accomplish?"

"Of course I do," Dismas said, turning toward her. "Please do not think me ungrateful. I am very thankful, and not unmindful of the risk you have taken in rescuing us."

"Then why do you question your freedom?"

"Because I wonder if God truly intended for me to go to Rome," he confessed. "Perhaps he wanted me to face my death on the cross, so that by my example the Lord might inspire the faithful in Ephesus."

"Dismas, put your mind at ease. You have done the correct thing," Marcella said.

"How can I be sure?"

"Didn't you tell me of a task given you by the apostle Paul? Your commission is not yet finished, is it?"

"It is not," Dismas admitted.

"And there is so much more to be done in the service of our Lord. Who, may I ask, is better prepared to serve than you, whose own father accompanied our Lord to Heaven? No, you were not meant for such a death. Not today."

"I hope you're right."

"I know I am," she said. "After all, if not for you, I would not now be counted among the faithful."

Dismas smiled and put his hand on her shoulder. "Perhaps you are right. Perhaps God is speaking to me, right now, through you."

Marcella returned the smile, then took her leave and walked over to a special chair that had been brought aboard for her, in keeping with her station.

Alone again at the rail, Dismas tried to convince himself that Marcella was right. Perhaps his work was not yet done. He thought of the love his brother had displayed in risking his life to save not only Dismas but a Roman centurion. And he did so despite being a nonbeliever.

Dismas prayed for Tibro, not only for his safety but that he might one day know the loving embrace of Jesus. He prayed also for the good Christians of Ephesus who had helped him escape. While he might question their decision to use force against soldiers who were only doing their job, he did not question the underlying motives that had moved them to act. They had put themselves in great danger to rescue him, and they would undoubtedly face the full wrath of Rufinus if he ever found out who they were.

After his prayers, Dismas prepared a makeshift table and took out the papyrus on which he had been writing his account of the life of Jesus:

For my preaching, I have received at the hand of my tormenters forty-minus-one lashes of the rod. I have been stoned near to death, and I have been thrown in prison under penalty of crucifixion. I have traveled by sea, I have been in danger from floods, robbers, and even from my own people who have not yet received our Lord.

And yet, through it all, the Lord my God has watched over me, has sent an angel to protect me, and has shown me the way.

As Marcella sat nearby, watching Dismas at work, she could see in each gesture the younger Tibro, and she longed to be in his presence again.

How could she feel such a thing? she chided herself. She was not only a married woman, she was a Christian. Surely such feelings for a man other than her husband were sinful in the eyes of God. But wasn't it that very God who had drawn them together?

As disconcerted as she was by the intensity of her feelings, she knew she could not get Tibro bar-Dismas out of her mind. What's more, she had no desire to do so.

She looked back across the water toward Ephesus, thinking of Tibro, hoping and praying that he was safe and was thinking of her.

TWENTY-SIX

WHEN FR. MICHAEL FLANNERY RETURNED TO JERUSALEM, HE DID NOT immediately notify Preston Lewkis or the rest of the research team. Instead, he took a room at a small hotel with a courtyard of aromatic lemon and orange trees. He had dinner in the courtyard, finishing off his meal with a very rich coffee, liberally doctored with heavy cream and sugar.

After dinner, Flannery headed into the Old City to one of the most sacred places in Christendom, the Church of the Holy Sepulcher, located deep in the Muslim quarter. As he walked, he felt beneath his feet the ancient stones, worn smooth under the footfalls of millions of pilgrims over two millennia. He was sure that Jesus' own feet had trod this pathway, and that Jesus had smelled the same scents of cheese, olives, vinegar, oiled wood, and a cacophony of spices—even the faint odor of urine.

Around him, merchants enticed tourists and pilgrims with gaudily colored candles, holy water from the River Jordan, rosaries, and vials of soil from the Holy Land.

The large church was filled with worshippers, many holding candles that flickered and smoked and dripped hot wax onto the floor. Flannery moved through the chanting, praying, swaying crowd, then made his way up a steep flight of 19 steps to a chapel hung with gold lamps and a large Byzantine crucifix, the site of the twelfth station of the cross—Golgotha, the place of crucifixion. As he approached the marble altar, he gazed at the life-size icons of Christ on the cross flanked on his right by the Virgin Mary and on his left by the apostle John.

Dropping to his knees below the altar, Flannery thrust his hand through a gold-rimmed hole in the floor that marked where Jesus' cross had been raised. He felt a smooth, flat stone, cool to the touch, Golgotha's summit.

When his prayers were done, he returned downstairs and visited the thirteenth station—the marble slab where Jesus' body was washed before burial. The slab was covered with rose petals and wet with pools of water. Many worshippers were dipping their rosaries and crosses into the water, then bathing their faces in it as they prayed. A couple of Israeli security guards walked by, rifles slung casually over their shoulders.

After standing before the final station, a large marble structure housing the remains of the rock-hewn tomb of Christ, Flannery headed back into the street, his spirit renewed as he followed the Via Dolorosa, the Way of Sorrow, back to his Jerusalem hotel.

———

THE NEXT MORNING, Flannery rented a car and drove south on Road 90 along the Dead Sea to Ein-Gedi. Eighteen kilometers south of Ein-Gedi he turned west for two kilometers, ending up in a parking lot at the foot of a steep and barren mountain.

Getting out of the Ford, he looked up at the summit plateau that held the Masada fortress. When he had visited the fortress previously, he had been whisked there by helicopter. The usual route was via a cable car that led from the parking lot to the peak. More adventurous visitors could make the assent on a narrow path that snaked back and forth up the steep mountain slope, though this path was officially closed due to the danger of falling rocks.

Flannery took neither the cable car nor the path but instead got back in the car and continued on the road toward Sdom. Several kilometers from Masada, he turned off the main road onto a narrow, rocky lane that led to a small compound near the banks of the Dead Sea. The simple, almost nondescript main building housed the Monastery of the Way of the Lord, the very monastery to which Father Leonardo Contardi had once been assigned. Abandoned for many years, it had maintained a Christian presence almost steadily since the earliest days of the Church. Now it was the place of archaeologists and scholars seeking to understand the intertwined history of Christians and Jews.

As he drove up to the monastery, an armed Israeli guard stopped him. Flannery had not expected security at such an obscure site and considered it a testament to the tension of the times. He showed the guard the security badge he had been given during his last visit to Israel, hoping it would do the trick. The guard examined it closely, then nodded and waved Flannery through.

As he parked near the main entrance and got out of the car, he saw several workers examining a section of the outer foundation. The three men all wore *yarmulkes,* while the woman was dressed in traditional Palestinian garb. The woman noticed him approaching, and as she took her leave of the others and came over, Flannery recognized her at once.

"You're Azra, aren't you?"

"Azra Haddad, yes," she said, lowering her gaze. "And you are Father Michael Flannery, from the Vatican."

"Yes," he replied, surprised that she remembered his name following their last, brief meeting. He pointed toward the workers. "I'm surprised to see Israelis interested in an old Catholic monastery."

"Some believe this present structure was built on the site of a small community of Essenes," Azra explained.

"Ah, the Essenes. Then I can understand their interest," Flannery said. He was familiar with the sect of Jewish ascetics that flourished before and during the time of Jesus. The most famous Essene community, Qumran, lay to the north in the Palestinian West Bank region. That was where most of the Dead Sea Scrolls had been found in jars, like the Dismas document, though not as well preserved.

"What brings you here, Father?" Azra asked. "I thought you were in Jerusalem, working on the scroll."

"I had a friend who lived here during its final days as an active monastery."

Azra turned and looked toward the building, then back at the priest. "Is he older than you?"

"No, he's about...that is, he was about my same age," Flannery said. "He died last week."

"You are talking about Father Leonardo Contardi?"

Flannery was visibly stunned. "How do you know that?"

"We have a document listing all who were assigned here during the past century. Father Contardi was here in the early eighties, and he's about your age. We only just learned of his death, and so I put two and two together."

Flannery chuckled. "Two and two is simple math. What you just did was trigonometry. What else do you know about this place?"

"Many believe the monastery was founded by James, the brother of Jesus, and continued uninterrupted as a Christian church until the end of the first millennium, when Muslims slaughtered the monks and took it over. They, in turn, were ousted in 1099 by the crusaders. The crusaders established a new Catholic order here, one that survived through the Mongolian, Egyptian, Turkish, French, and British occupation, then Israel. It closed in 1986, and the Vatican negotiated an agreement whereby the monastery and grounds returned to Israel."

"I must say, I am very impressed. You've learned a lot working on this site."

"Most of what I know came from my husband."

"Is he an archaeologist?"

She shook her head. "Like your friend Father Contardi, my husband served here as a monk."

"A monk?" he said in surprise.

"He left the Church before we were married," Azra explained. "But he always had a fascination with this place—until his death," she added, her tone calm and even, as if she had long ago buried her sorrow.

"Are you Christian, Azra?"

"I am a Palestinian Muslim and a citizen of Israel."

"You said your husband was fascinated with this place. Because of its possible connection to the Essenes?"

"Partly," she replied. "But mostly because of a legend he learned during his days as a monk."

"Legend?"

"That somewhere nearby there lay buried a secret account of the life and ministry of Jesus—one lost since the days of the fall of Jerusalem."

Flannery wanted to ask if she was talking about the Dismas Gospel. After all, she herself had found the urn at Masada, which was only a few kilometers away. But he held his question in check, uncertain if she knew—or had the security clearance to be told—the full nature of the scroll that had been discovered inside that urn.

"You speak of secret writing," he said, choosing his words carefully. "Do you mean like the Dead Sea Scrolls?"

"Certainly their discovery at Qumran fueled the legend," Azra replied. "It became something of an initiation rite for each new monk to spend several years in an active search for the Messiah's lost teachings. Some never gave up the quest, while others grew disenchanted and departed, either to go to another monastery or to seek life outside the Church, as my husband did."

"Did everyone believe there was such a document?"

"There were those who believed, while others were convinced it didn't exist in the physical realm but was like the Holy Grail sought by King Arthur's knights."

"What about you, Azra? Do you think a lost gospel was hidden near here?" Flannery asked.

"I have always believed that the truth lies in both worlds, the tangible and the ethereal."

He saw the hint of a smile touch Azra's lips, and though she was long past being considered a young woman, Flannery couldn't help but be reminded of the woman with the most famously ineffable smile of all, Mona Lisa.

"All right, I'll accept that," he said, his words slowing as he considered precisely what he wanted to ask. "But that brings me to another question—one that may also have a connection to this monastery."

"What is that?"

"Do you know of an organization named Via Dei?"

A shadow replaced Azra's smile, and she looked around quickly, as if checking to see if anyone was listening. "Where did you hear of those people?"

"Then, you *do* know about Via Dei?"

"I've heard of them."

"Tell me everything you know."

"Father Flannery, why are you pursuing this?"

"It has...recently come up," he replied, careful not to be specific. "I believe Father Contardi was involved with Via Dei in some way."

"Did that involvement have something to do with his death?"

"I...I don't know," Flannery replied, surprised by the question. In fact, he did suspect a connection between his friend's death and the secret organization of his youth. Perhaps Flannery himself was the agent of Contardi's demise, having upset him so terribly by raising memories the fragile priest was not equipped to handle.

"You do know something about Via Dei, don't you?" Flannery pressed.

"I'm not sure that I can differentiate between what I know and what I suspect," Azra replied.

"Then what do you suspect?"

"That over the years this monastery has been affiliated in some manner with Via Dei...perhaps going all the way back to the time of the crusaders."

"But not before?" Flannery asked.

"Before?"

"I'm trying to find out how long this Via Dei has been around. Could it have been in existence before the Crusades? Or did the crusaders create it as a secret order, rather like the Knights Templar?"

"It may predate the Crusades," Azra said flatly. "It may have been involved in creating the Knights Templar."

"Azra, was your husband a member of Via Dei?"

She shook her head emphatically. "No. If he had been, he would never have been able to leave the brotherhood, and we never would have been allowed to marry."

"But he did know about Via Dei, did he not? And he told you about it."

"Yes, he knew enough to be frightened away from this monastery and out of the Church."

"Yet he maintained a lifelong fascination with this monastery...isn't that what you said?"

"Fear and fascination," she said in a hush. "So often they are entwined." She looked up at the priest, her eyes almost beseeching. "Perhaps we have spoken enough of this Via Dei, and I can give you a tour of the monastery." She gestured toward the entrance, inviting him inside.

Flannery was convinced the woman knew more, but he didn't want to press too hard, fearful he had already frightened her. Perhaps she suspected he was a member of the secret order and was trying to determine what she knew and how much of a threat to the organization she might be.

As if reading his mind, Azra said, "Father Flannery, I will take a chance that you don't belong to Via Dei."

"I am not a member," he assured her.

"But you have been approached to become a member?"

"It was a long, long while ago. In my youth."

"Then you already know something of Via Dei. I will not tell you to cease your investigation; you appear to be a man of courage, and a few words from an old woman like me will not stop you. I will ask, however, that you be very careful in your quest. Know who can and cannot be trusted, and it will not be easy to discern between the two."

"Why are you so afraid?" Flannery asked.

She looked at him curiously. "I have no fear of Via Dei. I am but a poor woman who digs in the dirt for whatever scraps the soil may yield. Why would they take notice of someone as...invisible as me? But a great man of the Church such as yourself? Great stature carries great visibility, something a secret organization such as Via Dei shall always fear...shall seek always to destroy."

Suddenly the darkness left her eyes, and she grinned broadly.

"It is time now for that monastery tour I promised you."

Turning, she pointed first at the main entrance before them, then at a smaller door about twenty feet to its left and another one twenty feet to its right.

"There are three paths upon which you may enter the Monastery of the Way of the Lord. Choose wisely."

He examined the three entrances. At first he thought the doors to the left and right were identical, but then he noticed that this was only an illusion and that, in fact, the one to the right was a bit shorter and narrower. He immediately made his selection with a nod of the head.

"Did I make the right choice?" he asked as Azra led him down the walkway to the smallest of the three doors.

"All choices are correct," she proclaimed, "whether the doorway you choose opens upon Heaven or Hell or...Via Dei."

TWENTY-SEVEN

Daniel Mazar took a sip of his morning coffee as he studied a section of the Dismas scroll he had printed out from the computer image files. He preferred working on paper, not only because he had learned his craft long before computers became ubiquitous, but because it allowed him to scrawl notes on the copy and sketch connections between portions of text.

When the embedded Hebrew sections were discovered, Yuri Vilnai had used their presence to challenge the scroll's authenticity. While the earliest copies of the Old Testament were in Hebrew, virtually all New Testament writers used Greek, and none interspersed snippets of Hebrew, as they had found in the Dismas document.

Though Mazar had vociferously defended the scroll, he, too, was puzzled by the juxtaposition of Hebrew with Greek. There was no discernible pattern to the author's usage. Sometimes only a single Hebrew word appeared, other times a complete passage was in Hebrew.

As he studied one of the longer passages, his attention drifted, so that he wasn't actually reading the text but seeing it almost as an image, a complex pattern of sorts. As the text began to blur, several characters stood out. They were not side by side but were spaced evenly apart. They caught his eye because when taken together, they formed a familiar word he had often practiced writing as a child. Almost absent-mindedly he drew a line under each one. From right to left—the direction in which Hebrew is read—they were the letters Mem, Zayin, Resh.

Ancient Hebrew did not use vowels, and they were not needed for the professor to translate the word into English, which he whispered aloud: "Mazar." Coincidence, he told himself. But then he counted back an equal number of letters before those three and underlined the letters Dalet, Nun, Yod, Lamed.

"Daniel Mazar," he said numbly.

Slowly, painstakingly, he counted the spacing between each letter, and indeed they were evenly distributed, with each one precisely eight letters from the next.

"Eight..." Mazar shook his head in disbelief.

Throughout his life, he had been fascinated by Jewish mysticism, numerology in particular. The letters of the Hebrew alphabet did not only signify a sound, they held a numeric value. He had worked out the value of his own name numerous times, and yet he did so again, writing above each character, right to left, Dalet to Resh, its sacred value:

2007403010504
ReshZayinMemLamedYodNunDalet

On a piece of notepaper, he totaled the numbers: 341. Then he added each of the individual digits—3 + 4 + 1—which reduced the combined value to a single digit: 8—the precise spacing of the letters in the Dismas scroll.

"This can't be real," he said aloud. His scientific mind could not accept that this was more than mere coincidence. His mystic mind knew that coincidence was simply a manifestation of the perfection of God's plan.

He continued to study the Hebrew passage that contained his name, seeking other patterns that might be revealed by counting off the letters with different spacings. Nothing else emerged.

Mazar knew the appearance of his name could be random. Or perhaps Daniel had been encoded, and the subsequent letters M Z R were random. The idea that an ancient Hebrew text might contain secret messages encoded by a divine hand was nothing new. For centuries, Jewish mystics had searched for the so-called Torah code, information hidden within the first five books of the Old Testament, which by legend had been transmitted letter by letter from the Lord to Moses.

Some of the most famous research into Bible codes had been done in the early 1980s by Eliyahu Rips, a colleague of Mazar's at Hebrew University. His work had been popularized by journalist Michael Drosnin in his 1997 best-seller "The Bible Code." And while numerous debunkers had shown that similar prophecies could be found in everything from "War and Peace" to "Moby Dick," Mazar still found himself intrigued at the notion that Dismas bar-Dismas might have included Hebrew as a means of encoding messages that might have been too heretical to state plainly.

Realizing the computer was the perfect tool to test such a hypothesis, he sat back down at one of the terminals and called up a copy of the scroll that had been converted from images to text, containing the full document formatted with Greek and Hebrew fonts. Copying the file, he first deleted all of the Greek text, leaving just the Hebrew passages. Then he called up a program that analyzed text based on the complex formula worked out by Eliyahu Rips.

Using one and then another equidistant letter sequence, or ELS, Mazar searched the text for word patterns. The program compared the strings of letters against a Hebrew dictionary, seeking common words or phrases. Numerous words were identified, but none of them held any significance. Mazar tried different sequences until, an hour into the search, a familiar name appeared: Masada, the site where the scroll had been found. Using that name to set the starting point and ELS, Mazar reran the sequence, creating a matrix of letters surrounding the name. The program beeped as it found and highlighted another word crisscrossing Masada, then beeped a second and third time as additional words emerged. Like a scene emerging from the fog, Mazar stared in wonder as a series of phrases appeared, surrounding the key word Masada. Snatching up his notepad, he began translating the words into English, until he had the following three phrases:

Mountain of Jewish patriots
Scroll revealed for a short time
Returned to darkness

The professor stared in dumbfounded amazement at the words before him. He tried to chalk it up to coincidence, but he could not see how a message so specific to the scroll could be the result of a random pattern.

And what did it mean? he wondered. Was Dismas predicting that his scroll would be seen briefly during his lifetime, then returned to darkness when it was buried in Masada? While that was possible, Mazar had the strange feeling that "revealed for a short time" referred to the present and that the scroll would soon disappear again, perhaps forever.

He decided to rerun the program, using the appearance of his name to determine the starting point and equidistant letter spacing. He had seen his Hebrew name spaced apart in an eight-letter sequence. To check it against the Torah code worked out by Eliyahu Rips, he set the program to create a matrix of letters using an ELS of eight surrounding his name. As the matrix took form, words again began to be highlighted. His eyes fixed on the first one: *Ratsach*. Murderer.

Mazar sat immobile, staring at the screen as the full meaning of the message became clear. Was it a warning, or the prediction of something that could not be changed?

He made an encrypted copy of the computer file and attached it to an e-mail message, which he sent to his personal e-mail address. Then to further ensure the information would not be lost were something to happen to him, he plugged a small digital camera to the USB port of the computer, tucked the cable out of sight behind some objects on the desk, and hid the Web cam between some books on a shelf just above the work station.

He launched a video capture program on the computer, then picked up the phone and punched in a number. As it began to ring, he pressed the speakerphone button and replaced the receiver on the cradle.

After a few rings, a man answered, his voice a bit thin but clear through the phone's small speaker: "You're early, Sarah. I thought you weren't coming until nine."

Mazar was momentarily taken aback, then realized Preston Lewkis had been expecting a call from Sarah Arad.

"Preston, this is Daniel," he said a bit awkwardly.

"Oh, jeez, Daniel, I should be more careful how I answer the phone," Preston replied with a chuckle. "I might say something I'll regret."

"How soon can you get down to the lab?" Mazar asked, avoiding further pleasantries.

There was a moment's hesitation, then Preston replied, "I'm expecting Sarah in about an hour...at nine. I'll see if she can get here sooner. Has something happened?"

"It's not what has happened but what is going to happen," Mazar said. "That is, if I am correct."

"Correct about what? Daniel, my friend, you're being very, very mysterious. What's all this about?"

"If I told you, you'd think I was crazy. You'll have to see for yourself."

"Will it wait until I get there?"

"It's waited two thousand years—I suppose it can wait another hour."

"I'll be there as soon as I can."

After hanging up the phone, Mazar sat back down at the computer, using additional letter spacings to search out word patterns. As he worked, he provided a running narration of what he was doing. Common sense, reason, education and experience told him he was headed down a false path, but as additional phrases emerged from the scroll, they reinforced what he had already discovered.

"Careful, Daniel," he said in a moment of doubt. "Remember the ossuary. You ended up looking like a fool."

And how much more a fool he would look if he pursued analyzing the scroll using the Torah code, which most researchers dismissed as bunk.

Still, Mazar felt compelled to record his findings, even if it only served to provide ammunition to those who would seek to cast doubt on the document's authenticity. He opened his notebook and began writing the messages he had discovered so far. He had just finished the first entry, when he heard a door slam somewhere out in the hall.

"Preston?" he whispered, then glanced over at the wall clock and shook his head. There was no way his colleague could have gotten there so soon. Besides, Preston wouldn't slam a door like that.

Nobody would slam a door like that, he thought as he heard another loud bang.

Hurrying across the room, he jerked open the lab door and looked down the hall. He caught a glimpse of one of the security guards running with his gun drawn toward the front entrance. Suddenly the man fired into the distance, the muzzle flash lighting up the shadowed interior.

He hadn't been hearing doors slamming, but gunshots.

Mazar pulled closed the door and locked it. As he looked around the lab, his mind raced through a hundred scenarios. Was it a Palestinian hit team? Why would terrorists come here? Didn't they generally strike where they could kill the most people? But Mazar and the guards were the only ones here right now...

"My God!" he said. "The prophecy is true!"

Mazar hurried back to the computer. The entire Dismas document was loaded. In addition, the matrix of Hebrew letters was in the foreground, with several words highlighted as the result of his search patterns.

He hit the close button at the top of the window, and a message popped open asking if he wanted to save changes to the document. He clicked the "no" button, and the Torah code page disappeared from view. He then closed the scroll document and, leaving the computer running, turned off the monitor so it would appear to be shut down. Tearing a page out of his notebook, he stuffed it in his pocket. Finally, he rushed over to the safe, where the scroll and urn were kept. The double locks required two people to open, with Yuri Vilnai and himself knowing the combination for the right-hand tumbler and the chief security officer knowing the other. But Mazar had long been secretly aware of both combinations, though he had been careful not to reveal this knowledge by making use of it. But this was an emergency, and so he spun one dial left and right several times, then the second. There was a loud click, and he grasped the handle and pulled open the door.

The safe was more like a small closet with carefully controlled temperature and humidity. The shelves normally held various ancient manuscripts, but all had been moved to another location when the Dismas scroll had been brought in. The urn sat alone on one of the lower shelves, with the scroll wrapped in cloth on the shelf just above.

Leaving the urn in place, Mazar quickly but carefully lifted the scroll and, cradling it in his arms, carried it out into the lab. As more gunshots sounded outside, he looked for a suitable hiding place. Hurrying over to a tall filing cabinet, he put down the scroll and then pulled out and removed the bottom drawer. There was a fairly large gap below the drawer, and he slid the scroll inside and lowered it to the floor, then replaced the drawer and closed it.

After locking the safe, Mazar went to the shelf where the Web cam was hidden between the books. It was still recording on the computer with the monitor turned off. Looking into the camera, he spoke quickly, describing what he was happening and what he had discovered. He was nearly finished when someone banged on the door. As he backed across the room, there was a burst of gunfire that tore a hole where the lock had been. Then the door was thrown open and three men burst in, all wearing the dark outfits and full-face masks that were the common garb for terrorists.

"Who are you?" Mazar asked. "What do you want?"

"Open the safe!" one of them shouted in Arabic, then repeated the demand in heavily accented English.

When Mazar did not move, one of the others said, "We don't need him." Turning to the Israeli scholar, he raised his pistol and squeezed the trigger three times.

Mazar felt the slugs slam into his chest, throwing him back against the wall. As he slid numbly to the floor, his vision blurred, the muffled voices growing dull and indistinct. He saw the masked men huddled around the safe, the heavy door swinging open. And then everything was silent...everything went dark.

TWENTY-EIGHT

Yuri Vilnai had just parked his car when he saw three men in black face masks come running through the front doorway, two of them brandishing guns while the third carried something in his arms. Vilnai dropped down in his seat so he wouldn't be seen. He waited a full minute or so, and when he cautiously rose back up, they were gone.

Hurrying into the building, he saw the first security guard lying behind the front desk in a pool of blood. His face was almost blown away, and there was no need to check his pulse to confirm he was dead. Two more guards were in the hallway that led to the lab room. They, too, were dead.

As Vilnai cautiously approached the lab, he saw the badly damaged door hanging by one hinge from a splintered frame. Easing forward, he took a quick glance inside, then pulled back as his mind absorbed what he had just seen. Suddenly he shouted "Daniel!" and rushed to where the older man lay slumped against the far wall. "Daniel," he repeated over and over again as he checked Mazar for signs of life.

There was a harsh gasp as Mazar drew in a breath and struggled to open his eyes.

"Rest easy," Vilnai said as he fumbled for his cell phone. "Don't try to move. I'll call for help."

Mazar reached out and grasped the younger man's sleeve. In a choking rasp, he said, "D-Did you s-s-see them, Yuri? There...there were th-three."

"Yes," Vilnai answered. "I saw them."

"And the g-guards?"

"Dead," Vilnai replied somberly. "They are all dead."

Mazar coughed, and blood spattered on his lips.

"Did they get—?" Yuri started to ask, then saw the open, empty safe. He realized at once that the third masked man had been carrying the urn with the scroll inside.

Mazar tried to speak but broke into a fit of coughing, and more blood frothed at his lips. Vilnai urged him to lie still, but Mazar shook his head, saying, "S-sorry. I couldn't stop them, even though I...I knew they were c-coming."

"Of course you couldn't—" Vilnai said but interrupted his comment in midsentence. "You knew they were coming?"

"The c-c-code," Mazar stammered. "The code said it would happen."

"Daniel, what are you talking about? What code?" Vilnai asked, but Mazar had lost consciousness. Gently shaking him, he whispered, "Daniel, Daniel, wake up."

Mazar's eyes half opened, and he tried to speak.

"Daniel, you said something about a code. What code are you talking about?"

"My p-pocket," Mazar managed to gasp. "P-Paper...in my pocket."

Vilnai rifled through Mazar's clothes, taking little notice of the grimaces of pain elicited by his rough search. Finding a sheet torn from Mazar's notebook, he saw two phrases written in Hebrew and translated into English:

Murderer of Daniel Mazar
Not who it seems

"Daniel, what is this?" Vilnai asked.

"The code...the code of Dr. R-Rips."

"The Torah code? That's ridiculous," Vilnai said, but Mazar grabbed his lapel and almost pulled himself upright.

"The Dismas scroll. T-Tell Preston to run the code. He will know." Again he lost consciousness.

From outside the building came the discordant, wailing sirens of several approaching police vehicles. Suddenly Vilnai remembered his cell phone, lying on the floor where he had absently dropped it, having forgotten his promised call for assistance.

Stuffing the phone back into his coat pocket, he looked down at his colleague. "Help is coming," he said.

Mazar, breathing laboriously, was still unconscious.

"Did you hear me, Daniel? The ambulance is here."

Mazar did not respond.

Vilnai looked again at the notepaper he clutched in his fist. Deep in thought, he carefully folded it and tucked it into his pocket. Glancing around to reassure himself that they were alone, he softly stroked Mazar's cheek, then slid his hand across the older man's face. Holding his palm over Mazar's mouth, he pinched the nostrils between his thumb and forefinger.

Mazar's eyes shot open, and he stared up at Vilnai in surprise and confusion. Yet he didn't fight back or even try to jerk his head. His expression softened with acceptance, and he closed his eyes and died.

The sound of sirens faded from Vilnai's awareness as he wrapped Daniel Mazar in his arms, hugging his body close as he gently rocked from side to side. With tears streaming down his cheeks, he murmured a mournful dirge:

> *Yeetgadal v' yeetkadash sh'mey rabbah*
> *B'almah dee v'rah kheer'utey*

Vilnai was still chanting the Kaddish when the first police officer came through the doorway, gun at the ready. Close behind were Sarah Arad and Preston Lewkis, who had come in response to Mazar's earlier telephone call.

"My God! What happened?" Preston cried as he rushed to where Vilnai was cradling the dead professor in his arms.

Vilnai looked up, his face a mask of utter devastation. "Terrorists!"

he gasped, choking back tears. "They killed Daniel...and they've stolen the scroll."

———

FR. Michael Flannery pulled out onto the main road that led north to Jerusalem. As the desert dust swirled up around the vehicle, he reviewed his visit with Azra Haddad at the Monastery of the Way of the Lord. He had learned much from the fascinating Muslim woman, and he suspected there was a lot more still to be revealed.

He had just passed Masada when his cell phone rang. Snatching it from the cup holder, he greeted the caller with a simple, "Hello."

"Michael, where are you?"

Flannery recognized the caller and noted an urgency in his voice. "Preston? Is something wrong?"

"Where are you?" his friend repeated.

"I'm..." Flannery hesitated, not wanting to reveal yet that he had met with Azra at the monastery. "I'm on Road 90, just north of Ein-Gedi."

"Why are you...? Never mind, just come to the lab as quickly as you can."

"Something happened. What is it?"

"Yes." Preston's sigh was audible above the road noise. "It's Daniel. He's been killed."

"Professor Mazar? My God! How did it happen?"

"A terrorist squad—Palestinian, it seems," Preston replied. "He was in the lab when three gunman broke into the building, killed several guards and Daniel."

Flannery was silent for a moment as he prayed for the professor and the other victims.

"Michael, are you still there?"

"Yes," the priest replied. "They were Palestinians?"

"That's what the police think. Yuri Vilnai, too. He arrived just as they were making their escape. Apparently they were after the scroll."

"But it's locked up in the—"

"They got into the safe," Preston cut him off. "Somehow they knew the combinations. The door was wide open, and the urn and scroll are gone."

Flannery felt his heartbeat quicken. "I'll be there as quickly as I can."

As he shut the cell phone and tucked it back into the cup holder, he saw something dark ahead. Approaching, he made out a pair of vehicles blocking the road. One of them had a portable emergency light rotating on the roof, and Flannery saw a uniformed policeman standing beside it, waving for him to pull to a halt.

Stopping at the roadblock, Flannery retrieved the car rental agreement from the glove compartment. As he straightened back up and turned toward the approaching officer, the second car pulled out on the shoulder and circled behind his vehicle, hemming him in.

"What is this?" he asked, lowering his window.

Seeing that the officer was staring back at the second car, Flannery spun around on his seat just as two masked men came running up along his side of the car.

The priest managed to get the window closed and the doors locked but found the man in the uniform aiming his pistol at him through the windshield.

"Unlock the doors!" the man shouted. "Unlock them now, or I will kill you!"

Reluctantly, Flannery released the lock. The masked men jerked open the door and dragged him from the seat.

"Who are you?" Flannery demanded. "What do you want?"

"No talking," the one in the uniform said as his companions roughly bound Flannery's wrists behind his back with some sort of plastic pull tie. Then they dragged him over to the lead vehicle and shoved him into the back seat. A third masked man was seated behind the wheel.

"You've made some kind of mistake," Flannery said.

He was cut off by the man masquerading as an officer, who climbed in beside him and slapped him hard across the face. His ears rang, and he tasted blood in his mouth.

"I said no talking!"

Flannery nodded numbly. The driver then tossed something into the back seat, and the man in the uniform snatched up what turned out to be a black hood. As it was jerked down over Flannery's head, he caught a glimpse of his rental car and the rear vehicle pulling away and speeding north up the highway. A moment later, Flannery felt their car move forward and turn sharply back onto the road, then race after the other vehicles.

TWENTY-NINE

Tibro bar-Dismas raised his flagon, signaling the owner of the *kahn* that he wanted more wine. The innkeeper summoned one of his employees, and a moment later someone brought a pitcher over to their table in a darkened corner of the room. As the fellow refilled the flagon, Tibro looked around to reassure himself that he and his three companions were not attracting notice.

The inn, located just off the Street of Weavers in a working district of Jerusalem, was named the House of One Thousand Blessings, a rather extravagant appellation for an establishment that consisted of a single nondescript room filled with a jumble of bare wooden tables and no decorations to speak of. The smoke of guttering candles had streaked the once-white walls, with fainter patches revealing where a few paintings had once hung. Seated around the dozen or so tables were perhaps two dozen patrons, an egalitarian mix of merchants, laborers, and scholars who all appeared to be speaking simultaneously, sharing the latest news and street rumors.

Tibro waited until the server departed before resuming his conversation. "I'm not sure this is the right thing to do," he said, keeping his voice low.

"It has been ordered by the Sanhedrin," replied the oldest of the group, a gray-bearded fellow named Kedar. "We are to locate and remove the two in question."

"I know the orders," Tibro said, understanding that by *remove* the Sanhedrin meant *assassinate*. "Still, I do not like such an assignment."

"Do you not agree that these two men, by their very presence, are committing blasphemy against our religion?" the one named Menahem asked. "They are not even of our race, yet they would have us abandon our God."

"Yes," agreed Shimron, the fourth and youngest of the group. He was also the showiest, dressed in a blue robe with gold trim that Tibro feared might draw unwanted attention. "It was bad enough when our own brethren accepted Jesus as Messiah," Shimron said. "We could forgive them; they were our families, our friends, our own people. But this Christian movement has spread beyond our borders, beyond our people. These two, Rufus and Alex—"

He stopped abruptly, seeing their disapproving looks and remembering he was not supposed to speak aloud the names of the intended victims.

Lowering his voice to a near-whisper, he continued, "These two are uncircumcised, unclean, and black as night. How dare they come to Jerusalem and preach the gospel of the false prophet."

"But to kill someone who isn't hurting you...it is a hard thing to do," Tibro said. "It's not an action to be taken lightly."

"If their deaths serve God and our people, then it is not hard," Kedar insisted.

"But is it God's will? Or merely the will of the Sanhedrin?" Tibro countered.

"The Sanhedrin speak for God," Kedar said.

"Yes, I suppose that is true," Tibro agreed.

"Yet you would defy them?"

Tibro's eyes flashed with anger at the older man. "When have I ever defied a direct order from the Sanhedrin? I will carry out their wishes, even though I may question their wisdom."

"Are you thinking of your brother?" Menahem put in, his tone softer, as if seeking to smooth things between the two strong-willed men. "I realize Dismas is a Christian."

"I've neither seen nor heard from him in years."

Kedar frowned. "You saved his life in Ephesus at the risk of your own, and how did he repay you? By going to Rome not to fight Romans but to spread his false doctrine."

"When did you last see him?" Menahem asked.

"Ten years ago in Ephesus."

"That's a long time. Perhaps he has seen the error of his ways. Perhaps he has abandoned his false prophet and—"

"If you believe that, you don't know my brother," Tibro said. "I don't agree with Dismas, but I do know that he is a man of principle and courage. If he has accepted this man Jesus as his Lord, then he shall remain true to him until the day of his death."

"I see no problem with killing blasphemers," Shimron put in, stroking the sparse stubble of beard he was attempting to grow. "But I don't like the idea of dumping their bodies at the temple. Why desecrate a holy place with bodies of the unclean? Why not leave them where they fall?"

"No," Tibro said. "If we must do this thing, then it should serve a greater purpose. To leave them where they fall would be little more than murder. But in bringing their bodies to the temple—not inside holy ground, but within the outer walls—it will serve as a warning to others who would abandon the faith. And it will also justify the killings, for all know that death is the penalty for any non-Jew who would defile the temple."

"Tibro," Kedar whispered, nodding toward the door.

Tibro turned and saw a man in a blue girdle and a turban of rough brown cloth—the prearranged sign of recognition. As the man looked around the room, Tibro exchanged his flagon with Kedar's. Recognizing the return sign, the man in the turban came over to their table.

"God's grace be with you," he said.

"And his protection with you," Tibro replied.

Standing beside Tibro, the man reached inside his tunic and took out a small scroll. "This will tell you all you need to know," he said, handing it over.

"You have done God's work," Tibro said as he untied the cord around the scroll.

"Yes, I believe I have."

There was something in the man's tone, a sureness and arrogance, that caused Tibro to look up at him, but he had already turned and was weaving his way back through the tables toward the door.

"What is it?" Shimron asked.

Tibro studied the document, then nodded somberly. "It tells where to find the men we seek—the location of the house and the room in which they are lodged."

"When do we go?" Menahem asked.

"Now," Tibro replied, pushing his chair back and standing. He dropped a coin on the table, then led the group out to the street.

———————

"GET BACK," Tibro whispered, raising his arm.

He and his three companions slipped into a shadowed alley. Two Roman soldiers in full battle dress, with swords strapped to their hips, passed in and out of the shafts of light cast through the windows of the houses that lined the street. One laughed aloud at some remark of the other.

Tibro waited in silence until they were gone, then he signaled his friends to follow him out of the alley. "We're very near, now," he said as they continued up the street.

A hundred yards farther, Tibro turned into another alley, lit only by the brightness of the moon. As they approached a building at the far end, a cat wailed and leaped in front of them, then scampered into the darkness. All four men jumped reflexively.

Kedar chuckled softly. "What brave Sicarii we are, to be frightened by a cat."

"Quiet," Tibro hissed, pointing to a dark set of steps in front of them. "This is the place."

"How do we get in?"

"The message said it is never latched," Tibro replied. As he reached the foot of the steps, he looked at the others, then pulled his knife and held it forth, the blade gleaming in the moonlight. "Death to the Christian infidels," he declared.

Repeating the invocation, the others drew their daggers and touched the blades together. The knives inadvertently formed a cross, the sign that one day would symbolize the very sect they wished to destroy.

The four men crept up the steps to the back door. Tibro pushed it open, and they slipped inside. A single flickering lantern dimly illuminated the narrow hallway.

"It's the room at the far end," Tibro whispered, and they moved silently ahead.

They were halfway to the door when it swung open and several armed men rushed into the hall.

"It's a trap!" Shimron cried.

"Withdraw!" Tibro shouted, but it was too late, because more armed men were spilling from a room behind them, cutting off retreat. The four Zealots were caught in the narrow hallway, with armed Christians on either side.

Amid shouts of anger and fear, the Christians closed on the Zealots. Tibro stabbed one of the attackers, then turned his knife blade edge up so that as the man fell, the blade enlarged the wound. Feeling the man's warm blood running off the hilt and over his hand, Tibro spun around to take on another of the attackers. Beside him, Shimron dropped to his knees, a gaping wound in his belly, then Kedar and Menahem fell beneath the Christians' swords. Even as Tibro was watching Menahem, he felt a burning pain from a stab wound to the thigh. Someone knocked him down, then leaped upon him, a dagger raised for the killing thrust.

"No! Do not kill him!"

The deep voice reverberated through the narrow hallway and had an immediate effect on the man straddling Tibro, and he put aside his dagger. Tibro tried to jerk free, twisting to one side as he looked to see who had called out and spared his life. But he was met by a vicious kick from one of the other men. A second kick snapped his head back, and everything went black.

THIRTY

TIBRO BAR-DISMAS STRUGGLED TO OPEN HIS EYES, TO LIFT HIMSELF OUT
of the darkness that had enveloped him. Slowly he began to hear
sounds, see shadows and shapes moving around him. A voice, deep
and soothing, called to him.

"Dismas...are you all right? Dismas?"

Tibro felt someone patting his cheek, and he forced open his eyes,
blinking against the lantern-light.

"Dismas? What are you doing here?"

The shapes began to take form, and Tibro saw that the speaker
who hovered over him was as large and commanding as his voice, his
skin as black as the night.

"D-D-Dismas," Tibro stammered. "He's my b-brother."

The big man leaned closer, moving Tibro's face from side to side.
Slowly he began to nod, then he stood and turned to the others. "Bring
him into the meeting room."

Tibro felt strong hands clutching his arms and legs, and he was
hoisted from the floor and carried down the hall and through one of
the doorways. There he was propped unceremoniously in a large chair
that sat amid other chairs and benches that faced what appeared to be
a makeshift altar. As he looked around the large, undecorated room,

he recognized it as a smaller version of the house church he had visited in Ephesus.

The big black man, who appeared to be a leader among these Christians, turned one of the chairs to face Tibro, then sat down.

"How badly are you hurt?" he asked, gesturing at the gash on Tibro's thigh. When Tibro did not reply, he turned to one of the others and said, "Dress his wound."

"But he's a Zealot. He came to do us harm."

"He's the one who killed Aaron," another put in.

"I know this man. He will do us no more harm. He is the brother of Dismas, whom we all know to be a faithful follower of Christ. See to his wound." Turning back to Tibro, he said, "You don't remember me, do you?" His lips quirked into a smile. "We have met before, Tibro."

Tibro's eyes widened at hearing the man use his name. "How do you know me?"

"Think back, my friend, and you will recall when we met."

One of the Christians brought over a basin of water, some gauze, and soothing salve and began tending to the knife wound. Tibro winced as the man cleaned the gash, but he did not move or cry out, keeping his focus on the stranger who professed to know him.

"I remember now," Tibro finally said, nodding as he examined the man. Three decades had passed, which would make him perhaps sixty, yet he didn't look any older than Tibro's forty-nine years. "You're Simeon, aren't you? You were with my brother when they crucified Jesus. You carried the cross for him."

"Yes, except my name is Simon." He scooted his chair a little closer and looked at Tibro a long moment, then asked, "Why did you come here tonight?"

Tibro sighed. "I think you know why I'm here," he replied. "You must have been warned I was coming, or you wouldn't have been waiting."

"Yes, we knew someone was coming," Simon admitted.

Tibro was about to ask how they found out, when he realized that one of the group was the very man who had delivered the instructions back at the inn.

"You," he said to the messenger. "You would betray us? You would ally yourself with infidels who profane the one true God?"

"In following the Son of God, we serve the one true God," the man said resolutely.

Tibro shook his head. He knew from dealings with his brother that true believers such as these would not easily be dissuaded from their new faith. As he looked around at the rest of the group, he noticed a pair of younger black men who bore a strong resemblance to Simon. No doubt they were Tibro's intended victims, Rufus and Alexander.

The two men returned Tibro's stare, their faces contorted by the same anger that seemed to fill everyone except Simon. He alone looked upon Tibro with what appeared to be true compassion and even love. Fortunately for Tibro, he was clearly in charge, and because of that, the Zealot did not fear for his life.

"You wanted to kill my sons, didn't you?" Simon asked, indicating the two younger men.

Tibro realized Simon would see through any lie, so he declared, "Yes, we came to kill Rufus and Alexander."

"Why? What harm have they done to you?"

"They blaspheme before God, and that alone is enough," Tibro replied. "But even worse, they come as outsiders into our city and would lead our faithful away from God."

"But we all worship the same God," Simon said. "Can you not see that?"

"You follow a false prophet and dare to declare him the son of God."

"If the teachings of Jesus instruct us to love God, then how can he be a false prophet?"

"Enough," Tibro exclaimed, raising his hand. "I know only that God is God."

"Then we have no argument," Simon replied.

By now Tibro's wound had been cleaned, treated with salve, and bandaged.

"Stand up. See if you can walk," Simon directed.

Tibro stood and gingerly took a few steps. While the leg was painful, he could walk.

Another man came into the room and announced, "Simon, we have removed the bodies, as you ordered."

"What have you done with my friends?" Tibro demanded. "They must be taken to their families for proper burial."

"You were going to dump my sons in the temple courtyard, were you not?" Simon asked. "They would have been buried in Potters Field with everyone else you consider unclean."

Tibro could not deny the truth of Simon's words.

"Don't worry, Tibro, we aren't like that. Your friends will be taken to where the Sanhedrin will find them."

"And what about me? I hope you don't think that because you spared my life, I will join your movement. I will never become a Christian."

"Good."

Tibro raised his eyebrows. "You surprise me, Simon."

"Oh? And how is that?"

"Isn't it your mission to convert everyone to Christianity?"

"It is my mission to speak the truth," Simon replied. "Whether you accept that truth is between you and God. And for now, it is better for me that you continue a Zealot." He grinned. "In fact, I came to Jerusalem hoping to find you—though I confess not in so dramatic a manner."

"Me? Why were you looking for me?"

"I want you to arrange a meeting with the Zealot leaders."

"Why would you want to meet your sworn enemies?"

"Oh, but they aren't my enemies," Simon declared. "I have nothing but love for everyone."

"You love the Zealots?"

"Yes."

"All Jews, even those who crucified your master?" Tibro asked in growing disbelief. "And Ephesians, Romans?"

"I told you, I have no enemies," Simon repeated. "Will you arrange a meeting?"

"For what purpose?"

"To tell them what I just told you," Simon said. "That we are not enemies—that we worship the same God."

Tibro shook his head. "I will not arrange your death. Unlike you, the Zealots have enemies. They would kill you."

"I will take that chance."

"No," Tibro said emphatically. "I will not be responsible for your death."

Simon looked at Tibro for a long moment, then suddenly he erupted in laughter.

"Why are you laughing?"

"Can't you see the humor of this, Tibro?" Simon asked. "A few moments ago, you came in here determined to kill my sons—me, too, if you'd had the chance. Now you won't arrange a meeting because you fear for my life."

Realizing the irony, Tibro grinned. "Yes, I see your point. But even if I tried to arrange a meeting, they would want nothing to do with you —other than to kill you."

"Tibro is right," Alexander said, coming over to his father. "They will kill you."

"But surely, reasonable men can discuss the worship of God in a reasonable manner."

"No, Father, listen to Alexander," Rufus put in. "We have been here many months; you have not. What Tibro says is true. I beg of you, do not attempt this foolish thing. The Zealots have no wish to make peace with us."

"Is that true, Tibro?" Simon asked. "Do you not think the tent of God is big enough to provide peaceful shelter for all his children?"

"You talk of sheltering all under God's tent," Tibro said. "And yet, three of my friends lie dead, killed by your people. Is that the act of peacemakers?"

"Were you not coming to kill my sons?"

"Yes, but..." Tibro pinched the bridge of his nose. "Do not confuse me."

"It is true that Jesus was the bearer of peaceful tidings, the one who said to turn the other cheek. But we are not prohibited from defending ourselves."

Just then a man appeared in the doorway. Recognizing him, Simon grinned broadly and went to greet him.

"Lemuel, my friend. It is good to see you after so long. Come, rest yourself. Do you require food or drink?"

"Yes, some water...food if you have."

Alexander brought over a dipper of water, and Lemuel drank

thirstily, tipping it so steeply that the cool liquid dribbled down his beard.

Rufus, meanwhile, came over and reported, "We have bread, cheese, and a little wine."

"Bring it quickly," Simon told his son, then turned back to the new arrival. "Come, Lemuel, rest yourself on some pillows."

"Thank you." Lemuel wiped his hand across his beard. As he sat among the other men, he glanced over and noticed Tibro, then gasped in surprise. "Dismas, you eluded the Romans? But how?"

"This is Tibro, brother of Dismas," Simon told him. "What do you mean 'eluded the Romans'?" he added, his dark eyes narrowing in concern.

"You haven't heard? Years ago the Roman Senate declared Christianity *strana et illicita*—strange and illegitimate. They took no action then, but now they are using that old edict as a pretext to persecute us. In particular they are hunting for our leaders and teachers, and Dismas is one they want badly to arrest."

"Is my brother all right?" Tibro asked. "They haven't taken him, have they?"

Rufus brought over a plate of bread and cheese, and Lemuel voraciously tore off a chunk of the bread and stuffed it into his mouth, followed by a piece of cheese. Around mouthfuls, he managed to say, "They haven't found him yet, because he is being aided by a lady of influence."

"Is her name Marcella?"

Tibro's question caused Lemuel to stop chewing and look at him in surprise. Finally he swallowed, gulped some wine, and nodded. "Yes, it is Marcella, daughter of Senator Porcius, wife of Rufinus Tacitus. You know this woman?"

"We met when her husband was governor of Ephesus."

Often over the last ten years, Tibro had found himself thinking of the beautiful young woman, even though she was married, and to a Roman governor, no less.

"She has been a great help to our faithful in Rome," Lemuel said. "But I'm afraid that even she will not be able to protect Dismas if the Romans find him."

"Then they shall not find him," Simon declared. "I shall go to

Rome and bring him to safety."

"No, Father," Alexander said in concern. "It's too dangerous for you there."

"He's right," Rufus added. "You can't hide among the Romans, and if they even suspect you are a Christian..."

Simon chuckled. "What, you don't think I can pass myself off as a Roman?"

"I'm serious, Father," Rufus said. "It would be very dangerous—and foolhardy."

"I know the danger, son. But Dismas is not only an important leader of our movement, he is my friend and has been for over thirty years. I must do what I can to rescue him, even if it means disguising myself as a Roman slave."

Rufus started to object, but Alexander raised a hand and said, "Father is right. This is something he must do."

Rufus sighed, then nodded in acceptance. "Then I will accompany you, Father."

"As will I," Alexander added.

"No, three black-skinned men will attract too much attention. It will be easier for me to slip into the city alone. Unless..." He looked over at Tibro, then asked, "Will you join me? A Jewish merchant traveling with his slave will raise few eyebrows."

"Me?" Tibro said incredulously. "Why should I go to Rome—except to kill Romans?"

"Dismas is my brother in Christ, but he's your brother in the flesh."

Tibro shook his head. "I rescued him once and tried to convince him to return to Jerusalem. Instead he chose Rome and whatever fate his God holds for him there."

"It was a great deed you accomplished that day," Simon said. "One we believers shall long remember and honor."

"And what good did it do, if he faces the same fate in Rome that he did in Ephesus?"

"It did ten years of good and, God willing, many more to come. Ten years in which hundreds, perhaps thousands, heard your brother and received salvation."

Tibro frowned. "The salvation of dreamers who would fight Rome with a kiss and crush her with an embrace."

Simon chuckled. "And you Zealots? You would face the Roman engines of war with wooden staffs and stones, yet you call us naïve?" He shook his head. "No, Tibro, we are really not that different. Our paths to overcoming Rome may differ, yet we are both sure in the conviction that Rome and her many gods shall eventually fall and the kingdom of the one true God shall reign supreme."

"And my elder brother has chosen between those paths. If he is again in trouble, I bear no further responsibility for him."

"Are you prepared to stand before God, like Cain, and declare that you are not your brother's keeper?"

Tibro's eyes flashed. "What right have you to quote the Holy Word to me?"

"I have the right of a Christian, for the words that you hold holy are also holy to me. I ask you again, Tibro. Are you your brother's keeper?"

As Tibro considered Simon's words—as he wondered how he would feel if his brother died at the hands of Rome—he realized it was not Dismas he was envisioning but the beautiful face of Marcella. To see her again after so many years, to hear her voice one more time...

His thoughts were interrupted by an argument that had broken out between Simon and his sons. "You cannot be serious, Father," Alexander was saying. "Would you really allow this unbeliever to accompany you to Rome?"

"I would be honored," Simon replied. "He proved his bravery and resourcefulness in Ephesus. No one can doubt his love for his brother."

"Ten years ago in Ephesus?" Rufus scoffed. "What about this very night in Jerusalem? He's only here now because he was trying to murder Alexander and me."

"I know," Simon said. "But even Paul persecuted us before he became a Christian."

"Yes, but Paul *was* converted. But this man here?" Rufus glowered at Tibro. "You will never accept Jesus, will you?" he declared, more a statement than a question.

"No, I will not be converted," Tibro replied. Even before he realized what he was doing, he gripped Simon's shoulder and said, "But I will offer my pledge of loyalty until we find my brother and bring him home to Jerusalem."

THIRTY-ONE

T<small>IBRO BAR</small>-D<small>ISMAS</small> <small>STOOD AT THE OPEN WINDOW OF THE LITTLE</small> apartment, looking out at the forest of masts of the boats anchored in the harbor. He was in the coastal town of Sidon, having arrived with Simon to arrange for passage across the Mediterranean on their journey to Rome. But it was proving much harder to find a boat than they had expected. This was the stormy season, when sudden winds could easily destroy a vessel, and there were few sailors who would put to sea under such conditions.

Three ship's captains had offered to take them in two month's time. But Simon feared that every day they waited, the danger faced by Dismas was greatly increased, so he continued to haunt the docks every day to plead his case.

Tibro was about to turn away from the window when he saw Simon returning, and this time he wasn't alone but was accompanied by a short, bald man with bushy eyebrows and a prominent nose. As they climbed the outside stairs, Tibro crossed the room and opened the apartment door.

"I have very good news!" Simon said by way of greeting. "We have secured passage."

"Excellent." Tibro examined Simon's elderly companion and said dubiously, "Is this the captain?"

The bald stranger laughed aloud. "A captain, yes, but of my soul, as all of us are. I have never commanded a boat, nor, I'm sure, shall I ever."

"This is a friend of your brother's, Paul of Tarsus," Simon said. "Paul, this is Tibro bar-Dismas."

Paul stared at Tibro a long moment. "You are right," he told Simon. "He is the image of Dismas."

"I haven't seen my brother in ten years," Tibro said. "Perhaps we no longer look as much alike."

"I was with him in recent years," Paul said. "You are still each other's mirror."

"Paul's boat is recently arrived from Caesarea," Simon explained. "He spoke to the captain on our behalf, and we'll be aboard when it departs."

Tibro's caution eased slightly, and he allowed himself the hint of a smile. "Thank you, Paul. We're fortunate that you're on good terms with the captain."

Again Paul laughed, a resonant rumble from deep in his belly. "It is not the ship's captain whose ear I have, but that of Legatus Julius, an officer in the Emperor's Regiment. He leads an army detail on the boat."

"A Roman officer?" Tibro asked guardedly. "You are a Jew, are you not? And you have befriended a Roman officer?"

"He's not so much my friend as my jailer."

"Jailer? I don't understand."

"The boat is taking prisoners to Rome. As it happens, I am one of them."

"What have you done?"

"Preach the resurrection of our Lord Jesus," Paul replied. "It seems I have upset the Sanhedrin enough for them to call for my death."

"Paul has been held a prisoner at Caesarea these past two years," Simon put in. "The only thing that kept him alive is that he's a citizen of Rome and appealed his case to the emperor. Julius is taking him there now."

"And yet, this Julius has allowed you, a prisoner, to come ashore. How is that?"

"I have given Julius my word that I'll make no effort to escape, so he has granted me permission to visit with friends and gather provisions for the journey." He turned to Simon and laughed again. "It turns out that the provisions I've gathered today are you two fine gentlemen."

———

AFTER SIMON PAID their fare of five denarii each, the captain directed one of his men to show them to where Paul and a couple of other passengers were seated near the ship's stern; the rest of the prisoners were kept in chains below. Then he went off to oversee the crew as they weighed anchor and raised the sail.

While Simon joined Paul on one of the benches, Tibro headed to the aft rail and stood alone, listening to the creaking and groaning of wood and rope as the boat sailed out of the port. The buildings of Sidon grew ever smaller and finally disappeared from view, replaced by vast expanses of arid desert along the starboard side of the vessel as they sailed north along the coastline.

Tibro, who had studied geography, knew this was not the way to Italia, and he approached Paul and Simon.

"Why is it we're headed north, when to reach Rome we should be sailing west to Cyprus?"

Paul, whose many years evangelizing throughout the Mediterranean had given him a thorough knowledge of the sea, raised a finger overhead and nodded. "The winds are against us, just as the captain predicted. But have faith, Tibro, for I tell you truly, you shall reach Rome safely, and when you do, you will find your brother Dismas alive and well and doing the work of our Lord."

While Tibro was not pleased at the delay, he accepted the explanation and tried not to bother the others with his worries. He spent most of his time either standing at the rail or seated with his older companions, keeping out of the way of the crew and avoiding the Roman soldiers. Tibro was most intrigued by the seemingly effortless movements of the sailors as they worked the ropes to angle the sail into whatever wind they could catch. The boat, well trimmed and expertly handled, moved swiftly through the water, leaving a wake that rolled and glistened on the surface of the sea. Often they were followed by flying fish, some of which actually landed on the deck, where they were eagerly scooped up to augment the meager rations.

Two weeks after leaving Sidon, they were still coasting Asia Minor but had finally rounded the eastern end of the Mediterranean and were at last headed west. This brought them through a channel between Cilicia in Asia Minor to the north and Cyprus to the south.

They took on supplies in Kyrenia on northern Cyprus, then sailed past Cilicia and Pamphylia before arriving in Myra, their boat's final destination. There, Legatus Julius found another boat to take his soldiers and the prisoners in his charge to Italia.

This new vessel was also a merchantman, loaded with grain and oil. Though skillfully crewed, it sailed slowly, making little progress in the heavy seas and contrary winds. Finally they reached Crete, putting in at Lasea. They spent several days there, remaining in harbor even beyond the Day of Atonement. Then, on the day they were making ready to get under way, Paul climbed onto a capstan and called for attention.

Tibro watched with fascination. Though Paul was but a passenger, he commanded the respect and attention of soldiers, sailors, and fellow prisoners alike.

"We have stayed too long in this place," he began. "I see now that our voyage will be dangerous from here on; there will be great damage to the cargo and to the boat, and loss of life, as well."

"That's nonsense," the captain said. He rapped his knuckles on the railing. "We have a stout boat, manned by a crew of skilled sailors. We will have no difficulty."

"We would do well to winter here in Lasea," Paul continued.

Julius looked back and forth between the captain and prisoner, uncertain who to believe.

"If we are to winter anywhere, it should be at Phoenix, on the south side of Crete," the captain said, directing his comments to Julius. "This harbor will not be hospitable when the weather turns. The harbor at Phoenix faces south and west; it will provide the shelter we need."

Julius considered the matter, then said, "Let us sail for Phoenix. If the weather turns bad, we will accept Paul's counsel and winter there."

The other sailors and soldiers voiced their approval, and despite Paul's warning, the little boat set sail.

FOR THE REST of the afternoon, a warm, favorable wind blew from the south, and Tibro convinced himself that Paul's warning had been the work of an overactive imagination. But then, just after nightfall, a strong wind rose, lifting the seas and setting the boat bobbing atop the churning waves.

As a particularly large wave rose beneath them, the deck of the merchantman heaved and rolled to starboard, then dipped sharply to the opposite side. The boat hung there, and for several agonizing seconds Tibro had the terrifying sensation it wouldn't recover but would keep going until it capsized. Then slowly, laboriously, the boat righted itself before rolling hard again to the right.

All but the crew went below to ride out the storm as the vessel dipped and climbed on monstrous swells, rolling back and forth as it pitched through the sea. But the northeaster did not let up, the wind so fierce that the crew could not bring the boat around but were forced to let her run before it as they were driven farther from Phoenix and the coast of Crete, out into the rough waters of the Ionian Sea between Greece and Italia.

The gale continued unabated for a fortnight, tossing the boat about like a child's toy. It was all the crew could do to keep the sails and ropes patched and the boat from splitting apart, which they managed by running cables around the hull and lashing them to the deck.

Below deck was a shambles. A table and some benches were securely bolted in place, but everything else went sliding around. Cabinet doors swung open and closed, emptying their myriad contents onto the floor, which was covered with torn sacks of wheat and barley and with broken crockery that was smashed into ever smaller shards as it was tossed back and forth.

As the days passed and the storm did not let up, Tibro and the others began to despair of ever reaching land safely. Their concern multiplied when the captain came below to seek volunteers to help bail the leaking hold.

The captain sought to reassure Legatus Julius and the passengers that the boat was not at risk of breaking up under the pounding waves.

His words did little to ease their fears, and several of the Roman soldiers began to berate him for having led them into such dire straits.

Tibro considered coming to the captain's defense. After all, most of the others had supported the decision to set sail. Even Tibro, in his eagerness to reach his brother in Rome, had sided with him, leaving Paul alone to urge caution. That was why he was so surprised when it was Paul who now spoke up on the captain's behalf.

"Do not abandon hope or forswear our good captain," Paul exclaimed, shouting to be heard over the thrashing waves and the wailing screech of wind. "Men, you should have listened to me and not set sail from Crete and suffered this damage and loss. However, now I beg of you to keep up your spirits, for not one life is going to be lost, though we shall lose the ship."

"How do you know this?" Julius shouted back. "Surely you cannot believe we will survive this terrible storm!"

"I know because last night, the angel of the God to whom I belong, and whom I serve, stood by me and said, 'Have no fear, Paul! You must stand before Caesar. And God, as a mark of his favor toward you, has granted you the lives of those who are sailing with you.' Take courage then, men, for I believe God, and I am certain that everything will happen exactly as I have been told. But we shall have to run the ship ashore on some island."

"Our lives and our boat shall be saved?" Tibro asked.

"I didn't promise that," Paul replied, and Tibro thought he saw a twinkle of humor in his eyes. "We shall be driven ashore, the boat cast upon the rocks and shattered. But not even a hair on your heads shall be lost."

"Do you believe him?" one of the Roman soldiers asked, looking back and forth between Julius and the others. "Do you believe that no one will be killed?"

"I believe Paul to be a man of God," Simon replied. "If he says an angel of God promises all will survive, then I believe it shall be so."

While most remained unconvinced, the tension of the moment was eased, and the captain was able to return to his duties, with Legatus Julius organizing his soldiers to assist with bailing out the hold.

———

WHEN MORNING AT LAST BROKE, the storm was still a force to contend with, though it had lessened in fury somewhat. The boat continued to leak, and Tibro and the other passengers and prisoners were helping the soldiers bail the water. Several of the sailors, meanwhile, were attempting to repair some of the larger tears in what remained of the tattered sail.

When someone shouted out that land had been sighted, everyone rushed up onto the deck to see for themselves. Bracing himself against the starboard rail, Tibro stared into the stinging spray until he at last made out a thin strip of dark coastline.

None of the crew recognized where they were, but the captain spied what appeared to be a sheltered bay with a beach, and he decided they would attempt a landing. Jettisoning the anchors, they let out what remained of the sail and headed for shore.

The boat ran quickly before the wind as it raced toward the beach. Then the boat struck a sandbar and came to a jarring halt. Tibro was thrown to the deck so hard that a large knot rose quickly on his arm. But he could still move it and was thankful no bones were broken.

Even as he counted his blessings, the back of the boat began breaking up under the violent pounding of the waves.

"Abandon the boat!" the captain called. "Everyone! Swim for shore!"

Amid the commotion, several sailors leaped over the side of the foundering vessel and made for the beach, leaving soldiers, prisoners, and passengers behind.

"How is your arm?" Simon asked, kneeling beside his younger friend. "Can you swim?"

"It's painful but not broken," Tibro replied. He chuckled grimly. "But it doesn't matter. I can't swim."

"Neither can I," Simon said with a laugh.

"Then it ends here," Tibro declared. He looked up at Simon. "You are not of my religion, my people, or my race. Yet when I came to kill your sons, you showed mercy—even love. I didn't think I could befriend an infidel, but you have become my brother. May God have mercy on you."

Simon smiled. "Don't give up yet. Don't you remember? Paul said no one shall perish, and I believe him."

"But how are we to survive if neither of us can swim?"

"If it is God's will, my friend, then he shall provide a way."

Just then an enormous wave struck the stern and spun the boat to the side. Simon grabbed hold of Tibro, even as Tibro was grabbing onto the railing, as the boat rolled onto its side and began to capsize. The first wave washed over them; the next split the boat in two and swept them from what remained of the deck and out into the sea.

Tibro was pulled under the water, and as he came up struggling for air, he managed somehow to maintain his grip on the heavy wooden rail, which had broken free of the deck. He felt something tight around his waist, and then he heard someone sputtering and gasping and realized Simon was still holding onto him.

Wrapping a leg over the rail, Tibro shouted, "Hold tight!" as another wave struck, hurling them like a javelin through the foaming sea.

THIRTY-TWO

As Paul had promised, not one passenger on the ill-fated boat was lost. Like Tibro and Simon, those who couldn't swim made it to the beach by clinging to whatever wreckage they could grab onto. Individually and in small groups, they washed ashore and crawled up onto the sand, cold, drenched, exhausted, but alive. And thankful that the storm had at last passed, the sun emerging from the clouds for the first time in two weeks.

They were soon greeted by a small band of natives, who came down to the beach to put to sea in their crude fishing boats. One of the sailors understood their language and explained that this was the island of Melita, known today as Malta. The natives offered to build a fire to warm and dry the survivors, and everyone joined in gathering twigs and driftwood.

Paul made quite an impression on the islanders when, while gathering sticks, he disturbed a poisonous viper and it fastened onto his hand. The natives took this as a sign that he must be a murderer who escaped the sea but now would face justice from the bite of a serpent. They watched and whispered, waiting for him to swell up and fall down dead, but Paul merely shook off the viper and went on with his work, none the worse for the encounter. The sailor who was serving as a translator explained they were now convinced that Paul was no murderer but a god.

After the men were dry and rested, the natives took them to the estate of the governor, a Roman named Publius. He prepared a generous banquet, to which all—even the prisoners—were invited. And his generosity increased many times over when Paul and Simon visited the governor's father, who lay sick with fever and dysentery. The two Christians prayed over the man, and Paul laid his hand upon him and ordered the sickness to depart. Publius's father was cured, and soon the islanders were coming to see this stranger who healed the sick and had dominion over vipers.

Simon and Tibro were eager to continue their journey, and the grateful governor arranged passage for them on a small trade vessel that was about to set sail for Italia. The boat was not large enough for the rest of the group, whose sojourn on the island would last another three months. And so it was that with Paul's blessing and the good wishes of Julius, the captain and his crew, Simon and Tibro set off alone on the final leg of their journey.

The grain boat made a swift crossing to Syracuse in Sicily, where the two men caught another vessel heading up the coast to Rhegium and then Puteoli, a port on the north side of the Bay of Naples. From there, they walked the remaining 150 miles to Rome, disguised as a Jewish merchant and his slave. They chose olive oil as their trade so as to draw upon Simon's years of experience in that business.

Simon had been to Rome before, but this was Tibro's first visit, and as they passed through the gate he was struck by the size and vitality of the city. They slipped in among the crowds that streamed through the streets, losing themselves among the merchants, laborers, scholars, householders, soldiers, slaves, and foreigners who went about their business, seemingly oblivious to the many differences in their state and status.

They skirted the Forum, with its government buildings and temples, and followed the Tiber River past the great Circus Maximus. This huge, dominating edifice was six hundred yards long and almost half as wide, with an exterior three stories high, completely encircled by columns. Overhanging it on Palatine Hill were the palaces of the

Caesars, great brickwork structures with arched roofs, totally encased in shining marble.

Equally impressive was the beautiful temple of Apollo, fashioned of white marble but surrounded by porticos with columns of yellow marble. The temple contained sculptures of Apollo, Latona, and Diana.

"What do you think of it?" Simon asked, gesturing to the temple.

"I think too much time, effort, and beauty have been wasted on pagan gods," Tibro replied.

Simon chuckled. "That is one religious question we can both agree on."

"Do you have any idea where we might find my brother?" Tibro asked, growing a bit exasperated at their seemingly endless meandering around the city.

"I know where to look, and that is where we are headed." He raised an arm and pointed beyond the nearby Tiber River. "The Trastevere quarter. Come."

Tibro followed Simon to a footbridge that took them across the river to the first inhabited area on the west bank. Here the scenery changed. Gone were the pagan temples and the grand, columned estates of the Roman elite. Tibro felt immediately at home and commented that they could be in a neighborhood of Jerusalem.

"Yes," Simon replied. "Over the years many Jews have relocated to Rome, and they have all settled in this area."

As they walked down the Via Portuensis, Simon appeared to be hunting for something, pausing on occasion to push vegetation away from a wall or gate to examine beneath it.

"What are you doing?" Tibro asked at last.

"Searching for a sign."

"What sort of sign?"

"Ahh, one just like this," Simon declared as he pulled aside the branch of a flowering oleander to reveal a fish carved on a post.

"A fish?" Tibro said. "You were looking for a fish?"

"Our Christ is a fisher of men." Simon patted the carving. "With this sign, we can recognize one another. We will be welcome here. Come."

They were greeted at the door by the owner of the house, a tall man about forty years old who was clean-shaven in the style increasingly popular among Christians. Tibro did not recognize him and was taken aback when the man rushed forward, saying, "Tibro! You've come to Rome!" Tibro started to reply, but the fellow had already turned to Simon, embracing him as he said, "What a great honor this is, Simon, to have you at my home."

As Tibro examined him more closely, he imagined the fellow a bit younger and sporting a close-cropped beard, and finally he remembered. "Gaius," he said, just as the man looked back to him.

"Ah, you remember."

"You look different than in Ephesus."

Gaius stroked his smooth chin. "I cut it the day I reached Rome. But you, my friend, look just the same."

Tibro frowned. "A decade older."

"Hardly a day," Gaius replied with a dismissive wave. He turned to Simon. "How long since your last visit? Three years? You spoke at the home of Josephus."

"Five years ago," Simon replied. He looked up at the impressive two-story house. "I don't recall you living in such splendor. You were sharing rather meager quarters above some stables, as I recall."

Gaius grinned. "I'm more caretaker than owner. Three years ago one of our Roman converts went home to the Lord and left this for us to use as one of our church houses. Come inside. My home—our church—is your home."

As Gaius ushered them through the portico, Tibro noticed a tile mosaic of a fish on the floor, evidence of the original owner's conversion to the Christian faith.

Gaius showed them around the house and took them to the room where they would stay as his guests. After they bathed and changed into fresh linens, they were treated to a sumptuous dinner. As they dined, Tibro asked about Dismas and learned that he was still a free man, thanks to the efforts of believers who provided Dismas and other Christian leaders with a number of secret lodgings throughout Rome and its environs. For the past week Dismas had been on a mission to one of the outlying communities on the road to Ariminum.

Gaius then explained that while his guests were freshening up, he had sent word to others in the Christian community of Rome and arranged for tonight's worship gathering to be held at his house church so that the guests, weary from their long journey, could easily attend. He hoped that Tibro would join them as an honored guest, if not a fellow believer.

When the Christians soon began arriving, Tibro politely greeted them, then took a seat alone in the back of the large colonnaded room that served as their place of worship. There he fought the urge to stand and castigate the assembly for turning from the one true God to worship a false messiah, instead reminding himself about the kindnesses he had been shown by Simon and Paul, and now by their host, Gaius.

One thing that surprised Tibro as the faithful continued to arrive was that they were as apt to be Romans as converted Jews. He could understand how a Jew might get caught up in this messianic business. Jesus, after all, was a Jew himself. But for a citizen of Rome to reject the very culture and society that had bestowed so many blessings and privileges—and at great personal risk should their allegiance be revealed—took the kind of courage and faith that Tibro did not expect from a Roman.

All such doubts evaporated when one of the Roman Christians entered the worship room. In her late-thirties, she carried herself with great self-assurance and had a serene beauty that added an ethereal glow to her features.

Tibro recognized Marcella Tacitus at once, and he rose from his seat and approached, but held back until all the others had warmly greeted her. She seemed to sense that someone was staring at her, and she turned toward him. For a moment there was some uncertainty in her eyes, then recognition, and she approached with her hand extended.

"Tibro," she said warmly. "How wonderful to see you again after all these years."

"The years have been particularly good to you, Marcella," he replied, reaching out to take her hand. As they touched, he felt a small spark.

"Oh, we've made lightning," Marcella said with a laugh.

Grabbing her hand more tightly, Tibro felt as if the tiny charge of static electricity were multiplied many times as it coursed through his body. He was surprised that after so much time, he could still experience such a reaction from being in the presence of this woman.

"Your husband?" Tibro asked, trying to keep his tone calm and level. "Is he still in Ephesus?"

"No, here in Rome. He's a member of the Comitia Curiata."

Tibro shook his head. "I don't know what that is."

"The Assembly of the Curiae is where former officials go when they retire," Marcella explained. "He has no real power now, his position is mostly ceremonial."

"I see," Tibro said, forcing a smile but deeply discouraged to learn she was still married.

"We are married in name only," Marcella said, as if sensing Tibro's disappointment. "He amuses himself with the servants. I have considered getting a divorce. Here in Rome such a thing requires no legal formalities, simply the mutual consent of both parties. But our house, our furnishings, nearly all we have are the result of my dowry, and according to law I would receive all of that. Rufinus knows this and will never consent to a divorce."

"I understand."

"No," Marcella said, squeezing his hand. "I'm not sure that you do understand. I'm not sure that I understand. There are times when I think that I would gladly give up all that I have, just to be free of him."

"Why haven't you?"

She gave a slight shrug as she looked deeply into Tibro's eyes. "Perhaps I have had no real incentive." Implied but not spoken were the words *until now.* "Of course," she continued, "under the circumstances, being married to him does have its advantages. Rufinus has always been a man with good contacts and a snooping nature, so he has been a great source of information for us."

"Then perhaps you can tell me of my brother," Tibro said. "I was told the Romans seek to arrest him."

"Yes, but through the help of his friends, he has managed to survive."

"Aided, no doubt, by information you have been able to provide," Tibro said. "Can you take me to him?"

At that moment there was a commotion at the entrance to the meeting room, and Marcella smiled. "There is no need to lead you to Dismas. He has arrived."

THIRTY-THREE

EMERGING FROM THE CHILL WATER, MARCELLA COVERED HERSELF IN A light wrap and walked through a connecting hall between the cold and hot rooms of the bathhouse. There she slipped out of the dressing gown and stood for just a moment at the top of the steps that led into the hot pool. Two other women taking the waters at the baths and were already in the large concrete tub.

"Good morning Marcella," one woman said. "Wasn't the cold water bracing this morning?"

"Good morning, Julia." As Marcella stepped into the pool, the warm water enveloped her naked body like a blanket. "The cold bath was bracing, but this feels much better." She moved into a corner.

"Domita was telling of the party given by Poppaea Sabina," Julia said. "Did you attend?"

"No," Marcella replied. She smiled politely to mask her displeasure at the prospect of listening to the latest gossip about Emperor Nero's scandalous mistress.

"Oh, then, please do continue, Domita," Julia begged her younger friend.

"It was the merriest party I've ever attended," Domita declared. "There was much wine and food, lyre music, and dancing of course.

Then we were entertained by two handsome young men—nude, mind you."

"Nude?" Marcella said, looking dubious.

"Totally nude. Their faces and bodies were painted with blood from goats that had been sacrificed to the gods for our meal. And the naked young men ran around the room, touching women with strips of goatskin."

"All the women?" Marcella asked.

"Not all. They only touched those who were of child-bearing age, because the idea was to make them fertile."

"And where did they touch you?" Julia asked.

"Here." She cupped her breasts, which were half out of the water. "And here, too." She reached beneath the water. Neither of the other women could see her hand, but they knew where it went.

"Oh, my. And was no one embarrassed?"

Domita smiled. "I think we had drunk too much wine to be embarrassed. And as the young men were quite handsome—and naked—I think all enjoyed it. I know I did."

"Domita, you are *awful*!" Julia said and giggled.

"Afterward we ate roasted goat meat. Then Nero himself made an appearance to sing and play the cithara. It was very entertaining."

There was a bit more small talk, and then Julia and Domita took their leave. Marcella remained in the bath awhile longer, enjoying the solitude. Then she emerged from the water, dried herself, and went into the nearby dressing room. There she wrapped her chest in a breast-band and stepped into a pair of very brief, sheer underpants. Next she put on a tunic, sleeveless because it was July and quite warm. Over the tunic she wore a *stola*, a toga-like dress fashioned of a rectangle of cloth that was wrapped around the body and reached to the ground. A purple border, or *institia*, lined the edge of the garment. Lastly she donned the *palla*, a four-cornered shawl draped over her left shoulder and under her right. Slipping into a pair of sandals, she pulled a corner of the *palla* over her head, then went outside and glanced toward the fountain.

Would he be there?

Yes! He was seated on the stone bench, as he had been every morning for the past four months.

Even though her morning meetings with Tibro had become commonplace, her heart still raced every time she saw him, and she hurried across the terrace. He was standing when she arrived, smiling as he took her hands in his.

"Marcella," Tibro greeted. "There is no need for the sun, for you brighten the day."

"And you my life," Marcella replied, blushing as she lowered her gaze.

"Please sit," Tibro urged. "There is something I would say to you."

She looked up at him in excitement and trepidation. "I'm listening," she said, remaining standing before him.

"I have been giving this much thought. I want you to divorce Rufinus. Leave Rome and come to Jerusalem with me. I want you for my wife."

Marcella had long expected such a request, yet she was stunned to actually hear him say the words. She inhaled a quick, sharp breath before she responded.

"Tibro, I fear that now is not the right time. So far Nero has left the Christians alone—your brother and our other leaders have not been harassed in many months. But there is much intrigue within the palace. Rufinus is certain there are plots afoot, and some would make our community of believers the scapegoat. I fear that with the slightest provocation, Nero could be persuaded to move against us, and everyone, Dismas included, would be at risk of their lives."

"Isn't that all the more reason to come away with me? If Nero causes trouble, you'll be safely out of Rome."

"What of the others? What of Simon and Paul and Peter? What of your own brother? If I stay here with Rufinus, I may learn information in time to warn them. Don't you see that every Christian in Rome might be depending on me?"

"I depend on you, as well," Tibro said. He gently stroked Marcella's cheek, and she quivered under his touch. "And I cannot bear any longer the thought of you married to that...that man."

She reached up and took his hand. "I have told you before, Rufinus and I are married in name only. We have not been husband and wife—not truly—these many years in Rome." She softly touched her lips to his fingers, her eyes moistening with tears. "I do not even think of him, except as a means of helping the people I love. It is you I think of daily, you I come to every day, as we have done the months you've been in Rome."

"No," Tibro said, pulling his hand free. "That isn't enough. I want more of you. I need more of you."

He grasped the back of her neck and squeezed gently, and she felt her blood turning to warm honey.

"I want to go to sleep with you at night, and wake with you in the morning, and lie with you in the moonlight." He leaned closer, his cheek against hers as he recited from Solomon's Song of Songs:

"What a magnificent woman you are!
How beautiful are your feet in sandals.
The curve of your thighs is like the work of an artist."

Marcella closed her eyes, feeling the caress of his words almost as if they were something physical, as if they were his hands, exploring her body.

"Your breasts are like bunches of grapes,
Your breath like the fragrance of apples,
Your mouth like the finest wine."

Her body quivered as his lips brushed her neck with the faintest of kisses. He leaned back and gazed into her eyes. He started to continue his recitation, but she held her hand to his mouth, her fingers exploring the contours of his lips as she answered him from the Song of Songs:

"Then let the wine flow straight to my lover,
Flowing over his lips and teeth.
I belong to my lover, and he desires me."

"You must come with me, Marcella," Tibro implored. "If you cannot, then you must give yourself to me, for surely I will go crazy from desire."

"I cannot. I am still married, and as a Christian, I cannot commit adultery."

"A Christian..." Tibro said with a grumble.

"You've been here for four months now. You have befriended Simon, Peter, and Paul. And you have the teaching of your own brother to guide you. How is it that you have not yet seen the truth?"

"There is no truth to see, other than the truth I live," Tibro declared. "I give my allegiance to God, the one who is creator of all... not to some false messiah."

Marcella's eyes rimmed with tears, and she dropped her hands from his. "Oh, Tibro," she whispered. "I love you, but until you come into the light, I fear that there can never be anything more between us."

"As long as you stay with that despot husband, there can be nothing between us anyway," Tibro said in barely suppressed anger. "Perhaps you should go to him now, rather than waste your morning with this Jew. I am sure he has some news you can share with your Christian friends."

"Tibro, please." Marcella's tears began to slide down her cheek. "Try to understand."

"Go," Tibro said, a bit more gently this time. "It wouldn't be good to be seen with me."

"Will you be here tomorrow?"

"I don't know."

"Oh, Tibro, I cannot bear to think of life without your love. I...I will do as you ask."

Tibro's eyes narrowed. "You will do what?"

"I will go with you. I will lie with you. I will put my soul in danger of eternal damnation for you."

Tibro wrapped his arms around her and pulled her to him. As she cried against his shoulder, he kissed her hair, then he sighed and released her. Placing his finger under her chin, he lifted her head so he could look into her eyes, still glistening with tears.

"No," he said.

"No?"

"I want more than just that part of you I can touch, hear, see, and taste. I want all of you. I want your soul, as well. And you cannot give that to me, if you believe that what you are doing is wrong. Go. Remain with your husband and protect your Christian friends."

"But, to do so and lose you would be—"

"You will not lose me," he declared. "I haven't the strength to walk away."

Smiling through her tears, Marcella squeezed his hands one more time, then turned away. When she reached the far end of the baths, she looked back and saw that he was still there, watching her. She smiled again, sure in her heart that he would always be there when she needed him.

THIRTY-FOUR

THE GREAT, WHITE MARBLE BUILDINGS OF ROME GLISTENED UNDER A bright full moon. In a small lean-to shed in a poor district near the Circus Maximus, coals glowed in a forge. The blacksmith had banked them to preserve his fire for the next day of work.

A sharp breeze came up, rustled the leaves of trees and bushes, rattled a door on its hinges. The wind whipped through the blacksmith's shed, swirling around the banked coals. Gleaming embers were drawn into the funnel of wind and were whipped up into the sky, adding a flurry of sparks to the winking blue stars above.

One ember did not follow the others. Instead it lodged in the shed wall, and within moments the dry, pulpy fibers surrounding it held their own golden gleam. The freshening wind fanned the glow into a tiny flame that licked upward along the wall. Soon the shed was fully involved, and minutes later an adjacent house was on fire, the leaping flames threatening the surrounding buildings.

By now, several residents of the immediate area had raised an alarm, but the fire was too large for them to extinguish. The inferno grew ever more intense until it was a roaring conflagration, leaping from building to building, even crossing streets and open plazas.

Hundreds of thousands of sparks, riding clouds of smoke, were carried aloft, the sky emblazoned with more red stars than blue. Soon wealthier neighboring districts were involved, their large homes adding fuel to the now self-sustaining firestorm. The rising column of heat drew air from around the ever-widening circumference. That air rushed in with hurricane force, superheating the fire, spraying sparks across an ever larger swath of the city.

———

BECAUSE OF THE oppressive July heat, Tibro bar-Dismas was asleep by an open window in Gaius's home when a roaring sound awakened him. As he wiped the sleep from his eyes and stared outside, he was shocked to see that a large part of the city on the east side of the Tiber River was on fire.

"Marcella!" he blurted, for even as he measured the length and breadth of the involved area, he realized that her house was directly in the conflagration's path, if it had not already succumbed to the flames.

Dressing quickly, Tibro ran outside and through the streets toward the river. As he sprinted across the footbridge over the Tiber, he passed increasing numbers of people who were hurrying away from the fire, many of them hobbling along with horrible burns and wounds, their clothing tattered and charred.

"Run for your life!" someone shouted at him.

"Don't go there, sir!" another cried, blocking Tibro's path. The man's eyes, set a brilliant white against his soot-blackened skin, widened in shock at the sight of someone heading toward the inferno. "You are crazy if you go there!" he insisted, grabbing Tibro's arm.

Tibro jerked free and spun past the man as he raced off the bridge and headed toward the center of the firestorm. Suddenly he halted, looked back at the bridge, and reversed direction. The man who had stopped him must have thought Tibro had come to his senses, and he waved him on encouragingly, but at the last moment Tibro turned from the bridge and scurried down the steep bank to the river's edge. Dropping into the water, he completely submersed himself, then scrambled back onto shore. Clambering up the embankment, he continued toward the fire, leaving behind him a trail of dripping water and a confused man waving feebly for him to stop.

As Tibro reached the edge of the conflagration, he thought wryly that he had just been baptized in water, and now would come the baptism of fire. Somehow he found a pathway through the flames, which curiously assisted him by lighting the streets as bright as midday. He was able to find pathways through the inferno, sometimes ducking under curls of flames, other times going around, and occasionally leaping over burning timbers. His soaking toga protected him from the heat but began to give off an eerie steam.

As he feared, the house of Rufinus Tacitus was ablaze, though fortunately it had not yet spread beyond the roof.

"Marcella!" he shouted, bursting through the front entrance. "Marcella!"

"Here!" he heard a faint voice cry in the distance. "In here!"

Clutching his toga to his nose to filter out the smoke, Tibro hurried toward the woman's voice. Several roof timbers had collapsed to the floor, and smaller pieces of flaming wood were raining from above. Tibro ducked around them as he headed to the nearby receiving room just off the atrium at the center of the house.

Entering the room, he saw that a large section of the roof had caved in, and Marcella was standing near the rubble, struggling with a large, smoldering beam.

"Over here!" Tibro shouted. "We have to get out!"

"I can't," Marcella called back.

"Are you trapped?" As he raced over, he saw that she was standing clear. "Come, Marcella, the roof is going to fall in on us."

"I can't leave him."

It was then that Tibro saw a leg sticking out from under the massive beam. He knew, without having to ask, that it was Rufinus Tacitus.

Tibro felt a charge of joy. "Leave him!" he cried.

"No, I can't!"

As Tibro moved closer to Marcella, he was able to see the former governor of Ephesus lying dazed amid the smoldering debris, his leg trapped by the heavy beam. The old man was alive and seemed to understand his predicament and probable fate. He stared up at Tibro with a mixture of hatred, disdain, and self pride. Tibro knew Rufinus would never ask for his help.

"Don't you see?" Tibro said, turning to Marcella. "God is offering you a way out."

She shook her head. "God would not want me to leave him here to die."

Tibro looked between Marcella, Rufinus, and what remained of the burning roof, which threatened to collapse at any moment on top of them. His fleeting joy faded, replaced with a sense of longing and guilt. At last he sighed and said, "You're right. I'll help you."

Just then another large beam came crashing down, only a few feet from where they were standing. Marcella jumped backward into Tibro's arms and began to cough and choke as hot smoke filled the area.

"We must hurry," Tibro said, wiping her face with his moist toga.

Together they lifted the timber, raising it just far enough for Rufinus to slide out from underneath. They were surprised to discover that, though the beam had trapped Rufinus, his leg had not been broken, and while badly bruised, he was able to stand and walk.

"Let's go!" Tibro grabbed Marcella by the arm and pulled her with him. When she hesitated and looked back at her husband, he said, "Don't worry about Rufinus. He can walk; he can find his way out of here."

———

RUFINUS STOOD WITHOUT MOVING, still stunned by his near death and somewhat in shock at seeing another man take his wife by the hand and lead her away. A section of the roof fell then, and he realized he had to get out now. Moving quickly, he followed his wife and the man through the smoke-filled house to the vestibule that led outside.

While trapped under the beam, Rufinus had thought only his own house was on fire. Once outside he saw that all of Rome appeared to be ablaze. He could hear the roar of a thousand fires, and the orange sky was as bright as day. In this bright light he saw his wife clasping hands with the stranger, who was acting far too familiar with her. It was at that moment that he recognized their rescuer.

"Dismas!" he shouted. "I sentenced you to death many years ago, and yet here you are." He pointed an accusatory finger. "That sentence still stands. I order you to place yourself under arrest to me."

"This isn't Dismas," Marcella said to her husband. "And besides, he just saved both of us."

"That doesn't buy his life," Rufinus said resolutely, then turned back to Tibro. "You were sentenced by tribunal, and I am placing you under arrest. I order you to stay here until an officer of the Praetorian Guard arrives."

"I told you, this isn't Dismas, it's—"

"Nobody is going to arrive," Tibro interrupted, as if not wanting his identity revealed just then. "And anyone who stays here is going to die. If you want to live, then you'll keep quiet and follow us away from here." Still holding Marcella's hand, he started down the street.

"Dismas!" Rufinus shouted. "Dismas, come back here! I order you to halt!"

Behind him, the remaining roof fell in on the house with a rushing roar, and flames shot up from the top of the burning building. The front wall collapsed, and a shower of sparks sprayed around Rufinus. He cried out in pain, then looked over at Marcella, who stood with Tibro about twenty yards away, framed by the orange glow of the burning city.

"Are you coming?" Tibro shouted at Rufinus as he pulled Marcella toward safety.

The anger in the old Roman's eyes was replaced by fear as he realized the precariousness of their situation. He took a few cautious steps forward, then hurried after his wife and her rescuer, calling out, "This isn't over, Dismas! I will deal with you later!"

THIRTY-FIVE

FR. MICHAEL FLANNERY HAD NO IDEA HOW FAR THEY HAD DRIVEN SINCE the kidnappers had taken him earlier that afternoon. Several times they had stopped for long periods. During one stop they ditched his rental car and their other vehicle, with those drivers piling into the remaining car, leaving Flannery pinned between two of the men in the back seat, with two others in the front.

They kept a black hood over his head and his hands tied behind his back for the entire afternoon and fed him only once. Even then they did not remove the hood but merely lifted it high enough to press small morsels of fruit and cheese to his lips.

It was early evening now—even hooded, Flannery could tell it was growing dark—and he knew no one would be able to see him through the vehicle's tinted windows.

Because of their turns and frequent stops, he didn't believe they were too far from where he had been abducted just north of Ein-Gedi on Road 90. And from the sounds of outside traffic, he guessed that they were in a city somewhere. The only question was, what city?

Once, when they were stopped, he heard the *Adhan*, the Muslim call to prayer. Had they crossed over into Palestine? Might they even be in East Jerusalem?

The musical lilt of the muezzin's chant was amplified so that it floated out over the city.

> "Allah u Akbar, Allah u Akbar
> Ash-hadu al-la Ilaha ill Allah
> Ash-hadu al-la Ilaha ill Allah
> Ash-hadu anna Muhammadan Rasulullaah
> Ash-hadu anna Muhammadan Rasulullaah
> Hayya la-s-saleah - Hayya la-s-saleah
> Hayya la-l-faleah - Hayya la-l-faleah
> Allahu Akbar, Allahu Akbar
> La Ilaha ill Allah"

During the muezzin's call, Flannery was left alone in the car, and though he couldn't see what his captors were doing, he believed they were responding to the prayer call, probably kneeling beside the road. If so, his abductors had to be Palestinians, or at least Muslims.

They conversed rarely, and when they did, they spoke very quietly in English. He didn't know if they were using English so he could understand them or to conceal their nationality. They might not know he had a passing knowledge of Arabic, and he had no intention of letting on.

The next time the car halted, the kidnappers piled out, and then he felt a hand on his shoulder.

"Please to get out of car," one of them said in a clipped accent that seemed almost a pretense.

As Flannery slid across the seat, the man helped him from the vehicle. Considering the situation, his captor was treating him very gently. The other three men also emerged from the car, and then they led him across roughly textured ground—cobblestones, Flannery guessed.

"There are steps down," his guide said. "Be careful."

Flannery walked down a long flight of steps. He guessed the stairway was narrow because he could feel a stone wall against his right shoulder, and the man on his left was pressed tight against him. The steps were also of stone, and as he descended, the air became cool and dank. There was also a very musty, familiar scent that he recognized at once, because he had been there several times before. Even without being able to see, he knew he was in the catacombs of Jerusalem.

He counted twenty-three steps to the bottom, and then they led him through a doorway and into a room, where at last they removed his hood and cut free the plastic tie binding his arms. As he stood rubbing his wrists, he looked around the long stone chamber. The area was lit by a few flickering candles, the light so faint that it only took a moment for Flannery to adjust from the darkness of the hood. He saw that he had been correct and was indeed in the catacombs. The ancient Christian graffiti revealed the precise location: the catacombs on the Mount of Olives, uncovered in the mid-1950s by the Franciscan archaeologist Fr. Bellarmino Bagatti.

Flannery was led through one of the passageways that headed off from the entry chamber to a second, smaller room. Lit by torches, this chamber was considerably brighter than the first one or the narrow passageways.

The room contained three ossuaries in the same positions they had occupied for the last two thousand years. One, he knew, was the stone coffin of Shimon Bar Yonah. Another, bearing cross marks, read "Shlom-zion, daughter of Simon the Priest." Flannery had been in this very spot before.

In the center of the room was a table covered with white linen. Seated behind the table were three men in white ecclesiastical robes. They wore masks, but not the hooded ones used by his kidnappers. These were the type worn by revelers at masked balls. Somehow, the masks with their pagan-like satiric connotations, paired with priestly vestments, seemed a sacrilege against the holy orders.

But what really caught his eye was the bright red symbol embroidered on the front of the linen. It was the sign of Via Dei, similar to but not precisely the same as the one on the scroll of Dismas bar-Dismas.

"Sit down please, Father Flannery," the man in the middle of the triumvirate said, indicating the facing chair. His voice held no anger, only a cajoling warmth.

"You know my name," Flannery said without surprise as he sat down across the table from the three men.

"Of course we do." He motioned for Flannery's kidnappers to

depart, and as they filed out of the room, he turned back to the priest. "In fact, Father Flannery, we know everything there is to know about you."

"Do you, now?"

"When you were seventeen, you won the Irish National fifteen-hundred-meter race. Your trainer, the famous Irish runner Ron Delaney, wanted you to work toward the Olympics, but even then, you wanted to enter the priesthood."

"That was in the newspapers," Flannery said. "It couldn't have been that hard for you to look up."

"What about Mary Kathleen O'Shaughnessy? Will I find her name in the newspapers? She thought you were going to marry her, didn't she? You broke her heart when you entered the priesthood."

Flannery didn't reply. That episode had been one of the most difficult periods of his life, and it wasn't something he wanted to talk about, especially with someone who had brought him here against his will.

"You have a cousin, Sean O'Neal, who was with the IRA," the apparent leader of the triumvirate continued. "He was killed in a skirmish with the British. His mother, your mother's sister, died of a broken heart, and even your own mother suffered because of it."

Flannery still didn't reply.

"Then you became a priest. Not a parish priest, mind you, but a Jesuit, an honored scholar, with a major in archaeology. You are now regarded as the leading religious archaeologist in the Catholic Church, and indeed, one of the leading archaeologists in the world." The man paused, his lips curling into a smile. "But, there came a time when you realized you had a problem...a drinking problem."

"I have not had a drink—"

"In eighteen years, nine months, two weeks, and three days," his inquisitor interjected.

"All right," Flannery acquiesced. "You do know quite a bit about me. Now I want to know who you are."

"I think you already know, Father Flannery." The man gestured toward the symbol on the linen covering. "After all, we did try to recruit you once. You do recall that, don't you?"

"Yes, I remember."

"We used Father Leonardo Contardi as our agent. But alas, Contardi proved to be...well, shall we politely say, unstable? And we feared that, by association, you might prove unstable as well."

"I see."

"No, I don't think you do see. Father Flannery, we are offering you a second chance now to join us...to become a member of Via Dei."

"Why would I want to do that?"

"Who exactly do you think we are?"

"A secretive organization, like the Knights Templar."

The inquisitor chuckled. "Do you know the song the Knights Templar marched to in their glorious Crusade?" When Flannery did not reply, the man began to sing:

> *"Vexilla regis prodeunt,*
> *Fulget crucis mysterium,*
> *Qua vita mortem pertulit*
> *Et morta vitam protulit."*

"The Breviary hymn by Venantius Fortunatus," Flannery said, then recited the English translation:

> *"Behold the royal ensigns fly,*
> *The Cross's shining mystery;*
> *Where Life itself gave up its breath*
> *And Christ by dying conquered death."*

"To answer your question, Father Flannery, we are not a modern-day Knights Templar, though indeed, one of our most illustrious members, Peter the Hermit, first preached the Crusades and was a founder of the Priory of Sion, which created the Knights Templar. Our members also served with the Legions of Constantine and the armies of Charlemagne. We advised Joan D'Arc; we were at the Battle of Constantinople, and with the founders of the New World. Ah, yes, Father Flannery, our movement is a noble and holy order, begun and ordained by Jesus Christ himself to protect the Church and his blessed name."

"You believe Via Dei was personally founded by Jesus?"

"I do."

"I have done some of my own research," Flannery said. "I know that Via Dei has been excommunicated from the Church. Why would the Church do that if, as you say, it was founded by Jesus?"

"We have our enemies, even within the Vatican."

"Is it any wonder you have enemies? The Church is blamed for the Spanish Inquisition, the murder of hundreds of thousands of Jews and Muslims during the Middle Ages, the slaughter of innocents in the New World. Upon closer examination, it appears that these acts were encouraged by a secret cabal within the Church. Might that be Via Dei?"

"If Via Dei appears sinister, Father Flannery, it is only a mask—like the ones we are wearing. We don such a mask in order to keep out prying eyes. Our members are not Church outcasts who have created their own society within the greater whole. Indeed, we count among our membership many of the popes who have sat on the throne of St. Peter."

"What do you want with me?" Flannery said impatiently.

"We have brought you before this tribunal to offer you a great honor. We will admit you, this very day, into our ranks, conferring not only full membership but knowledge of the deepest mysteries of our Mother Church. Father Flannery, these are secrets you have spent a lifetime trying to uncover. They are known to a precious few—to an elite even among Via Dei. All this, we offer you."

"That's why I was kidnapped?"

"I would prefer to say, that is why we had you brought to us."

"Do Islamist terrorists recruit all your initiates?" Flannery said pointedly. "Or, just me?"

"We have an unusual situation and a unique opportunity now," the leader of the tribunal replied. "As you know, 'misery acquaints a man with strange bedfellows,' And in our current situation, let's just say that it serves our interests to ally ourselves with some of those bedfellows against a mutual enemy."

There was something about the man's vocal pattern and the way he quoted Shakespeare's "The Tempest" that struck Flannery as familiar, but he couldn't quite place it.

"And who would that mutual enemy be?" Flannery asked.

"Join us, Father, and all secrets will be made known to you."

"What's the catch?" Flannery asked. "You can't want me because I'm such a prize. There has to be some catch."

"Ah, yes, the catch. Well, it is simple—something that, as a member of Via Dei, you will want to do, for once the full mysteries are revealed, you will understand that what we ask is merely the fulfillment of God's plan."

With that, he turned and nodded to the man on his right, who reached under the table and lifted a heavy object. Even as he was placing it atop the table, Flannery recognized it as the urn unearthed at Masada.

"Yes, the scroll of Dismas bar-Dismas," the leader continued.

His smile hardened into a scowl as he turned the urn onto its side to reveal that it was empty.

"We had made arrangements to obtain the scroll, but unfortunately, even the best laid schemes of Via Dei 'gang aft agley,' and leave us naught but grief and pain for promised joy," he said, paraphrasing the famous poem by Robert Burns about plans going astray. He seemed amused by his own verbal play, and his smile returned. "And so, the catch, as you so eloquently put it, is that you shall bring us the Dismas scroll."

"Why do you need the scroll?" Flannery asked. "Once our research is finished, its contents will be evaluated by the Church and a determination made as to whether or not it is to be included in the Holy Word. But even if it isn't, the full text will be published—the Israelis will insist on that. So either way, within or without the Church, you will have access to everything the scroll contains."

"That is not enough," the man shot back, the first hint of annoyance in his tone. "It is very meet, right, and our bounden duty that we should at all times, and in all places, have control of the scroll."

Flannery looked curiously at the masked man, who had used such an archaic expression. Even more peculiar was that it was not Catholic but from the Anglican Book of Common Prayer: *It is very meet, right, and our bounden duty, that we should at all times, and in all places, give thanks unto thee, O Lord, holy Father, almighty, everlasting God.* Either he was subtly pointing out that the influence of Via Dei extended beyond the Catholic Church, or this was but another example of the man's penchant for literary allusion.

Again Flannery was reminded of someone he knew but could not quite place. Filing away the observation for the time being, he leaned closer to the table and asked, "Does Via Dei wish to possess the scroll, or merely keep the world from learning its secrets?"

The spokesman sighed. "All right, Father Flannery, I am going to tell you something that has never been revealed to anyone outside Via Dei during the two thousand years of our existence."

"No," the masked man to the left said, shaking his head. The one to the right remained silent but laid a restraining hand on the spokesman's arm.

"Forgive me, my brothers," their leader said, looking at each of his comrades in turn. "But extraordinary circumstances call for the most extraordinary of measures."

The two other men looked at him a long moment, then turned to examine Flannery. First one and then the other nodded in acquiescence.

"Father Flannery," the leader said after gaining the consensus of the tribunal. "We know that the symbol—our symbol—is found on the Dismas document. Suppose I tell you that the symbol of Via Dei was given directly to Dismas bar-Dismas by Jesus Christ himself, who appeared to Dismas on the road from Jerusalem the day after his resurrection."

"It was given to Dismas?" Flannery asked.

"Yes."

"That is what your legend tells you?"

"It is not legend, sir, it is truth!" the leader declared, his tone sharpening noticeably.

"It is sometimes hard to separate legend from fact," Flannery countered.

"Fact, yes, but not truth. And surely, Father Flannery, you are intelligent enough to know the difference between the two."

"Yes, I know the difference. But in this case truth is not good enough. You are asking me to help you obtain one of the most important documents ever discovered in the history of Christianity, knowing full well that you will deny the world and the wider body of Christians access to that document. To even consider such an action, I will need fact. What facts have you?"

"We have the fact that Dismas wrote his gospel long before those of Matthew, Mark, Luke, John, or even any of Paul's epistles. We have the fact that Dismas gave his scroll to his successor, Gaius of Ephesus, who then founded Via Dei. Therefore the Gospel of Dismas, by rights, belongs to us. But somehow, at the very beginnings of Via Dei, the scroll was lost, and we alone, for two thousand years, have known of its existence and have searched the Earth for it."

As Flannery listened, he suddenly remembered where he had heard that voice before.

"What proof do we have?" the man continued. "Why, the Via Dei symbol itself. Do you think it mere coincidence that a first century document bears the very symbol long held sacred to our organization? Isn't that proof enough that Dismas bar-Dismas is the father of Via Dei, through his successor and our founder, Gaius of Ephesus, and that his Gospel must by all rights be returned to us?"

"And you want me to return it," Flannery stated.

"In so doing, you will be fulfilling an act of God."

"What about the murder of Daniel Mazar? Was that an act of God?"

The man hesitated, apparently unaware that Flannery knew of what happened at the lab. His tone grew strained, defensive, as he declared, "The professor was killed by Palestinian terrorists."

"But you are in possession of the urn."

"Yes."

"If terrorists killed Professor Mazar, how is it that you have the urn?" Flannery pressed. "Was it the work of those strange bedfellows you spoke of?"

"It...it wasn't supposed to happen that way," the man replied, sounding increasingly uncomfortable. "We sought only the scroll, not anyone's death."

"Those bedfellows of yours killed not only Daniel Mazar but three Israeli guards. When you unleashed them, did you really expect anything less would happen, or did you merely wash your hands of it?" When the man hesitated, Flannery added, "As you wash your hands of so many things at the Prefettura dei Sacri Palazzi Apostolici, Father Sangremano?"

The man seemed to reel back at being identified as Fr. Antonio Sangremano, one of the most powerful men in the Prefecture of the Sacred Apostolic Palaces, which administered the papal palaces and served as the State Department of the Vatican. Regaining his composure, he began to speak but was interrupted by one of his comrades.

"Michael, m'lad..."

Flannery turned in surprise to the man on the right. "My God," he gasped, for he knew this priest, as well. "Father Wester, you?"

Sean Wester, the archivist who had been Flannery's friend for so many years, sighed as he removed his mask and laid it on the table in front of him. He ran his hand through his hair, then shook his head, almost sadly. "Michael," he repeated. "Like a son, I have loved you all these years. Like a son."

THIRTY-SIX

"Is that all?" Yuri Vilnai asked, standing from his desk in his small, cluttered office at the secret "Catacombs" antiquities laboratory of Hebrew University. "I'd like to go home. It's been quite...quite a day."

Sarah Arad and Preston Lewkis rose from a small couch that was jammed between piles of books that filled the room. Flipping shut her notepad, Sarah said, "Yes, it must have been quite upsetting." She tapped the notepad. "You gave all of this to the investigators, didn't you?"

"Everything. But I fear I wasn't too helpful. I only saw them for a fleeting moment, really."

"But you believe they were Palestinians?"

Vilnai shrugged. "That's what I thought at the time. That's what I told your investigators."

"But they wore masks, didn't they?"

"Yes, but I caught a glimpse of one of them removing his mask in the car. I was too far for a good look, but he seemed Palestinian."

"Right. And thank you, Professor."

Sarah walked over to the door, and Preston followed her into the hall. Vilnai was close behind, pulling on his jacket and then closing and locking the door.

"We can reach you at home?" Sarah asked as Vilnai turned to leave.

"Yes, or anytime on my cell phone." Shaking his head, he muttered, "This is some terrible business. Daniel and I had our differences, but there's no one I respected more." Taking his leave, he headed down the hall. He paused as he approached the taped-off area where the laboratory was located, then turned down a side hallway that detoured around the crime scene.

"What do you think?" Preston asked Sarah as he followed her to a nearby conference room.

"I'm not convinced."

As they entered the room, Sarah glanced down the hallway, then shut the door. The room contained an oval table with six chairs, and a small workstation against the side wall with a telephone and fax machine.

"You think he's lying?" Preston said as they sat down at one end of the conference table. "He seemed genuinely upset, which is quite understandable."

"Perhaps not lying but exaggerating."

"About what?"

"Well, the Palestinian angle, for one," she replied.

"You don't believe they were Palestinians?"

"What I don't believe is that he has any idea if they were or weren't." She flipped through her notebook and tapped her finger on one of the entries. "Remember when he first described seeing them in the parking lot?"

"Yes."

"He saw three men, the first two brandishing firearms, and he dropped down on the seat so they wouldn't see him. He waited until they drove off before sitting back up."

"But he also said he glanced back up and saw one of them remove his mask. Isn't that reasonable?"

"He mentioned that later, when I pressed him about their nationality." She drummed her fingers on the notepad. "I don't know...I guess I just don't buy it. His first story makes more sense. He seems like a guy who would've dropped down and not moved a muscle until he was sure they were gone. The stuff about the mask...well, it just seemed an excuse, an explanation to back up why he thought they were Palestinians."

"So you *do* think he was lying."

"Not necessarily. I mean, most Israelis seeing masked men with guns, then finding the laboratory shot up, would jump to the conclusion it was Palestinians. Perhaps Yuri did the same, then concocted or even imagined he had seen one of them in order to justify that prejudice—not only to the police but to himself." She paused, shaking her head, then continued, "I mean, how easy is it to tell if someone's a Palestinian, especially from a quick glance at a distance? If you dress a group of Semitic Israelis and Arabs in the same clothes and put them in a lineup, not many could tell them apart."

"Who else could it have been?"

"That's what I'm wondering." She raised a finger. "Just a minute...I want to check something."

Sarah opened her cell phone. She started to dial, then snapped it shut again. "There's no signal in here."

"There's a phone." Preston gestured toward the workstation.

"Right." She went over to the small desk. Lifting the receiver, she punched in a number and waited. After a few rings, someone picked up and said, "Roberta Greene."

"Roberta, it's Sarah. I'm over at the university lab. I was wondering—"

"Sarah?" the woman interrupted. "I've been trying to reach you."

"My cell phone isn't working here," Sarah explained. "What's up?"

"It's about that Mercedes that was chasing you."

"That's what I was calling about. Did you find out anything from the license plate?"

"There are only three Mercedes with a plate that begins AL9. I was able to narrow it down to one, and it was stolen hours before the crash. But there's something else."

"What?"

"Just a minute."

Sarah heard her colleague shuffling some papers.

"There are two investigators assigned to this case," Roberta said. "Let's see, one's named Steinberg, the other, he's listed here somewhere..."

"Gelb. Bruce Gelb," Sarah said.

"That's right. Well, I went a bit off protocol and had a friend at police headquarters check their files. That produced the full license plate number and matched it to the stolen Mercedes. But there's something else."

"What?" Sarah said impatiently as she heard more papers shuffling.

"Here it is," Roberta blurted. "Sorry, there's such a pile on my desk."

"What is it, Roberta?" Sarah pressed.

"When they interviewed you, did they mention a ring?"

"No. What kind of ring?"

"A very curious one. It was found on one of the victims—the driver of the Mercedes. And through it they were able to ID the man. Let's see...yes, it's right here. Javier Murillo, of Spanish-Moroccan descent."

"A Muslim?" Sarah asked.

"No, Catholic—at least he was. There was some sort of scandal ten years ago, and he was excommunicated."

"Can you fax me the details?"

"Yes, and I'll send a photo of the ring. What's the fax number?"

Sarah saw that the fax machine was connected to the phone and did not have a dedicated line. She gave Roberta the phone number, then said, "I'll have to hang up to take the fax."

"Fine. I'll send it right now. Call back if you need me to do anything else."

"Thanks, Roberta." She hung up the phone.

"What is it?" Preston asked, coming over and standing behind Sarah.

"Maybe nothing. We'll know in a moment."

The phone rang, and Sarah pressed the fax machine's receive button. Soon the paper began to appear in the output tray. They watched as the close-up image of a ring came into view. As soon as the paper had fully ejected, Sarah snatched it up and raised it in front of them. The ring looked much like a school graduation ring, with a large black stone that bore a carved seal and lettering.

"What's that?" she asked, pointing at the stylized inscription that surrounded the seal.

Preston took the paper from her and ran his fingers over the letters as he intoned, *"In Nomine Patris."*

"In the name of the Father?" Sarah translated, questioning what he had said.

Preston nodded.

"And the seal?" she asked, pointing at the image of crossed keys surmounted by a crown.

"Where did you get this?" he asked.

"Why? What is it?"

"I'm not positive, but I believe it's the Vatican seal."

Sarah looked more closely and saw that, indeed, the crown was the Triregnum tiara of the Pope, with the keys representing the ones given the apostle Peter by Jesus.

"Who would have a ring like this?" Sarah asked.

"Certainly not Palestinians," Preston replied, stating the obvious. "But there's someone who might know."

"Father Flannery."

"Yes." Preston glanced at his watch. "In fact, he should be here by now. I called him hours ago to tell him about Daniel. Let me see what's taking so long." He picked up the receiver and dialed Michael Flannery's cell phone. As he waited for an answer, he looked up at Sarah. "Is there a connection between this ring and Daniel's death?"

"There may be. I'm not sure."

"Sarah, when you were talking to that Roberta woman, you said something about men chasing you. Are they connected to this ring or the attack on the lab?"

"I'll tell you all about it afterward." She gestured at the phone.

Preston shrugged. "It's still ringing. Either he's out of range or he's not answering." He waited a moment longer, then hung up the phone.

"How long ago did you call him?"

"Three, maybe four hours. He was just north of Ein-Gedi on Road 90."

"I don't like this," Sarah muttered with a frown. She redialed her office, and when Roberta Greene answered, she said, "It's Sarah again. I need you to put an immediate trace on Father Michael Flannery. Find out what car he's rented, and alert the police that he was last seen on Road 90 just north of Ein-Gedi."

She gave a few more details to her colleague, then ended the call.

"Come," she told Preston, leading him from the room. "There's something else I want to try."

Sarah led him out to where her Mini Cooper was parked. Opening the tailgate, she retrieved her small Sony VAIO laptop, then motioned for Preston to get in the car. She climbed into the driver's seat and, leaving her door open, flipped open the laptop. After it booted up, she launched a program, typed in her password, and started punching in a series of numbers.

"You're not seeing what I'm doing right now," she said almost casually.

"What do you mean?"

"This is pretty classified stuff, but I'll trust you to forget you've ever seen it."

"I don't understand..."

"Here." She angled the computer toward Preston.

"A map?"

"There's Ein-Gedi." She pointed at a spot on the map, indicating the oasis where King Solomon composed the Song of Songs. "And this is Road 90."

Her finger tracked a red line along the road, then followed it onto a side road. As it headed off the screen, she tapped the arrow keys to shift the map and bring it back in view. The red line meandered east and west as it moved slowly north toward Jerusalem. When the line came to a stop, she pressed one of the function keys several times, zooming in on the location.

"That's where Father Flannery is right now—or at least was about an hour ago. And the red line is the route he took to get there."

Preston looked at her incredulously. "How do you know?"

"That doesn't matter right now. The thing is, we've got to find out what he's doing—and why I'm not able to track him for the last hour."

"Where is this?" Preston asked, tapping the screen on the spot where the red line ended.

"East Jerusalem." She handed him the laptop. "You can navigate," she said, shutting her door and starting up the engine. A moment later they were spinning out of the parking lot, heading east across the city.

THIRTY-SEVEN

FR. MICHAEL FLANNERY STARED IN STUNNED DISBELIEF AT THE MAN WHO had just professed a father's love for him. "You, Father?" he muttered, shaking his head. "You, of all people, a party to this...to the murder of Professor Mazar and those Israeli guards?"

"We did not plan that," Fr. Sean Wester replied. "We asked only that they retrieve the scroll. The sin of murder lies upon them, not us."

"But surely you knew what would happen. Palestinians, conducting a raid in Israel?"

"It couldn't be helped," Wester said. "Sometimes decisive action must be taken for a greater good."

"And the greater good is what? To steal a gospel of our Lord so as to deny it to the world? You, Sean? A man who loves knowledge? Don't you realize that this document, if authenticated, could bring millions more to Christ?"

"The greater good is to protect Mother Church from the Jews, Muslims, scientists, humanists, journalists, politicians, and critics... aye, even the so-called evangelicals who distort and pervert the teachings of the one true Church."

"Don't attack the evangelicals for their zeal in worshipping the Lord," Flannery said. "Rather be glad that we can count them as our brothers and sisters in Christ. And remember also that our Lord himself was a Jew."

"The time has come, Michael, m'lad," Wester declared. "Where do your loyalties lie? Do they lie with the Holy Roman Catholic Church and Via Dei, an instrument of its protection, created and ordained by Jesus Christ himself? Or do you ally yourself with the enemies of the Church?"

Flannery shook his head. "I do not consider myself an enemy of the Church."

"Then you will lead us to that which is rightly ours? The sacred scroll of Dismas bar-Dismas?"

"I don't know where it is."

"You are lying, Father Flannery," the tribunal leader said from behind his mask. "You have been a part of their team from the very beginning. You have seen the scroll, you have touched it, smelled it, read it. Don't you see? You have already achieved something that generations of members of our organization have not been able to accomplish. That is why we consider you worthy of entry into the deepest level of Via Dei."

"Yes, I have done all those things," Flannery admitted. "But the scroll is still the property of the Israelis. After our initial inspection, we've had access only to photocopies. The scroll itself has been kept in a vault with the urn, and if it wasn't there when your agents raided the lab, then I have no idea where it is today. Or perhaps those bedfellows of yours found it but are holding out on you."

"Tell me this, Michael," Wester said. He placed his palms on the table and leaned toward Flannery. "And it's the truth I'll be wanting and expecting from an old friend. If you knew where the scroll was—and I understand you do not—but if you did, would you be willing to tell us?"

"Not for a minute," Flannery replied resolutely.

Wester leaned back in his chair, his eyes registering intense sorrow and regret. "I was afraid of that." He looked over at the other two. "We've done all we can do. We'll get nothing more from Father Flannery."

The man in the middle removed his mask then, confirming that he was Fr. Antonio Sangremano, first secretary to the sub-prefect of the

Prefettura dei Sacri Palazzi Apostolici, a powerful Vatican insider known for sprinkling his speech with quotations.

The third inquisitor also removed his mask, and Flannery recognized him as Boyd Kern, an American lawyer who served as counsel to the Inquisitor of the Tribunal of the Prefecture. Like Sangremano, Kern's position was quite high within the hierarchy of the Church.

As Flannery looked from one man to the other, he came to the sudden realization that he was undoubtedly the only non-member of Via Dei who could identify these three men as key members of an organization that for two thousand years had gone to great lengths to guard its secrecy.

"I'm not going to get out of here alive, am I?" Flannery said with no trace of fear or pleading in his voice. Rather he evinced a calm acceptance of his fate.

"I'm sorry, Michael," Father Wester replied.

"Tell me one thing first. How high does this go...in the Vatican, I mean."

"The Vatican?" Wester asked, looking momentarily confused. "You think all this is at the bidding of the Vatican? You don't understand Via Dei...not really. The Vatican is no more than a sideshow. A means. Via Dei is the end. The alpha and the omega."

"Tell me, Sean, are you the one who's going to kill me?"

"Father Wester is under enough strain," Sangremano interjected. "Do not increase that strain by pleading for your life."

"I have no intention of doing so," Flannery declared.

"That is to your credit, and it confirms why you would make a valuable addition to Via Dei. This is your last chance. Are you going to help us?"

"'What you are going to do, do quickly,'" Flannery stated, using the words Jesus had uttered in commanding Judas to deliver him to his death.

Raising his hand, Sangremano extended his thumb and two fingers and drew a cross in the air. *"In Nomine Patris, et Filii, et Spiritus Sancti. Amen,"* he intoned. "May God have mercy on your soul."

He turned toward the doorway that led to the entry hall and clapped three times. There was a single clap, sharper and louder, in return.

Sangremano clapped again and shouted, "Come in here!"

He was answered by a flurry of reports, and this time Flannery realized it wasn't hands clapping but the unmistakable sound of gunshots echoing through the catacombs. He looked back at Sangremano, and seeing the man's look of surprise and worry, he knew this was not something they were expecting.

"Father Flannery! Get down!" a woman's voice echoed from beyond the chamber.

With the athleticism that had made him a good runner in his youth, Flannery dove from the chair and rolled behind the ossuary of Shlom-zion. A bullet ricocheted off the wall behind him, and he spun around to see that Sangremano had pulled a revolver from beneath his robe and was waving it about wildly. Flannery ducked to avoid another shot, then saw that Father Wester had leaped in front of Sangremano and was struggling for the gun. There was a muffled report, and Wester's body jerked backward. He slumped to the floor, his lifeless hands releasing their grip on the other man's arm.

Someone appeared in the doorway, and Sangremano got off a round, forcing the person back. His next bullet centered Boyd Kern's chest, and as a crimson pool spread across the front of his snow-white vestments, he dropped to his knees, his lips silently mouthing the word "Why?" as he sprawled facedown on the stone floor, one arm reaching out toward his killer. But Sangremano was already gone, having snatched a torch off the wall and disappeared into a small passageway at the back of the chamber.

The gunshots continued for several more seconds, then there was an eerie silence that seemed to ring in Flannery's ears as he peered out from behind the ossuary and saw the distorted, torch-tossed shadows of someone coming into the chamber. Realizing it might be one of Sangremano's hired hit men, he pulled himself into a near fetal position to stay out of sight.

"Father Flannery? Are you here?"

It was the same voice that had warned him earlier, and Flannery peered around the edge of the stone coffin to see Sara Arad entering the room, her arms extended, a pistol in her hands. Seeing the two bodies, Sara moved cautiously toward them.

"They're dead," Flannery said, standing.

Reacting quickly, Sarah swung her pistol toward him.

"It's me!" Flannery shouted, thrusting his hands in the air.

With an embarrassed smile, she lowered her weapon. "Is there anyone else?"

"One more, but he escaped through there." Flannery pointed toward the rear of the chamber.

Torch in hand, Sarah ducked through the opening in the wall. She was gone about a minute before returning.

"He's gone. That passageway runs under the city and has a hundred or more exits." She crossed to the entryway and called into the hall, "Preston, it's all clear!"

A moment later, Preston Lewkis came into the chamber. He was also carrying a weapon, an AK-47 submachine gun.

"Where'd you get that?" Sarah asked.

"Off one of the guards," he replied, then hurried over to his friend. "Michael, are you all right?"

"Yes, yes," Flannery said, then asked Sarah, "Where are the police?"

"I *am* the police," Sarah said.

"Just you? It sounded like a whole force out there."

"Believe it, Michael," Preston put in. "Sarah is soldier, archaeologist, and secret agent, all in one."

Looking a bit embarrassed and eager to change the subject, Sarah said, "Father Flannery, there were four Palestinian guards, two outside the catacombs and two in the hallway. Do you know if there were any others, besides these two and the one you said got away?"

"These men aren't Palestinians," Flannery replied, pointing to the two bodies.

"And I'm not so sure about those guards," Preston said.

"What do you mean?" Sarah asked.

"When I was picking up this gun, I checked the fellow over. He looks European, maybe Mediterranean, and he's wearing the same ring as in that photo."

"What ring?" Flannery asked.

Sarah looked down at the two dead men. "They're from the Vatican, aren't they?" she asked, and Flannery nodded. "Some of the others wore a ring bearing the Vatican seal. They may have wanted us to think they were Palestinians, but I doubt any of them were."

Preston walked over to the table and ran his hand over the symbol emblazoned on the cloth. "That's just like the one on the scroll."

"Not exactly," Sarah said, coming over to examine it. "This one is topped with a circle, like an *ankh*. The Dismas symbol has an upward-pointing crescent moon."

"That's right," Flannery said. "This is the symbol of Via Dei, a very secret, very dangerous group within the Catholic Church. Only, they aren't exactly in the Church."

"Yes, Via Dei," Preston replied. "You mentioned them when you first saw the scroll. I thought they were from the Middle Ages. They still exist?"

"Apparently so. They fancy themselves as protectors of Christianity and the Church. But their overzealous excesses brought them into collision with Church tenets, and they were excommunicated more than a hundred years ago. They operate in even greater secrecy now and count some Vatican heavyweights among them." He gestured at the bodies.

"What are they doing here now?" Sarah asked. "And what did they want with you?"

"They were trying to obtain the Dismas scroll, which they believe is their birthright."

"Then the symbol on the scroll *is* related to this one, isn't it?"

"They believe it to be," Flannery told her. "But their symbol, like their organization, is a perversion of truth."

"And what is the truth?" Preston asked.

"That, my friend, is what I've been trying to find out."

"Do you know who they are?" Sarah asked, indicating the dead men.

Flannery felt uncertain about revealing all that he knew, but he realized he mustn't interfere with a murder investigation. "Yes, I knew all three. Especially Father Sean Wester." He knelt beside the body of the Vatican archivist as he prayed for his former friend.

"You can tell us about them while we're driving back to the city," Sarah said as Flannery finished his prayer.

The priest stood back up. "You saved my life, you know. They had just ordered my death when you arrived."

"That's our Sarah," Preston put in. "Like all good rescuers, she arrived just in the nick of time. All that was lacking was a bugler playing *The Charge*."

Flannery laughed and realized what a good feeling it was to be able to do so, given the circumstances. "Yes, I've seen those American movies with John Wayne and the U.S. cavalry. But tell me, Preston, how did you find me?"

Preston was about to answer, but Sarah cut in, saying, "First answer this. You were kidnapped near Ein-Gedi, weren't you?"

"How did you know?"

"I tracked you by satellite, and no one would've willingly driven the route you took to get here."

"Satellite? How did you do that?"

"I shouldn't reveal this, but I suppose you've a right to know. You still have that security ID that Preston gave you during your first visit to Masada?"

"It's in my pocket."

"It contains a microchip," she declared. "It not only allows our scanners and security personnel to identify you, but we can track it by GPS satellite."

"You knew where I was the whole time?"

"Don't worry—it's not something I'd normally check, and it required special access permission. But when we realized you were missing, I was able to track your movements over the past several hours, until the trail went dead not far from here."

"Went dead?" He slipped the ID from his pocket and held it forth. "But I'm still carrying it."

"The satellite can't pick it up down here in the catacombs. We tracked you to the entrance, and that was enough to figure out where you were."

"Amazing," Flannery said as he looked more closely at the nametag ID. "Truly amazing."

Preston grinned. "Yes. You might say that someone above was looking out for you."

THIRTY-EIGHT

Rome burned for nine days. Nearly seventy percent of the city was destroyed, and only four of Rome's fourteen districts were untouched. Three districts were totally devastated; the other seven were reduced to a few scorched and mangled ruins. Nero's palace was transformed into a charred mass, with all its art treasures forever lost.

Thousands were burned out of their homes, losing everything they owned. For a while there was little to differentiate Rome's wealthiest, most powerful citizens from the underprivileged and impoverished, for all were huddled together in hastily constructed shelters outside the city.

Marcella and Rufinus Tacitus were more fortunate than many, because they had another place to go. Marcella's parents had owned a villa in the Campagna just outside Rome, and the property had passed to her when they died. In the wake of the fire, Marcella had reluctantly parted with Tibro and accompanied her husband to the villa as part of an unspoken understanding that Rufinus would not pursue his threats against the man he thought to be Dismas bar-Dismas.

Even before the last of the embers had stopped smoldering, there were rumors that Emperor Nero had ordered the city torched so he could get rid of the slums and rebuild in even grander Greek style, but that the controlled fire he planned had gotten out of hand. In fact, there were stories of him standing on the summit of the Palatine, playing his lyre as flames devoured the city.

While it was true that Nero desired an ambitious rebuilding program, it was unlikely he would undertake it in so reckless a fashion. He wasn't even in Rome when the fire started, but he rushed back from his palace in Antium and moved about the city all that first night, not even waiting for his personal guards to accompany him. He directed efforts to quell the blaze and personally took a hand in rescuing some of the citizens. Despite that, rumors that he was the fire's architect were so persistent, the anger so palpable, that some of his supporters began to fear for his safety—and their own.

Rufinus was a strong backer of Nero, not so much out of agreement with his policies or appreciation of his artistic talents but because he believed his own power was dependent upon the emperor remaining on the throne. There were others who shared Rufinus's position, and on this day two of them, Cassius Avitus and Seneca Fabius, had come to the villa to discuss the situation. Marcella did not join the conversation but sat to one side, embroidering a pillow covering as she listened to their conversation.

"I don't believe it was Nero," Seneca declared. "I am convinced it was the Jews. Already their merchants profit from the rebuilding."

"Not the Jews. It was Christians," Cassius countered.

"Why do you say that?"

"They stand in direct opposition to the ancient social and religious practices of our society. I believe they are our sworn enemies. And few of them lost their houses."

"But aren't Jews and Christians the same?"

"Not at all. Jews have lived among us for centuries, and while a dirty and debased lot, they keep to themselves and cause trouble only in their own lands. These new Christians, on the other hand, seek to convert us to their cause. And I'm sorry to say, many citizens have professed their faith, proving themselves traitors to Rome."

"And yet the leader of the cult, the one called Jesus who was crucified many years ago, he was a Jew, was he not?" Seneca asked.

"He was, but the Jews disavowed him and called for his death," Cassius explained. "No, there is little love between Christian and Jew."

"What I cannot understand is how a cult will continue to follow a leader who is dead."

"The Christians believe this Jesus rose from the dead," Rufinus said, interjecting himself into the conversation. "Is that not right, Marcella?" He quickly added, "My wife is no Christian, but she had dealings with them during some unpleasantness in Ephesus."

"He rose from the dead?" Cassius said, his tone mocking. He and Seneca laughed, but Rufinus displayed no humor as he turned to Marcella.

"That is the Christian belief," she said softly without looking up from her work.

"So, what you are saying is that these Christians worship a ghost," Seneca said. "And not even the ghost of one of the gods, but the ghost of a crucified Jew?"

"What say you, Marcella?" her husband asked. "Is Jesus the Jew an apparition?"

"Those who saw him say he wasn't a ghost but appeared to them in the flesh," Marcella said.

Cassius laughed. "You speak as if you believe there actually were people who saw him." When Marcella didn't reply, he looked at Rufinus with more than a bit of suspicion. "Your wife is well versed in Christian doctrine. What was the unpleasantness that brought her such knowledge?"

"One of her childhood friends, Marcus Antonius, was a centurion in my personal guard when I was governor in Ephesus. He became a Christian, and Marcella, with my permission of course, sought to convince him of his error."

"A centurion became a Christian?" Seneca put in. "Is he still a Roman officer?"

Rufinus shook his head. "He was obstinate and refused my offers of mercy should he repent and disavow this Jesus. Ultimately my tribunal sentenced him to death, but he managed to escape. At least he no longer disgraces the empire by holding the rank of centurion. For many years I didn't know what happened to him, but my wife has since learned that he has married his Ephesian whore and is living the life of a fig-grower in Dalmatia."

"Dalmatia?" Seneca snickered. "I'd rather be executed."

Cassius looked with curiosity at Marcella. "How is it that she knows this?"

"You don't understand my wife." Rufinus forced a smile. "She is too tolerant and kind. I have counseled caution, but she makes no distinction between Roman and Christian and Jew when it comes to those she befriends."

"There's no law against knowing Christians," Marcella said, keeping her eyes down and voice low.

"Dear wife, would you please leave us?" Rufinus said with mock tenderness. "All this talk of religion and politics is unseemly for a woman."

"As you wish," she replied. Standing, she gave the three men a slight nod, then withdrew from the room.

Cassius started to speak, but Rufinus raised a hand, signaling him to wait until they were alone.

———

A MINUTE LATER, Marcella was seated in a small room on the second floor. Soon after moving into the villa, she had discovered that a system of grates used to transfer heat from room to room also carried voices. This particular room was directly above where her husband was receiving his guests, and she had no trouble hearing their conversation.

"Do you think it wise to allow your wife to consort with Christians?" Cassius was saying, his tone betraying both concern and disapproval.

"Allow?" Rufinus replied. "I don't just allow it, I encourage it."

"Why would you do such a thing?"

"Because it serves my purposes. You have said it yourself on many an occasion, Cassius. One must know one's enemy—or potential enemy. Do you not think I see the threat these Christians pose? More importantly, I see their usefulness, just as I see the usefulness of allowing my wife to consort with them, as you put it, and report back to me on what she learns."

"Then she is your spy?" Seneca asked.

Rufinus chuckled. "An unwitting one. She's far too delicate to play the spy. But how she loves to chatter, and I encourage her to prattle on about the customs and doings of Christians, Jews, and anyone else she befriends. As she enjoys telling me, there is no law against knowing a Christian or even becoming one."

"Might she have converted—?"

"By all the gods, no," Rufinus declared. "She is amused by people who are different, that is all. As for Marcella's devotion to the gods, she carries out all the necessary rituals and offerings. She is especially devoted to Apollo and prays to him daily."

Upstairs, Marcella smiled at her husband's mention of Apollo. So often when he had caught her in prayer, she had explained that she was worshipping the Son God, knowing he would take it to mean the sun god, Apollo.

"You would do well to keep a close eye on her," Cassius cautioned. "These Christians are a dangerous lot, and your wife, if you'll excuse me, seems impressionable."

"Aren't all wives?" Rufinus replied with a half-laugh. "But all this talk of Christians has given me an idea. If we can convince the good citizens of Rome that Christians started the fire, their anger at Nero will subside."

"How are we to do that?" Seneca asked.

"By getting Nero to say he has investigated the cause of the fire and determined it to be the work of Christians. Then have him pass a law making it a crime against the state to be a Christian."

"Would Nero agree to such a thing?" Cassius asked.

"He will do anything he believes is to his advantage," Seneca said.

"This would be very much to his advantage, and I think we could convince him of that, if we had a way to get his ear," Rufinus said.

"Perhaps I can talk to Laelius," Seneca suggested. "He, too, is a musician and has Nero's trust."

"Good, good." Rufinus grinned broadly. "Tell Laelius he must convince Nero to launch a campaign against the Christians. They are to be blamed for the fire and for every other evil that has befallen us. They must be rounded up and thrown in prison, and all their leaders executed."

Above, Marcella gasped, covering her mouth so as not to be heard.

"Are you certain this will work?" Cassius said dubiously. "We can offer no evidence that Christians were in any way involved, and Nero has allowed them to live freely among us. He may not wish to persecute them."

Rufinus laughed. "When Nero feared there was a plot against him, he killed his own mother. He also killed his wife and brother. If he realizes that the best way to preserve his throne is to declare the Christians outlaws, he will not hesitate to do so."

"Perhaps," Cassius agreed. "And if we're the ones who provide him a way out of his dilemma, we shall be forever in his favor." He turned to Seneca. "Rufinus is right, you must go to Laelius."

"At once," Seneca said.

Marcella heard a chair move, and footsteps as Seneca headed toward the door.

"I'll accompany you," Cassius offered, pushing back his chair and following.

"Seneca," Rufinus called. "You will tell the emperor that this was my idea?"

"Of course."

"Tell him also that I shall personally deliver one of the Christian leaders by name of Dismas bar-Dismas. That will further strengthen our position with Nero."

As the footsteps receded, Marcella stood and padded quietly to her room. She dropped in front of the small table that served as a makeshift altar and fought back the tears that welled within her. While she knew her fellow Christians had nothing to do with the fire, she didn't doubt it would be a simple matter to convince others—Nero included—that they had. They were especially at risk because most had settled in the Trastevere quarter, which had passed through the ordeal largely unscathed. While that may have been a blessing from God, it was also because Trastevere was separated from the city by the Tiber River, which had served as a firebreak. But the superstitious masses would be easily persuaded that the Christians' good fortune was proof of their guilt.

Marcella clasped her hands, her eyes shut tight as she repeated over and over again the prayer of her Lord:

"Thy will be done. Thy will be done."

THAT NIGHT, after Rufinus was asleep, Marcella left the villa and walked briskly along Via Appia until she came to the outskirts of Rome. The air was redolent with the smell of burnt wood and charred stone. A pall of smoke still hung over the destroyed city, and here and there she saw small groups of displaced people living outside because they had no other place to go.

Not until she started up Via Portuensis did she see whole buildings again. When she reached Gaius's house, she was welcomed inside, despite the late hour. The house was nearly full, as he had opened his doors to many who had lost their own homes.

Among those present were Tibro and Dismas. It heartened her to see the brothers together. Though there was no longer the bad blood that once separated them, there was still some strain in the relationship, due to their differing beliefs.

"Marcella! I didn't expect to see you so soon," Tibro said, hurrying over as she entered the large meeting room. "How are you? Are you safe?"

"Yes." She smiled demurely. "The house in the Campagna is quite secure and comfortable."

"That's good. I have worried about you."

"And I about you," she replied.

"Greetings, Marcella, I hope you are well," Dismas called out as he approached from across the room.

As Marcella looked up into his eyes, she could read the thoughts behind his simple greeting. She and Tibro had never told him of their mutual feelings, but it was obvious he knew they were in love. And while his eyes spoke of his approval, they revealed something else—an abiding concern over how difficult and tenuous their situation was. One was a nonbeliever, the other baptized in the name of Jesus; one a commoner and a Jew, the other of royalty and of Rome; one free to marry, the other another man's wife. Shaking off those thoughts, she returned Dismas's greeting.

Dismas smiled. "What brings you here? We have no meeting tonight."

Marcella drew in a long breath. When at last she spoke, her voice was calm but firm. "You're in danger. All of you are, but Dismas, you and Paul and Peter are in the most danger."

"Why?" Dismas asked.

"The fire. A plot is afoot to have the emperor blame Christians for the fire."

Gaius and some of the others came over just in time to hear the warning.

"But why would he blame us?" Gaius asked. "What reason would we have to burn down Rome? We have no quarrel with Nero. He has tolerated our religion."

"No reason is needed," she replied, shaking her head. "Don't you understand? We will be guilty simply because Nero says we are. He will make scapegoats of us in order to direct the anger of the citizens away from himself."

"But surely the citizens of Rome won't believe such an obvious falsehood," one of the others put in.

"It doesn't matter whether they believe it or not," Marcella replied. "All that matters is that Nero declares it to be so. He will use the false-hood to round up and execute first our leaders and then anyone who professes the faith. You must flee. All of you."

Dismas shook his head. "I'm not going anywhere. There is too much work to do here."

"You must go," Tibro urged. "What good works can you accomplish if you're dead?"

"Your brother is right, my friend," Gaius said. "You must leave, and it must be at once." He allowed himself a smile. "And I know the perfect place—the home of Phillip of Játiva on the road to Ariminum. He will take you in."

Dismas sighed and nodded. "I will take your advice, but only for the time being."

THIRTY-NINE

THE NEXT MORNING, MARCELLA WAS IN THE VILLA GARDEN WHEN AN officer from the Praetorian Guard arrived on horseback. Tying his horse to an iron ring in the fence, he nodded at Marcella and touched a hand to his highly polished helmet. "Good day to you, Madam Tacitus."

"Good day, Legatus Lucius Calpurnius," she replied.

"I have news for your husband. Is he in?"

"You will find him in the peristyle."

Again Calpurnius touched his helmet, then went inside. Marcella returned to the flowering wisteria until he was gone. Then she hurried to another entrance and hid behind one of the columns that surrounded the peristyle, an enclosed courtyard in the middle of the villa.

"Good news, Your Excellency. We have located Dismas bar-Dismas," the Roman officer announced.

"Wonderful!" Rufinus replied. "Is he in custody?"

"Not yet. I await only your word to seize him."

"Yes, by all means, go," Rufinus said impatiently.

"I shall gather my men and seize the criminal this very afternoon," Calpurnius declared with a smart salute.

Seeing the soldier turn to leave, Marcella hurried back to the garden. When Calpurnius came through the vestibule a moment later, Marcella was again busily attending to the wisterias.

"By your leave, my Lady," he said as he strode to his horse and untied it.

"Go in safety," Marcella replied.

Shortly after Calpurnius rode away, Marcella carried a basket of the wisteria blossoms to the peristyle. She found her husband sitting on a stone bench, smiling broadly. She forced herself not to react to his smug merriment.

"Rufinus, I am going to take leave for a while," she told him.

"Oh? And where will you go?" he asked distractedly, as if he had more important things on his mind. "The baths have all burned down."

"I wish to call upon some friends I haven't seen since the fire and inquire as to their welfare. I cut some flowers to bring them." She held forth the basket.

"You could send one of the servants," he said, then shook his head and gave a dismissive wave. "Yes, go ahead. Whatever you wish."

"Thank you, my husband," she said softly. Leaving him to his ruminations, she hurried away before he could change his mind.

———

"SHE'S GONE," a voice called from across the peristyle.

"You saw her leave?" Rufinus asked, standing as Calpurnius came into the courtyard.

"Yes, Your Excellency."

"Follow her. She will lead you to Dismas."

Calpurnius grinned. "You were right, Your Excellency. She listened to our conversation, and now she will go to warn him."

"Yes, but be careful to stay out of sight," Rufinus cautioned. "If she sees your men following her, she'll never lead you to him."

"We will be very careful," Calpurnius promised. "She will have no idea we are there."

———

REACHING GAIUS'S HOUSE CHURCH, Marcella found Tibro and Simon seated alone in a small anteroom. Hurrying over, she blurted, "Dismas is in grave trouble."

"What sort of trouble?" Simon asked.

"The soldiers know where he's hiding and plan to arrest him."

"How did they find out?"

She shook her head. "I only know that Legatus Lucius Calpurnius of the Praetorian Guard told my husband they have discovered where Dismas is hiding."

"He said this in front of you?" Tibro asked.

"No. They were in the courtyard, and I hid behind a column. Neither my husband nor Calpurnius knew I was there. I heard Calpurnius ask for permission to arrest Dismas."

"I'll bet that wasn't a hard decision for Rufinus to make. He hates my brother so."

"I'm so worried," Marcella said.

Tibro laid a reassuring hand on her shoulder. "Don't worry. I'll warn Dismas."

"I'm going with you," Marcella announced.

"That wouldn't be wise," Tibro said.

"I'm going," she insisted.

"And I shall go, as well," Simon declared, standing beside his friend. "My body may be old, but there is still strength in these arms and legs. I may be of some help should there be trouble."

"All right, all right," Tibro agreed. "We accomplish nothing standing here talking. Let's get started."

———

LEGATUS LUCIUS CALPURNIUS stood gripping the reins of his horse in what remained of a stone stable near the bridge leading to the Trastevere district. He looked up as one of his centurions dismounted and came rushing over.

"What is it, Horatius?"

"I followed the woman to the home of a Christian, and a few minutes later she emerged with the one named Dismas bar-Dismas and a black companion."

"You are certain it was Dismas?" Calpurnius asked of the centurion who often served him as a spy.

"I have seen him many times. It is Dismas."

"Where are they now?"

"On Via Flaminia heading toward Ariminum. I left Junius to follow them."

"Come," Calpurnius called to the nine other soldiers who stood with horses in hand. "We must move at once."

———

MARCELLA WAS the first to hear the approaching hoof beats. She tugged at Tibro's arm and gestured back the way they had come.

"Roman soldiers, I fear," Simon said, looking down Via Flaminia.

"Yes," Tibro agreed. "And they've already seen us, no doubt. It would be pointless to hide; better to try to bluff them if they stop."

As the dozen horsemen drew up alongside the trio of travelers, Marcella knew at once there would be no possibility of pretense. "Legatus Lucius Calpurnius," she said as the officer dropped down off his mount in front of her. "What are you doing here?"

"I might ask you the same, Madam Tacitus," he replied with a smirking grin.

"How impudent of you," she said angrily. "My husband will hear of this."

"Oh, yes indeed, he certainly will, my Lady, for I shall personally deliver you to the *curia lictor*," he said, using Rufinus's title as a member of the Assembly of the Curiae. "How he deals with you is up to him." He turned to Tibro. "And you, Dismas, shall finally face the justice you have so long avoided."

"He's not—"

"Afraid of your so-called justice," Tibro interrupted Marcella, signaling with his eyes that she should not tell Calpurnius that he had the wrong man. "I will willingly face a Roman tribunal," he went on. "For I believe that when the truth is known, I will be set free."

Marcella realized that Tibro was using himself to protect his brother, gambling that when he revealed his true identity, they would let him go. By then it would be too late for them to find Dismas.

"No, don't do this," Marcella warned him. "I fear you greatly underestimate the danger you face."

"Come, friends," Tibro told his companions. "Let us test Roman justice."

"No," Calpurnius declared. He pointed at Simon. "Not that one."

"What shall we do with the slave?" Horatius asked.

"You and Junius take him off the road, into the bushes," Calpurnius said.

Horatius and Junius looked uncertainly at each other, then Horatius asked, "And what then?"

Calpurnius grinned coldly. "Kill him, of course. No need to bother the tribunal with an extra defendant."

———

SIMON STOOD TALL, unflinching, as he watched the soldiers ride off toward Rome with their prisoners in tow, Marcella seated in front of the one named Calpurnius and Tibro tied and flung facedown across another horse in front of its rider.

The two soldiers who had been left behind stood a few feet away, swords drawn as the one named Horatius gestured for the prisoner to head down off the road into the thicket below. As Simon complied, he saw a hint of fear in their eyes and guessed that, despite serving in the guard, they had never had to kill a man—at least not up close.

"Shall we do it here?" Junius asked as he followed Horatius and Simon into the thicket.

"No, up ahead...see that clearing? We'll do it there." Horatius prodded Simon's back with the tip of his sword. "Move along, and be quick about you!"

They emerged from the thicket into a small clearing, and Simon moved to the far side and turned to face his executioners. "You don't have to do this," he said with a smile of genuine compassion. "You can simply leave and—"

"Shut up!" Horatius blurted, raising his blade menacingly. "Get down on your knees!"

As Simon complied, he raised his left hand and began to pray in Aramaic. His right hand slipped under his tunic, and when he removed it, he held not a hidden dagger but a simple patch of cloth. He drew it to his lips and kissed, then continued his prayer.

The soldiers looked at each other in confusion, then back at the kneeling prisoner. Horatius took a step forward and halted, as if frozen in position. He cocked his head to one side as his eyes fixed on Simon's, hypnotized by the man's gaze as he listened to words he could not understand. Junius was immobilized as well, his sword tip lowering as he tried to make out what he was hearing.

Suddenly Simon gasped and clutched the cloth to his belly. He started to tip forward, then caught his balance and kneeled there with his palms held forward to the soldiers. His hands and the cloth he was still clutching were soaked in blood, with more blood oozing through the front of his slashed tunic and spilling onto the earth.

The stunned soldiers looked at their swords and saw that the blades were also dripping with the man's blood.

"Lord, f-forgive them..." Simon muttered as he fell to his side and rolled motionless onto his back, a dark pool of blood spreading around him.

"Wh-What happened?" Junius asked as he backed away slowly. "I don't remember..." He stopped midsentence and looked again at his blood-drenched sword.

"We did our duty," Horatius replied, shaking his head in bewilderment.

He moved closer and gave Simon a nudge with his foot to confirm he was dead, then walked over to one of the bushes surrounding the clearing and wiped his sword on the leaves. Junius followed his lead, and the two men ducked back into the thicket and headed up to the road.

Simon lay in stillness as the sound of horses retreated into the distance. Then he rolled onto his side and sat up. He rubbed his belly, confirming that he wasn't wounded. In fact, his tunic was no longer torn and there was no sign of blood anywhere on the material or the ground. The only bloodstain was on the cloth in his hand, which he again raised to his lips and kissed tenderly.

"Oh Lord, from my enemies you have delivered me," he intoned. "And to you, I give thanks. Amen."

Returning to the road, he looked southwest down Via Flaminia and saw the dust of horses in the distance as the two frightened soldiers raced back to Rome. Turning in the opposite direction, he continued toward the nearby village where Dismas bar-Dismas was hiding.

Returning to the road, he looked southeast down Via Flaminia and saw the dust of horses in the distance as the two frightened soldiers raced back to Rome. Pausing in the opposite direction, he continued toward the nearby village where Flavius had been waiting.

FORTY

NIGHT BIRDS AND INSECTS FILLED THE AIR WITH MUSIC AS SIMON MOVED through the trees to the small house where Dismas bar-Dismas was staying. In the stable a donkey brayed, and a freshening breeze set the leaves rustling. He knocked on the door.

"Who comes?" a muffled voice called from within.

"I am Simon of Cyrene, a friend to—"

Before he could finish his reply, the door was jerked opened and a white-haired old man greeted him with a smile as crooked as his hunched back.

"Yes, I know who you are," the man declared. "Dismas has spoken well and often of you. I am Phillip of Játiva, though as you can see I'm a long way from Hispania. Please, come in and rest yourself. Do you require food or drink?"

"Both would be welcome, indeed," Simon replied.

"Wait in there." Phillip pointed to a room just off the vestibule. "Take this lamp, I will light another. Then I will wake Dismas and get cheese and wine."

"Thank you."

The flickering light of the oil lamp guided Simon's way as he entered the room. He sat on a backless couch, which was little more than an oblong wooden frame supported by six legs with a hard, straw-stuffed cushion. The wall fresco behind him depicted a meadow and trees, possibly the landscape outside the house or a memory of Phillip's former life in the Roman province of Spain. The floor was covered in an ornate mosaic of grapes, grains, and wine.

In a very short time Dismas came into the room, still tying the cincture that closed his tunic. "Simon, my friend, what a welcome surprise," he said warmly.

"Perhaps not as welcome when you learn why I'm here."

"What is it? Has something happened?"

"Marcella overheard that the Romans found out where you are," Simon explained. "We were on our way to warn you when we were stopped by soldiers an hour south of here."

Dismas looked around, as if expecting to see Marcella. "Where is she now?"

"The Romans took her—and Tibro. You know how alike you two are. They believe he is you."

"Surely he corrected them," Dismas said, then frowned. "No, I suppose he didn't. But they would believe Marcella."

"She didn't say anything, either. She wouldn't disobey Tibro's wishes—neither would I. He hopes to give you time to escape before revealing their mistake."

Dismas shook his head resolutely. "They won't care that they've blundered. They aren't stupid; they'll realize what he did and why. I won't let my brother put his life at risk for me. I'm going to Rome to set things right."

Phillip came into the room then with some bread, cheese, and wine.

"And just how do you intend to make things right?" Simon asked as he broke off a chunk of the bread.

"I'll tell them I'm the one they seek and insist they let him go."

"What's to keep them from arresting you both? Isn't that what happened in Ephesus?"

Dismas thought on it for a long moment. Finally he said, "It's a long journey back to Rome. Plenty of time to come up with a plan to assure his release in trade for me."

"Are you sure you want to do that?"

"Yes, I am certain."

"Many are blaming Nero for the fire, and he's determined to redirect their anger. You won't just be held in a prison, Dismas. You will be executed."

Dismas nodded. "If such is the will of God. But I cannot let my brother die in my place."

"Yes, I thought that's what you would do," Simon replied. "Let me finish eating and I will accompany you."

"There's no need to put yourself in danger."

"I will be in no danger," Simon said assuredly.

"Then I welcome your company. Finish your supper. There is something I must prepare for the journey."

———

THE TWO MEN had been walking for an hour, each bearing a staff provided by Phillip, with Dismas carrying a small sack of belongings over his shoulder. The flat paving stones of Via Flaminia gleamed a soft silver under the light of the moon. When they heard the gurgle of a brook, they left the road to slake their thirst.

Looking around, Simon realized they were near where the Roman soldiers had overtaken him earlier. He pointed to a small, grassy knoll. "Let's sit and rest for a spell."

"There's no time for rest," Dismas replied. "I fear we will not arrive in time to save Tibro. If only we had horses or a fast chariot."

"Fear not. We'll arrive in time. But we may not if we don't rest. We are old men now."

Dismas nodded and sighed. "Yes. I don't remember it happening, but I am older than my father."

Simon chuckled.

"Why do you laugh?" Dismas asked as he sat on the ground beside his friend.

"I was thinking of the time we first met. I was on my way to Jerusalem to sell olive oil. I stopped to rest only a few minutes in the shade of a fig tree, but the grass was soft and the shade was cool and I fell asleep." Simon held up a finger. "But sleep was not to be, for my pleasant dreams were interrupted by loud voices."

"Ah, yes, the thieves," Dismas said.

"'Give us your purse and you won't be hurt,' one of them called out. And what did you answer?"

Dismas laughed. "I told them if they wanted my money they were going to have to take it from me. Foolish talk from one man facing three."

"Brave talk, I would say."

"But as it turned out, I wasn't facing them alone. Fortunately for me, you appeared from nowhere, brandishing your staff as if you were Gideon, armed with God's might."

"And together we drove them off," Simon said. "We were much younger then, my friend."

"Yes. It has been a long but very rewarding journey since that day. And every step of the way has been walked in the path of our Lord."

"And you have recorded all of it," Simon noted. Seeing his friend's look of surprise, he gestured at Dismas's sack. "Are you not carrying a scroll bearing the account of your journey?"

"You know of the scroll? But I've told no one of its existence. I'm not even certain I shall ever finish it."

"For many years I have known of the scroll," Simon told him. "Even before you finally began to set it down in writing. You see, each of us is chosen for a task, and your commission, from God, is to write the things you have heard, seen, and experienced. Fifty generations from now, men and women will read and be inspired by your words."

"Two thousand years? Do you think my humble scroll will survive that long?"

"Yes," Simon said without elaboration.

"If, as you say, I was chosen to write this, I wonder why God didn't pick a more skilled or educated man." Dismas gave a small, self-deprecating laugh. "I didn't even write it all in one language but have jumped between tongues as the spirit moved me."

Simon smiled. "Yes, as the *spirit* moved you. For though the hand that holds the pen is yours, the mind that composed the words is animated by God."

"Yes," Dismas said, nodding. "I have often felt that power...and I have been frightened by it."

"It is an awesome thing."

As Dismas stared up at the bright moon, set in a curtain of stars, he felt a shiver run through him. "Simon...I confess that I feel that fear even now. I am reminded that on the night our Lord was betrayed, even he asked that the cup of suffering be taken from him."

"Don't fear the future, Dismas. The appointed time for each of us to leave this Earth is in the hands of God."

"How is it, Simon, that even though you face the same dangers, you always seem at peace...a peace that surpasses all understanding?"

"Perhaps because of this," Simon said cryptically. "Here, let me show you a secret of my own."

Dismas watched with interest as his friend reached under his tunic and withdrew a small leather pouch. Simon loosened the ties, reached inside and removed a patch of cloth, which he gently, reverently unfolded. The cloth was whiter than anything Dismas had seen before and seemed almost iridescent in the moonlight. And it bore a strange-looking mark in the most brilliant of reds.

"This is the blood of Jesus," Simon whispered, "shed on the way to Golgotha."

"But that was over thirty years ago," Dismas said. "See how fresh and new it looks."

"It has remained as fresh as when I tore this cloth from the hem of my shirt and wiped our Lord's brow."

"Then why isn't it all smeared? Instead it looks like...like someone has drawn a sign in blood."

Dismas leaned closer for a better look at the unfamiliar symbol. "What is this strange sign?"

"Our master called it Trevia Dei."

"Trevia Dei?"

"Three paths to God."

Dismas only half-heard as Simon related the story of meeting Jesus on the road to Cyrene after the crucifixion. Instead his attention was fixed on the image on the cloth. As he stared in wonder, the Trevia Dei began to shift and transform into three separate symbols, which slowly lifted into the air and pulled away from one another. The top rotated and formed a crescent moon and star. The pyramid doubled and folded upon itself into a six-pointed star. Finally, the transept of the cross lowered, forming a cross with four arms.

"What is this?" Dismas gasped.

Simon smiled as he pressed the cloth against Dismas's breast and placed his other hand upon Dismas's forehead. "Put your faith in God," he whispered, "and all shall be revealed."

The road and the dark forest grew ever brighter. The change was neither gradual nor sudden. It was as if Dismas had been granted the privilege of seeing a light that had always been there and would forever be present, even in the darkness. Strangely, the light seemed to be flowing outward from Simon's heart. And emblazoned there, over his chest, that same symbol took form. Although Simon's lips did not move, Dismas heard his friend intone the words, "Trevia Dei." Then the light disappeared, and once more they were bathed in the silver glow of the moon.

"Are you ready to resume the journey?" Simon asked.

Dismas felt a renewed strength of body and spirit, and he looked at Simon, knowing they had just been given a glimpse of the glory of God.

"Yes," he said. "I am ready for whatever may come."

FORTY-ONE

DISMAS BAR-DISMAS AND SIMON OF CYRENE WAITED JUST OUTSIDE THE Campagna villa until they saw Rufinus Tacitus depart. Then, praying it was safe, they went to the vestibule entrance and called out to Marcella.

As they had hoped, she came to the door rather than one of the servants. She looked quite distraught and uncharacteristically disheveled, but she managed a faint smile upon seeing Dismas. When she realized Simon accompanied him, she gasped and reached out to touch him. "It—it can't be. You were..."

"Killed?" Simon said with a chuckle. "No, Marcella, I'm no apparition."

"But the soldiers, Horatius and Junius, when they returned, they reported you were dead."

"We'll have to call him Simon the Magician from now on," Dismas put in.

"Please, no," Simon pleaded. "Simon Magus was rebuked by Peter for his false arts. Let's just say those soldiers were mistaken," he said without further explanation.

"May we come in?" Dismas asked.

"Of course...please, excuse me." She moved aside and ushered them into the villa. "I've been so upset, so distracted," she said as she led them into a small sitting room just off the vestibule. "But I'm over-joyed that you're all right." She smiled at Simon, then turned to Dismas and, her voice quavering now, said, "Tibro is in great danger. The Romans have taken him. He's a prisoner of Nero!"

"I know. Is there any further news of him?"

"None. But I'll find out when I reach the palace."

The two men looked at her curiously.

"I was waiting for my husband to leave. I intend to go to Nero and declare my faith—and my love. I shall die at Tibro's side."

"No," Dismas said resolutely. "It won't be necessary for either you or my brother to die. I will surrender myself in exchange for Tibro."

"What if it doesn't work?" Marcella asked. "Remember, once before you tried to trade yourself for a prisoner, but my husband condemned both you and Marcus Antonius."

"Your husband was but a petty governor. Nero is an emperor, and he understands the value of standing by his word. And I will not be so foolhardy as to present myself unannounced but will send an emissary to arrange the transfer." He glanced at Simon, who nodded to indicate he would be carrying out Dismas's plan.

"But even if he does accept your offer, it will mean your death," Marcella said. "And you are too important to the church."

"My time has come, and I am ready."

Dismas opened his sack and placed a cloth-wrapped object on a side table that was well illuminated by a small window. He carefully removed the cloth, revealing a scroll.

Marcella came over to the table. "What's this?"

"This, Marcella, is your destiny. Yours and Tibro's." He unrolled a portion of the scroll and used a small bowl to hold down the end so it wouldn't close back up.

As Marcella leaned closer, she saw that it was completely filled with writing, the Greek letters clear, bold, and very legible:

The Account of Dismas bar-Dismas.
Recorded in his own hand
in the 30th year from
the Death and Resurrection of the Christ,
set down in the City of Rome

at the command of Paul the Apostle
by a Servant and Witness.

"Dismas...you have made a written accounting," Marcella exclaimed. "Oh, what a wonderful thing!"

"Years ago in Ephesus I was charged with the task, and you helped me begin when you provided writing materials in your husband's prison. I have at last completed the work and transcribed it onto this scroll, and now my mission in this lifetime is at an end. All that remains is for this account to be brought to the believers in Jerusalem."

"Then you must leave," Marcella said. "You must leave at once and take it back."

"No, Marcella." Dismas gently touched her hand. "I will not be taking it. This is for you and Tibro to do."

"Why us? Tibro isn't a believer, and I'm not a Jew. Surely this mission should be undertaken by someone else. By yourself."

"No," Simon put in, coming up beside her. "It is vital that you and Tibro carry it to Jerusalem."

"But I don't understand. Why is it so important that we be the ones?"

"I don't know," Simon admitted. "I know only what I have seen—that in order for the scroll to be revealed when it is most needed, you must be the ones."

"Do you also know how we are to accomplish such a thing?" she asked. "I am virtually a prisoner in my own home, and Tibro is an actual prisoner of Nero."

"When the time comes, you'll know what to do," Simon said. "For now, it is only important that you accept this great commission."

Marcella took a deep breath, then let it out slowly as she nodded. "I will do as you request," she vowed. "I don't know how, but I will do it." She reached for the scroll.

"Wait," Dismas said. "There is one final task."

Standing over the scroll, Dismas drew a dagger from beneath his tunic. With his arm extended over the bowl that held down the papyrus, he cut his wrist at the precise spot one of the nails pierced Jesus' flesh. When enough blood had collected in the bowl, he wrapped a cloth around his arm. Then using a pen from his sack and the blood as ink, he drew something at the beginning of the text.

Marcella stared at the strange drawing. "What symbol is that?"

"Trevia Dei," Dismas replied.

"Trevia Dei?" she repeated. "What does that mean?"

"Ask Simon. He is Keeper of the Sign."

She looked up questioningly at Simon.

"It speaks of three great paths to God, but it means that for the believer, all sacred paths ultimately lead to the one true Lord."

As Marcella turned back to the scroll, she saw that Dismas was using what remained of the blood to write something later in the text.

"For some reason I had left a space when I first wrote Simon's name, and now I understand why," Dismas explained. He gestured at the finished work, and Marcella saw that he had drawn a smaller version of the Trevia Dei symbol between the Greek words for "Simon" and "the Cyrene."

When the symbols in blood were dry, Marcella rolled up the scroll, wrapped the cloth around it, and took it to her private chambers. She had just rejoined her friends when they were surprised by her husband's unexpected arrival.

"Rufinus!" Marcella blurted, startled at seeing him in the doorway.

"How did you escape?" Rufinus asked Dismas, ignoring his wife.

"I didn't," Dismas told him. "I was never in custody. The man Nero is holding is my brother."

"He speaks the truth," Marcella said. "Nero has arrested his younger brother, Tibro. And it was Tibro, not Dismas, who saved your life during the fire."

"Tibro?" Rufinus said, stroking his chin. "And is it this Tibro whom you have been meeting at the baths?"

Marcella gasped but didn't answer.

Rufinus held up his hand. "Do you think I didn't know, my dear? That I wouldn't have you watched? I knew from the very beginning that you were seeing another."

"Rufinus, I have never been unfaithful to you."

"If you mean you have never lain with him, I know that, too," Rufinus said dismissively. He laughed, though it held no humor. "In truth, I wouldn't have cared if you had bedded with him. Such trivialities mean nothing to me now." He turned his attention back to Dismas. "You're the man I sentenced to death many years ago, are you not?"

"I am," Dismas replied.

"So, what are we to do with you now? Will you run again and allow your brother to die in your place?"

"No," Dismas said resolutely. "I have come here to correct the error. I intend to surrender myself to Nero in exchange for my brother's life."

"How...Christian of you." Rufinus smirked. "Very well, come with me and I will explain it all."

"No!" Marcella said quickly. "Dismas, remember what happened at Ephesus."

"Yes, I do remember. I shall not go with you."

"As you wish. Whether you die or your brother dies, it makes no difference to me."

"I would make you a bargain, Rufinus Tacitus."

"What sort of bargain?"

"Go to Rome. Get my brother and bring him here so I may see that he is free. When I know he's safe, I will surrender myself to you."

"Why should I do that?"

"Because Nero wants to make scapegoats of Christians, and I am a leader among the believers. I'm certain he would rather have me than an ordinary Jew, which is what he possesses in my brother. Tibro has never professed the faith—he is not a Christian."

Rufinus looked surprised. "Tibro is not a Christian?"

"No, he isn't," Marcella said. "I have tried, many times, to bring him to the Lord, but he will not see."

"And what about you, my dear? Are you a Christian?"

"I am. But you already knew that, didn't you?"

"Of course. I just wanted to see if you would lie to me," Rufinus said. "But I always knew you were incapable of lying, which is why I have never asked you that question before. But whether or not you are a Christian is of no consequence to me. I will deal with you later. For now," he looked over at Dismas, "I accept your offer. I will send a message to the prison and have Tibro brought here. I'll even give you an opportunity for a brotherly goodbye before I take you away forever."

———

TWO HOURS LATER, Rufinus opened the front door to receive Legatus Lucius Calpurnius and three of his soldiers. They led the shackled Tibro bar-Dismas through the villa and out to the peristyle courtyard, where Marcella was standing beside Dismas. He hurried toward his younger brother, but one of the soldiers stepped between them to block the way.

Seeing how the brothers' close resemblance, Calpurnius shook his head and said to Rufinus, "I am sorry, Your Excellency, for the error."

"It has been made right," Rufinus replied.

"Shall I take the prisoner back now?" he asked, indicating Dismas.

"I promised them a short visit," Rufinus said, then looked at Marcella. "And I am a man of my word."

At a signal from Calpurnius, one of his soldiers removed Tibro's chains, and he was turned out into the courtyard.

"Enjoy your visit," Rufinus said. "But not for too long. Dismas has an appointment with the cross, and he is already ten years late. As for any thoughts of escape, there will be a soldier at each exit." He nodded at Calpurnius, who motioned for his men to take up positions in each doorway that led from the villa's inner courtyard.

When Rufinus entered the house and they were at last alone, Tibro embraced his brother and then Marcella. Suddenly he noticed Simon standing near one of the columns, and he called, "You're alive! We thought you were dead."

"I am not, as you can see." Simon approached and grasped Tibro's forearm in friendship.

Tibro turned back to his brother. "Dismas, they told me you're trading your life for mine. Is this true?"

"Yes."

"I won't allow you to—"

"You won't allow me? You are my younger brother, Tibro. It is not for you to allow or disallow me anything."

"Then I will return with you and die at your side."

"But you are not a Christian."

"No, but I am your brother. And I am a Jew, and like you, I oppose Rome."

Dismas put his hand on Tibro's shoulder. "I know you do this out of love, but if you truly love me, you will live for me. You must live, for there is something I would have you do."

"I will do anything you ask," Tibro said, "except stand by and watch them murder you."

"I have given Marcella a scroll. The two of you must deliver it to the apostles still in Jerusalem. If you cannot give it to them, hide it in a safe place so it won't fall into the hands of nonbelievers and be destroyed."

"But I am one of those nonbelievers, my brother. How do you know I will not destroy it?"

"Because you are a man of honor, and if you give me your word to protect this scroll, I know you will do so." Seeing his brother hesitate, Dismas pulled him close and whispered into his ear, "You must do this not only for me, but for Marcella. This is her only chance—your only chance to be together. If through stubborn pride you refuse, what do you think will become of her? Do you want her to share my fate? She is your wife in spirit, Tibro. Your duty lies with her."

Dismas kissed his brother hard on each cheek, then pulled back and released him.

Tibro looked between Dismas and Marcella, then nodded. "I will do as you ask. I give my word." He turned to Simon. "And what of you? Will you accompany us to Jerusalem?"

"I am going to Rome with Dismas," Simon announced.

"No, Simon," Dismas said. "You mustn't place yourself in danger over me."

"I am in no danger," Simon declared. "They will not see me."

"How will you hide from them?"

"There are ways to walk without being seen." Simon turned to Marcella. "Did you not think it strange that your husband took no notice of me when he returned home? And Calpurnius—he made no mention of seeing an apparition come back to life."

Just then, Rufinus, Calpurnius, and the soldiers came back into the courtyard. One of the soldiers was carrying the set of irons that had been on Tibro, and he signaled for Dismas to extend his hands. Dismas complied, and the shackles were locked in place.

"Move," Calpurnius ordered Dismas. "I wish to reach Rome before nightfall."

As Calpurnius gave the order, Simon walked directly in front of him, blocking his view of Dismas. But the officer took no notice, as if he were staring right through a specter. Simon continued past him, then looked back at his friends and smiled.

"They will not see me," he repeated, and indeed Calpurnius, Rufinus, and the soldiers neither saw him nor heard anything he said.

As the soldiers led Dismas—with Simon following—back through the villa and out to the larger contingent of troops on horseback outside, Rufinus signaled Calpurnius to remain behind. "Please stay a moment with one of your soldiers," he told the officer. "I have need of you."

"Very well, Your Excellency," Calpurnius replied, then called to one of his men, "Darius, you remain here. Send the prisoner on his way with the others. We'll catch up with them shortly."

When Calpurnius and Darius returned to the courtyard, Rufinus pointed at Tibro and ordered, "Bring him inside."

"But you promised to set him free!" Marcella cried out as the two soldiers approached.

"Bring him inside," he repeated, ignoring her.

Darius grabbed hold of one arm, and when Tibro tried to pull free, Calpurnius struck him across the face with the hilt of his sword, stunning him. They hoisted him between them and hauled him into the villa.

Marcella hurried after them as Tibro was dragged down the hall to the same room where Dismas had given her the scroll. It was hidden away, but as she entered the room, she saw with alarm that Dismas's knife was still lying beside the bowl that had contained his blood. Fearful that Rufinus would notice and ask questions, she moved in front of the table, shielding the bloody knife from view.

"Hold him right there," Rufinus said as he entered the room and walked over to a cabinet.

Tibro, still dazed from Calpurnius's blow, shook his head to clear it as he squirmed weakly in their tight grip.

"He saved your life, Rufinus. You promised to let him go," Marcella implored.

"You would like that, wouldn't you? Then you could run off with him. Well, my dear, that isn't going to happen." He opened the cabinet door and removed a short broadsword.

"What are you going to do?" she asked anxiously.

"What I should have done a long time ago. I am going to kill your lover."

Rufinus raised the sword as he moved past Marcella. In desperation, she reached behind her and grabbed Dismas's knife. Rufinus glimpsed her movement as she brought it around, and she found herself standing face to face with him, the knife tip inches from his chest.

Rufinus looked down at the blade, then up at his wife, and he started to laugh. "Go on, woman," he declared, lowering his broadsword. "Plunge it in my heart. Isn't that what your Jesus teaches you to do?"

Her hand shook as she looked between her husband and the man she loved, who hung unconscious in the grip of the Romans. She tried to speak, to cry out, but no sound would come. Her eyes welled with tears as the knife began to slip from her fingers.

"Just as I thought," Rufinus declared, swatting her hand with the hilt of his sword and sending the blade clattering across the room. "You are of no more worth to me, woman. You are no longer my wife."

He drew back the broadsword, his jaw tightening as he prepared to thrust it into her chest. Suddenly he staggered forward, his eyes widening with shock. He opened his mouth to speak, but blood trickled from the corner of his mouth. He dropped to his knees in front of her, his left hand clawing at her stola as he toppled facedown on the floor, the hilt of a dagger protruding from his back.

In his place, Marcella saw the figure of a man who had just come rushing into the room. It was Gaius of Ephesus, and he seemed shocked by what he had done as he stood frozen in place, rubbing his blooding hands.

Calpurnius had already released his grip on Tibro's arm, and he drew his sword and moved toward Gaius. "Bastard!" he cursed. "You killed the *curia lector!*"

Tibro was hanging limply in Darius's arms, but suddenly he shoved the soldier aside, knocking him to the floor. Leaping forward, he snatched up the sword Rufinus had dropped and, swinging it in a wide arc, slashed through Calpurnius's thigh, just below the armor.

Surprised by the attack, Calpurnius spun his own sword around. He was even more shocked to see the flash of metal as Tibro thrust the sword tip into the soft flesh at the base of the soldier's throat, just above the breastplate. Tibro was in so close that Calpurnius only struck him weakly with the hilt of his sword. Then the Roman slid to the floor, gurgling as the life flowed out of him.

Even as Calpurnius was falling, Tibro whirled toward the other soldier, who was already bolting through the doorway. He chased Darius outside and sent him running down the road.

Racing back into the room, Tibro embraced Marcella, who fell into his arms and stood weeping on his shoulder. As he held her close, he felt something release from within her—and from within him, as well. It was as if all distance between them had disappeared, as if this were the very first time they had embraced. He knew with a certainty that they would never again be parted, in this life or the one to come.

Tibro looked over at Gaius, who seemed to be coming back to his senses. "That was a brave thing you did."

"I...I killed him," Gaius muttered, staring down at Rufinus's lifeless body.

"You saved our lives. In the eyes of God—and we worship the same God—what you did was right." He paused a moment, then added, "But we must be away now. That soldier will bring others back with him."

With Gaius following, Tibro led Marcella from the villa, away from the scene of death.

FORTY-TWO

The morning after Fr. Michael Flannery was rescued from the catacombs at the Mount of Olives, Sarah Arad met him and Preston Lewkis at the antiquities laboratory. The building had been closed following the raid, but Sarah had no trouble gaining access due to her position as a special agent of YAMAM, Israel's elite counter-terrorism unit.

As Sarah and her companions headed down the hallway to the lab where Daniel Mazar was shot, she paused a moment to speak with the head police officer on duty.

"Lieutenant Lefkovitz," she said, reading the man's ID tag, "Might we view the security camera videotape?"

Lefkovitz shook his head. "I'm sorry, Agent Arad, but there was no tape."

"That can't be. There's a security camera in the lab."

"Yes, but there was no tape in the machine. Evidently it hadn't been loaded."

"I see," she replied. "Can we have some time alone in the lab? We'll follow protocol."

He looked at her dubiously but thought better than to deny admittance to a member of YAMAM. "Just take precautions." He gestured at a table in the hallway just outside the lab. On it were boxes of surgical gloves and paper slippers, as well as evidence bags and other items needed by the forensics teams.

Lefkovitz walked over to the lab and peered inside to confirm no one was on hand, then turned back to Sarah. "If you need me, I'll be at the front station." He headed back down the hallway.

"What do we do first?" Preston asked as he donned the shoe coverings and gloves.

"Find the scroll," she replied.

"I expect it's still here somewhere," Flannery said as he also donned the protective wear.

"Why do you say that?"

"Well, Via Dei had information it was in the lab, but all they found was the urn we recovered last night. Somehow they overlooked it."

"We'll soon find out," Sarah said as she led them in.

The door of the safe remained open, as it had been when Mazar's body was found. Sarah carefully examined the interior, then turned back to them, shaking her head.

"It's completely empty. And there's no way they could have overlooked the scroll, had it been here."

"Perhaps they lied to you," Preston said to Flannery. "Maybe they had it all the time and were testing you, to see if you'd be willing to turn it over."

"I don't think so. No, if they had the scroll, they wouldn't have gone to all that effort to kidnap me. They wouldn't have needed me to join them."

"I agree," Sarah said, standing away from the safe. "There's only one other explanation. Someone else with access to the safe removed it before the raid."

"Such as whom?" Preston asked.

"Me, for one." She grinned. "As security officer on this project, I had access to one of the two combinations." She saw their confused expressions and added, "Don't worry, I didn't take the scroll. I was just making a point. I know that combination, and it's on file at headquarters and might have been compromised. Professors Mazar and Vilnai knew the other combination."

"Maybe they forced Daniel to open the safe," Preston offered.

"Perhaps, but why then kill him?" she mused aloud. "I mean, when they realized the scroll was missing, wouldn't they try to use him to discover its location? The same way they tried to use you, Father?"

"Maybe Daniel hid it," Flannery suggested. "If he realized the lab was under attack, he might not have trusted the safe."

"Then where is it? Our people have been all through this laboratory."

She walked around the room, taking care where she stepped so as not to compromise any evidence. She stopped by a small wall panel in the corner of the room and swung open the door. On a shelf inside was a VCR. It was turned on, and she pressed the eject button several times to confirm there was no videotape inside.

"There's something strange here," she muttered. "This VCR captures images from the camera over there." She indicated a security camera above the door. "Lieutenant Lefkovitz said that someone must've forgotten to load the tape, but no one ever loads or unloads this VCR. The same tape continually recycles. It's an endless loop that records six hours and then erases the earlier recording. It's a pretty simple system and usually quite effective."

"Unless someone knows where the VCR is located," Preston put in.

"Precisely. The people who killed Professor Mazar must've known about the system and taken it."

Flannery was not listening to their conversation but was examining something that had caught his eye. He called the others over and said to Sarah, "When you mentioned a security camera, I looked in the wrong place and saw this one over here. Is it connected to the same VCR?"

Sarah saw a small Web cam wedged between some books on a shelf over one of the workstations. "It's not part of the security system." Moving the books aside for a closer inspection, she followed the cable from the shelf and behind the workstation desk to where it was plugged into the USB port of the computer on the floor. "This computer is turned on," she said in surprise, standing back up.

"No it isn't," Preston said. "They're all shut down."

"Not this one." She examined the monitor. "Someone turned off the screen but left the CPU running."

She pressed the monitor's power button. It crackled with static electricity, and slowly the screensaver appeared. She clicked the mouse button, and the swirling pattern disappeared, revealing the PC desktop behind.

"There's a Web cam capture program. It's still launched, but it must've timed out and shut down."

Moving the cursor, she clicked the "back" button to jump to the start of the recording, then clicked "play."

At first, all they saw was a pair of hands looming large in the foreground. Then the hands pulled back, revealing Daniel Mazar adjusting the camera on the shelf.

"SARAH," Yuri Vilnai said as he appeared in the laboratory doorway. "I'm glad you sent for me. I tried to come earlier, but those fools out front wouldn't let me pass. Obviously you've got more pull with the police."

"Yes," Sarah replied, "Please come in."

"The scroll—have you found it?" he asked eagerly.

"How did you know it was missing?"

"It was the first thing I checked for when I came in here and found poor Daniel dead."

"You mean you looked in the safe?"

"Certainly. But it wasn't there, so I figured it was inside the urn, and that's what his killers must've been carrying from the building."

"How do you suppose they got it?" Sarah pressed. "I mean, the safe was locked, wasn't it?"

"I assume so. Perhaps they forced Daniel to open it."

"But he only had one combination."

Vilnai looked a bit sheepish. "I believe Daniel could have opened the safe without difficulty had he needed to."

"Just as you could," Sarah said without elaboration. "But never mind that. To answer your first question, no, we haven't found the scroll. But we did find something else."

"Really? What else matters but the scroll?" He looked at Preston and Flannery, who stood watching him in silence.

"You might want to take a look at this," Sarah said, walking over to the workstation. She clicked the mouse, restarting the video Daniel Mazar had captured.

"What is this? What's going on?" Vilnai asked as the image of the professor adjusting the Web cam appeared.

"Just watch," Sarah replied.

Vilnai dropped almost woodenly into the chair in front of the computer. On the screen, Mazar began speaking, his voice somewhat thin and reedy through the computer speaker.

The recording began with Mazar's phone call asking Preston to hurry to the lab. When Preston asked if something had happened, Mazar replied, *"It's not what has happened but what is going to happen. That is, if I am correct."*

"Correct about what? Daniel, my friend, you're being very, very mysterious. What's all this about?"

"If I told you, you'd think I was crazy. You'll have to see for yourself."

"Will it wait until I get there?"

"It's waited two thousand years—I suppose it can wait another hour."

Following that call, Mazar continued with his work on the computer, all the while providing a running narration:

"I'm working with a photocopy of the scroll, because it is necessary for me to make some annotations in order to bring out the code."

"The code? What code?" Vilnai asked, interrupting the playback.

"Shh," Sarah said. "Just listen."

"Some may be familiar with the work of my colleague, Dr. Eliyahu Rips, one of the world's leading experts in group theory, a field of mathematics that underlies quantum physics. Dr. Rips discovered a hidden code in the Torah that appears to reveal the details of events thousands of years after the scriptures were written.

"Amazingly, I have found just such a code, embedded in the Hebrew portions of our Dismas scroll. One entry says that the scroll will lie buried in the 'mountain of Jewish patriots' until it is time for it to be revealed. The date of that revelation, given in the Hebrew calendar, coincides with the very day the scroll was unearthed on Masada. Even more incredible, the coded message says that the Gospel will be coveted by many, and that not long after its discovery, it will be snatched back into the darkness by human hands. The length of time between the discovery of the scroll and its disap-

pearance was given in days and revealed that it would be stolen this very day."

On the monitor, Mazar was seen looking up into the camera.

"I don't know if such messages are warnings or absolute predictions, but working on the theory it is a warning, I plan to remove the scroll from its normal place."

Yuri Vilnai stared at the screen as if hypnotized, watching as Mazar was interrupted by a banging noise that grew into the unmistakable sound of gunfire. He saw the professor rush away from the workstation, heard the lab door opening and closing, listened transfixed as Mazar exclaimed, *"My God! The prophecy is true!"*

As the video played out, Vilnai saw Mazar head toward to the safe, which was off camera, then reappear soon after with the scroll. He was just in view at the very edge of the screen as he removed one of the file cabinet drawers and placed the scroll inside, then replaced the drawer.

Vilnai spun around toward the filing cabinet. The drawer was on the floor, and nothing was visible inside.

"Keep watching," Sarah said, gesturing at the monitor.

Vilnai started to shake as Mazar said directly into the camera, *"I fear this will be my last words on this Earth. Take care of the scroll. Protect it with your lives. It is that important."*

A moment later the gunmen burst into the room, and the final moments of Daniel Mazar's life played out as they shot him at point-blank range, opened the safe, and made their escape.

Still shaking, Vilnai stood and backed away from the computer. "Daniel...he recorded his own death," he said, his voice breaking.

"Wait," Sarah said. "There's more."

"No, turn it off. I don't want to see any more."

"Are you sure?"

"I...please..." Vilnai slumped into a chair and covered his face with his hands. "Please," he begged, his voice muffled. "Turn it off."

Sarah stopped the program. "Why, Dr. Vilnai?" she asked. When he didn't respond, she continued, "You realize that the recording shows everything, don't you? What the two of you said...what you did to him... how you later stole the security videotape to cover up your crime."

Vilnai still did not speak.

"Why did you kill him?"

"I had nothing to do with the raid," Vilnai blurted, his eyes wide with fright as he looked up at her. "I want you to know that. I swear, I had nothing to do with it."

"But you did kill him," Preston said, coming closer.

Vilnai nodded, tears streaming down his cheeks. "Yes. Yes, I killed him."

"I ask you again. Why?" Sarah pressed.

"He was going to die anyway. His wounds were so terrible. He was barely hanging on."

"But it was life that he was hanging onto," Flannery said. "You had no right to play God."

"You don't understand. Nobody does," Vilnai said. "It was Daniel who made the mistake with the ossuary of James. He authenticated it. It was his sloppy research. I proved he was in error, but was I heralded for this? Quite the opposite. People thought I had stabbed a colleague in the back. And Daniel, despite his error, still commanded more respect than I did."

"So you killed him?" Preston said incredulously.

"When he told me about the Torah code...I couldn't bear that he would get all the credit. Posthumously, no less. I would always remain in his shadow. No, better for him to remain quiet, while I carried on his work."

"You are under arrest, Dr. Yuri Vilnai, for the murder of Dr. Daniel Mazar," Sarah said authoritatively.

"I...I won't resist," Vilnai said faintly.

"Things may go easier for you if you'll turn over the scroll," she added.

Vilnai looked up in surprise. "What do you mean?"

"The scroll," Preston said. "What did you do with it?"

"I didn't do anything with the scroll. Wasn't it in that filing cabinet?"

Sarah shook her head. "It wasn't there."

"Then the terrorists must have gotten it."

"No," she said. "It's clear from the video that they left without it. Someone returned to the room and removed it from the filing cabinet after the recording timed out."

"I swear to you, I don't know where the scroll is," Vilnai protested.

"Why should we believe you?" Preston asked.

"I have just confessed to murder. Do you think I would confess to murder, but lie about a theft?"

"I wouldn't put that or anything else past you," Preston said, his voice dripping with disdain.

"We'll worry about that later," Sarah declared. "Now it's time for the professor to take a ride down to police headquarters and get used to his future surroundings."

―――

TWO HOURS LATER, a woman punched in a number on her cell phone. When the other party picked up, she said, "Hello, Father Flannery. This is Azra Haddad. You are looking for the Gospel of Dismas, are you not?"

"Azra?" Flannery replied. "Who told you it was missing?"

"You seek the scroll, do you not?"

"Yes. Yes, we're looking for it."

"I have some information you may find helpful."

"What do you mean?" Flannery asked. "Do you know where it is?"

"Meet me at four-thirty this afternoon," Azra told him. "But this information is only for you. Please, bring no one along, and tell no one else about the meeting."

"Where shall we meet?"

"At the Masada dig," she replied. "But you must come alone."

There was a slight pause, and then Flannery said, "I'll be there. Alone."

Turning off her cell phone, Azra stood and walked over to a table in the corner of one of the monk's cells at the former Monastery of the Way of the Lord. Spread out on the table was a long scroll of papyrus. Ever so carefully, she began rolling up the Gospel of Dismas bar-Dismas.

FORTY-THREE

DISMAS BAR-DISMAS'S BACK ACHED FROM STANDING ON THE STONE FLOOR for so long. Before dawn he had been dragged from the prison to a great hall in the palace, where he joined Peter, Paul, and dozens of other Christians who had been rounded up and brought together for trial. Their prosecutor was Emperor Nero himself, who also served as judge and jury. They were not allowed a defense attorney.

Nero looked nothing like prosecutor or judge or even emperor. Instead he wore the gaudy costume of a stage performer, his hair perfumed and bleached, his cheeks colored with rouge.

"Do you know how many died because of your deceit?" Nero asked as he strode back and forth in front of the defendants. "Do you know how many have been made homeless because of your evilness? Do you know how many beautiful statues and works of art were destroyed by the treachery of you...Christians?"

Nero dragged out the word, as if it were unclean.

"You are the one called Peter?" he asked as he stopped in front of an old, gaunt man with a curly black beard and eyebrows so thin they were almost invisible.

Peter looked Nero directly in the eye. "Yes, I am."

Nero seemed discomfited by the prisoner's unflinching gaze, and he lifted his hand in front of his face and examined his own fingernails. They glistened purple from the paint he had recently applied. Without looking back at Peter, he continued his interrogation.

"And you have been preaching of this man Jesus? He is dead, is he not? Why would you worship a god who is dead?"

"He was dead, yet he lives," Peter declared.

Nero chuckled. "Yes, I have heard that you claim he rose from the dead. Do you actually believe that?"

"I, myself, saw his resurrected body."

"You saw it, did you?" Nero scoffed. He turned again to the prisoner. "Tell me this. If by renouncing this false prophet you could spare your life, would you do so?"

"No."

"Remember, I have the power of life and death. Do you want to die?"

"Death has no dominion over those who have accepted Jesus," Peter replied.

"A courageous statement. But you will regret such bravado when you feel the nails bite into your flesh."

Moving down the line, Nero stopped before several other prisoners, offering them the same opportunity to spare their lives by a public renunciation of Jesus. Not one person accepted his offer of clemency.

"I don't understand," he told the last one in line. "I have made a good-faith offer to spare the lives of any who renounce your god, yet none of you accepted. Why is that?"

"Your offer would save our bodies but cannot redeem our souls," the prisoner replied. "And while life on Earth is temporary, the soul is eternal."

"And you are...?"

"I am Dismas bar-Dismas."

"I have heard of you. Your father died on the cross alongside Jesus, did he not?"

"That is true."

"Then, like father, like son," Nero quipped, giggling at his own wit. "Quintus, hand me my lyre."

He reached toward a heavily made up and very feminine-looking young man, who brought over the musical instrument.

"Such a beautiful boy," Nero said admiringly. Then to the prisoners, "Now I shall play and sing for you."

> *"Guarded from winds that sigh*
> *You watch the solitary hours flee.*
> *Ivy wrapped columns rise on high*
> *Surrounding statues of me.*
>
> *"Scattered stones upon the trail,*
> *Guide your feet along their way.*
> *You have made your own travail*
> *And come to this, your judgment day."*

――――――

LATER THAT MORNING, Tibro and Marcella returned to the Campagna villa to retrieve the hidden scroll and gather items for their journey to Jerusalem. After confirming the bodies of Rufinus and Calpurnius had been removed the night before and no soldiers were on hand, Tibro led Marcella into the now-vacant home, abandoned even by the servants.

"Don't take too much," Tibro cautioned as she began packing. "It's a long journey, most of it on foot."

"I'm sorry," Marcella said, putting aside some of the clothes she had gathered. "I'm used to traveling with servants and transportation."

He chuckled. "Your days as a highborn Roman citizen are no more. I hope you won't miss them too much."

"I won't miss them at all," Marcella promised. "I am happy to put Rome behind me." She sighed. "And I will be happy to be away from this place."

"There is one more thing I wish to do before we leave Rome," Tibro said.

"I know." She placed her hand upon his. "You want to rescue Dismas. But Tibro, we are both wanted for murder. We have taken a great risk just by returning here. And it will be Nero's own prison where he is held; I have no access to it as I did the prison in Ephesus."

"Of course you are right. Still, I feel as if I'm betraying him."

"But you aren't." Marcella held up the scroll. "Your brother has charged you with a mission he holds as dear to his heart as life itself. If we succeed in getting this to Jerusalem, you will not be betraying but serving him."

"I hope you're right." He slung the straps of their two travel sacks over his shoulder. "Are you ready?"

Marcella tucked the scroll in a smaller bag and slipped the strap over her head. She took a final look around the room. The villa had belonged to her parents, and she had spent many happy hours there as a young girl. She tried to hold those images in her mind and not the darker memories of recent days.

"Yes," she said, nodding. "I am ready."

As they headed back through the villa, they heard footsteps in the vestibule, and Tibro pulled Marcella into a darkened anteroom and signaled for her to be quiet. Lowering the travel sacks to the floor, he drew a dagger from his belt and edged closer to the door. He peered down the hallway, waiting to see if the Roman soldiers had returned to search the premises.

A man emerged from the vestibule, and Tibro ducked away from the door, then suddenly realized who he had seen. Sheathing his knife, he stepped out from the anteroom and called, "Gaius!"

Startled, the man seemed ready to run, then he cocked his head and stared at the figure in the hall. "Tibro?"

"I thought you returned home."

"Yes," Gaius replied as he came over to Tibro, and Marcella joined them in the hallway. "But I decided to try to see Dismas at the prison before they discovered those bodies and things got even more complicated." He looked nervous as he gestured toward the room where he had killed Rufinus Tacitus the night before.

"The bodies are gone," Tibro reassured him. "The soldier who escaped must've returned with others and retrieved them."

"Did you see Dismas?" Marcella asked eagerly.

Gaius nodded. "A few gold coins smoothed my way past the night guards."

"How is he?"

"Strong...and resolute. He's ready for whatever the Lord plans for him."

"It's Nero's plans that concern me," Tibro commented.

"We'll know that soon enough. He was taken for trial this very morning."

"Then why aren't you there?"

"No one is allowed at the trial. Nero himself is conducting it."

"Is there nothing we can do?" Marcella asked.

"Not now," Gaius replied. "Perhaps after things quiet down in a few days, Nero can be persuaded to show mercy. He is fond of condemning a man only to later grant pardon—provided a suitable ransom is offered. And our community will raise more than enough to tempt even an emperor."

"What brought you back here today?" Tibro asked. "Were you looking for us."

"Well, yes," Gaius said a bit uncertainly. "And something else."

"What is it?" Tibro pressed.

"Dismas spoke of a scroll. He said he asked you to carry it to Jerusalem."

Tibro glanced at Marcella, debating how much he was at liberty to reveal.

"You do have Dismas's scroll, don't you?" Gaius asked.

Tibro nodded. "And you came here to take it."

"Why, yes, of course," Gaius admitted, looking a bit surprised at Tibro's accusatory tone. "I mean, what if something had happened after we parted? The soldiers might have arrested you—or worse. And no matter our own fate, the Gospel of Dismas must be protected."

"It will be," Tibro assured him.

"Then we must bring it to Rome. The faithful will be eager to read what—"

"We are taking it to Jerusalem."

"Of course, just as Dismas wishes. But first we must make copies. The original will be hidden and preserved, and in a few days you'll carry the very first copy to the apostles in Jerusalem."

"Not a copy, but this one," Tibro declared, pointing to the small bag Marcella carried. "And not in a few days, but right now."

"But that is madness."

"I made a vow to my brother."

"The journey is too dangerous. The scroll could be lost forever. Surely Dismas wouldn't want that."

"Did he say that?" Marcella asked. "Was this his idea?"

Gaius hesitated, then smiled and began to nod. "Yes, yes, it is his desire. When I suggested this course of action, he urged me to find you and give you his assent."

Tibro's expression hardened, his green eyes flashing with anger. "Lying doesn't become a Christian like you." He turned to Marcella. "Come, we've a long journey ahead."

"But you mustn't!" Gaius exclaimed, and he continued to protest as Tibro retrieved their travel sacks. When it became clear Tibro wouldn't be dissuaded, he said, "If you must go, at least let me see it. Dismas told me of the scroll, so surely he wouldn't object to my seeing it."

He directed his plea to Marcella, who recognized the genuine longing in his eyes and finally turned to Tibro and said, "For just a few minutes."

Tibro started to object, then sighed and nodded.

They moved to the well-lit vestibule, where Marcella unwrapped the cloth-covered scroll and placed it on a marble side table. As she slowly unrolled the papyrus, Gaius leaned closer, his hand shaking as he followed the text with his forefinger. He read silently, his lips forming the words as he hurried through the document, as if trying to commit to memory as much as possible.

"It is time," Tibro said after about ten minutes. "We aren't safe here; we must be on our way." He started to roll up the scroll.

"One moment. There is something that confuses me." He pointed to the red symbol Dismas had drawn at the beginning of the document. "This sign...what does it mean?"

"He called it the Trevia Dei," Marcella explained.

"Three roads to God? I don't understand."

"Nor do we," Tibro snapped, rolling up the remainder of the scroll and wrapping the cloth around it. "Get my brother out of that prison and he can tell you about it."

"Go to Simon," Marcella told Gaius. "The Master himself made him Keeper of the Sign." She returned the scroll to her bag and slung it over her shoulder.

"And now we must be away," Tibro said.

He started forward, but Gaius blocked his path and said, "I must ask you once more...let me bring this gospel to our people for safe-keeping."

Tibro noticed Gaius's right hand on the hilt of his dagger. He stared at the weapon a long moment, then looked up at Gaius. "Are you so desperate that you would desecrate Dismas's gospel with the blood of his own brother? And this good Christian?" he added, indicating Marcella.

She reached forward and placed a gentle hand on Gaius's. "Let any Christian blood that is spilled be at the hands of Nero, not each other." Feeling Gaius's grip on the knife ease, she withdrew her hand. "Return to Rome," she told him, her smile warm and sincere. "I fear Dismas is in need of you today. And worry not about the scroll. Dismas has already had a vision of it safe in Jerusalem."

She took Tibro's arm and walked with him into the front garden, leaving Gaius of Ephesus watching from the vestibule doorway.

————

IT WAS late morning as Tibro and Marcella walked down Via Appia, which would take them from Rome to Capua and onward by sea to Greece and regions to the east. There were many others traveling along the road, and Tibro guessed that most were Christians fleeing the persecutions Nero had unleashed back in the city.

Tibro sensed Marcella's fear, and he wanted to embrace her and promise to protect her. He believed that he could, under most circum-stances. But there was no way to protect her from the Roman army, should their flight be discovered.

Suddenly Tibro felt very small and insignificant. It was a feeling magnified a thousandfold as they crested a small rise and gazed upon the spectacle ahead.

"My God!" Marcella gasped, covering her mouth.

Even Tibro was stunned as he looked out upon a seemingly endless line of T-shaped crosses, stretching along both sides of the road and disappearing in the distance. For an instant he thought they bore the bodies of all the Christians Nero had sworn to execute. But they were empty, and he remembered that they stood as silent witnesses to the six thousand slaves Spartacus had led in a failed uprising almost one hundred fifty years before.

That they were empty did little to erase the revulsion he felt, and he shuddered as he looked away and wrapped Marcella in his arms. They stood a long moment, gathering strength together, then turned back to the road and continued their journey in the shadows of the crucified.

———

TWENTY-FOUR HOURS after Tibro and Marcella passed beneath the crosses on the Appian Way, three hundred of them were no longer empty. They had again been put into service of the emperor, bearing the tortured figures of Christians suffering their final, excruciating torment.

Absent from the group was Paul of Tarsus. Being a citizen of Rome, he had been spared the ordeal of crucifixion, though not the sentence of death. He was beheaded, even before his companions were sent to the cross.

As Dismas was tied to the crossbeam and nails were driven into his wrists and ankles, he told himself that he had cheated the cross in Ephesus, and now that debt must be repaid. He took heart from the joy he had seen in Paul's eyes as the apostle had faced the executioner and prepared to face his Lord.

Dismas clenched his teeth with each blow of the soldier's hammer, determined not to cry out. When he could bear the pain no longer, he closed his eyes and prayed first to Jesus and then to his own father, who had been promised a place in Heaven. He felt something like a hand caressing his forehead, and the sharp pain grew duller, his arms and legs turning numb.

As the worst of the pain subsided, he opened his eyes and looked over at the cross beside him. The old, frail apostle Peter had been dragged there by two of the soldiers and was about to suffer Dismas's fate.

Seeing the way Peter was arguing with the soldiers, Dismas recalled how, on the night Jesus was arrested, the apostle had denied three times that he knew Jesus. Was it possible that Peter, facing a similar death, had lost faith and was again denying the Lord to save his own life? But Dismas's heart soared with pride at the courage of his spiritual leader when he heard why the old man was protesting.

"No!" Peter shouted. "I'm not worthy of dying in the same manner as my Lord. Please, I beg of you, when you place me on the cross, hang me upside down."

"Upside down?" one of the soldiers repeated and laughed. "This old fool wants to look at the ground," he told his partner. "Let's not disappoint him."

Dismas turned away, feeling it was somehow immodest to watch his friend and teacher suffer this final indignity. When the soldiers had finished their work and moved off to carry out the next execution, Dismas looked over at Peter. The old man's legs were spread apart, his ankles nailed to the crossbeam. His hands were drawn together over his head and nailed at the wrists to the base of the upright post.

"Peter..." Dismas called, his voice weak as he struggled to catch his breath.

The old man opened his eyes and smiled at Dismas. He managed a nod of the head, and he moved his lips to speak, but no words emerged. Dismas blinked his eyes against the sweat that was running down his face as he struggled to make out what Peter was saying.

"Praise the Lord," Peter silently mouthed. Then he closed his eyes and the breath went out of him. His suffering was over.

Dismas knew that his own death, in this upright position, would not come so quickly.

As he returned his thoughts to the passion of Jesus and his own father, he felt the rest of his body growing numb and cold. He could hear people calling out in despair as they hung from their own cross, and he was aware of the sobs of grief from those who had gathered in the road to wait out the sufferings of friends and loved ones. There were others on hand who were not so sympathetic to the victims' plight. Some looked on with morbid fascination, relishing the spectacle. Others were curious but detached, as unmoved as if they were watching a flock of birds perched in the trees.

Dismas turned his head as far as he could and stared down along the long line of crosses. So many martyrs. So many new saints would be welcomed in Heaven this day.

When Dismas looked back down, he saw several of his family of believers gathered around Gaius of Ephesus, whom they were restraining from coming closer. Their concern was well-founded, for a soldier approached and accused them of being Christians. Realizing the danger they faced, Gaius composed himself and told the soldier they had nothing to do with the sect, and the others voiced their assent. The lie saddened Dismas, but he forgave them their weakness and gave a silent blessing.

The soldier ordered the group to disperse or face a similar fate, and as Gaius led them away, he looked a final time at Dismas. The older man smiled and nodded, as if to say, *My time is at an end; you must now lead our flock.*

"He shall lead them into darkness, for he has not your understanding," a voice said, and Dismas looked down at the foot of the cross to see Simon of Cyrene standing at the edge of the road. Apparently no one else could see or hear him, for the Roman soldiers passed in front of him several times without taking the slightest notice.

Simon's expression bore love rather than pity, hope rather than horror. Although he spoke no words aloud, his voice could be heard resonating within Dismas's mind and heart. Such communication could not be silenced by the mere destruction of a man's flesh, Dismas realized as he closed his eyes and listened.

While the many paths to God are but one, Gaius would see only his own and deny all others. Via Dei—the one path to God—all-embracing, it brings salvation, but wielded as a weapon, it brings destruction.

Dismas tried to understand what his friend was saying. Via Dei? But hadn't he called it Trevia Dei?

It shall all happen as the Master warned. His teachings shall be twisted, until the many paths that are one becomes the one path that denies all others. It has already begun, as it was written and as it must be.

"But you must stop them," Dismas pleaded. "Go to Gaius and the others. Tell them of their error."

There is no error. As the Master proclaimed, 'He who has ears to hear, let him hear.' But do not fear, my friend. The true message is always there to be heard. And in time, it will be revealed for all the world to see. You have made it so, by your very hand. And so, my friend, your pain and suffering will soon be over, and you will be in a place far more beautiful than this. You will be home.

Dismas saw now that Simon was not alone. A man in unfamiliar black garb, with some sort of stiff white collar, was at his side. This curiously dressed man was looking on with horror and bewilderment as he witnessed the spectacle of the mass crucifixion.

Dismas turned to Simon, trying to understand who this stranger was. As death approached, he began to find answers, not only to this mystery, but to every question he had ever voiced. As he looked a final time down the Appian Way, the distances shrank, and he could see beyond the horizon to where Tibro and Marcella were journeying, then farther still to the very walls of Jerusalem.

His vision traversed not only distance but time. He observed the apostles still living, and leaders of the Church not yet born. Events of past, present, and future flashed before his inner eye, and he realized, without knowing how, that this man in black garb and white collar lived in that distant place and time. And he was no longer a stranger to Dismas but a dear and welcome friend.

The images grew lighter, brighter, the details less distinct as they filled with a radiance Dismas could perceive with each of his senses. The last earthly image he recognized was a fortress upon a tall desert plateau. *Masada? Why Masada?* he wondered. And there, under the walls of the fortress, lay the bodies of the dead, their final prayers still rising to the heavens:

> *Yeetgadal v' yeetkadash sh'mey rabbah*
> *B'almah dee v'rah kheer'utey*

And there amid so much death and destruction stood the man in black, his arms cradling Dismas's scroll.

Yes, Dismas sighed as a final understanding filled his awareness. *It is finished. And so it begins.*

FORTY-FOUR

Fr. Michael Flannery jerked upright in the chair, waking himself up. Looking around, he realized he was in his room at the hotel. He must have dozed off, and he turned quickly to the clock on the bed stand. Only a few minutes had passed; he still had plenty of time to drive to Masada and meet Azra Haddad at four-thirty.

He started to stand but felt drained and dizzy. An image flashed in his memory—the remembrance of a dream. *The passion of the Lord?* he wondered as he recalled a fleeting glimpse of someone on a cross. But no, it wasn't Christ on Golgotha, for there were dozens, no hundreds of martyrs in a line of crosses that stretched to the horizon. And one in particular who gazed down at him from above.

Flannery blinked his eyes, clearing the memory, not wanting to revisit whatever it was he had envisioned. He took a few calming breaths, then stood and walked to the dresser. Pocketing the keys to the car he had rented that afternoon, he reached for his security ID. He hesitated, his hand hovering over the tag that had been so crucial to his rescue at the catacombs near the Mount of Olives.

Some inner sense fought against picking it up. But that was ridiculous, he told himself, snatching the card from the dresser. He started to slip it into his pocket, but his hand froze in place. His fingers felt strangely numb, and a single word emanated from within: *Faith.*

As the word played through him like a mantra, he watched his hand move back up to the dresser, his fingers release the ID. He stared at it a long moment as he heard himself whisper, "Not my will but thine be done."

Turning quickly, he hurried from the room, heading down to the car and south on the road to Masada.

———

A BUBBLE of light flared as Gavriel Eban lit a cigarette. Shielding his eyes against the afternoon sun, he glanced over at the low stone structure that two millennia ago had held grain and other provisions for the final holdouts at the fortress of Masada. Silhouetted in an open doorway were a half dozen men and women, members of the archaeology team spending their break huddled around the door to take advantage of the cooling breeze spilling from within. Eban was too far away to make out more than an occasional word, but he fantasized that they were Zealot fanatics debating how to defeat the Roman troops who had laid siege to their mountaintop stronghold. And he pictured himself a Zealot guard with a broadsword strapped to his side rather than the 9mm Jericho 941 handgun that was standard issue for Israeli security police.

In his musings, the final assault had begun, and it would soon fall to him and the handful of other security officers—no, Zealot warriors —to bring glory to the Jewish nation at the point of their swords.

But this wasn't the first century, it was the twenty-first, Eban reminded himself. There were no Roman soldiers, no Zealot uprising to alleviate the numbing boredom of another long, hot day working security at an archaeology dig where the only enemy assault was by the dust devils that swept across the desert valley surrounding Masada.

Eban took a long drag on the cigarette and dropped it to the ground, crushing it into the dirt with his boot, remembering his promise to Livya that he'd quit. He smiled at the image of her waiting for him in their Hebron apartment. A few more hours and he'd be home, climbing under the covers beside her.

A shuffling movement caught his attention from off to the side.

Turning directly into the sunlight, he saw the figure of a man approaching from around one of the fort's small outer buildings.

"Moshe?" he called, squinting as he tried to make out if it was one of the other guards on duty. "Moshe, what are you doing out here? I thought you were at the—"

A silver blade flashed once, then sliced across Eban's throat. He felt a sting, then wetness as blood from his carotid artery spilled down his neck. He opened his mouth, but the windpipe was severed, his scream silent as he dropped to his knees and clawed at his neck. He looked up at his attacker, his expression beseeching, his lips forming the word: *Why?*

Only the man's fierce, blazing eyes were visible from behind the dark headdress that covered his face. His reply was as cold as the steel in his hand as he leaned over and thrust the blade upward into Eban's heart, then kicked his lifeless body onto its back in the dirt.

The assassin's raised arm and clenched fist summoned others, and eleven more men in dark headdresses and clothing materialized from behind the nearby rocks and stone walls.

With hand signals and gestures, he directed their gruesome task. Unsuspecting and unarmed, the victims went down under the knives and garrotes of the assault team.

The assassin walked among the bodies, rolling each onto its back to examine the face, as the rest of his team searched the area. One of them came hurrying over and said with a shrug, "It's not here."

"It's nearby," he replied, not bothering to look up at the fellow. "She said it was here, and I believe her."

"Look for yourself, it's not here, I tell you."

"Have you checked inside all the buildings?" he asked.

"Of course."

"Search them again." He gave a dismissive wave. "Find the woman." He didn't bother with her name. His team had been drilled for countless hours; they knew all too well who and what they had come here for. "Find her, but be careful she isn't harmed. She will lead us to it."

A SHUDDER OF FEAR—OF death—passed through Fr. Michael Flannery, but he managed to shake it off as he parked near the cable car that carried tourists and workers to the top of the plateau on which the Masada fortress sat.

The tram was not moving and seemed deserted, and even though the ruins were closed to the public today, Flannery knew there should be an attendant on hand to transport workers and security personnel to the top.

"Hello!" he called. "Anyone here? Please! I need a ride to the top! Anyone here?" The only response was the echo of his words off the wall of the cliff.

Flannery walked to the ticket window at the cable car office. Someone's half-finished coffee sat on the counter, and he reached through the semicircular opening in the window to feel the cup. It was cold.

He stared through the window at the small office but saw no one. A slight breeze fluttered the pages of a magazine on one of the desks and set the cord of the Venetian blinds tapping against the windowsill.

"Hello?" he called, leaning close to the ticket-window opening. "Is anyone here?"

Deciding that everyone must have come down from the ruins and left for the day, Flannery debated returning to Jerusalem. But there was something compelling about the way Azra Haddad had urged him to meet her. He looked over at his car, then back toward the plateau high above. Nodding in acceptance, he headed across the parking lot to the base of the same footpath the Jewish Zealots had used two thousand years earlier when they captured Masada and made their final stand.

As Flannery began the steep climb to the Masada fortress more than four hundred feet above the desert floor, he was besieged by a flood of emotions and memories: Father Leonardo Contardi, Via Dei, the Dismas Gospel with its strange symbol, the tragic death of Daniel Mazar.

Stopping to rest halfway to the top, he sat on a flat boulder and leaned against an even larger stone. As he closed his eyes, he saw images of people and events he had been recalling during the climb. It was like a waking dream at first, but slowly the imagery shifted, transformed into something far more real, something he had never seen before.

Flannery stood alone in an unfamiliar terrain. No, not alone, for now he could see people around him, a great crowd in antiquated costumes who filled what appeared to be an ancient, hand-constructed road. He heard women weeping, men crying out in pain. He felt a presence beside him, and when he turned to find out what it was, he saw a powerfully built black man dressed in a coarse homespun robe.

"You," Flannery muttered. "You were in St. Peter's Basilica."

The old man merely nodded and gestured with one hand, directing Flannery to look behind him.

Turning, Flannery saw someone in the armor of a Roman soldier standing alongside the road, his hand resting on the hilt of his broadsword. Then Flannery looked up and gasped. There, but a few feet above him, a man was nailed and crucified. For an instant he thought it might be his Savior, but then he gazed down the length of the road and realized there were not three crosses—not three men crucified—but scores, perhaps hundreds.

"God in Heaven!" he cried, looking away. "What is this?"

The dream, he told himself. *I'm having the dream again.*

He struggled to wake himself up, wondering if he would find himself still sitting in his hotel room.

"Faith," came the answer, and he felt the black man's hand upon his shoulder. "Look upon him in faith."

Flannery lifted his gaze to see the dying man looking down at him, and something passed between them—hope, recognition, love.

"Dismas bar-Dismas..." Flannery whispered, closing his eyes, unable any longer to witness such suffering.

The wind strengthened, the vision faded, and when Flannery opened his eyes again, he was back on the footpath leading up to Masada. He stood slowly and looked around for any sign of the black man or the road of many crosses.

He heard the distant call of a crow.

———

NINE YEARS HAD PASSED since Tibro bar-Dismas and Marcella Tacitus left Rome. They had married along the way, in Ephesus where they had first met. It had taken more time than expected to arrange safe passage to Jerusalem, and when they had finally reached the city, the situation had become so chaotic that they had been unable to fulfill their promise to Dismas.

With the Romans putting great pressure on the city, the situation had worsened for Christians. The Zealots, considering them collaborators, had increased their attacks, assassinating many of their leaders and forcing most of the believers to flee Judea. With no established leadership and little security against the Zealots and Romans alike, Tibro had thought it best to delay turning over his brother's scroll.

Eventually the situation in Jerusalem had grown untenable even for the Jews, with Titus Flavius Vespasianus laying siege to the city. And so Tibro and Marcella had joined hundreds of other Jews in following the Zealot leader and high priest Eleazer ben-Yair to the desert fortress of Masada. Among the precious few things they had been able to take with them was the Gospel of Dismas.

Now, three years after the fall of Jerusalem, the Jews of Masada had managed to hold off a force of fifteen thousand Roman soldiers under the command of Flavius Silva, the governor of Judea. Silvia's siege had lasted for two years, but still he was not been able to storm the plateau and take their stronghold. But he had spent those long months constructing an earthen ramp, which had brought the Romans close enough to launch their final assault. During the previous night, his forces finally succeeded in setting fire to the wooden roofs of the fortress, the fire raging most of the night before finally burning itself out.

Soon after daybreak, while a pall of smoke hung over the fortress, Tibro stood on one of the parapets, looking down at the iron-plated towers that had been brought forth during the siege. From within these towers, the Romans used *ballistas* to hurl large stones high up into the fortress. The constant pounding of the barrage as missiles slammed into the barricades had unnerved the defenders, and with the latest assault by fire, he knew their fate was sealed.

"Tibro," someone called, and he turned to see Eleazer ben-Yair climbing a ladder to the parapet.

"Here," Tibro offered, extending his hand and helping the older man off the ladder and onto the rampart.

Eleazer brushed his hands together, then straightened his clothes as he walked to the edge and looked down at the Roman encampment, which during the siege had taken on the appearance of a town.

"Our time has come to an end," the high priest said. "Last night they were close enough to set fires. By tomorrow, they will have scaled the summit and be at our walls."

Even as Eleazer spoke, a catapulted boulder brought down a large section of charred wood and stone. Tibro could hear the cries of fear and alarm from the defenders inside the fortress.

"Is there a way we can strengthen the walls and stop their advance?" Tibro asked.

Eleazer shook his head. "We have no material left, no more time. I have called a meeting, Tibro."

"Of the leaders?"

"Of every man, woman, and child, for this concerns all."

"I understand," Tibro said solemnly.

Half-an-hour later, even as the barrage continued, Eleazer was speaking to his followers in the large central courtyard of the complex.

"Long ago, my generous friends, we resolved never to be servants to the Romans nor to any other but God himself, who alone is the true and just Lord of mankind. The time is now come to make that resolution true in practice. It is now clear that Masada will be taken within a day's time. But though the Romans may breach our walls, they need not breach nor break our spirit."

Some of the assembly voiced their approval, others called for Eleazer to explain what they must do.

"First, let us destroy our belongings and our money and put to the torch what remains of the fortress, so that the Romans shall not claim what little earthly wealth we still possess. But let us not destroy our provisions, for they will serve as a testament that we were not subdued for want of food but that we chose death over slavery."

He paused as he looked around the room, taking in each of the nearly one thousand people present.

"And finally, my faithful friends, let us indeed choose death, at our own hands, so that no Roman sword may stain this sacred ground with Jewish blood."

"But suicide is a sin, is it not?" someone called out.

"Yes, and the final sin," another said, "for there is no asking God for forgiveness."

"It is a sin," Eleazer admitted. "But I have contrived a way in which the sin would rest on only one of us. Ten will be chosen to execute all the others. They will then draw lots among them, and one of those ten will execute the nine, leaving the sin of suicide on him alone."

"Yes, that is the way we must do it," a man shouted, and others took up the cry, until the entire assembly was shouting its assent.

"When do we do this thing?" someone asked.

"In a few minutes," Eleazer replied. "I have already sought volunteers from among our greatest warriors, and from them I have chosen ten who shall be the instruments of our glory. Let us use the time that remains to embrace our beloveds and to offer up prayers in praise of our Lord."

Eleazer called out the names of the ten executioners, and as they took up their swords and joined their leader in the center of the courtyard, others went about setting fire to what remained of the fort. The rest of the assembly gathered in small groups, sharing kisses and warm embraces, chanting and singing of the glory of God.

As the executioners began their terrible work, Tibro and Marcella slipped away, not to avoid death but because they had their own mission to fulfill. Knowing for many weeks that their fate was sealed, they had already prepared an earthen jug, placing Dismas's gospel inside and filling the cavity with straw, then sealing the lid with wax to protect the scroll for the day it might be found.

They retrieved the urn from their quarters and brought it to a room they had chosen deep in the fortress. Tibro carried a shovel to dig a hole large enough for the urn.

Even through the thick stone walls, they could hear the terrifying sounds from above, the moans and cries and prayers of the dying.

"Hurry," Marcella said. "We must not let it be found."

Tibro dropped to his knees to scoop up dirt with the short-handled shovel, the pungent odor of freshly turned earth assailing his nostrils.

"Hurry," she urged. "We don't have much time!"

"I'm almost deep enough." He gasped for breath as he increased his labor.

Another scream, this one so close as to make both of them jump. Then a mournful dirge:

> *May His great Name grow exalted and sanctified*
> *in the world that He created as He willed.*

"Give it here," he said, dropping the shovel and reaching up toward the vase.

"Is it deep enough? This must not fall into the wrong hands," Marcella said, handing it to him.

"It has to be. We have no time left."

> *May his great name be blessed forever and ever.*
> *May his great name be blessed forever and ever.*

Above, the chanting of the Kaddish grew fainter as the voices trailed off one by one.

Marcella kept vigil by the stairs as Tibro quickly filled the hole, tamped the dirt, and tossed the shovel to one side. "The shovel," she whispered excitedly, gesturing at where it lay.

"Of course," he said, realizing it was evidence of the burial site. He snatched it back up, then scraped his foot over the ground, hiding any remaining marks of the dig.

Marcella was again peering up the stairs at the doorway above as her husband came over and placed a hand on her shoulder.

"It's time for us to go."

"Do you think it's safe?" she asked, fear evident in her eyes as she looked up at him.

"We have done all we can do. Whether the door opens upon Heaven or Hell is now up to God."

Outside, the cries and prayers were stilled, replaced now by the soft whisper of the wind.

When Tibro and Marcella emerged from below, they discovered the killings were complete, the ten executioners also dead at the hands of the one they had chosen by lot. It was a gruesome sight, and yet they were not horrified, for there was something peaceful, almost poetic, in the way these patriots of Israel lay in one another's last embrace.

Tibro thought he heard sounds from within the fortress, and he guessed there were a few who had faltered in their resolve and had hidden during the mass killings. They would face an uncertain fate when the Romans stormed Masada. Perhaps a few might even live to relate the glorious and terrible events that had taken place this day.

For a moment he considered joining them, not to save himself but for the sake of his wife, whom he loved with all his being. Marcella must have sensed his thoughts, for she kissed his cheek and whispered, "Leave them to their path; we have chosen ours. We shall not be made to part."

And so together they walked through the still and silent courtyard, past the bodies of parent and child, warrior and priest, then through the fortress gates and out to the edge of the Masada cliff. There they gazed down upon the Roman troops, who were already gathering for a final assault up their crude earthen ramp.

Tibro and Marcella prayed aloud together, first to his God and then to hers, realizing that it was the same God, be they Christian or Jew. With a final embrace, they stepped forward and leaped into the void.

FORTY-FIVE

Fr. Michael Flannery felt a curious mixture of foreboding and excitement as he reached the Masada summit and walked toward the ruins of the fortress. The sun was closing on the horizon, yet he was strangely unperturbed at the possibility of being trapped there after dark, unable to make his way back to the car.

It was eerily silent as he moved through the ruins. He realized why as he approached the building where the scroll had been unearthed and came upon the first body. The man wore the uniform of a security guard, and a nametag on his blood-soaked shirt read Gavriel Eban. The poor fellow lay sprawled on his back, a deep gash across his throat, his eyes open wide and fixed.

Fighting the urge to flee, Flannery continued toward the building. At the doorway he came upon half a dozen other bodies, men and women wearing the casual work clothes of the archaeological team. Some also had their throats cut, others bore multiple stab wounds to torso and face.

Flannery gagged, closing his eyes, struggling not to vomit. He leaned in the doorway, forcing himself to breathe slowly, calmly, as he considered what to do. Remembering his cell phone, he flipped it open, then shook his head in dismay at finding he was not in range of cellular service.

Though he knew he should hurry back to his car and go for help, something compelled him to check inside the building. He headed slowly down the stairs to the chamber where the urn had been found. As he entered the room, he discovered there was enough light spilling through the small, high windows to illuminate the area.

The hole where the urn had been found was considerably larger now, and there was something dark at the bottom. As Flannery approached, he saw it was the body of one of the archaeology team leaders, whom he recognized from his earlier visit. It looked as if the man had been trying to hide when his killers found him. Unlike the other victims, this man had been shot. There were two other bodies in the far corner of the room, and they also had been shot.

As Flannery looked around the room, he noticed that the walls had been spray-painted with Muslim symbols and slogans. He walked over and confirmed the paint was still wet. He was proficient enough in Arabic to translate:

There is no God but Allah!
Israel is the spawn of Satan!
Death to the Jews!

He was still staring at the words when a soft voice intoned: "Via Dei."

Flannery spun around to find Azra Haddad standing at the foot of the stairs.

"Don't be fooled by appearances," she said, nodding toward the slogans. "It wasn't Palestinians who did this. It was the work of Via Dei. They came for the scroll."

"It certainly looks like terrorists," Flannery said, looking her over suspiciously as he noted her traditional Muslim clothing and head scarf. "What makes you suspect Via Dei? And why would they come to Masada for the scroll?"

"Because they knew I had it. They knew I would bring it here."

"You?" He stared at her, mystified. "You have the scroll?"

"I took it from where Professor Mazar hid it inside the file cabinet."

"How did you know about that?" he demanded. "No one has been told what he did."

"There are ways to know without being told."

"Even if you knew, the lab was always under guard. You would've been stopped if you tried to walk in there."

"There are ways to walk without being seen," she replied, equally cryptically.

"I...I don't understand." He ran a hand through his hair. "I mean, why would you bring the scroll here?"

"To give it to Via Dei."

"What?" he said, stunned. "You handed it over to them, just like that? Why?"

"I know Via Dei—far better and far longer than you can imagine," she replied. "I knew they wouldn't forsake their quest, and that the murder of Daniel Mazar was but the start."

"But the other day—at the catacombs—two of their leaders were killed, the third is on the run."

"Do not be fooled by appearances," she repeated. "There are many to step into the shoes of those who fall. And Sangremano on the run is far more dangerous than hiding in the shadows of the Vatican."

"You know Father Sangremano?"

"I know Via Dei. But there are some things even I didn't count on. I came here because I knew that when Sangremano failed to steal the scroll from the lab, he'd send his men to see if it had been brought back to Masada. And it was time for the killing to stop. But I was too late." She looked over at the bodies. "I was unable to prevent their deaths, and though I willingly turned over the scroll, I fear the killing is not at an end."

"Why did you give it to them?" he demanded, his voice rising in anger. "You had no right. The scroll doesn't belong to you."

"I was the one who found it, just a few feet from where we now stand."

"Just because you were lucky enough to stumble upon—"

"It was no accident," she said, raising a hand to silence him. "For many years I have known where it lay buried. I came to Masada and joined the archaeology team precisely so that I could stumble upon it, as you put it."

"Years?" he said incredulously. "But how could you have known?"

"It was revealed to me."

"By whom?"

"The Keeper."

Flannery shook his head in confusion. "Excuse me, Azra, but you aren't making sense right now."

"Do you recall the symbol on the Dismas scroll?"

"Yes, the Via Dei."

"No, Father Flannery. Not Via Dei."

"I realize it's different, but only slightly."

"Trevia Dei...the symbol that Dismas bar-Dismas drew in his own blood upon the scroll is the Trevia Dei."

"Blood?" he said, envisioning it on the papyrus. "Yes, that's what it looked like. But what's Trevia Dei?"

"The true sign. Over the centuries it was corrupted by the followers of Dismas, just as they became corrupt."

"But Father Sangremano said that their symbol was given to them by Jesus himself."

"The true sign of Trevia Dei was revealed by Jesus to the Keeper, and—"

"That's the second time you mentioned him. Who, or perhaps I should ask what, is the Keeper?"

"The first Keeper of the Sign was Simon of Cyrene, who revealed it to Dismas bar-Dismas. Via Dei traces its roots to Dismas's successor, Gaius of Ephesus, but he learned of the Trevia Dei secondhand. Over the centuries the organization he founded was forced underground, and the symbol became corrupted, its true meaning lost."

"How is it that you know all these things?" Flannery asked.

"There isn't much time," she said, turning and starting up the stairs. "Come with me."

He followed her up onto the plateau, away from the building and the bodies. As they walked toward the setting sun, she continued her discourse.

"In time, Father Flannery, you will know the full story, how Jesus visited Simon following the crucifixion, how a cloth soaked in the Master's blood came to bear the Trevia Dei, how Jesus anointed Simon as Keeper of the Sign and charged him with its protection, not just in his lifetime but for fifty generations to come."

Flannery stopped short. "This doesn't make sense. None of it."

"Think upon all you have seen and done," she softly urged. "The sign...the one in the scroll. Of what elements is it composed?"

Closing his eyes, he visualized the image he had seen so often in his mind's eye. "A pyramid...a cross...a crescent moon and a star."

"Trevia Dei," she intoned. "The three great paths to God. The pyramid doubled...the Star of David. The Cross of your faith. The Star and Crescent of my Islam."

"But that's nonsense," he said, opening his eyes. "None of those symbols existed two thousand years ago. Of the three religions, only Judaism existed, and they didn't adopt the Star of David for centuries to come. And Islam? Hundreds of years before Muhammad's birth? Impossible."

"All things are possible to he who created the universe and time. That is the great mystery of Trevia Dei, which speaks not only of three paths but of the unity of all paths that lead to the one true home, in the embrace of the Lord."

"Trevia Dei..." Flannery whispered, his head nodding slightly. "Via Dei...the one road to God."

She smiled.

"They've altered it completely," he declared, his voice urgent, eager.

"Yes, Michael, you understand. And so much more will be made clear to you in time."

A feeling of warmth, acceptance, came over Flannery as Azra used his given name for the first time.

"Now, Michael, it is time. The Keepers are waiting."

"Keepers? But you only mentioned one."

"Until today, there have been forty-nine. When Simon came to the end of his days, he found someone worthy to bear the great treasure. That treasure was handed down, one to another, as each Keeper in turn anointed the one who would follow. That anointing has continued century after century, through Dark Ages and Renaissance, plagues, wars, and Holocaust. Each had a role to play, a special task to fulfill. One stood beside Pope Leo the Great at the gates of Rome when he confronted Attila, known to Christians as *Flagellum Dei*, the Scourge of God. Another stood with Muhammad when the Prophet received the light of Allah and the Star and Crescent. More recently, a Keeper came to the New World and helped found a nation based upon religious freedom and tolerance, unheard of before that time."

Azra began walking again, and Flannery followed her further from the ruins. Suddenly he was struck by an awareness that seemed so simple, so familiar.

"My God," he exclaimed, not as an oath but filled with awe and fear. "You are one of them, aren't you? One of the Keepers of the Sign."

Azra smiled in reply.

"But why are you telling me all this?" Flannery asked. "Why reveal the secret now?"

"The secret...and the treasure."

Reaching up, she lifted a thin silver chain over her head. The chain bore a silver case, larger than most lockets and exquisitely detailed, with geometric patterns and vines that surrounded the carved symbol of Trevia Dei. She held it forth.

"This vessel was a gift from Muhammad to the Keeper who influenced his conversion. What it contains was a gift to Simon, the first Keeper of the Sign."

Azra carefully opened the hinged case and lovingly removed and unfolded a patch of brilliant white cloth, emblazoned with the bright-red image of Trevia Dei.

"This," she whispered, "is the blood of Christ."

"Sanguis Christi," Flannery repeated in awe. "But how can it be so fresh?"

"Because it is the blood of Christ," she replied, explaining it all with that one statement.

Azra slipped the necklace over his head, then handed him the cloth.

"A gift," she said, "from one Keeper to the next."

"What?" Flannery gasped, staring down at the cloth in his hands, feeling its warmth flowing up his arms, filling his heart. "But...but I'm not worthy of this."

"It is my appointed hour, and I must leave. Indeed, I've been waiting only for you to arrive."

"But how do you know I'm the one?"

"Don't you understand, Michael? You have always been the Keeper. You always shall be the Keeper."

She started to move past him.

"Wait!" he called after her. "There's so much I want to know, so much you must tell me."

"Put your faith in Trevia Dei and in God, and you will know all that needs to be known."

"Yes," Flannery whispered, accepting his commission, under- standing that in God lay all answers.

"Your time of trial has begun," Azra said, coming closer and standing before him. "I know you will serve God faithfully, but you must be very cautious, Michael, because Via Dei will come after you now. And they will not be the only ones. But do not assume that all are your enemies. There are those, even within Via Dei, who upon seeing the truth will recognize its light."

"But the scroll...they have the scroll," Flannery said. "How will I get it back? Or is it lost forever?"

"They have only paper. The truth of Dismas's gospel abides. And it is not lost, but waiting. All will be made clear in time. Until then, we will be nearby."

"We?"

"The Keepers who came before, and those who shall follow. Always, we'll be there. Look with your true eyes and you will see. Listen with your true heart and all will be revealed."

Azra placed one hand upon his forehead and the other over his heart. As Flannery stared into her eyes, he saw the faces of many others, of the long line of Keepers back to those dark, penetrating eyes of the very first one. Then, suddenly, another pair of eyes looked upon him, so brilliant and all-embracing that he could hardly bear the intensity of their gaze.

Flannery felt as if he were rising from the ground, floating above everything, and he struggled to see the world around him.

"We are with you always, even until the end of the world," she said as she walked toward the very spot where, two thousand years before, Marcella and Tibro had flung themselves into the valley.

Flannery watched in stunned silence as Azra continued toward the cliff. He wanted to run after her, to stop her from what she was about to do, but he had no control over his body. He watched immobilized as she strode without hesitation to the edge of the precipice and beyond.

Amazingly, she did not fall to her death. Instead, she continued out over the abyss, toward a circle of men and women who awaited her with open arms.

Some inner sense caused Flannery to glance to his right, and he saw someone lying nearby. It was the body of Azra Haddad, her throat slashed, her torso riddled with bullets from the Via Dei hit team when they stormed Masada and snatched the scroll of Dismas from her hands.

Looking back out over the abyss, he watched as a tall black man moved forward from the waiting group, embraced Azra, and drew her into their fold. Flannery recognized him as the one who came to him in spirit months earlier during a Pontifical service, and again when he was witness to the mass crucifixions. He knew now that this was Simon of Cyrene. And there, beside Simon, was the old man Flannery had seen among the crucified on the Appian Way: Dismas bar-Dismas, whose Gospel had set Flannery on his quest.

As the other Keepers closed around Simon and Azra, their shimmering bodies grow fainter, more ethereal, until finally they disappeared.

Michael Flannery, the new Keeper of Trevia Dei, was left alone, holding the cloth of Jesus, feeling the Master's hand still resting upon his forehead and upon his heart.

"Father," he prayed. "Please give me the strength to carry out your great commission."

AUTHORS' NOTE

Portions of the account of Dismas bar-Dismas that appear in this book in English are not an official translation but were commissioned by the authors from a theologian and scholar at Seton Hall University who was given access to the scroll found in the Masada jar and wishes to remain anonymous.

Biblical scholars working on translating the Dismas document have agreed to allow the authors to reproduce the opening in its original Greek and Hebrew. Their official translation will not be available until their work is completed and released to the public.

The Account of Dismas bar-Dismas, as found in the Masada jar:

ΔΙΗΓΗΣΙΣ ΔΙΣΜΑΣ ΒΑΡΔΙΣΜΑΣ ΑΝΑΓΕΓΡΑΦΑΜΕΝΗ ΕΝ ΧΕΙΡΙ
ΑΥΤΟΥ
ΕΝ ΕΤΕΙ ΤΡΙΑΚΟΣΤΩΙ ΑΠΟ ΤΟΝ ΘΑΝΑΤΟΝ ΚΑΙ ΑΝΑΣΤΑΣΙΝ
ΤΟΥ ΧΡΙΣΤΟΥ
ΜΝΗΜΟΝΕΥΘΗΣΟΜΕΝΗ ΕΝ ΤΗΙ ΠΟΛΕΙ ΡΟΜΑΙ
ΥΠΟ ΤΗΣ ΕΝΤΟΛΗΣ ΠΑΥΛΟΥ ΤΟΥ ΑΠΟΣΤΟΛΟΥ
ΔΙΑ ΔΟΥΛΟΥ ΚΑΙ ΜΑΡΤΥΡΟΥ

ΕΓΟ ΔΙΣΜΑΣ ΥΙΟΣ ΤΟΥ ΔΙΣΜΑΣ ΓΑΛΙΛΗΟΥ ΚΑΙ ΑΓΓΕΛΟΣ
ΙΗΣΟΥ ΧΡΙΣΤΟΥ ΥΠΟ ΤΗΣ ΒΟΥΛΗΣ ΘΕΟΥ ΠΑΤΡΟΣ ΔΙΑ

ΘΕΛΗΜΑΤΟΣ ΑΓΙΟΥ ΠΝΕΥΜΑΤΟΣ ΕΝΤΑΥΘΑ ΠΡΟΤΙΘΗΜΙ ΔΙΑΘΗΚΗ ΠΙΣΤΕΥΟΝΤΟΥΣΙ ΚΑΙ ΠΙΣΤΕΥΣΟΝΤΕΣΙ ΚΑΤΑ ΒΟΥΛΗΝ ΑΥΤΟΥ

ΜΑΡΤΥΡΙΟΝ Ο ΕΓΟ ΔΕΔΩΚΑ ΠΑΝΤΩΝ Α ΙΗΣΟΥΣ ΤΕΤΕΛΕΥΤΗΚΕ ΚΑΙ ΕΠΑΙΔΕΥΣΕ ΠΡΟ ΣΤΑΥΡΩΣΙΝ ΑΥΤΟΥ ΥΠΟ ΠΟΝΤΙΟΥ ΠΙΛΑΤΟΥ ΗΓΗΜΟΝΤΙΣ ΡΟΜΑΝΟΥ ΙΟΥΔΑΙΑΣ ΥΠΕΡ ΔΕΔΟΤΑΙ ΕΚ ΤΗΝ ΣΤΩΜΑΤΩΝ ΑΓΙΩΝ ΑΠΟΣΤΟΛΩΝ ΑΥΤΩΝ ΠΡΟΣ ΕΜΕ ΑΛΛΑ ΠΕΡΙ ΣΤΑΥΡΟΣΕΩΣ ΑΥΤΟΥ ΦΕΡΩ ΜΑΡΤΥΡΠΟΝ ΙΔΙΟΝ ΚΑΙ ΠΕΡΙ ΤΩΝ ΑΚΟΛΟΥΘΗΣΕΩΝ ΜΕΧΡΙ ΑΝΑΒΕΒΗΚΕ ΕΙΣ ΤΟΝ ΟΥΡΑΝΙΟΝ ΠΡΟΣ ΔΕΞΙΑΙ ΤΟΥ ΠΑΤΡΟΣ ΠΑΓΚΡΑΤΟΥ

ΤΑΥΤΑ ΕΣΤΙΝ Α ΟΙ ΠΙΣΤΕΥΟΝΤΕΣ ΑΠΟΜΑΡΤΥΡΟΝΤΑΙ ΑΛΗΘΗ ΟΤΙ ΠΑΙΣ ΕΤΕΧΘΗ ΜΑΡΙΑΜ ΝΑΖΑΡΕΘ ΕΝ ΗΣ ΥΣΤΕΡΑ ΚΥΡΙΟΣ ΑΥΤΟΣ ΥΠΟ ΔΥΝΑΜΕΩΣ ΠΝΕΥΜΑΤΟΣ ΑΓΙΟΥ ΠΑΡΑΔΕΔΗΚΕ ΥΙΟΝ ΕΙΝΑΙ ΒΑΣΙΛΕΑ ΤΗΣ ΒΑΣΙΛΕΙΑΣ ΥΠΕΣΧΗΜΕΝΗΣ ΟΥΡΑΝΙΗΣ ΟΤΙ ΠΑΙΣ ΜΑΡΙΑΜ ΓΑΜΕΤΙΔΟΣ ΙΩΣΗΦ ΕΞ ΟΙΚΟΥ ΔΑΥΙΔ ΤΗΣ ΑΝΕΥ ΜΙΑΣΜΑΤΟΣ ΚΑΙ ΜΗΤΡΟΣ ΤΟΥ ΚΥΡΙΟΥ ΜΕΜΑΝΤΕΥΕΤΑΙ ΥΠΟ ΤΩΝ ΠΡΩΦΗΤΩΝ ΙΣΡΑΕΛ ΣΩΤΗΡ ΚΑΙ ΣΗΜΕΙΟΝ ΤΟΥ ΘΕΟΥ ΜΕΤΑ ΗΜΩΝ ΠΑΙΔΩΝ ΑΥΤΟΥ ΤΗΣ ΔΙΑΘΗΚΗΣ ΟΤΙ ΟΝΟΜΑ ΑΥΤΟΥ ΙΗΣΟΥΣ

ΚΑΙ ΟΤΕ ΙΗΣΟΥΣ ΠΑΡΑΓΙΝΕΤΑΙ ΑΠΟ ΤΗΣ ΓΑΛΙΛΑΙΑΣ ΕΠΙ ΤΟΝ ΙΟΡΔΑΝΗΝ ΠΡΟΣ ΙΩΑΝΝΗΝ ΘΟΡΥΒΗΤΟ ΒΑΠΤΙΣΘΗΝΑΙ ΙΩΑΝΝΗΣ ΛΕΓΩΝ ΔΙΔΑΣΚΑΛΕ ΔΙΟΤΙ ΕΡΩΤΑΣ ΕΜΕ ΒΑΠΤΙΖΕΙΝ ΟΤΕ ΕΓΩ ΧΡΕΙΑΝ ΕΧΩ ΥΠΟ ΤΟΥ ΥΙΟΥ ΑΝΘΡΩΠΟΥ ΒΑΠΤΙΣΘΗΝΑΙ ΣΕ ΔΙΑΘΗΝΗ ΠΙΣΤΕΩΣ

ΚΑΙ ΑΠΟΚΡΙΘΕΙΣ Ο ΙΗΣΟΥΣ ΕΙΠΕΝ ΑΥΤΩΙ ΑΦΕΣ ΑΡΤΙ ΟΥΤΩΣ ΔΙΑΘΗΚΗ ΠΙΣΤΕΩΣ ΗΜΩΝ ΚΑΙ ΟΤΕ ΙΗΣΟΥΣ ΑΝΕΒΗ ΕΚ ΤΟΥ ΥΔΑΤΟΣ ΚΑΙ ΙΔΟΥ ΗΝΕΩΙ ΧΘΗΣΑΝ ΟΙ ΟΥΡΑΝΟΙ ΚΑΙ Ο ΘΕΟΣ ΕΥΔΟΚΗΣΕ

ΚΑΙ ΠΕΡΙΗΓΕΝ Ο ΙΗΣΟΥΣ ΠΑΝΤΑΣ ΤΑΣ ΚΩΜΑΣ ΚΑΙ ΠΟΛΕΑ ΔΙΔΑΣΚΩΝ ΕΝ ΤΑΙΣ ΣΥΝΑΓΩΓΑΙΣ ΚΑΙ ΚΗΡΥΣΣΩΝ ΤΟ ΕΥΑΓΓΗΛΙΟΝ ΤΗΣ ΒΑΣΙΛΕΙΑΣ ΣΥΝ ΜΑΘΗΤΑΙΣ ΟΙ ΕΙΣΙ ΣΙΜΩΝ

Ο ΛΕΓΟΜΕΝΟΣ ΠΕΤΡΟΣ ΚΑΙ ΑΝΔΡΕΑΣ Ο ΑΔΕΛΦΟΣ ΑΥΤΟΥ ΙΑΚΩΒΟΣ Ο ΤΟΥ ΖΕΒΕΔΑΙΟΥ ΚΑΙ ΙΩΑΝΝΗΣ Ο ΑΔΕΛΦΟΣ ΑΥΤΟΥ ΦΙΛΙΠΠΟΣ ΚΑΙ ΒΑΡΘΟΛΟΜΑΙΟΣ ΘΩΜΑΣ ΚΑΙ ΜΑΤΘΑΙΟΣ Ο ΤΕΛΩΝΗΣ ΙΑΚΩΒΟΣ Ο ΤΟΥ ΑΛΦΑΙΟΥ ΚΑΙ ΘΑΔΔΑΙΟΣ ΣΙΜΩΝ Ο ΚΑΝΑΝ ΑΙΟΣ ΚΑΙ ΙΟΥΔΑΣ Ο ΙΣΚΑΡΙΩΤΗΣ Ο ΚΑΙ ΠΑΡΑΔΟΥΣ ΤΟΝ ΚΥΡΙΟΝ

ויבא אל נצרת אשר גדל שם וילך כמשפטו ביום השבת אל בית הכנסת ויקם לקרא: והיתה רוח יהוה עליו לבשר הבשורה: ואיש היה בבית הכנסת ובו רוח שטן ויצעק לאמר הניחה לנו ישוע הנצרי: ויצו ישוע את השטן לצאת ממנו ויראו כלם את אלה ותפל אימה על כלם כי בשלטן ובגבורה מצוה לשטן לצאת: וידברו בו בבתים ובבתי הכנסיות ויגדל שם ישוע בכל מקמות הככר: ויאמר ישוע כי הוא יבשר גם לערים האחרות את מלכות האלהים כי לזאת שלח: ויהי קורא בבתי הכנסיות ולעם עד למסר אתו יהודה:

ΜΕΤΑ Ο ΚΥΡΙΟΣ ΠΡΟΔΕΔΕΤΕΤΑΙ ΠΑΝΤΕΣ ΟΙ ΑΡΧΙΕΡΕΙΣ ΚΑΙ ΟΙ ΠΡΕΣΒΥΤΕΡΟΙ ΕΖΕΤΟΥΝ ΚΑΤΑ ΤΟΥ ΙΗΣΟΥ ΜΑΡΤΥΡΙΑΝ ΕΙΣ ΤΟ ΘΑΝΑΤΩΣΑΙ ΕΝ ΤΗΙ ΑΥΤΗΙ ΩΡΑΙ ΒΑΡΑΒΒΑΣ Ο ΖΕΛΩΤΗΣ ΚΑΤΑΔΙΚΑΣΘΗΣΕΤΑΙ ΠΡΟΣ ΤΟΝ ΘΑΝΑΤΟΝ ΚΑΙ ΑΥΤΩΣ ΚΗΣΤΟΣ ΚΑΙ ΔΙΣΜΑΣ Ο ΠΑΤΗΡ ΕΜΟΥ

ΚΑΤΑ ΕΟΡΤΗΝ ΕΙΩΘΕΙ Ο ΗΓΕΜΩΝ ΑΠΟΛΥΕΙΝ ΕΝΑ ΔΕΣΜΙΟΝ ΚΑΙ ΠΙΛΑΤΟΣ ΠΡΟΣΕΚΑΛΕΣΕ ΤΟΝ ΟΧΛΟΝ ΕΡΩΤΑΝ ΟΝ ΗΘΕΛΟΝ ΠΑΡΕΔΟΘΗ ΠΡΟΣ ΣΕΑΥΤΟΙΣ Ο ΟΧΛΟΣ ΠΡΟΣΕΚΑΛΕΣΕ ΒΑΡΡΑΒΑΣ ΚΑΣΙ ΚΑΤΑ ΝΟΟΝ ΑΥΤΩΝ ΒΑΡΡΑΒΑΣ ΑΦΕΙΤΑΙ ΟΙ ΑΛΛΟΙ ΔΕΣΜΙΟΙ ΚΗΣΤΑΣ ΔΙΣΜΑΣ ΚΑΙ ΙΗΣΟΥΣ ΣΤΑΥΡΟΥΝΤΑΙ

ΠΑΡΑ ΤΗΝ ΣΤΑΥΡΩΣΙΝ ΤΟΥ ΧΡΙΣΤΟΥ ΔΙΣΜΑΣ ΠΑΤΗΡ ΕΜΟΥ ΠΡΟΣΕΚΑΛΕΣΕ ΙΗΣΟΥΝ ΜΝΗΜΟΝΕΥΕΙΝ ΣΕΑΥΤΟΝ ΟΤΑΝ ΕΛΘΗΙ ΕΝ ΤΩΙ ΠΑΡΑΔΕΙΣΩΙ ΚΑΙ ΘΝΗΣΚΩΝ ΕΝ ΤΩΙ ΣΤΑΥΡΩΙ ΨΥΧ ΤΟΥ ΠΑΤΡΟΥ ΕΜΟΥ ΕΣΩΘΗ

ΟΤΕ ΙΗΣΟΥΣ ΣΤΟΥΡΟΥΤΑΙ ΚΑΙ ΕΤΕΘΗ ΕΝ ΤΩΙ ΜΝΗΜΕΙΩΙ ΑΥΤΟΥ ΗΓΕΡΘΗ ΕΚ ΤΟΥ ΘΑΝΑΤΟΥ ΑΠΟ ΤΟΥ ΑΝΑΣΤΑΣΕΩΣ ΑΥΤΟΥ ΕΦΑΝΗ ΠΡΩΤΟΝ ΣΙΜΩΝΙ ΕΝ ΤΩΙ ΟΔΩΙ ΚΥΡΑΝΑΙΩΙ ΚΑΙ

ΩΙ ΤΟΝ ΣΥΜΒΟΛΟΝ ΔΕΔΩΚΕ ΤΟΤΕ ΚΕΦΩΙ ΤΟΤΕ ΤΩΙ ΔΩΔΕΚΑ
ΚΑΙ ΑΠΟ ΤΟΥΤΩΝ ΤΟΙΣ ΑΔΕΛΦΟΙΣ ΠΕΝΤΑΚΟΣΙΟΙΣ ΑΥΤΟΘΕ

ΔΙΑ ΚΗΡΥΞΕΩΣ ΕΜΟΥ ΑΠΟΔΕΔΕΓΜΑΙ ΥΠΟ ΤΩΝ
ΒΑΣΑΝΙΖΩΝΤΩΝ ΕΜΕ ΤΕΣΣΑΡΑΚΟΝΤΑ ΠΑΡΑ ΜΙΑΝ ΤΩΝ
ΙΜΑΣΘΛΙΩΝ ΕΛΙΘΑΣΘΗΝ ΣΧΕΔΟΝΠΡΟΣ ΘΑΝΑΤΟΝ ΚΑΙ ΕΝ
ΦΥΛΑΚΑΙΣ ΑΠΕΙΛΟΜΕΝΟΣ ΠΡΟΣ ΤΗΝ ΣΤΑΥΡΩΣΙΝ
ΕΝΕΠΟΡΕΥΘΗΝ ΕΝ ΤΩΙ ΠΕΛΑΓΩΙ ΕΚΙΝΔΥΝΕΥΣΕ ΤΑ ΡΕΥΜΑΤΑ
ΚΑΙ ΤΟΥΣ ΟΔΟΥΡΟΥΣ ΚΑΘΑΠΕΡ ΤΟΝ ΛΑΟΝ ΕΜΟΝ ΟΙ ΜΗ
ΕΛΑΒΟΝ ΤΟΝ ΚΥΡΙΟΝ ΑΥΤΩΝ

ΚΑΙ ΤΟΙ ΔΙΑ ΠΑΝΤΩΝ Ο ΚΥΡΙΟΣ ΘΕΟΣ ΕΜΟΥ ΠΕΦΥΛΑΚΕ ΕΜΕ
ΚΑΙ ΕΠΕΜΨΕ ΤΟΝ ΑΓΓΕΛΟΝ ΕΠΙΣΚΟΠΕΙΝ ΕΜΕ ΚΑΙ
ΑΠΟΔΕΔΕΙΓΤΑΙ ΤΗΝ ΟΔΟΝ

A LOOK AT PEOPLE OF THE BOOK PART TWO: ARMOR OF GOD

In the riveting follow-up to The Masada Scroll, delve into a compelling and thought-provoking narrative that remains as relevant today as ever.

In Masada, the discovery of a previously unknown gospel sets in motion a powerful chain of events that rocks religious communities across the globe. This sacred scroll, penned by Dismas bar-Dismas, introduces an enigmatic symbol uniting elements of Christianity's Cross, Judaism's Star of David, and Islam's Crescent and Star. Bar-Dismas also espouses the concept of unity among Christians, Jews, and Muslims by outlining the three paths to God. The gospel's existence attracts the attention of Via Dei, a dangerous sect hell-bent on perpetuating religious conflict.

Father Michael Flannery, the prophesied Keeper of the Sign, is destined to bring peace to the world through this gospel. Once a translator of the scroll, he narrowly survives an assassination attempt while en route to a historic symposium in New York, where the world's largest religious groups gather. Via Dei is determined to silence Father Flannery and prevent his message from reaching the world.

Woven into the fabric of this contemporary suspense are the trials of Tobias Garlande, a scholar living during the First Crusade. Plagued by visions of future calamities, Tobias, too, is a Keeper of the Sign, and his warning to Father Flannery reverberates across centuries: Failure is not an option.

Combining international intrigue and suspense with fascinating historical detail, *Armor of God* explores the ramifications of true faith with a compelling tale of past and present religious turmoil and touching human drama.

AVAILABLE JANUARY 2024

ABOUT ROBERT VAUGHAN

Robert Vaughan sold his first book when he was nineteen. That was several years and nearly three-hundred books ago. Since then, he has written the novelization for the mini-series Andersonville, as well as written, produced, and appeared in the History Channel documentary Vietnam Homecoming.

Vaughan's books have hit the *New York Times* bestseller list seven times. He has won the Spur Award, the Porgie Award in Best Paperback Original, the Western Fictioneers Lifetime Achievement Award, the Will Rogers Medallion Award, the Readwest President's Award for Excellence in Western Fiction, and is a member of the American Writers Hall of Fame and a Pulitzer Prize nominee.

Vaughan is also a retired army officer, helicopter pilot with three tours in Vietnam, who has received the Distinguished Flying Cross, the Purple Heart, the Bronze Star with three oak leaf clusters, the Air Medal for valor with 35 oak leaf clusters, the Army Commendation Medal, the Meritorious Service Medal, and the Vietnamese Cross of Gallantry.

ABOUT PAUL BLOCK

Paul Block is an author, editor, photographer, and journalist. After graduating from the State University of New York, he worked at newspapers in San Pedro, CA, and Albany, NY. His photography has been featured in newspapers and on book covers.

Paul formerly served as creative director and editor-in-chief of Book Creations Inc., a book producer specializing in historical fiction, where he conceived, produced, and marketed more than a dozen historical series that included 100+ titles, with millions of copies sold.

Paul's published books include thirteen historical novels, two mystery-thrillers, a young-adult novel, and a collection of poetry and photography. He currently lives in a historic village in upstate New York, where he is working on a murder mystery. His work can be seen at paulblock.com.